DUDLEY PUBLIC LIBRARIES

The loan of this book may be renewed if not required by other readers, by contacting the library from which it was borrowed.

The Rumours
COLLECTION

July 2019

August 2019

September 2019

October 2019

November 2019

December 2019

Rumours: The Dishonoured Copelands

JANE PORTER

MILLS & BOON

First Published in Great Britain 2019
By Mills & Boon, an imprint of HarperCollins *Publishers*
1 London Bridge Street, London, SE1 9GF

RUMOURS: THE DISHONOURED COPELANDS
© 2019 Harlequin Books S.A.

The Fallen Greek Bride © Jane Porter 2013
His Defiant Desert Queen © Jane Porter 2015
Her Sinful Secret © Jane Porter 2017

ISBN: 978-0-26327673-2

1119

MIX
Paper from
responsible sources
FSC™ C007454

THE FALLEN
GREEK BRIDE

For Randall Toye--thank you
for the friendship and support.

CHAPTER ONE

"WELCOME HOME, MY WIFE."

Morgan froze inside Villa Angelica's expansive marble and limestone living room with its spectacular floor-to-ceiling view of blue sky and sea, but saw none of the view, and only Drakon's face.

It had been five years since she'd last seen him. Five and a half years since their extravagant two-million-dollar wedding, for a marriage that had lasted just six months.

She'd dreaded this moment. Feared it. And yet Drakon sounded so relaxed and warm, so *normal,* as if he were welcoming her back from a little holiday instead of her walking out on him.

"Not your wife, Drakon," she said softly, huskily, because they both knew she hadn't been his anything for years. There had been nothing, no word, no contact, not after the flurry of legal missives that followed her filing for divorce.

He'd refused to grant her the divorce and she'd spent a fortune fighting him. But no attorney, no lawsuit, no amount of money could persuade him to let her go. Marriage vows, he'd said, were sacred and binding. She was his. And apparently the courts in Greece agreed with him. Or were bought by him. Probably the latter.

"You are most definitely still my wife, but that's not a conversation I want to have across a room this size. Do come in,

Morgan. Don't be a stranger. What would you like to drink? Champagne? A Bellini? Something a little stronger?"

But her feet didn't move. Her legs wouldn't carry her. Not when her heart was beating so fast. She was shocked by Drakon's appearance and wondered for a moment if it really was Drakon. Unnerved, she looked away, past his broad shoulders to the wall of window behind him, with that breathtaking blue sky and jagged cliffs and azure sea.

So blue and beautiful today. A perfect spring day on the Amalfi Coast.

"I don't want anything," she said, her gaze jerking back to him, although truthfully, a glass of cool water would taste like heaven right now. Her mouth was so dry, her pulse too quick. Her head was spinning, making her dizzy from nerves and anxiety. Who *was* this man before her?

The Drakon Xanthis she'd married had been honed, sleek and polished, a man of taut, gleaming lines and angles.

This tall intimidating man in front of the picture window was broader in the shoulders and chest than Drakon had ever been, and his thick, inky brown and black hair hung in loose curls to almost his shoulders, while his hard fierce features were hidden by a dark beard. The wild hair and beard should have obscured his sensual beauty, rendered him reckless, powerless. Instead the tangle of hair highlighted his bronzed brow, the long straight nose, the firm mouth, the piercing amber gold eyes.

His hair was still damp and his skin gleamed as if he'd just risen from the sea, the Greek god Poseidon come to life from ancient myth.

She didn't like it. Didn't like any of this. She'd prepared herself for one thing, but not this....

"You look pale," he said, his voice so deep it was almost a caress.

She steeled herself against it. Against him. "It was a long trip."

"Even more reason for you to come sit."

Her hands clenched into fists at her sides. She hated being here. Hated him for only seeing her here at Villa Angelica, the place where they'd honeymooned for a month following their spectacular wedding. It'd been the happiest month of her life. When the honeymoon was over, they had left the villa and flown to Greece, and nothing was ever the same between them again. "I'm fine here," she said.

"I won't hurt you," he replied softly.

Her nails pierced her skin. Her eyes stung. If her legs would function, she'd run. Protect herself. Save herself. If only she had someone else to go to, someone else who would help her, but there was no one. Just Drakon. Just the man who had destroyed her, making her question her own sanity. "You already did that."

"You say that, my love, and yet you've never told me how—"

"As you said, that isn't something to discuss across a room of this size. And we both know, I didn't come here to discuss us. Didn't come to rehash the past, bring up old ghosts, old pain. I came for your help. You know what I need. You know what's at stake. Will you do it? Will you help me?"

"Six million dollars is a lot of money."

"Not to you."

"Things have changed. Your father lost over four hundred million dollars of what I gave him."

"It wasn't his fault." She met his gaze and held it, knowing that if she didn't stand up to him now, he'd crush her. Just as he'd crushed her all those years ago.

Drakon, like her father, played by no rules but his own.

A Greek shipping tycoon, Drakon Sebastian Xanthis was a man obsessed with control and power. A man obsessed with amassing wealth and growing his empire. A man obsessed with a woman who wasn't his wife. Bronwyn. The stunning Australian who ran his Southeast Asia business.

Her eyes burned and her jaw ached.

But no. She wouldn't think of Bronwyn now. Wouldn't wonder if the willowy blonde still worked for him. It wasn't important. Morgan wasn't part of Drakon's life anymore. She didn't care whom Drakon employed or how he interacted with his female vice presidents or where they stayed on their business trips or what they discussed over their long dinners together.

"Is that what you really believe?" he asked now, voice almost silky. "That your father is blameless?"

"Absolutely. He was completely misled—"

"As you have been. Your father is one of the biggest players in one of the biggest Ponzi schemes ever. Twenty-five billion dollars is missing, and your father funneled five billion of that to Michael Amery, earning himself ten percent interest."

"He never saw that kind of money—"

"For God's sake, Morgan, you're talking to me, Drakon, your husband. I know your father. I know exactly who and what he is. Do not play me for a fool!"

Morgan ground her teeth together harder, holding back the words, the tears, the anger, the shame. Her father wasn't a monster. He didn't steal from his clients. He was just as deceived as they were and yet no one would give him an opportunity to explain, or defend himself. The media had tried and convicted him and everyone believed the press. Everyone believed the wild accusations. "He's innocent, Drakon. He had no idea Michael Amery was running a pyramid scheme. Had no idea all those numbers and profits were a lie."

"Then if he's so innocent, why did he flee the country? Why didn't he stay, like Amery's sons and cousins, and fight instead of setting sail to avoid prosecution?"

"He panicked. He was frightened—"

"Absolute rubbish. If that's the case, your father is a coward and deserves his fate."

She shook her head in silent protest, her gaze pinned to Drakon's features. He might not look like Drakon, but it was definitely him. She knew his deep, smooth voice. And those eyes. His eyes. She'd fallen in love with his eyes first. She'd met him at the annual Life ball in Vienna, and they hadn't danced—Drakon didn't dance—but he'd watched her all evening and at first she'd been discomfited by the intensity of his gaze, and then she'd come to like it. Want it. Crave it.

In those early weeks and months when he'd pursued her, Drakon had seduced her with his eyes, examining her, holding her, possessing her long before he'd laid a single finger on her. And, of course, by the time he did, she was his, completely.

The last five years had been brutal. Beyond brutal. And just when Morgan had found herself again, and felt hopeful and excited about her future, her world came crashing down with the revelation that her beloved, brilliant financier father, Daniel Copeland, was part of Michael Amery's horrific Ponzi scheme. And instead of her father handling the crisis with his usual aplomb, he'd cracked and run, creating an even bigger international scandal.

She drew a slow, unsteady breath. "I can't leave him in Somalia to die, Drakon. The pirates will kill him if they don't get the ransom money—"

"It would serve him right."

"He's my father!"

"You'll put yourself in debt for the rest of your life, just to buy his freedom, even though you know that his freedom will be short-lived?"

"Yes."

"You do understand that he'll be arrested the moment he tries to enter any North American or European country?"

"Yes."

"He's never going to be free again. He's going to spend

the rest of his life in prison, just like Michael Amery will, once he's caught, too."

"I understand. But far better for my father to be in an American prison than held by Somali pirates. At least in the United States he could get medical care if he's sick, or medicine for his blood pressure. At least he could have visitors and letters and contact with the outside world. God knows what his conditions are like in Somalia—"

"I'm sure they're not luxurious. But why should the American taxpayer have to support your father? Let him stay where he is. It's what he deserves."

"Do you say this to hurt me, or is it because he lost so much of your money?"

"I'm a businessman. I don't like to lose money. But I was only in four hundred million of the five billion he gave to Amery. What about those others? The majority were regular people. People who trusted your father with their retirement money…their life savings. And what did he do? He wiped them out. Left them with nothing. No retirement, no security, no way to pay the bills now that they're older and frailer and unemployable."

Morgan blinked hard to clear her vision. "Michael Amery was my father's best friend. He was like family. Dad trusted him implicitly." Her voice cracked and she struggled to regain her composure. "I grew up calling him Uncle Michael. I thought of him as my family."

"Yes, that's what you told me. Just before I gave your father four hundred million dollars to invest for me. I nearly gave him more. Your father wanted more. Twice as much, as a matter of fact."

"I am so sorry."

"I trusted your father." His gaze met hers and held. "Trusted you. I know better now."

She exhaled slowly. "Does that mean you won't help me?"

"It means…" His voice faded, and his gaze narrowed as

he looked at her, closely, carefully, studying her intently. "Probably not."

"Probably?" she repeated hoarsely, aware that if Drakon wouldn't help her, no one would. The world hated her father, and wanted him gone. They all hoped he was dead. And they all hoped he'd suffered before he died, too.

"Surely you must realize I'm no fan of your father's, *glykia mou.*"

"You don't have to be a fan of my father's to loan me the money. We'll draft a contract, a legal document that is between you and me, and I will pay you back in regular installments. It will take time, but it'll happen. My business is growing, building. I've got hundreds of thousands of dollars of orders coming in. I promise—"

"Just like you promised to love me? Honor me? Be true to me for better or worse, in sickness and in health?"

She winced. He made it sound as if she hadn't ever cared for him, when nothing could be further from the truth. The truth was, she'd cared too much. She'd loved him without reservation. And by loving him so much, she'd lost herself entirely. "So why haven't you divorced me then? If you despise me so much, why not let me go? Set me free?"

"Because I'm not like you. I don't make commitments and run from them. I don't make promises and then break them. I promised five and a half years ago to be loyal to you, and I have been."

His deep gravelly voice was making her insides wobble while his focused gaze rested on her, examining her, as if she were a prized pet that had been lost and found.

"Those are just words, Drakon. They mean nothing to me. Not when your actions speak so much louder."

"My actions?"

"Yes, your actions. Or your lack of action. You only do something if it benefits you. You married me because it benefited you...or you thought it would. And then when times were difficult…when I became difficult…you disappeared. You wouldn't grant me a divorce but you certainly didn't come after me, fight for me. And then when the world turned against us, where were you again? Nowhere. God knows you wouldn't want your name sullied by connection with the Copeland family!"

He studied her for an endless moment. "Interesting how you put things together. But not entirely surprising. You've inherited your mother's flair for the dramatic—"

"I hate you! I do." Her voice shook and her eyes burned, but she wouldn't cry, wouldn't give him the satisfaction. He'd taken everything from her, but not anymore. "I knew you'd mock me, humiliate me. I knew when I flew here, you'd make it difficult, but I came anyway, determined to do whatever I had to do to help my father. You'll let me plead with you, you'll let me beg—"

"That was a very passionate speech, so please forgive my interruption, but I'd like to clarify something. I don't believe you've begged. You've asked for money. You've demanded money. You've explained why you needed money. But there's been very little pleading, and absolutely no begging, at all."

A pulse beat wildly in her throat. She could feel the same wild flutter in her wrists and behind her ears. Everything in her was racing, raging. "Is that what you want? You'd like for me to beg you to help me?"

His head cocked, and he studied her, his gaze penetrating. "It'd certainly be a little more conciliatory, and far less antagonistic."

"Conciliatory." She repeated the word, rolling it over in her mouth, finding it sharp and bitter.

He said nothing, just watched her, and she felt almost breathless at the scrutiny, remembering how it had been between them during their four weeks here on their honeymoon. It was in this villa she'd learned about love and lust, sex and pleasure, as well as pain and control, and the loss of control.

Drakon never lost control. But he'd made sure she did at least once a day, sometimes two or three times.

Their sex life had been hot. Explosive. Erotic. She'd been a virgin when she'd married him and their first time together had been uncomfortable. He was large and it had hurt when he entered her fully. He'd tried to make it pleasurable for her but she'd been so overwhelmed and emotional, as well as let down. She couldn't respond properly, couldn't climax, and she knew she was supposed to. Knew he wanted her to.

He'd showered with her afterward, and kissed her, and beneath the pulsing spray of the shower, he lavished attention on her breasts and nipples, the curve of her buttocks and the cleft between her thighs, lightly playing with her clit until he finally accomplished what he hadn't in bed—she came. One of his arms held her up since her legs were too weak to do the job, and then he'd kissed her deeply, possessively, and when she could catch her breath, he'd assured her that the next time he entered her, it wouldn't hurt. That sex would never hurt again.

It hadn't.

But that didn't mean sex was always easy or comfortable. Drakon liked it hot. Intense. Sensual. Raw. Unpredictable.

He loved to stand across the room from her—just as he was doing now—and he'd tell her what to do. Tell her what he wanted. Sometimes he wanted her to strip and then walk naked to him. Sometimes he wanted her to strip to just her panties and crawl to him. Sometimes he wanted her to wear nothing but her elegant heels and bend over…or put a foot on a chair and he'd tell her where to touch herself.

Each time Morgan would protest, but he'd look at her from beneath his black lashes, his amber gaze lazy, his full mouth curved, and he'd tell her how beautiful she was and how much he enjoyed looking at her, that it gave him so much pleasure to see her, and to have her trust him....

Obey him...

She hated those words, hated the element of dominance, but it was part of the foreplay. They had good sex in bed, but then they had this other kind of sex—the sex where they played erotic games that pushed her out of her comfort zone. It had been confusing, but inevitably she did what he asked, and then somewhere along the way, he'd join her, and his mouth would be on her, between her legs, and his hands would hold her, fingers tight on her butt, or in her hair, or gripping her thighs, holding them apart, and he'd make love to her with his mouth and his fingers and his body and he'd arouse her so slowly that she feared she wouldn't ever come, and then just when the desire turned sharp and hurt, he'd relent. He'd flick the tip of his tongue across that small sensitive nub, or suck on her, or stroke her, or enter her and she'd break. Shatter. And the orgasms were so intense they seemed to go on forever. Maybe because he made sure they went on forever. And by the time he was finished, she was finished. There was nothing left. She was drained, spent, but also quiet. Compliant.

He loved her flushed and warm, quiet and compliant. Loved her physically that is, as long as she made no emotional demands. No conversation. No time, energy or patience. Required no attention.

Morgan's chest ached. Her heart hurt. She'd been so young then, so trusting and naive. She'd been determined to please him, her beautiful, sensual Greek husband.

Their honeymoon here, those thirty days of erotic lovemaking, had changed her forever. She couldn't even think of this villa without remembering how he'd made love to her in every single room, in every way imaginable. Taking her on chairs and beds, window seats and stairs. Pressing her naked back or breasts to priceless carpets, the marble floor, the cool emerald-green Italian tiles in the hall…

She wanted to throw up. He hadn't just taken her. He'd broken her.

"Help me out if you would, Drakon," she said, her voice pitched low, hoarse. "I'm not sure I understand you, and I don't know if it's cultural, personal or a language issue. But do you *want* me to beg? Is that what you're asking me to do?" Her chin lifted and tears sparkled in her eyes even as her heart burned as if it had been torched with fire. "Am I to go onto my knees in front of you, and plead my case? Is that what it would take to win your assistance?"

He didn't move a muscle and yet the vast living room suddenly felt very small. "I do like you on your knees," he said cordially, because they both knew that on her knees she could take him in her mouth, or he could touch her or take her from behind.

She drew a ragged breath, locked her knees, praying for strength. "I haven't forgotten," she said, aware that she was in trouble here, aware that she ought to go. Now. While she could. While she still had some self-respect left. "Although God knows, I've tried."

"Why would you want to forget it? We had an incredible sex life. It was amazing between us."

She could only look at him, intrigued by his memory of them, as well as appalled. Their sex life had been hot, but their marriage had been empty and shallow.

Obviously that didn't trouble him. It probably didn't even cross his mind that his bride had feelings. Emotions. Needs. Why should it? Drakon's desires were so much simpler. He just needed her available and willing, as if she were an American porn star in a rented Italian villa.

"So on my knees it is," she said mockingly, lifting the hem of her pale blue skirt to kneel on his limestone floor.

"Get up," he growled sharply.

"But this *is* what you want?"

"No. It's not what I want, not like this, not because you need something, want something. It's one thing if we're making love and there's pleasure involved, but there's no pleasure in seeing you beg, especially to me. The very suggestion disgusts me."

"And yet you seemed so charmed by the memory of me on my knees."

"Because that was different. That was sex. This is..." He shook his head, features tight, full mouth thinned. For a moment he just breathed, and the silence stretched.

Morgan welcomed the silence. She needed it. Her mind was whirling, her insides churning. She felt sick, dizzy and off balance by the contradictions and the intensity and her own desperation.

He had to help her.

He had to.

If he didn't, her father was forever lost to her.

"I've no desire to ever see my wife degrade herself," Drakon added quietly, "not even on behalf of her father. It actually sickens me to think you'd do that for him—"

"He's my father!"

"And he failed you! And it makes me physically ill that you'd beg for a man who refused to protect you and your sisters and your mother. A man is to provide for his family, not rob them blind."

"How nice it must be, Drakon Xanthis, to live, untouched and superior, in your ivory tower." Her voice deepened and her jaw ached and everything in her chest felt so raw and hot. "But I don't have the luxury of having an ivory tower. I don't have any luxuries anymore. Everything's gone in my family, Drakon. The money, the security, the houses, the cars, the name...our reputation. And I can lose the lifestyle, it's just a lifestyle. But I've lost far more than that. My family's shattered. Broken. We live in chaos—"

She broke off, dragged in a breath, feeling wild and unhinged. But losing control with Drakon wouldn't help her. It would hurt her. He didn't like strong emotions. He pulled away when voices got louder, stronger, preferring calm, rational, unemotional conversation.

And, of course, that's what she'd think about now. What Drakon wanted. How he liked things. How ironic that even after five years, she was still worrying about him, still turning herself inside out to please him, to be what *he* needed, to handle things the way *he* handled them.

What about her?

What about what she needed? What she wanted? What about her emotions or her comfort?

The back of her eyes burned and she jerked her chin higher. "Well, I'm sorry you don't like seeing me like this, but this is who I am. Desperate. And I'm willing to take desperate measures to help my family. You don't understand what it's like for us. My family is in pain. Everyone is hurting, heartsick with guilt and shame and confusion—how could my father do what he did? How could he not know Amery wasn't investing legitimately? How could he not protect his clients...his friends...his family? My sisters and brother—we can't even see each other anymore, Drakon. We don't speak to each other. We can't handle the shame of it all. We're outcasts now. Bottom feeders. Scum. So fine, stand there and mock me with your principles. I'm just trying to save what I can. Starting with my father's life."

"Your father isn't worth it. But you are. Stop worrying about him, Morgan, and save yourself."

"And how do I do that, Drakon? Have you any advice for me there?"

"Yes. Come home."

"Home?"

"Yes, home to me—"

"You're not home, Drakon. You were never home."

She saw him flinch and she didn't like it, but it was time he knew the truth. Time he heard the truth. "You asked me a little bit ago why I'd want to forget our sex life, and I'll tell you. I don't like remembering. It hurts remembering."

"Why? It was good. No, it was great. We were unbelievable together—"

"Yes, yes, the sex was hot. And erotic. You were an incredibly skillful lover. You could make me come over and over, several times a day. But that's all you gave me. Your name, a million-dollar diamond wedding ring and orgasms. Lots and lots of orgasms. But there was no relationship, no communication, no connection. I didn't marry you to just have sex. I married you to have a life, a home. Happiness. But after six months of being married to you, all I felt was empty, isolated and deeply unhappy."

She held his gaze, glad she'd at last said what she'd wanted to say all those years ago, and yet fully aware that these revelations changed nothing. They were just the final nail in a coffin that had been needing to be sealed shut. "I was so unhappy I could barely function, and yet there you were, touching me, kissing me, making me come. I'd cry after I came. I'd cry because it hurt me so much that you could love my body and not love me."

"I loved you."

"You didn't."

"You can accuse me of being a bad husband, of being cold, of being insensitive, but don't tell me how I felt, because I know how I felt. And I did love you. Maybe I didn't say it often—"

"Or ever."

"But I thought you knew."

"Clearly, I didn't."

He stared at her from across the room, his features so hard they looked chiseled from stone. "Why didn't you tell me?" he said finally.

"Because you hated me talking to you." Her throat ached and she swallowed around the lump with difficulty. "Every time I opened my mouth to say anything you'd roll your eyes or sigh or turn away—"

"Not true, either."

"It is true. For me, it's true. And maybe you were raised in a culture where women are happy to be seen and not heard, but I'm an American. I come from a big family. I have three sisters and a brother and am used to conversation and laughter and activity and the only activity I got from you was sex, and even then it wasn't mutual. You were the boss, you were in control, dictating to me how it'd be. Strip, crawl, come—" She broke off, gasping for air, and shoved a trembling hand across her eyes, wiping them dry before any tears could fall. "So don't act so shocked that I'd beg you to help me save my father. Don't say it's degrading and beneath me. I know what degrading is. I know what degrading does. And I've been there, in our marriage, with you."

And then she was done, gone.

Morgan raced to the door, her heels clicking on the polished marble, her purse on the antique console in the grand hall close to the front door, her travel bag in the trunk of her hired car.

She'd flown to Naples this morning from London, and yesterday to London from Los Angeles, almost twenty hours of traveling just to get here, never mind the tortuous winding drive to the villa perched high on the cliffs of the coast between Positano and Ravello. She was exhausted and flattened. Finished. But she wasn't broken. Wasn't shattered, not the way she'd been leaving him the first time.

Count it as a victory, she told herself, wrenching open the front door and stepping outside into the blinding sunshine. *You came, you saw him and you're leaving in one piece. You did it. You faced your dragon and you survived him.*

CHAPTER TWO

DRAKON WATCHED MORGAN spin and race from the living room, her cheeks pale, her long dark hair swinging. He could hear her high-heeled sandals clicking against the gleaming floor as she ran, and then heard the front door open and slam shut behind her.

He slowly exhaled and focused on the silence, letting the stillness and quiet wash over him, calm him.

In a moment he'd go after her, but first he needed to gather his thoughts, check his emotions. It wouldn't do to follow her in a fury—and he was furious. Beyond furious.

So he'd wait. He'd wait until his famous control was firmly in check. He prided himself on his control. Prided himself for not taking out his frustrations on others.

He could afford to give Morgan a few minutes, too. It's not as if she would be able to go anywhere. Her hired car and driver were gone, paid off, dispensed with, and the villa was set off the main road, private and remote. There would be no taxis nearby. She wasn't the sort to stomp away on foot.

And so Drakon used the quiet and the silence to reflect on everything she'd said. She'd said quite a bit. Much of it uncomfortable, and some of it downright shocking, as well as infuriating.

She'd felt degraded in their marriage?

Absolute rubbish. And the fact that she'd dare say such

a thing to his face after all these years made him want to throttle her, which seriously worried him.

He wasn't a violent man. He didn't lose his temper. Didn't even recognize the marriage she described. He had loved her, and he'd spoiled her. Pampered her. Worshipped her body. How was that degrading?

And how dare she accuse him of being a bad husband? He'd given her everything, had done everything for her, determined to make her happy. Her feelings had been important to him. He'd been a respectful husband, a kind husband, having far too many memories of an unhappy childhood, a childhood filled with tense, angry people—namely his mother—to want his wife to be anything but satisfied and content.

His mother, Maria, wasn't a bad woman, she was a good woman, a godly woman, and she tried to be fair, just, but that hadn't made her affectionate. Or gentle.

Widowed at thirty-five when Drakon's father died of a heart attack at sea, Maria had found raising five children on her own overwhelming. The Xanthis family was wealthy and she didn't have to worry about money, but that didn't seem to give her much relief, not when she was so angry that Drakon's father, Sebastian, had died leaving her with all these children, children she wasn't sure she'd ever wanted. One child might have been fine, but five was four too many.

Drakon, being the second eldest, and the oldest son, tried to be philosophical about her anger and resentment. She came from a wealthy family herself and had grown up comfortable. He told himself that her lack of affection and attention wasn't personal, but rather a result of grief, and too many pregnancies too close together. And so he learned by watching her, that she was most comfortable around her children if they asked for nothing, revealed no emotion or expressed no need. Drakon internalized the lesson well, and by thirteen and fourteen, he became the perfect son, by having no needs, or emotions.

But that didn't mean he didn't enjoy pleasing others. Throughout his twenties he had taken tremendous pride in spoiling his girlfriends, beautiful glamorous women who enjoyed being pampered and showered with pretty gifts and extravagant nights out. The women in his life quickly came to understand that he didn't show emotion and they didn't expect him to. It wasn't that he didn't feel, but it wasn't easy to feel. There were emotions in him somewhere, just not accessible. His girlfriends enjoyed his lifestyle, and his ability to please them, and they accepted him for who he was, and that he expressed himself best through action—doing or buying something for someone.

So he bought gifts and whisked his love interests to romantic getaways. And he became a skilled lover, a patient and gifted lover who understood the importance of foreplay.

Women needed to be turned on mentally before they were turned on physically. The brain was their largest erogenous zone, with their skin coming in second. And so Drakon loved to seduce his partner slowly, teasing her, playing with her, whetting the appetite and creating anticipation, because sex was how he bonded. It's how he felt close to his woman. It was how he felt safe expressing himself.

And yet she hadn't felt safe with him. She hadn't even enjoyed being with him. Their lovemaking had disgusted her. He had disgusted her. He'd turned off Morgan.

Drakon's stomach heaved. He swallowed the bitter taste in his mouth.

How stupid he'd been. Moronic.

No wonder she'd left him. No wonder she'd waited until he had flown to London for the day. He had only been away for the day, having flown out early on his jet, returning for a late dinner. But when he had entered their villa in Ekali, a northern suburb of Athens, the villa had been dark. No staff. No dinner. No welcome. No Morgan.

He remembered being blindsided that night. Remembered

thinking, he could go without dinner, could live without food, but he couldn't live without Morgan.

He'd called her that night, but she didn't answer. He'd left a message. Left another. Had flown to see her. She wasn't to be found.

He'd called again, left another message, asking her to come home. She didn't. She wouldn't even speak to him, forcing him instead to interact with her trio of attorneys as they informed him that their client was filing for divorce and moving on with her life, without him.

His surprise gave way to frustration and fury, but he never lost his temper with her. He tried to remain cool, focused, pragmatic. Things had a way of working out. He needed to be patient, and he refused to divorce her, insisting he wouldn't agree to a divorce until she met with him. Sat down and talked with him. In person.

She wouldn't. And so for two years her attorneys had battled on her behalf, while Drakon had battled back. His wife would not leave him without giving him a proper explanation. His wife could not just walk away on a whim.

While the Copeland attorneys filed their lawsuits and counter lawsuits, Drakon had made repeated attempts to see Morgan. But every attempt to reach her was stymied. Her cell phone was disconnected. He had no idea where she was living. Her family would only say she'd gone away indefinitely. Drakon had hired private investigators to find her, but they couldn't. Morgan had vanished.

For two and a half years she'd vanished into thin air.

And then in October she had reappeared, emerging again on the New York social scene.

The private investigators sent Drakon her address, a high-rent loft in SoHo, paid for by her father. She'd started her own business as a jewelry designer and had opened a small shop down the street from her loft, locating her little store close to big hitters.

Drakon immediately flew to New York to see her, going straight from the airport to her boutique, hoping that's where he'd find her at 11:00 a.m. on a Wednesday morning. Before he even stepped from his limousine, she walked out the shop's front door with her youngest sister, Jemma. At first glance they looked like any glamorous girls about town, slim and chic, with long gleaming hair and their skin lightly golden from expensive spray-on tans, but after that first impression of beauty and glamour, he saw how extremely thin Morgan was, dangerously thin. She looked like a skeleton in her silk tunic and low-waisted trousers. Wide gold bangles covered her forearms, and Drakon wondered if it was an attempt to hide her extreme slenderness, or perhaps accent her physique?

He didn't know, wasn't sure he wanted to know. The only thing he knew for certain was that she didn't look well and he was baffled by the change in her.

He let her go, leaving her with Jemma, and had his driver take him to her father's building on 53rd and Third Avenue. Daniel Copeland could barely hide his shock at seeing Drakon Xanthis in his office, but welcomed him cordially—he was, after all, taking care of Drakon's investment—and asked him to have a seat.

"I saw Morgan today," Drakon had said bluntly, choosing not to sit. "What's wrong with her? She doesn't look well."

"She hasn't been well," Daniel answered just as bluntly.

"So what's wrong with her?" he repeated.

"That's her business."

"She's my wife."

"Only because you won't let her go."

"I don't believe in divorce."

"She's not happy with you, Drakon. You need to let her go."

"Then she needs to come tell me that herself." He'd left Daniel's office after that, and for several weeks he'd expected a call from Morgan, expected an email, something to say she was ready to meet with him.

But she didn't contact him. And he didn't reach out to her. And the impasse had continued until three days ago when Morgan had called him, and requested a meeting. She'd told him up front why she wanted to see him. She made it clear that this had nothing to do with them, or their marriage, but her need for a loan, adding that she was only coming to him because no one else would help her.

You are my last resort, she'd said. *If you don't help me, no one will.*

He'd agreed to see her, telling her to meet him here, at Villa Angelica. He'd thought perhaps by meeting here, where they'd embarked on their married life, they could come to an understanding and heal the breach. Perhaps face-to-face here, where they had been happy, he could persuade Morgan to return to Athens. It was time. He wanted children, a family. He wanted his wife back where she was supposed to be—in his home, at his side.

Now he realized there was no hope, there never had been, and he felt stupid and angry.

Worse, he felt betrayed. Betrayed by the woman he'd vowed to love and protect, a woman he'd continued to love these past five years, because it was his duty to love her. To be faithful to her. To provide for her.

But he was done with his duty. Done with his loyalty. Done with her.

He wanted her gone.

It was time to give her what she wanted. Time to give them both what they needed—freedom.

Drakon ran a hand over his jaw, feeling the dense beard, a beard he'd started growing that day he'd learned she intended to end their marriage without uttering a single word, or explanation, or apology to him.

He'd vowed he'd grow his beard until his wife returned home, or until he'd understood what had happened between them.

It had been an emotional, impulsive vow, but he'd kept it. Just as he'd kept hope that one day Morgan, his wife, would return to him.

And she had returned, but only to tell him how much she hated him. How much she despised him. How degrading she'd found their marriage.

Drakon exhaled slowly, trying to control the hot rush of emotion that made his chest ache and burn. He wasn't used to feeling such strong emotions. But he was feeling them now.

He headed into the small sitting room, which opened off the living room to his laptop and his briefcase. He took a checkbook to his personal account out of his briefcase and quickly scrawled her name on a check and filled in the amount, before dating it and signing it. He studied the check for a moment, the anger bubbling up, threatening to consume him, and it took all of his control to push it back down, suppressing it with ruthless intent.

He wasn't a failure. She was the failure. She was the one who had walked out on him, not the other way around. He was the one who had fought to save their marriage, who had honored their vows, who had honored her by thinking of no other woman but his wife, wanting no other woman than Morgan.

But now he was done with Morgan. He'd give her the money she wanted and let her go and once she left, he wouldn't waste another moment of his life thinking or worrying about her. She wanted her freedom? Well, she was about to get it.

Morgan was standing on the villa's front steps gazing out at the sweeping drive, with the stunning view of the dark green mountains that dropped steeply and dramatically into the sapphire sea, anxiously rubbing her nails back and forth against her linen skirt, when she heard the front door open behind her.

Her skin prickled and the fine hair at her nape lifted. She knew without even turning around it was Drakon. She could feel his warmth, that magnetic energy of his that drew everything toward him, including her.

But she wouldn't allow herself to be drawn back into his life. Wouldn't give him power over her ever again.

She quickly moved down the front steps, putting distance between them. She refused to look at him, was unable to look at him when she was filled with so much anger and loathing.

"You had no right to send away my car," she said coolly, her gaze resolutely fixed on the dazzling blue and green colors of the coast, but unable to appreciate them, or the lushness of the dark pink bougainvillea blooming profusely along the stone wall bordering the private drive. Panic flooded her limbs. He was so close to her she could barely breathe, much less think.

"I didn't think you'd need it," he said.

She looked sharply at him then, surprised by his audacity, his arrogance. "Did you imagine I was going to stay?"

"I'd hoped," he answered simply.

She sucked in a breath, hating him anew. He could be so charming when he wanted to be. So endearing and real. And then he could take it all away again, just like that. "You really thought I'd take one look at you and forget my unhappiness? Forget why I wanted the divorce?"

"I thought you'd at least sit down and talk to me. Have a real conversation with me."

"You don't like conversation, Drakon. You only want information in bullet form. Brief, concise and to the point."

He was silent a moment, and then he nodded once, a short, decisive nod. "Then I'll be brief in return. The helicopter is on the way for you. Should be here soon. And I have this for you." He handed her a folded piece of paper.

Morgan took it from him, opened it. It was a check for seven million dollars. She looked up at Drakon in surprise. "What's this?"

"The money you begged for."

She flinched. "The pirates are only asking for six."

"There will be other expenses. Travel and rescue logistics. You'll want to hire an expert to help you. Someone with the right negotiation skills. There are several excellent firms out there, like Dunamas Maritime Intelligence—"

"I'm familiar with them."

"They won't be cheap."

"I'm familiar with their fees."

"Don't try to do it on your own, thinking you can. Better to pay for their expertise and their relationships. They know what they're doing, and they'll help you avoid a trap. The Somali pirates sound like they're a ragtag organization, but in truth, they're being funded by some of the wealthiest, most powerful people in the world."

She nodded, because she couldn't speak, not with her throat swelling closed. For the first time in a long, long time, she was grateful for Drakon Xanthis, grateful he had not just the means to help her, but knowledge and power. There weren't many people like Drakon in the world, and she was suddenly so very glad he had been part of her life.

"Use whatever is left after you pay your management fee to pay your father's travel expenses home. There should be enough. If there isn't, let me know immediately," he added.

"Thank you," she whispered huskily.

His jaw tightened. "Go to London before you return to New York, cash the check at the London branch of my bank. There won't be any problems. They'll give you the six million in cash you need for the ransom. You must have it in cash, and not new bills, remember that. But I'm sure your contact told you that?"

"Yes."

His lashes dropped, concealing his expression. "They're very particular, *agapi mou.* Follow the instructions exactly. If you don't, things could turn unpleasant."

"As if storming my father's yacht off the Horn of Africa, and killing his captain, wasn't unpleasant enough—" She broke off, hearing the distinctive hum of the helicopter. It was still a distance from them, but it would be here soon.

For a moment neither said anything, both listening to the whir of the helicopter blades.

"Why have you kept the news of your father's kidnapping private?" he asked her. "I would have thought this was something you'd share with the world...using the kidnapping to garner sympathy."

"Because it wouldn't garner sympathy. The American public hates him. Loathes him. And if they discovered he was kidnapped by Somali pirates, they'd be glad. They'd be dancing in the streets, celebrating, posting all kinds of horrible comments all over the internet, hoping he'll starve, or be killed, saying it's karma—"

"Isn't it?"

She acted as though Drakon hadn't spoken. "But he's my father, not theirs, and I'm not using their money. Not spending government funds, public funds or trust funds. We haven't gone to the police or the FBI, haven't asked for help from anyone. We're keeping this in the family, handling it on our own, and since my brother and sisters don't have the means, I'm using my money—"

"You mean my money."

She flushed, and bit hard into her lower lip, embarrassed. His money. Right. They weren't married, not really, and she had no right to spend his money, just because she had nothing left of her own.

"I stand corrected," she whispered. "Your money. I'm using your money. But I will pay you back. Every penny. Even if it takes me the rest of my life."

A small muscle popped in his jaw. "There is no need for that—" He paused, glancing up at the dark speck overhead. The helicopter.

One of the reasons Drakon had chosen this villa for their honeymoon five and a half years ago was that the outdoor pool had a special cover that converted it into a heli landing pad, making the remote villa far more appealing for a man who needed to come and go for meetings in Naples, Athens and London.

"No need to pay me back," Drakon said, picking up his broken train of thought, "because I'm calling my attorney this afternoon and asking him to process the paperwork for the divorce. He will make sure the dissolution is expedited. By the end of the month, it will be over."

It will be over. For a moment Morgan couldn't take this last bit in. What was he saying? He'd finally agreed to the divorce?

He was giving her the money *and* granting her the divorce?

She just looked up at him, eyes burning, too overwhelmed to speak.

He dipped his head and raised his voice in order to be heard over the hum of the helicopter, which had begun to descend. "You will receive your full settlement once the dissolution occurs. With the current state of affairs, I'd suggest you allow me to open a personal account for you in London or Geneva and I can deposit the funds directly into the account without fear of your government freezing it. I know they've frozen all your family accounts in the United States—"

"I don't want your money."

"Yes, you do. You came here for my money. So take what you came for—"

"I came to see you for my father, and that was the only reason I came here today."

"A point you made abundantly clear." He smiled at her

but his amber gaze looked icy, the golden depths tinged with frost. "So I am giving you what you wanted, freedom and financial security, which fulfills my obligation to you."

She shivered at the hardness in his voice. She had never heard him speak to her with so much coldness and disdain and it crushed her to think they were ending it like this—with contempt and anger.

"I'm sorry," she whispered, her heart beating too fast and aching far too much.

He didn't answer her, his gaze fixed on the helicopter slowly descending. Morgan watched him and not the helicopter, aware that this just might be the last time she would see Drakon and was drinking him in, trying to memorize every detail, trying to remember him. This.

"Thank you," she added, wanting him to just look at her, acknowledge her, without this new terrible coldness.

But he didn't. He wouldn't. "I'll walk you to the landing pad," he said, putting his hand out to gesture the way without touching her or looking at her.

Perhaps it was better this way, she told herself, forcing herself to move. It was hard enough being near him without wanting to be closer to him. Perhaps if he'd been kind or gentle, she'd just want more of him, because she'd always wanted more of him, never less. The doctors had said she was addicted to him, and her addiction wasn't healthy. He wasn't the sun, they lectured her, and Drakon, despite his intense charisma and chemistry, couldn't warm her, nor could he actually give her strength. She was the only one who could give herself strength, and the only way she could do that was by leaving him, putting him behind her.

And so here she was again, leaving him. Putting him behind her.

So be strong, she told herself. *Prove that you're strong on your own.*

Morgan blinked to clear her vision, fighting panic as they

rounded the villa and walked across the lawn for the oper pool terrace where the helicopter waited, balancing like a peculiar moth on the high-tech titanium cover concealing the pool. The roar from the helicopter's spinning blades made conversation impossible, not that Drakon wanted to talk to her.

One of the household staff met them at the helicopter with Morgan's travel bag and Drakon set it inside the helicopter then spoke briefly to the pilot before putting out his hand to assist Morgan inside.

She glanced down at his outstretched hand, and then up into his face, into those unique amber eyes that had captivated her from the start. "Thank you again, Drakon, and hope you'll be happy."

His lips curved, but his eyes glittered with silent fury. "I: that a joke? Am I supposed to be amused?"

She drew back, stunned by his flash of temper. For a moment she could only stare at him, surprised, bewildered, by this fierce man. This was a different Drakon than the mar she'd married. This was a Drakon of intense emotions and yet after they'd married she'd become convinced that Drakon felt no emotion. "I'm serious. I want you to be happy You deserve to be happy—"

"As you said I'm not one for meaningless conversation, so I'm going to walk away now to save us from an embarrass ing and uncomfortable goodbye," he said brusquely, cutting her short, to propel her into the helicopter. Once he had he inside, he leaned in, his features harsh, and shouted to her "Don't try to cut corners, Morgan, and save money by handling the pirates yourself. Get help. Call Dunamas, or Blue Sea, or one of the other maritime intelligence companies Understand me?"

His fierce gaze held hers, and she nodded jerkily, even a her stomach rose up, and her heart fell. If he only knew...

If he only knew what she had done....

And for a split second she nearly blurted the truth, how she had been negotiating with the pirates on her own, and how she'd thought she was in control, until it had all gone terribly wrong, which was why she was here...which was why she needed Drakon so much. But before she could say any of it, Drakon had turned around and was walking away from the helicopter.

Walking away from her.

Her eyes burned and her throat sealed closed as the pilot handed Morgan a set of headphones, but she couldn't focus on the pilot's instructions, not when she was watching Drakon stride toward the villa.

He was walking quickly, passing the rose-covered balustrade on the lower terrace then climbing the staircase to the upper terrace, and the entire time she prayed he'd turn around, pray he'd acknowledge her, pray he'd wave or smile, or just *look* at her.

He didn't.

He crossed the terrace to the old ballroom and disappeared into the great stone house without a backward glance.

So that was it. Done. Over. She was finally free to move on, find happiness, find love elsewhere.

She should be happy. She should feel at peace. But as the helicopter lifted off the pad, straight into the air, Morgan didn't feel any relief, just panic. Because she didn't get the help she needed, and she'd lost him completely.

It wasn't supposed to have gone like this. The meeting today...as well as their marriage. Because she had loved him. She'd loved him with everything she was, everything she had, and it hadn't been enough. It should have been enough. Why wasn't it enough? In the beginning she'd thought he was perfect. In the beginning she'd thought she'd found her soul mate. But she was wrong.

Seconds passed, becoming one minute and then another as the helicopter rose higher and higher, straight up so that the villa fell away and the world was all blue and green, with the sea on one side and the sharp, steep mountains on the other and the villa with its famous garden clinging to that bit of space on the rock.

Fighting tears, her gaze fell on the check she still clutched in her hand. Seven million dollars. Just like that.

And she'd known that he'd help her if she went to him. She'd known he'd come through for her, too, because he'd never refused her anything. Drakon might not have given her much of his time or patience, but he'd never withheld anything material from her.

Guilt pummeled her, guilt and fear and anxiety, because she hadn't accomplished everything she'd come to Villa Angelica to accomplish. She needed more from Drakon than just a check. She needed not just financial assistance, but his help, too. There were few men in the world who had his knowledge of piracy and its impact on the shipping industry. Indeed, Drakon was considered one of the world's leading experts in counter piracy, and he'd know the safest, quickest method for securing her father's release, as well as the right people to help her.

Morgan exhaled in a rush, heart beating too hard.

She had to go back. Had to face Drakon again. Had to convince him to help her. Not that he'd want to help her now, not after everything that was said.

But this wasn't about pride or her ego. This was life and death, her father's life, specifically, and she couldn't turn her back on him.

Swallowing her fear and misgivings, Morgan grabbed at her seat belt as if throwing on brakes. "Stop, wait," she said to the pilot through the small microphone attached to her headphones. "We have to go back. I've forgotten something."

The pilot was too well-trained, and too well-paid, to question her. For a moment nothing seemed to happen and then he shifted and the helicopter began to slowly descend.

* * *

Drakon didn't wait for the helicopter to leave. There was no point. She was gone, and he was glad. While climbing the stairs to his bedroom suite, he heard the helicopter lift, the throbbing of the rotary blades vibrating all the way through the old stone walls.

In his bathroom, Drakon stripped his clothes off and showered, and then dried off, wrapping the towel around his hips and prepared to shave. It would take a while. There was a lot of beard.

He gathered his small scissors and his razor and shaving cream, and as he laid everything out, he tried not to think, particularly not of Morgan, but that was impossible. He was so upset. So angry.

What a piece of work she was. To think he'd wanted her back. To think he'd loved her. But how could he have loved her? She was shallow and superficial and so incredibly self-centered. It was always about her…what she wanted, what she needed, with no regard for anyone else's needs.

As he changed the blade on his razor, he felt a heaviness inside, a dull ache in his chest, as if he'd cut his heart. And then Drakon took the razor to his beard.

He had loved her, and he had wanted her back. Wanted her home with him. But that was before he understood how disgusted she was with him, how disgusted she'd been by their marriage.

Disgust.

He knew that word, and knew disgust produced shame. His mother used to be disgusted by emotion, and as a young child, Drakon had felt constant shame in her presence, shame that he had such strong emotions, emotions she found appalling. He still remembered how wild he'd felt on the inside as a little boy, how desperate and confused he'd felt by her rejection, and how determined he'd been to win her affection, even if it meant destroying part of himself. And so that became the goal, his sole objective as a child. To master his hideous emotions. To master want and need, to stifle them, suppress them, thereby winning his mother's approval and love.

He succeeded.

Drakon rinsed the shaving cream from his face and studied his smooth, clean jaw in the mirror. He'd forgotten what his face looked like without a beard, had forgotten how lean his cheeks were above his jutting chin. He had a hard chin, a stubborn chin, which was fitting since he knew he'd become a very hard, stubborn man.

A knock sounded on the outer door of his suite. Drakon mopped his damp face, grabbed a robe and crossed his room to open the door, expecting one of the villa staff.

It wasn't one of the staff. It was Morgan.

Something surged in his chest, hot and fierce, and then it was gone, replaced by coldness. Why was she back? What game was she playing now? He leaned against the door frame, and looked her up and down, coolly, unkindly. "Need more money already?"

Color stained her cheeks, making her blue eyes even deeper, brighter. "You...shaved."

"I did."

"We need to talk."

He arched an eyebrow. "Thank you, but no. I've heard more than enough from you already. Now if you'd be so good as to see yourself out, and get back into the helicopter—"

"The helicopter is gone. I sent him away."

"That was foolish of you. How are you getting back home?"

"We'll figure that out later."

"You mean, you can figure that out later. There is no more we. I'm done with you, and done helping you. You've got your check, and in a month's time you'll receive your settlement, but that's it. That's all there is. I've nothing more for you. Now if you'll excuse me, I have things to do."

Her eyebrows lifted and she walked past him, into his room, glancing around the impressive bedroom where they'd spent the first month of their marriage. "Looks just as I remembered," she said, turning to face him. "But you don't. You've changed."

"Yes, I grew a beard, I know."

"It's not just the beard and hair. It's you. You're different."

"Perhaps you weren't aware. My wife left me. It wasn't an easy thing."

She gave him a long, level look. "You could have come after me."

"I did."

"You did not."

"I *did*."

"I'm not talking about phone calls, or emails or texts. Those don't count."

"No, they don't, and they don't work, either, not once you turned your phone off. Which is why I flew repeatedly to New York, drove up to Greenwich—"

"You didn't!"

His hands clenched at his sides. "Good God, if you contradict me one more time, I will throttle you, Morgan, I will. Because I did go after you, I wanted you back, I wanted you home and I did everything I could to save our marriage. I visited your father at work. I appeared on your parents' doorstep. I spoke—repeatedly—to each of your siblings—"

"I can't believe it," she whispered.

"Believe it," he said grimly, moving toward her, stepping so close he could smell the hint of fragrance from her shampoo, and the sweet clean scent of her perfume on her skin. He loved her smell. Loved her softness. Loved everything about his woman.

But that was then, and this was now, and he was so done with the craziness and the chaos that had followed their marriage.

His gaze caught hers, held, and he stared down into her eyes, drinking in that intense blue that always made him think of the sea around his home in Greece. Tiny purple and gold flecks shimmered against the deep blue irises…like the glimmer of sun on the surface of water. He used to think her eyes perfectly expressed who she was…a woman of magic and mystery and natural beauty.

Now he knew he'd been tricked. Tricked and deceived by a beautiful face, by stunning blue eyes.

Bitterness rolled through him and his gut clenched, his jaw hardening, anger roiling. He really didn't like remembering, and he really didn't like feeling the fury and rejection again, but it was what it was. They were what they were. Such was life.

"And if you don't believe me, make some enquiries. Ask your brother, or your sister Tori, or Logan, or Jemma. Ask them all. Ask why no one would tell me anything. Demand answers, if not for you, then for me. Find out why the entire Copeland family turned their backs on me. I still don't know why. Just as I don't know why you disappeared, or where you went, but you were gone. I even hired private investigators, but you were nowhere to be found."

Morgan bundled her arms across her chest and drew a slow, unsteady breath. A small pulse beat wildly at the base of her throat. "You really came after me?"

"Of course I came after you! You were my wife. You think I just let you go? You think I'd just let you leave?"

She swallowed hard, her blue eyes shining. "Yes."

He swore softly, and walked away from her, putting distance between them. "I don't know what kind of man you think you married, but I am not he. In fact, you, my wife, know nothing about me!"

She followed him, her footsteps echoing on the tiled floor. "Maybe that's because you never gave me a chance to get to know you, Drakon."

He turned abruptly to face her, and she nearly bumped into him. "Or maybe it's because you didn't stay long enough to get to know me, *Morgan.*"

Morgan took a swift step backward, stunned by his blistering wrath. She squeezed her hands into fists, crumpling the check in her right hand.

The check.

She'd forgotten all about it. Her heart ached as she glanced down at the paper, creased and crumpled in her hand. "If that is truly the case," she said, voice husky, "I'm sorry."

"If," he echoed bitterly, his upper lip lifting. "I find it so ironic that you don't believe a word I say, and yet when you need something, you'll come running to me—"

"I didn't want to come to you."

"Oh, I'm quite sure of that." He made a rough sound and turned away, running a hand over his newly shaven jaw. "My God, what a joke. I can't believe I waited five years for this."

"What does that mean?"

"Forget it. I don't want to do this." He turned and looked at her, cheekbones jutting against his bronzed skin, his amber gaze hard. "I have finally come to the same realization you did five years ago. That we don't work. That we never worked. That there is no future. And since there is no future, I've nothing to say to you. You have the money, you have what you came for—"

"I didn't just come for money. I need your help."

"That's too bad, then, because the check is all you're getting from me."

She inhaled sharply. He sounded so angry, so bitter, so unlike her husband. "Drakon, please. You know how the pirates operate. You've dealt with them before—"

"No. Sorry. I'm not trying to be ugly, just honest. I'm done. Done with you. Done with your family. Done with your father—my God, there's a piece of work—but he's not my problem anymore, because I'm not his son-in-law anymore, either. And I never thought I'd say this, but I'm actually glad to be done…glad to have a complete break. You've exhausted every one of my resources, and I've nothing more to give. To you, or the rest of the Copeland family."

She winced and looked away, hoping he didn't see the tears that filled her eyes. "No one told me you came after me," she said faintly, her gaze fixed on the view of the sea beyond the window. "But then, in that first year after I left you, no one told me anything."

"I don't see how that is relevant now."

"It probably won't mean anything to you now, but it's relevant to me. It's a revelation, and a comfort—"

"A *comfort?*" he repeated sarcastically.

She lifted her chin a fraction, squared her shoulders. "Yes, a comfort, knowing you didn't give up on me quickly, or easily."

"Unlike you, who gave up so quickly and easily."

"I'm sorry."

"I'm sure you are, now that the privileged Copelands are broke."

She laughed to keep from crying. He was so very, very changed. "We're broke," she agreed, "every last one of us, and struggling, but my brother and sisters, they're smart. They'll be fine. They'll come out of this okay. Me…I'm in trouble. I'm stupid—"

"If this is a play for my sympathy, it's not working."

"No. I'm just telling you the truth. I'm stupid. Very, very stupid. You see, I didn't come to you first. I tried to handle the pirates on my own. And I've already given them money—"

"What?"

She licked her lower lip. "We didn't want it known about my father, and so we kept the details to ourselves, and I tried to manage freeing my father on my own, and I gave them money. But they didn't free my father."

Drakon just looked at her, his jaw clenched, his lips a hard flat line. She could see the pulse beating at the base of his throat. His amber gaze burned. He was furious.

Furious.

Morgan exhaled slowly, trying to calm herself, trying to steady her nerves, but it wasn't easy when her heart raced and the blood roared in her ears. "I didn't want to have to bother you, Drakon. I thought I could manage things better than I did."

He just kept staring at her, his spine stiff, his muscles tensed. He was clearly at war within himself and Morgan felt his anger and frustration. He wanted to kick her out of the villa but he didn't run from responsibilities, or from providing for his family.

He was Greek. Family was everything to him. Even if he didn't enjoy his family.

His tone was icy cold as he spoke. "You should have never tried to handle the pirates on your own. You should have gone to Dunamas or Blue Sea immediately—"

"I didn't have the money to pay for outside help or expertise," she said softly, cutting him short, unable to endure another lecture. "I didn't even have enough to pay the three million ransom. You see, that's what they asked for in the beginning. Three million. But I couldn't come up with exactly three million, and I'd run out of time, so I made the sea drop with what I had, thinking that almost three million was better than nothing, but I was wrong. The pirates were really angry, and accused me of playing games, and they were now doubling the ransom to six million and I had just two weeks or they'd execute Dad."

"How much were you short?"

"A hundred thousand."

"But you dropped two-point-nine million?"

She nodded. "I was so close to three million, and to get it I emptied my savings, sold my loft, liquidated everything I had, but I couldn't get more. I tried taking out personal loans from family and friends but no one was able to come up with a hundred thousand cash in the amount of time we had."

"You didn't come to me for the hundred thousand."

"I didn't want to involve you."

"You have now."

"Because there was no one else who would help me. No other way to come up with six million without my father's situation becoming public knowledge."

"One hundred thousand would have been a hell of a lot cheaper than six million."

"I know." Her stomach heaved. She felt so terribly queasy. "But then, I told you I was stupid. I was afraid to come to you, afraid to face you—"

"I wouldn't have hurt you."

"No, but I have my pride. And then there were all those feelings—" she broke off, and gulped air, thinking she might just throw up "—because I did have feelings for you, and they confused me, but in the end, I had to come. Had to ask you for help…help and money, because the pirates are playing games. They're toying with me and I'm scared. Scared of botching this, scared of never seeing my father again, scared that they have all the power and I have none."

She opened her fist, smoothed the creased check, studied the number and sum it represented. "I know you're angry with me, and I know you owe me nothing. I know it's I that owe you, but I need your help, Drakon. At the very least, I need your advice. What do I do now? How do I make sure that they will release my father this time?" Her gaze lifted, met his. "Who is to say that they will ever release him? Who is to say that he's even…he's even…" Her voice drifted off, and she gazed at him, unable to finish the thought.

But she didn't have to finish the thought. "You're afraid he might not be alive," Drakon said, brutally blunt.

She nodded, eyes stinging. "What if he isn't?"

"That's a good question."

"So you see why I need you. I've already given them three million. I can't give them another six without proof, but they refuse to let me speak to him, and I don't know what to do. I'm frightened, Drakon. And overwhelmed. I've been trying to keep it together, but I don't know how to do this—"

"You and your father sing the same tune, don't you?"

She just stared at him, confused. "What does that mean?"

"The only time I hear from you, or your father, is when one of the Copelands needs money. But I'm not a bank, or an ATM machine, and I'm tired of being used."

Morgan struggled to speak. "I never meant to use you, Drakon. And I certainly didn't marry you for money, and I'm ashamed my father asked you to invest in his company, ashamed that he'd put you in that position. I didn't agree with it then, and I'm shattered now that he lost so much of your personal wealth, but he is my father, and I can't leave him in Somalia. It might be acceptable…even fiscally responsible, but it's not morally responsible, not to me. And so I'm here, begging for your help because you are the only one who can help me."

She paused, swallowed, her gaze searching his face, trying to see a hint of softening on his part. "You might not want to hear this right now, Drakon, but you'd do the same if it were your family. I know you…I know who you are, and I know you'd sacrifice everything if you had to."

Drakon looked at her hard, his features harsh, expression shuttered, and then turned away, and walked to the window where he put his hand on the glass, his gaze fixed on the blue horizon. Silence stretched. Morgan waited for him to speak, not wanting to say more, or rush him to a decision, because she knew in her heart, he couldn't tell her no…it'd go against his values, go against his ethics as a man, and a protective Greek male.

But it was hard to wait, and her jaw ached from biting down

so hard, and her stomach churned and her head throbbed, but she had to wait. The ball was in Drakon's court now.

It was a long time before he spoke, and when he did, his voice was pitched so low she had to strain to hear. "I have sacrificed everything for my family," he said roughly. "And it taught me that no good deed goes unpunished."

Her eyes burned, gritty, and her chest squeezed tight with hot emotion. "Please tell me I wasn't the one who taught you that!"

His hand turned into a fist on the window.

Morgan closed her eyes, held her breath, her heart livid with pain. She had loved him...so much...too much....

"I need to think, and want some time," Drakon said, still staring out the window, after another long, tense silence. "Go downstairs. Wait for me there."

CHAPTER THREE

DRAKON WAITED FOR the bedroom door to close behind Morgan before turning around.

His gut churned with acid and every breath he drew hurt.

He wasn't going to do it. There was no way in hell he'd actually help her free her father. For one—he *hated* her father. For another—Drakon had washed his hands of her. The beard was gone. The vigil was over. Time to move forward.

There was no reason he needed to be involved. No reason to do more than he had. As it was, he'd gone above and beyond the call of duty. He'd given her the money, he'd told her what to do, he'd made it clear that there were those who knew exactly what to do, he'd named the people to call... he'd done everything for her, short of actually dialing Dunamas on his cell phone, and good God, he would not do that.

Drakon stalked back to the bathroom, stared at his reflection, seeing the grim features, the cold, dead eyes, and then suddenly his face dissolved in the mirror and he saw Morgan's instead.

He saw that perfect pale oval with its fine, elegant features, but her loveliness was overshadowed by the worry in her blue eyes, and the dark purple smudges beneath her eyes, and her unnatural pallor. Worse, even here, in the expansive marble bathroom, he could still feel her exhaustion and fatigue.

She'd practically trembled while talking to him, her thin arms and legs still too frail for his liking and he flashed back to that day in New York where he'd spotted her walking out of her shop with Jemma. Morgan might not be sick now, but she didn't look well.

Someone, somewhere should be helping her. Not him… she wasn't his to protect anymore…but there should be someone who could assist her. In an ideal world, there would be someone.

He shook his head, not comfortable with the direction his thoughts were taking him. She's not your problem, he told himself. She's not your responsibility. Not your woman.

Drakon groaned, turned away from the mirror, walked out of the bathroom, to retrieve his phone. He'd make a few calls, check on a few facts, see if he couldn't find someone to work with her, because she'd need someone at her side. Not him, of course, but someone who could offer advice and assistance, or just be a source of support.

Standing outside on his balcony he made a few calls, and then he made a few more, and a few more, and each call was worse than the last.

Morgan Copeland was in trouble.

She'd lost her home, her company, her friends, her reputation. She was a social outcast, *and* she was broke. She was overdrawn in her checking account and she'd maxed out every credit card she owned.

Drakon hung up from his last call and tossed the phone onto the bed.

Dammit.

Dammit.

He was so angry with her.…

And so angry with her rarified world for turning on her.

She had lost everything. She hadn't been exaggerating.

Morgan was standing in the living room by the enormous wall of windows when Drakon appeared, almost an hour after she'd left him in his bedroom. He'd dressed once again in the off white cashmere V-neck sweater he'd worn earlier, his legs long in the pressed khaki trousers, the sweater smooth over his muscular chest. He'd always had an amazing body, and his perfect build allowed him to wear anything and now with the beard gone she could see his face again and she couldn't look away.

She couldn't call him beautiful, his features were so strong, and his coloring so dark, but he had a sensuality and vitality about him that fascinated her, captivated her. "How long had you been growing that beard?" she asked.

"A long time."

"Years?"

"I'm not here to discuss my beard," he said curtly, crossing the room, walking toward her. "While upstairs I did some research, made a few phone calls, and you did sell your loft. Along with your boutique in SoHo."

Energy crackled around him and Morgan felt her insides jump, tumble. He was so physical, always had been, and the closer he got, the more the tension shifted, growing, building, changing, binding them together the way it always had. The way it always did. "I had to," she said breathlessly, "it was the only way to come up with the money."

"You should have told me immediately that you'd given the Somali pirates ransom money and that they'd failed to release your father."

"I thought you might not have helped me, if you knew...." Her voice faded as Drakon closed the distance between them. He was so alive, so electric, she could almost see little sparks shooting off him. Her heart pounded. Her tummy did another nervous, panicked flip.

She shouldn't have sent away the helicopter. She should have gone while she could. Now it was too late to run. Too late to save herself, and so she stared at him, waited for him, feeling the energy, his energy, that dizzying combination of warmth and heat, light and sparks. This was inevitable. He was inevitable. She could run and run and run, but part of her knew she'd never escape him. She'd run before and yet here she was. Right back where they'd honeymooned, Villa Angelica.

She'd known that coming here, to him, would change everything. Would change her.

It always did.

It already had.

Her legs trembled beneath her. Her heart pounded. Even now, after all these years, she felt almost sick with awareness, need. This chemistry and energy between them was so overwhelming. So consuming. She didn't understand it, and she'd wanted to understand it, if only to help her exorcise him from her heart and her mind.

But all the counselors and doctors and therapists in the world hadn't erased this...him.

Why was Drakon so alive? Why was he more real to her than any other man she'd ever met? After Drakon, after loving Drakon, there could be no one else...he made it impossible for her to even look at anyone else.

He'd reached her, was standing before her, his gaze fierce, intense, as it traveled across her face, making her feel so bare, and naked. Heat bloomed in her skin, blood surging from his close inspection.

"What did you do, Morgan?"

"I don't understand."

"You've sold everything," he added harshly. "You have nothing and even if you get your father back to the United States, you'll still have nothing."

"Not true," she said, locking her knees, afraid she'd collapse, overwhelmed by emotion and memories, overwhelmed by him. She'd been up for two days straight. Hadn't eaten more than a mouthful in that time. She couldn't, knowing she would soon be here, with him again. "I'd have peace of mind."

"Peace of mind?" he demanded. "How can you have peace of mind when you have no home?"

He could mock her, because he didn't know what it was like to lose one's mind. He didn't know that after leaving him, she'd ended up in the hospital and had remained there for far too long. It had been the lowest point in her life, and by far, the darkest part. But she didn't want to think about McLean Hospital now, that was the past, and she had to live in the present, had to stay focused on what was important, like her father. "I did what I had to do."

"You sacrificed your future for your father's, and he doesn't have a future. Your father—*if* alive, *if* released—will be going to prison for the rest of his life. But what will you do while he's in his comfortable, minimum security prison cell, getting three square meals a day? Where will you sleep? What will you eat? How will you get by?"

"I'll figure it out."

"You are so brave and yet foolhardy. Do you ever look before you leap?"

She flashed to Vienna and their wedding and the four weeks of honeymoon, remembering the intense love and need, the hot brilliant desire that had consumed her night and day. She hated to be away from him, hated to wake up without him, hated to breathe without him.

She'd lost herself completely in him. And no, she hadn't looked, hadn't analyzed, hadn't imagined anything beyond that moment when she'd married him and became his.

"No," she answered huskily, lips curving and heart aching. "I just leap, Drakon. Leap and hope I can fly."

If she'd hoped to provoke him, she'd failed. His expression was impassive and he studied her for a long moment from beneath his thick black lashes. "How long has it been since you've spoken to your father?"

"I actually haven't ever spoken to him. My mother did, and just that first day, when they called her to say they had him. Mother summoned us, and told us what had happened, and what the pirates wanted for a ransom."

"How long did she speak to your father?"

"Not long. Just a few words, not much more than that."

"What did he say to her?"

"That his yacht had been seized, his captain killed and he had been abducted, and then the pirates got back on the phone, told her their demands and hung up."

"Has anyone spoken with your father since?"

She shook her head. "No."

"Why not?"

"They won't let us. They say we haven't earned the right."

"But you've given them three million."

Her lips curved bitterly and her gaze lifted to meet his. "I can't sleep at night, knowing I was so stupid and so wasteful. Three million dollars gone! Three million lost forever. It would have been fine if we'd saved my father, but we didn't. I didn't. Instead it's all gone and now I must start over and worse, the ransom has doubled. I'm sick about it, sick that I made such a critical error. I didn't mind liquidating everything to save my father, but it turns out I liquidated everything for nothing—"

"Stop."

"You are right to despise me. I am stupid, stupid, stupid—"

He caught her by the shoulders and gave her a hard shake. "Enough. You didn't know. You didn't understand how the pirates operated, how mercurial they are, how difficult, how unpredictable. You had no way of knowing. There is no handbook on dealing with pirates, so stop torturing yourself."

With every sentence he gave her a little shake until she was thoroughly undone and tears filled her eyes, ridiculous tears that stung and she swiped at them, annoyed, knowing they were from fatigue, not sadness, aware that she was exhausted beyond reason, knowing that what she wanted was

Drakon to kiss her, not shake her, but just because you wanted something didn't mean it was good for you. And Drakon wasn't good for her. She had to remember that.

He saw her tears. His features darkened. "We'll get your father back," he said, his deep voice rumbling through her, his voice as carnal as the rest of him, drawing her into his arms and holding her against his chest, comforting her.

For a moment.

Morgan pulled back, slipping from Drakon's arms, and took several quick steps away to keep from being tempted to return. He'd been so warm. He'd smelled so good. His hard chest, covered in cashmere, had made her want to burrow closer. She'd felt safe there, secure, and yet it was an illusion.

Drakon wasn't safe. He was anything but safe for her.

He watched her make her escape. His jaw jutted, his brow lowered, expression brooding. "We'll get your father back," he said, repeating his promise from a few moments ago. "And we'll do it without giving them another dollar."

She looked up at him, surprised. "How?"

"I know people."

She blinked at him. Of course he knew people—Drakon knew everyone—but could he really free her father without giving the pirates more money? "Is that possible?"

"There are companies…services…that exist just for this purpose."

"I've looked into those companies. They cost millions, and they won't help me. They loathe my father. He represents everything they detest—"

"But they'll work with me."

"Not when they hear who they are to rescue—"

"I own one of the largest shipping companies in the world. No maritime agency would refuse me."

Hope rose up within her, but she didn't trust it, didn't trust anyone or anything anymore. "But you said…you said you wouldn't help me. You said since you'd given me the check—"

"I was wrong. I was being petty. But I can't be petty. You're my wife—" he saw her start to protest and overrode her "—and as long as you are my wife, it's my duty to care for you and your family. It is the vow I made, and a vow I will keep."

"Even though I left you?"

"You left me. I didn't leave you."

Pain flickered through her. "You owe me nothing. I know that. You must know that, too."

"Marriage isn't about keeping score. Life is uneven and frequently unjust and I did not marry you, anticipating only fun and games. I expected there would be challenges, and there have been, far more than I anticipated, but until we are divorced, you are my wife, and the law is the law, and it is my duty to provide for you, to protect you, and I can see I have failed to do both."

She closed her eyes, shattered by his honesty, as well as his sense of responsibility. Drakon was a good man, a fair man, and he deserved a good wife, a wife less highly strung and sensitive…a wife who craved him less, a wife who could live and breathe without him at her side….

Morgan wasn't that woman. Even now she wanted to be back in his arms, to have his mouth on hers, to have him parting her lips, tasting her, filling her, possessing her so completely that the world fell away, leaving just the two of them.

That was her idea of life.

And it was mad and beautiful and impossible and bewitching.

"It's not your fault," she whispered, wrapping her arms around her, wishing she'd needed less talk and tenderness and reassurance. "It's mine. Maybe even my father's. He spoiled me, you know, and it infuriated my mother."

"Your mother did say at our wedding that you were your daddy's little girl."

Morgan's breath caught in her throat and she bit into her bottom lip. "Mother had Tori and Branson and Logan, and yes, I was Daddy's girl, but they were Mother's darlings, and you'd think since she had them living with her, choosing her, she wouldn't mind that I chose to live with Father, but she did."

"What do you mean, they lived with her, and you lived with Daniel? Didn't you all live together?"

Morgan shook her head. "Mother and Father lived apart most of the time. They'd put on a show for everyone else—united front for the public, always throwing big parties for the holidays or special occasions…Christmas party, New Year's party, birthdays and anniversaries. But behind closed doors, they could barely tolerate each other and were almost never in the same place at the same time, unless there was a photo shoot, or reporter about. Mother loved being in the society columns, loved having our lavish, privileged lifestyle featured in glossy magazines. She liked being envied, enjoyed her place in the sun. Father was different. He hadn't grown up with money like Mother, and wasn't comfortable in the spotlight. He lived far more quietly…he and I, and Jemma, when she joined us. We'd go to these small neighborhood restaurants and they weren't trendy in the least. We loved our Mexican food and Greek food and Indian food and maybe once every week or two, we'd send out for Chinese food. After dinner, once my homework was done, we'd watch television in the evening…we had our favorite show. We had our routines. It was lovely. He was lovely. And ordinary." She looked up at Drakon, sorrow in her eyes. "But the world now won't ever know that man, or allow him to be that man. In their eyes, he's a greedy selfish hateful man, but he wasn't. He really wasn't—" She broke off, drew a deep breath and then another.

"Mother used to say I was a demanding little girl, and she hated that Father humored me. She said he spoiled me by taking me everywhere with him, and turning me into his shadow. Apparently that's why I became so clingy with you. I shifted my attachment from my father onto you. But what a horrible thing for you…to be saddled with a wife who can't be happy on her own—"

"You're talking nonsense, Morgan—"

"No, it's true."

"Well, I don't buy it. I was never saddled with you, nor did I ever feel encumbered by you. I'm a man. I do as I please and I married you because I chose you, and I stayed married to you because I chose to, and that's all there is to it."

She looked away, giving him her profile. It was such a beautiful profile. Delicate. Elegant. The long, black eyelashes, the sweep of cheekbone, the small straight nose, the strong chin, above an impossibly long neck. The Copeland girls were all stunning young women, but there was something ethereal about Morgan…something mysterious.

"You're exhausted," he added. "I can see you're not eating or sleeping and that must change. I will not have you become skin and bones again. While you're here, you will sit and eat real meals, and rest, and allow me to worry about things. I may not have been the patient and affectionate husband you wanted, but I'm good at managing chaos, and I'm damn good at dealing with pirates."

He didn't know what he expected, but he didn't expect her to suddenly smile at him, the first smile he'd seen from her since she arrived, and it was radiant, angelic, starting in her stunning blue eyes and curving her lips and making her lovely face come alive.

For a moment he could only look at her, and appreciate her. She was like the sun and she glowed, vital, beautiful, and he remembered that first night in Vienna when she'd turned and looked at him, her blue eyes dancing, mischief playing at her mouth, and then she'd spotted him, her eyes meeting his, and her smile had faded, and she'd become shy.

She'd blushed and turned away but then she'd peek over her shoulder at him again and again and by the end of the ball he knew he would have her. She was his. She would always be his. Thank God she'd felt the same way. It would have created an international scandal if he'd had to kidnap her and drag her off to Greece, an unwilling bride.

"I am happy to allow you to take the lead when it comes to the pirates," she said, her smile slowly dying, "and you may manage them, but Drakon, you mustn't try to manage me. I won't be managed. I've had enough of that these past five years."

Drakon frowned, sensing that there was a great deal she wasn't saying, a great deal he wouldn't like hearing, and he wanted to ask her questions, hard questions, but now wasn't the time, not when she was so fragile and fatigued. There would be time for all his questions later, time to learn just what had dismantled his marriage, and who and what had been managing her, but he could do that when she wasn't trembling with exhaustion and with dark purple circles shadowing her eyes.

"I'm concerned about you," he said flatly.

"There's been a lot of stress lately."

He didn't doubt that, and it crossed his mind that if he'd been a real husband, and a more selfless man, he would have gone to Morgan, and offered her support or assistance before it'd come to this. Instead, he, like the rest of the world, had followed the Copeland family crisis from afar, reading about the latest humiliation or legal move in the media, and doing nothing.

"I can see that, but you'll be of no use to your father, if you fall apart yourself," he said. "I'll make some calls and the staff can prepare us a late lunch—"

"Do we really need lunch?"

"Yes, we do. And while I understand time is of the essence, not eating will only make things worse. We need clear

heads and fierce resolve, and that won't happen if we're fainting on our feet."

Morgan suddenly laughed and she shook her head, once
again giving him a glimpse of the Morgan he'd married...
young and vivacious and full of laughter and passion. "You
keep using 'we,' when we both know you mean me." She
paused and her gaze lifted, her eyes meeting his. "But I do
rather like the image of you fainting on your feet."

His gaze met hers and held and it was all he could do to
keep from reaching for her. He wanted her. Still wanted her
more than he'd wanted anyone or anything. "Of course you
would," he said roughly. "You're a wicked woman and you
deserve to be—"

Drakon broke off abruptly, balling his hands into fists
and he realized how close he'd come to teasing her the way
he'd once teased her, promising her punishment, which was
merely foreplay to make her hot, to make her wet, to make
her shudder with pleasure.

It used to give him such pleasure that he brought her pleasure. He wasn't good at saying all the right words, so he
used his body to say how much he adored her, how much he
desired her, how much he cherished her and would always
cherish her.

But only now did he know she'd hated the way he'd pleasured her.

That she'd been disgusted—

"Don't," she whispered, reaching out to him, her hand settling on his arm. "Don't do that, don't. I know what you're
thinking, and I'm sorry. I shouldn't have said what I did,
shouldn't have said it how I did. It was wrong. I was wrong.
I was upset."

His body hardened instantly at her touch, and he glanced
down at her hand where it clung to his forearm. He could feel
her warmth through the softness of the cashmere, and the

press of her fingers, and it was nothing at all, and yet it was everything, too. Nothing and everything at the same time.

He looked away from her hand, up into her eyes, angry with her all over again, but also angry with himself. How could he have not known how she felt? How could he have not realized that she didn't enjoy…him…them?

"Rest assured that I will not take advantage of you while you are here," he said, trying to ease some of the tension rippling through him. "You are safe in the villa," he continued, hating that he suddenly felt like a monster. He wasn't a monster. Not even close. It's true he could be ruthless in business, and he had a reputation for being a fierce negotiator, a brilliant strategist, an analytical executive, as well as a demanding boss, but that didn't make him an ogre and he'd never knowingly hurt a woman, much less his wife. "You are safe from me."

"Drakon."

"I'll have your bag taken up to the Angelica Suite," he said. "It's the second master suite, on the third floor, the suite one with the frescoed ceiling."

"I remember it."

"It's in the opposite wing of where I'm staying but it should give you privacy and I think you'll find it quite comfortable. I can show you the way now."

"There's no need to take me there," she said hoarsely. "I remember the suite."

"Fine. Then I'll let you find your way, and as I have quite a few things to do, I'll eat as I work, and I'll have a light lunch sent to you in your room, but we'll need to meet later so I can fill you in on the arrangements I've been able to make for your father."

Morgan was glad to escape to her room, desperate to get away from Drakon and that intense physical awareness of him….

She'd hurt him. What she'd said earlier, about their sex

life, about their marriage, it'd hurt him terribly and she felt guilty and sorry. So very sorry since she knew Drakon would never do anything to hurt her. He'd always been so protective of her but he was also so very physical, so carnal and sexual and she was a little afraid of it. And him. Not when she was with him, making love to him, but later, when he was gone, separated from her. It was then that she analyzed their relationship, and what they did and how they did it and how little control she had with him.

It frightened her that she lost control with him.

Frightened her that he had so much power and she had so little.

It had niggled at her during their honeymoon, but their picnics and dinners out and the afternoon trips on his yacht were so fun and romantic that she could almost forget how fierce and shattering the sex was when he was charming and attentive and affectionate. But in Athens when he disappeared into his work life, his real life, the raw nature of their sex life struck her as ugly, and she became ugly and it all began to unravel, very, very quickly.

Upstairs in her suite, Morgan barely had time to open the two sets of French doors before a knock sounded on the outer bedroom door, letting her know her overnight bag had arrived. She thanked the housemaid and then returned to the first of the two generous balconies with the stunning view.

She had never tired of this view. She couldn't imagine how anyone could tire of it.

The Amalfi Coast's intense blues and greens contrasted by rugged rock had inspired her very first jewelry collection. She'd worked with polished labradorite, blue chalcedony, pāua shell, lapis lazuli and Chinese turquoise, stones she'd acquired on two extensive shopping trips through Southeast Asia, from Hong Kong to Singapore to Bali.

It'd been a three-month shopping expedition that big sister

Tori had accompanied her on for the first month, and then Logan came for the second month, and Jemma for the third.

By the time Morgan returned to New York, she'd filled two enormous trunks of stones and had a briefcase and laptop full of sketches and the first orders from Neiman Marcus and Bergdorf Goodman. The designs were pure fantasy—a stunning collection of statement-making collars, cuffs and drop earrings—and had cost her a fortune in stone. It had tested her ability to execute her ideas, but had ended up being worth every stress and struggle as the Amalfi Collection turned out to be a huge success, generating significant media attention, as well as the attention of every fashion designer and fashion publicist of note, never mind the starlets, celebrities and socialites who all wanted a Morgan Copeland statement piece.

Morgan's second collection, Jasper Ice, had been inspired by her love of the Canadian Rockies and ski trips to Banff and Lake Louise. The collection was something that an ice princess in a frozen tundra would wear—frosty and shimmering pieces in white, silver, blush, beige and pale gold. The second collection did almost as well as the first, and garnered even more media with mentions in virtually every fashion magazine in North America, Europe and Australia, and then photographed on celebrities and young royals, like the Saudi princess who had worn a gorgeous pink diamond cuff for her wedding.

Morgan was glad Jasper Ice did well, but the cool, frozen beauty of the collection was too much like her numb emotional state, when she'd been so fiercely, frantically alive and in love with Drakon Xanthis.

Drakon, though, was the last person she wanted to think of, especially when she was enjoying the heady rush of success, and for a while she had been very good at blocking him out of her mind, but then one October day, she had been walking with Jemma to lunch and she had spotted a man in a limousine. He'd had a beard and his hair was long but his eyes reminded her so much of Drakon that for a moment she thought it was him.

She had kept walking, thinking she'd escaped, but then a block away from her shop, she'd had to stop, lean against a building and fight for air.

She'd felt like she was having a heart attack. Her chest hurt, the muscles seizing, and she couldn't breathe, couldn't get air, couldn't even speak. She opened her mouth, stared at Jemma, wanting, needing help, but she couldn't make a sound. Then everything went black.

When she woke up, she'd been in an ambulance, and then when she woke again, she was in a bed in the emergency room. She'd spent the next ten days in the hospital, six in ICU, being seen by cardiac specialists. The specialists explained that her extreme weight loss had damaged her heart, and they warned her that if she didn't make immediate and drastic changes, she could die of heart failure.

But Morgan hadn't been dieting. She didn't want to lose weight. She had just found it impossible to eat when her heart was broken. But she wasn't a fool, she understood the gravity of her situation, and recognized she was in trouble.

During the day they'd fed her special shakes and meals and at night she'd dreamed of Drakon, and the dreams had been so vivid and intense that she'd woke desperate each morning to actually see him. She made the mistake of telling Logan that she was dreaming about Drakon every night, and Logan had told their mother, who then told the doctors, and before Morgan knew it, the psychiatrists were back with their pills and questions and notepads.

Did she understand the difference between reality and fantasy?

Did she understand the meaning of wish fulfillment?

Did she want to die?

It would have been puzzling if she hadn't been through all this before at McLean Hospital in Massachusetts, and then at the Wallace Home for a year after that. But she had been through it before so she found the doctors with their clipboards and questions and colorful assortment of pills annoying and even somewhat amusing.

She'd refused the pills. She'd answered some questions. She'd refused to answer others.

She wasn't sick or crazy this time. She was just pushing herself too hard, working too many hours, not eating and sleeping enough.

Morgan had promised her medical team and her family she'd slow down, and eat better, and sleep more and enjoy life more, and for the next two plus years she did. She began to take vacations, joining her sisters for long holidays at the family's Caribbean island, or skiing in Sun Valley or Chamonix, and sometimes she just went off on her own, visiting exotic locations for inspiration for her jewelry designs.

She'd also learned her lesson. She couldn't, wouldn't, mention Drakon again.

Those ten days in the hospital, and her vivid, shattering dreams at night, had inspired her third collection, the Black Prince, a glamorous, dramatic collection built of ruby hues—garnets, red spinels, pink sapphires, diamonds, pave garnets, watermelon tourmaline, pink tourmaline. The collection was a tribute to her brief marriage and the years that followed, mad love, accompanied by mad grief. In her imagination, the Black Prince was Drakon, and the bloodred jewels represented her heart, which she'd cut and handed to him, while the pink sapphires and delicate tourmalines were the tears she'd cried leaving him.

But, of course, she had to keep that inspiration to herself, and so she came up with a more acceptable story for the public, claiming that her newest collection was inspired by the Black Prince's ruby, a 170-carat red spinel once worn in Henry V's battle helmet.

The collection was romantic and over-the-top and wildly

passionate, and early feedback had seemed promising with orders pouring in for the large rings, and jeweled cuffs, and stunning pendulum necklaces made of eye-popping pale pink tourmaline—but then a week before the official launch of her collection, news of the Michael Amery scandal broke and she knew she was in trouble. It was too late to pull any of her ads, or change the focus of the marketing for her latest Morgan Copeland collection.

It was absolutely the wrong collection to be launched in the middle of a scandal implicating Daniel Copeland, and thereby tarnishing the Copeland name. The Black Prince Collection had been over-the-top even at conception, and the finished pieces were sensual and emotional, extravagant and dramatic, and at any other time, the press and fashion darlings would have embraced her boldness, but in the wake of the scandal where hundreds of thousands of people had been robbed by Michael Amery and Daniel Copeland, the media turned on her, criticizing her for being insensitive and hopelessly out of touch with mainstream America. One critic went so far as to compare her to Marie Antoinette, saying that the Black Prince Collection was as "frivolous and useless" as Morgan Copeland herself.

Morgan had tried to prepare herself for the worst, but the viciousness of the criticism, and the weeks of vitriolic attacks, had been unending. Her brother, Branson, a media magnate residing in London, had sent her an email early on, advising her to avoid the press, and to not read the things being written about her. But she did read them. She couldn't seem to help herself.

In the fallout following the Amery Ponzi scandal, the orders that had been placed for her lush Black Prince Collection were canceled, and stores that had trumpeted her earlier collections quietly returned her remaining pieces and closed their accounts with her. No one wanted to carry anything with the Copeland name. No one wanted to have an association with her.

It was crushing, financially and psychologically. She'd invested hundreds of thousands of dollars into the stones, as well as thousands and thousands into the labor, and thousands more into the marketing and sales. The entire collection was a bust, as was her business.

Fortunately, there was no time to wallow in self-pity. The phone call from Northern Africa, alerting her that her father had been kidnapped, had forced her to prioritize issues. She could grieve the loss of her business later. Now, she had to focus on her father.

And yet…standing here, on the balcony, with the bright sun glittering on the sapphire water, Morgan knew she wouldn't have had any success as a designer, or any confidence in her creative ability, if it hadn't been for her honeymoon here in this villa.

And Drakon.

But that went without saying.

CHAPTER FOUR

MORGAN HAD ONLY packed her traveling clothes and the one blue linen top and skirt she'd changed into after arriving in Naples, and so before lunch arrived, she slipped into her comfortable tracksuit to eat her lunch on the balcony before taking a nap. She hadn't meant to sleep the afternoon away but she loved the breeze from the open doors and how it fluttered the long linen curtains and carried the scents of wisteria and roses and lemon blossoms.

She slept for hours in the large bed with the fluffy duvet and the down pillows all covered in the softest of linens. The Italians knew how to make decadent linens and it was here on her honeymoon that she'd come to appreciate cool, smooth sheets and lazy afternoon naps. She'd fall asleep in Drakon's arms after making love and wake in his arms and make love yet again and it was all so sensual, so indulgent. It had been pure fantasy.

She'd dreamed of Drakon while she slept, dreamed they were still together, still happy, and parents of a beautiful baby girl. Waking, Morgan reached for Drakon, her hand slipping sleepily across the duvet, only to discover that the other side of her big bed was empty, cool, the covers undisturbed. Rolling onto her side, she realized it was just a dream. Yet more fantasy.

Tears stung her eyes and her heart felt wrenched, and the heartbreak of losing Drakon felt as real as it had five years ago, when her family had insisted she go to McLean Hospital instead of return to Drakon in Greece.

You're not well. This isn't healthy. You're not healthy. You're too desperate. This is insanity. You're losing your mind… .

Her throat swelled closed and her chest ached and she bit into her lip to keep the memories at bay.

If she hadn't left Drakon they probably would have children now. Babies…toddlers…little boys and girls…

She'd wanted a family with him, but once in Greece Drakon had become a stranger and she had feared they were turning into her own parents: distant, silent, destined to live separate lives.

She couldn't do it. Couldn't be like her parents. Wouldn't raise children in such an unhealthy, unsuitable environment.

Stop thinking about it, she told herself, flipping the covers back and leaving the bed to bathe before dinner. In her grand bathroom with the soaring frescoed ceiling and the warm cream-and-terra-cotta marble, she took a long soak in the deep tub before returning to the bedroom to put her tired linen skirt and blouse back on. But in the bedroom the crumpled blue skirt and blouse were gone and in their place was a huge open Louis Vuitton trunk sitting on the bench at the foot of the bed.

She recognized the elegant taupe-and-cream trunk—it was part of the luggage set her father had given her before her wedding and it was filled with clothes. Her clothes, her shoes, her jewelry, all from the Athens villa. Drakon must have sent for them. It was a thoughtful gesture and she was grateful for clean clothes and something fresh to wear, but it was painful seeing her beautiful wardrobe…so very extravagant, so much couture. So much money invested in a couple dozen dresses and blouses and trousers. Thousands more in shoes and purses.

Morgan sorted through the sundresses and evening dresses

and chic tunics and caftans. Her sisters were far more fashionable than she was, and constantly pushing her to be a bit more trendy, but Morgan liked to be comfortable and loved floaty dresses that skimmed her body rather than hug every curve, but she needed something more fitted tonight, something to keep her together because she was so close to falling apart.

She settled on a white eyelet dress with a boned corset and small puffy sleeves that made her feel like a Gypsy, and she added gold hoop earrings and a coral red shawl worn loosely around her shoulders. Morgan didn't wear a lot of makeup and applied just a hint of color to her cheeks and lips, a little concealer to soften the circles that remained beneath her eyes and then a bit of mascara because it gave her confidence.

The sun was just starting to set as she headed downstairs. She remembered her way to the dining room, but one of the villa staff was on hand at the foot of the stairs to escort her there. Before she'd even entered the dining room she spotted Drakon on the patio, through the dining room's open doors. He was outside, leaning against the iron railing, talking on the phone.

She hesitated before joining him, content for a moment to just look at him while he was preoccupied.

He'd changed from the cashmere sweater to a white linen shirt and a pair of jeans for dinner. His choice in wardrobe surprised her.

Jeans.

She'd never seen him wear jeans before, and these weren't fancy European denim jeans, but the faded American Levi's style and they looked amazing on him. The jeans were old and worn and they outlined Drakon's strong thighs and hugged his hard butt and made her look a little too long at the button fly that covered his impressive masculine parts.

How odd this new Drakon was, so different from the sophisticated, polished man she'd remembered all these years ago. His beard and long hair might be gone, but he still wasn't the Drakon of old. He was someone else, someone new, and that kept taking her by surprise.

The Drakon she'd married had been an incredibly successful man aware of his power, his wealth, his stature. He'd liked Morgan to dress up, to wear beautiful clothes, to be seen in the best of everything, and Drakon himself dressed accordingly. He wouldn't have ever worn a simple white linen shirt halfway unbuttoned to show off his bronze muscular chest. He'd been too controlled, too tightly wound, while this man…he oozed recklessness. And sex.

Drakon had always had an amazing body, but this new one was even stronger and more fit now and Morgan swallowed hard, hating to admit it, but she was fascinated by him. Fascinated and a little bit turned on, which wasn't at all appropriate given the situation, especially considering how Drakon had promised not to touch her….

Drakon suddenly turned, and looked straight at her, his amber gaze meeting hers through the open door. Despite everything, heat flickered in his eyes and she swallowed hard again, even as she blushed hotly, aware that she'd been caught staring.

Nervous, she squared her shoulders and briskly crossed the dining room before stepping outside onto the patio. Drakon had just ended his call as she joined him outside and he slipped the phone into the front pocket of his jeans.

Those damn faded jeans that lovingly outlined his very male body.

There was no reason a Greek shipping magnate needed a body like that. It was decadent for a man who already had so much. His body was beautiful. Sexual. Sinful. He knew how to use it, too, especially those lean hard hips. Never mind his skillful fingers, lips and tongue.

"Hope I didn't keep you waiting long," he said.

Cheeks hot, insides flip-flopping, she reluctantly dragged

her gaze from his button fly up to his face with its newly shaven jaw and square chin. "No," she murmured, almost missing the dark thick beard and long hair. When she'd first arrived, he'd looked so primitive and primal. So undeniably male that she wouldn't have been surprised if he'd pushed her up against the wall and taken her there.

Perhaps a little part of her wished he had.

Instead he'd vowed to stay away from her, and she knew Drakon took his vows seriously. Was it so wrong of her to wish he'd kissed her properly before he'd made that vow? Was it wrong to crave his skin even though he'd made the vow already?

Just thinking of his skin made her glance at his chest, at that broad expanse of hard muscle, and her body reacted, her inner thighs tightening, clenching, while her lower belly ached with emptiness. She hadn't been honest with him. She had loved to make love with him, loved the way he felt inside of her, his body buried deeply between her thighs and how he'd draw back before thrusting back in, over and over until she raked her nails across his shoulders and gripped his arms and arched under him, crying his name.

And just remembering, she could almost feel the weight of him now, his arms stretching her arms above her head, his hands circling her wrists, his chest pressed to her breasts. He'd thrust his tongue into her mouth even as his hard, hot body thrust into hers, burying himself so deeply she couldn't think, feel, want anything but Drakon.

Drakon.

And now she was here with him. Finally. After all these years.

Morgan, it's not going to happen, she told herself. He's letting you go. You're moving on. There will be no sex against the wall, or sex on the floor, or sex on the small dining table painted gold and rose with the lush sunset.

But wouldn't it feel good? another little voice whispered.

Of course it'd feel good. Everything with Drakon had felt good. Sex wasn't the problem. It was the distance after the sex that was.

"Something to drink?" he asked, gesturing to the bar set up in the corner and filled with dozens of bottles with colorful labels. "I can make you a mixed drink, or pour you a glass of wine."

"A glass of wine," she said, as a breeze blew in from the sea, and caught at her hair, teasing a dark tendril.

"Red or white?"

"Doesn't matter. You choose."

He poured her a glass of red wine. "Were you able to sleep?" he asked, handing her the goblet, and their fingers brushed.

A frisson of pleasure rushed through her at the brief touch. Her pulse quickened and she had to exhale slowly, needing to calm herself, settle herself. She couldn't lose focus, had to remember why she was here. Her father. Her father, who was in so much danger. "Yes," she said, her voice pitched low, husky with a desire she could barely master, never mind hide.

Drakon stiffened at the sudden spike of awareness. Morgan practically hummed with tension, her slim figure taut, energy snapping and crackling around her. It was hot and electric, she was hot and electric, and he knew if he reached for her, touched her, she'd let him. She wanted him. Morgan had been right about the physical side of their relationship. There was plenty of heat…intense chemistry…but she'd been the one that brought the fire to their relationship. She'd brought it out in him. He'd enjoyed sex with other women, but with her, it wasn't just sex. It was love. And he'd never loved a woman before her. He'd liked them, admired them, enjoyed them…but had never loved, not the way he loved her, and he was quite sure he would never love any woman this way again.

"For hours," she added, blushing, her voice still husky. "It was lovely. But then, I always sleep well here."

"It's the air, I think," he said. "You look beautiful, by the way," he said.

Her cheeks turned pink and her blue eyes glowed with pleasure. She looked surprised, touched. His beautiful woman. Part of him wanted to shake her, kiss her, make her his again, and another part of him wanted to send her away forever.

"Thank you for sending for my clothes," she said, fighting the same tendril of hair, the one the breeze loved to tease. "That was very kind of you."

"Not kind, just practical," he answered. "Since you're not returning to Ekali, there's no point keeping your things at the villa there anymore. Which reminds me, I have another trunk with your winter clothes and ski things ready to go home with you when you leave for New York. It's in one of the storage rooms downstairs. Didn't see any reason to drag it up three flights of stairs only to drag it down again in a few days.

A shadow passed across her face. "Is that how long you think I need to be here?"

"We'll know better once Rowan arrives. I expect him in late tonight or early tomorrow."

"Rowan?"

"Rowan Argyros, from Dunamas Maritime Intelligence. He's the one I work with when my ships have been seized. His headquarters are in London, but when I phoned him this afternoon I learned that he's in Los Angeles and he's promised to fly out this afternoon."

"But if you are a maritime piracy expert, why do you need outside help?"

"Because while I know shipping, and I've becoming quite knowledgeable about counter-piracy, it takes more than money to free a seized ship, or crew being held hostage. It takes a team of experts, as well as information, strategy and decisive action, and in your father's case, it will take extraordinary action. As you can imagine, it's crucial to do everything exactly right. There is no room for error in something like this. Even a small mistake could cost his life."

She paled. "Perhaps it's too dangerous."

"Rowan won't act unless he's sure of a positive outcome."

He watched her bite nervously into her lower lip and his gaze focused on that soft bottom lip. For a few seconds, he could think of nothing but her mouth. He loved the shape, the color, the softness of it. Always had. Her lips were full and a tender pink that made him think of lush, ripe summer fruit—sweet strawberries and cherries and juicy watermelon.

"We don't even know if my father is alive," she said after a moment, looking up into his eyes.

He knew from her expression that she was looking for reassurance, but he couldn't give it, not yet, not until Rowan had finished his intelligence work. And yet at the same time, there was no reason to alarm her. Information would be coming soon. Until then, they had to be positive. "We don't know very much about his condition at the moment, but I think it's important to focus on the best outcome, not the worst."

"When do you think this…Rowan…will have news for us?"

"I expect he'll have information when he arrives."

Morgan's eyes searched his again and her worry and fear were tangible and he fought the impulse to reach for her, comfort her, especially when she was so close he could feel her warmth and smell her light, delicate fragrance, a heady mix of perfume and her skin.

"It's difficult waiting," she said softly, the tip of her tongue touching her upper lip. "Difficult to be calm and patient in the face of so much unknown."

The glimpse of her pink tongue made him instantly hard. He wanted her so much, couldn't imagine not wanting her. It was torture being this close and yet not being able to kiss her, hold her, and he hardened all over again at the thought of kissing her, and tasting her and running his tongue across the seam of her lips.

He'd been with no one since Morgan left. For five years he'd gone without a woman, gone without closeness, intimacy, gone without even a kiss, and he suddenly felt starved. Ravenous. Like a man possessed. He needed her. She was his. His wife, his woman—

Drakon stopped himself. He couldn't go there, couldn't think of her like that. She might be his legally, but the relationship itself was over. "But that is life," he said grimly. "It is nothing but the unknown."

His staff appeared on the patio, lighting candles and sconces, including the heavy silver candelabra on the round white-linen covered table. "It appears dinner is ready," he added, glad for the diversion. "Shall we sit?"

Morgan realized with a start that the sun had dropped significantly and now hung just above the sea, streaking the horizon red, rose and gold. It would be a stunning sunset and they'd be here on the patio to see it. "Yes, please," she said, moving toward the table, but Drakon was already there, holding a chair for her.

She felt the electric shock as she sat down, her shoulder briefly touching his chest, and then his fingers brushing across the back of her bare arm. Her shawl had slipped into the crook of her elbow and the unexpected sensation of his skin on hers made her breath catch in her throat and she held the air bottled in her lungs as she pressed her knees tightly together, feeling the hot lick of desire and knowing she had to fight it.

"It will be a gorgeous sunset," she said, determined to think of other things than the useless dampness between her thighs and the coiling in her belly that made her feel so empty and achy.

His amber gaze met hers, and the warm tawny depths were piercing, penetrating, and it crossed her mind that he *knew*.

He knew how she felt, he knew she wanted him, and it was suddenly too much...being here, alone with him.

"Must grab my camera," she said, leaping to her feet. "Such an incredible sunset."

She rushed off, up to her room, where she dug through her things and located her phone, which was also her camera, but didn't return to the dining room immediately, needing the time to calm herself and pull her frayed nerves back together.

He's always done this to you, she lectured herself. *He seduced you with his eyes long before he ever touched you, but that doesn't mean anything. It's lust. He's good at sex. That doesn't mean he should be your husband.*

Morgan returned downstairs, head high. As she approached the patio through the dining room, the sunset bathed the patio in soft golden light. The small, round dining table seemed to float above the shimmering green tiles on the patio. The same green tiles extended all the way into the dining room and from the kitchen she caught a whiff of the most delicious aromas—tomato and onion, garlic, olive oil, herbs—even as the breeze rustled her skirts, tugging at her air, whispering over her skin.

So much light and color and sound.

So much sensation. So much emotion. It was wonderful and terrible...bittersweet. Drakon and Villa Angelica had made her feel alive again.

Drakon rose as she stepped out onto the patio. "The sun is almost gone," he said, holding her chair for her.

She glanced out at the sea, and he was right. The bright red ball of sun had disappeared into the water. "I did miss it," she said, hoping she sounded properly regretful as she sat back down.

"Maybe next time," he said, with mock sympathy.

She looked up at him and then away, aware that he was playing her game with her. Pretending she'd wanted a photo when they both knew she just needed to escape him.

"I'll have to keep my phone close by," she said, reaching for her water glass and taking a quick sip.

His gaze collided with hers and then held, his expression one of lazy amusement. "Photos really help one remember things."

She felt herself grow warm. "I have a purely professional interest in the scenery."

"Is that so?"

She hated the way one of his black eyebrows lifted. Hated that curl of his lips. It was sardonic, but also quite sexy, and she was sure he knew it. "I use them for inspiration, not souvenirs," she said coolly, wanting to squash him, and his amusement. There was no reason for him to take pleasure in her discomfiture. No reason for him to act superior.

"Interesting," he drawled, and Morgan had to restrain herself from kicking him beneath the table because she knew he didn't mean it. And he didn't believe her. He probably was sitting there arrogantly thinking she was completely hung up on him...and imagining she was obsessing about having great sex with him...which was ludicrous because she wasn't thinking about having great sex with him anymore. At least not when she was talking about the scenery and inspiration.

"I use the inspiration for my work," she said defiantly, not even sure why she was getting so upset. "But you probably don't consider it work. You probably think it's silly. Superficial."

"I never said that."

"Perhaps you didn't say it, but you think it. You know you do."

"I find it interesting that you feel compelled to put words into my mouth."

His ability to be so calm and detached when she was feeling so emotional made her even more emotional. She leaned toward him. "Surely you've wondered what drove you to marry a flighty woman like me…a woman so preoccupied with frivolous things."

"Are you flighty?"

"You must think so."

He leaned forward, too, closing the distance between them. "I'm not asking you to tell me what I think. I'm asking you—are you flighty?"

Her chin jerked up. "No."

"Are you preoccupied with frivolous things?" he persisted.

Her cheeks burned hot and her eyes felt gritty. "No."

"So you're not flighty or frivolous?"

"No."

His eyes narrowed. "Then why would I think you are?"

She had to close her eyes, overwhelmed by pain and the wave of grief that swept over her.

"Morgan?"

She gave her head a small shake, refusing to open her eyes until she was sure they were perfectly dry. "I am sorry," she said huskily. "You deserved better than me."

"And I'd like to hear more about your jewelry and your ideas, unless you're determined to hold onto this bizarre fantasy of yours that I don't care for you or what's going on inside that beautiful, but complicated head."

She suddenly seethed with anger. Why was he so interested in her thoughts now, when he hadn't been interested in anything but her body when they'd lived together? "I loved what I did," she said shortly. "I was really proud of my work, and I am still proud of those three collections."

She glared at him, waiting for him to speak, but he simply sat back in his chair and looked at her, and let the silence grow, expand and threaten to take over.

The silence was beginning to feel uncomfortable and he was examining her a little too closely. She felt herself grow warm, too warm. "They were jewelry, yes," she said, rushing now to fill the silence, "but they were also miniature works of art, and each collection had a theme and each individual piece told a story."

"And what were those stories?"

"Life and death, love and loss, hope and despair..." Her voice faded, and she looked away, heart aching, because the collections had really been about him, them, their brief fierce love that became so very dangerous and destructive.

"I liked them all, but my favorite collection was your last one. The one you called a failure."

Her head jerked up and she had to blink hard to keep tears from welling up. "You're familiar with my three collections?"

"But of course."

"And you liked my designs?"

"You have such a unique vision. I admired your work very much."

She exhaled slowly, surprised, touched, grateful. "Thank you."

"I was proud of you, my wife. I still am."

The tears she'd been fighting filled her eyes and she didn't know what affected her more—his words or his touch. "My short-lived career," she said, struggling to speak, trying to sound light, mocking, but it had hurt, closing her business. She'd truly loved her work. Had found so much joy in her work and designs.

He caught one of her tears before it could fall. "I don't think it's over. I think you're in the middle of a transition period, and it may feel like death, but it's just change."

"Well, death certainly is a change," she answered, deadpan, flashing him a crooked smile, thinking she liked it when Drakon talked to her. She'd always liked his perspective on things. She found it—him—reassuring, and for her, this is how she connected to him. Through words. Language. Ideas.

If only they'd had more of this—time and conversation—perhaps she wouldn't have felt so lost in Greece. Perhaps they'd still be together now.

He suddenly reached out and stroked her cheek with his thumb, making her heart turn over once again.

"I liked it when you smiled a moment ago," he said gruffly, his amber gaze warm as he looked at her. "I have a feeling you don't smile much anymore."

For a moment she didn't speak, she couldn't, her heart in her mouth and her chest filled with hot emotion.

She was still so drawn to him, still so in love with him. But there was no relationship anymore. They were mostly definitely done—finished. No turning back.

He was helping her because she needed help, but that was all. She had to remember what was important—her father and securing his release—and not let herself get caught up in the physical again because the physical was maddening, disorienting and so incredibly addictive. She hadn't known she had such an addictive personality, not until she'd fell for Drakon.

"There hasn't been a great deal to smile about in the past few months," she said quietly. "Everything has been so grim and overwhelming, but just being here, having your support, gives me hope. If you hadn't agreed to help me, I don't know what I would have done. I'm so very grateful—"

"Your father's not home yet."

"But with your help, he soon will be."

"Careful, my love. You can't say that. You don't know that."

She averted her head and blinked hard, gazing out across the water that had darkened to purple beneath a lavender sky. The first stars were appearing and the moon was far away, just a little crescent of white.

"I'm not saying that it's hopeless," Drakon said. "Just that there is still a great deal we do not know yet."

"I understand. I do."

CHAPTER FIVE

MORGAN PASSED ON coffee and returned to her room, finding it far too painful to sit across from Drakon and look at him, and be so close to him, and yet not be part of his life anymore. Better to return to her suite and pace the floor in privacy, where he couldn't read her face or know how confused she felt.

How could she still want him so much even now? How could she want him when she knew how dangerous he was for her?

She needed to go home, back to New York, back to her family. There was no reason to remain here. Surely this man, Rowan whatever-his-name-was, from Dunamas Intelligence, didn't need her here for his work. He could email her, or call, when he had news....

Morgan nearly returned downstairs to tell Drakon she wanted to leave tonight, that she insisted on leaving tonight, but as she opened her door she realized how ridiculous she'd sound, demanding to go just when Rowan was set to arrive. No, she needed to calm down. She was being foolish. As well as irrational. Drakon wouldn't hurt her. He wasn't going to destroy her. She just needed to keep her head, and not let him anywhere close to her body.

Morgan went to bed, thinking she'd be too wound up to sleep, but she did finally sleep and then woke up early, her room filled with dazzling morning sunlight. After showering, she dressed simply in slim white slacks and one of her favorite colorful tunics and headed downstairs to see if she could get a coffee.

One of the maids gestured to the breakfast room, which was already set for two. Morgan shook her head. "Just coffee," she said, unable to stomach the idea of another meal with Drakon. "An Americano with milk. Latte," she added. "But nothing to eat."

The maid didn't understand and gestured again to the pretty table with its cheerful yellow and blue linens and smiled winningly.

"No, no. Just coffee. Take away." Morgan frowned, wondering why she couldn't seem to remember a single word of Italian. She used to know a little bit, but her brain wasn't working this morning. She was drawing a total blank.

The maid smiled. "Coffee. Americano, *si. Prego.*" And she gestured to the table once more.

Morgan gave up and sat down at the table, needing coffee more than argument. She ended up having breakfast alone and enjoyed her warm pastries and juice and strong hot coffee, which she laced with milk.

The sun poured in through the tall leaded windows, and light dappled the table, shining on the blue water glasses and casting prisms of delicate blue on the white plaster walls.

Morgan studied the patches of blue glazing the walls. She loved the color blue, particularly this cobalt-blue glass one found on the Amalfi coast, and could imagine beautiful jewelry made from the same blue glass, round beads and square knots mixed with gold and shells and bits of wood and other things that caught her fancy.

Her fingers suddenly itched to pick up a pencil and sketch some designs, not the extravagant gold cuffs and collars from her Amalfi collection, but something lighter, simpler. These pieces would be more affordable, perhaps a little bit of a splurge for younger girls, but within reach if they'd saved their pennies. Morgan could imagine the trendy jet-setters buying up strands of different colors and textures and pairing them with easy bracelets, perfect to wear to dinner, or out shopping on a weekend, or on a beach in Greece.

"What are you thinking about?" Drakon asked from the doorway.

Startled, she gazed blankly at him, having forgotten for a moment where she was. "Jewelry," she said, feeling as if she'd been caught doing something naughty. "Why?"

"You were smiling a little...as if you were daydreaming."

"I suppose I was. It helps me to imagine designing things. Makes the loss of my company less painful."

"You'll have another store again."

"It'd be fiscally irresponsible. My last collection nearly bankrupted me."

One of the kitchen staff appeared with an espresso for Drakon and handed it to him. He nodded toward the table. "May I join you?"

"Of course you may, but I was just about to leave," she said.

"Then don't let me keep you," he answered.

His voice didn't change—it remained deep, smooth, even—but she saw something in his face, a shadow in his eyes, and she suddenly felt vile. Here he was, helping her, supporting her, extending himself emotionally and financially, and she couldn't even be bothered to sit with him while he had breakfast?

"But if you don't mind my company," she added quickly "I'll have another coffee and stay."

There was another flicker in his eyes, this one harder to read, and after sitting down across from her, he rang the bell and ordered another coffee for her, along with his breakfast

They talked about trivial things over breakfast like the weather and movies and books they'd read lately. Morgan was grateful their talk was light and impersonal. She was finding it hard to concentrate in the first place, never mind carry on a conversation. Drakon was so beautiful this morning with his dark hair still slightly damp from his shower and his jaw freshly shaven. The morning light gilded him, with the sun playing across his strong, handsome features, illuminating his broad brow, his straight Greek nose, his firm full mouth.

It was impossible to believe this gorgeous, gorgeous man had been her husband. She was mad to leave him. But then, living with him had made her insane.

Drakon's black brows tugged. "It's going to be all right. Rowan should be here in the next hour. We'll soon have information about your father."

"Thank you," she said quietly.

"Last night after you'd gone to bed I was thinking about everything you said yesterday—" He broke off, frowning. "Am I really such an ogre, Morgan? Why do you think I would judge you...and judge you so harshly?"

His gaze, so direct, so piercing, unnerved her. She smoothed the edge of the yellow square cloth where it met the blue underskirt. "Your corporation is worth billions of dollars and your work is vital to Greece and world's economy. I'm nothing. I do nothing. I add little value—"

"Life isn't just about drudgery. It is also about beauty, and you bring beauty into the world." The heat in his eyes reminded her of their courtship, where he'd watched her across ballrooms with that lazy, sensual gleam in his eyes, his expression one of pride and pleasure as well as possession. She'd felt powerful with his eyes on her. Beautiful and important.

"But I don't think important thoughts. I don't discuss relevant topics."

"Relevant to whom?"

"To you! I bore you—"

"Where do you get these ideas from?"

"From you." She swallowed hard and forced herself to hold

his gaze even though it was so incredibly uncomfortable. "I annoyed you when we lived together. And I don't blame you. I know you find people like me irritating."

His black eyebrows pulled and his jaw jutted. "People like you? What does that mean?"

She shrugged uneasily, wishing she hadn't said anything. She hadn't meant anything by it.

No, not true. She had. She still remembered how he had shut down her attempts at conversation once their honeymoon had ended and they'd returned to Greece, remembered their silent lonely evenings in their sprawling modern white marble villa. Drakon would arrive home from work and they'd sit in the dining room, but it'd been a silent meal, with Drakon often reviewing papers or something on his tablet and then afterward he'd retreat to a chair in the living room and continue reading until bed. Once in the bedroom, things changed. Behind the closed door, he'd want hot, erotic sex, and for twenty minutes or sixty, or even longer depending on the night, he'd be alive, and sensual, utterly engrossed with her body and pleasure, and then when it was over, he'd fall asleep, and in the morning when she woke, he'd be gone, back to his office.

"People like me who don't read the business section of the newspaper. People like me who don't care passionately about politics. People like me who don't make money but spend it." She lifted her chin and smiled at him, a hard dazzling smile to hide how much those memories still hurt. "People who can only talk about fashion and shopping and which restaurants are considered trendy."

He tapped his finger on the table. "I do not understand the way you say, 'people like you.' I've never met anyone like you. For me, there is you, and only you."

She leaned forward, her gaze locking with his. "Why did you marry me, Drakon?"

"Because I wanted you. You were made for me. Meant for me."

"What did you like about me?"

"Everything."

"That's not true."

"It is true. I loved your beauty, your intelligence, your warmth, your passion, your smile, your laugh."

She noticed he said *loved,* past tense, and it hurt, a hot lance of pain straight through her heart. Perhaps it was merely a slip, or possibly, a grammatical error, but both were unlikely. Drakon didn't make mistakes.

"But you know that," he added brusquely.

"No," she said equally roughly, "I didn't know that. I had no idea why you cared about me, or if you even cared for me—"

"How can you say such a thing?"

"Because you never talked to me!" she cried. "After our honeymoon ended, you disappeared."

"I merely went back to work, Morgan."

"Yes, but you worked twelve- and fourteen-hour days, which would have been fine, but when you came home, you were utterly silent."

"I was tired. I work long days."

"And I was home alone all day with servants who didn't speak English."

"You promised me you were going to learn Greek."

"I did, I took lessons at the language school in Athens, but when you came home at night, you were irritated by my attempts to speak Greek, insisting we converse in English—" She compressed her lips, feeling the resentment and frustration bubble up. "And then when I tried to make friends, I kept bumping into your old girlfriends and lovers. Athens is full of them. How many women have you been with, Drakon?"

"You make it sound like you met dozens of exes, but you bumped into just three."

"You're right, just three, and in hindsight, they were actually much nicer than the Greek socialites I met who were furious that I'd stolen Greece's most eligible bachelor from under their noses." Morgan's eyes sparkled dangerously. "How could I, a trashy American, take one of Greece's national treasures?"

"It wasn't that bad."

"It was that bad! Everybody hated me before I even arrived!" She leaned across the table. "You should have warned me, Drakon. Prepared me for my new married life."

"I didn't know…hadn't realized…that some of the ladies would be so catty, but I always came home to you every night."

"No, I didn't have you. That was the problem."

"What do you mean?"

Morgan laughed coolly. "You came home to dinner, a bed and sex, but you didn't come home to me, because if you had, you would have talked to me, and tried to speak Greek to me, and you would have helped me meet people, instead of getting annoyed with me for caring what Greek women thought of me."

He swore violently and got up from the table, pacing the floor once before turning to look at her. "I can't believe this is why you left me. I can't believe you'd walk out on me, and our marriage, because I'm not one for conversation. I've never been a big talker, but coming home to you was my favorite part of the day. It's what I looked forward to all day long, from the moment I left for my office."

She swallowed around the lump filling her throat. "And yet when Bronwyn called you at home, you'd talk to her for hours."

"Not for hours."

"For thirty minutes at a time. Over and over every night."

"We had business to discuss."

"And could nothing wait until the morning? Was everything really a crisis? Or could she just not make a decision without you?"

"Is that why you left me? Because of Bronwyn?"

Yes, she wanted to say. Yes, yes, yes. But in her heart she knew Bronwyn Harper was only part of the issue. Drakon's close relationship with his Australian vice president only emphasized how lonely and empty Morgan felt with him. "Bronwyn's constant presence in our lives didn't help matters. Every time I turned around, she was there, and you did talk to her, whereas you didn't talk to me."

The fight abruptly left her, and once her anger deserted her, she was exhausted and flattened, depressed by a specter of what they had been, and the illusion of what she'd hoped they'd be. "But it's a moot point now. It doesn't matter—" She broke off. "My God! You're doing it now. Rolling your eyes! Looking utterly bored and annoyed."

"I'm frustrated, Morgan, and yes, I do find this entire conversation annoying because you're putting words in my mouth, telling me how I felt, and I'm telling you I didn't feel that way when we were married."

"Don't you remember telling me repeatedly that you had people—*women*—talking at you at work, and that you didn't need me talking at you at home? Don't you remember telling me, you preferred silence—"

"I remember telling you that *once,* because I did come home one day needing quiet, and I wanted you to know it wasn't personal, and that I wasn't upset with you, that it had simply been a long day with a lot of people talking at me." He walked toward her, his gaze hard, his expression forbidding. "And instead of you being understanding, you went into hysterics, crying and raging—"

"I wasn't hysterical."

"You had no right to be upset, though." He was standing before her now. "I'd just lost two members of my crew from a hijacked ship and I'd had to tell the families that their loved ones were gone and it was a bad, bad day. A truly awful day."

"Then tell me next time that something horrific has happened, and I'll understand, but don't just disappear into your office and give me the silent treatment."

"I shouldn't have to talk if I don't want to talk."

"I was your wife. If something important happens in your world, I'd like to know."

"It's not as if you could do anything."

"But I could care, Drakon, and I would at least know what's happening in your life and I could grieve for the families of your crew, too, because I would have grieved, and I would have wanted to comfort you—"

"I don't need comforting."

"Clearly." Hot, sharp emotions rushed through her, one after the other, and she gave her head a fierce, decisive shake. "Just as you clearly didn't need me, either, because you don't need anything, Drakon Xanthis. You're perfect and complete just the way you are!"

She brushed past him and walked out, not quickly, or tearfully, but resolutely, reassured all over again that she had done the right thing in leaving him. He really didn't want a wife, or a partner, someone that was equal and valuable. He only wanted a woman for physical release. In his mind, that was all a woman was good for, and thank God she'd left when she had or he would have destroyed her completely.

Drakon caught up with her in the narrow stairway at the back of the villa. It had once been the staircase for the servants and was quite simple with plain plaster walls and steep, small stairs, but it saved Morgan traversing the long hallway.

He clasped her elbow, stopping her midstep. "You are so very good at running away, Morgan."

She shook him off and turned to face him. He was standing two steps down but that still put them on eye level and she stared into his eyes, so very full of anger and pain. "And you are so good at shutting people out!"

"I don't need to report to you, Morgan. You are my wife, not my colleague."

"And funny enough, I would rather have been your colleague than your wife. At least you would have talked to me!"

"But then there would have been no lovemaking."

"Perhaps it will surprise you to know that I'm actually far more interested in what's in your brain than what's in your trousers." She saw his incredulous expression and drew a ragged breath, horrified all over again that their entire relationship had been based on sex and chemistry. Horrified that she'd married a man who only wanted her for her body. "It's true. Lovemaking is empty without friendship, and we had no friendship, Drakon. We just had sex—"

"Not this again!"

"Yes, this again."

"You're being absurd."

"Thank God we'll both soon be free so we can find someone that suits us both better. You can go get another pretty girl and give her an orgasm once or twice a day and feel like a real man, and I'll find a man who has warmth and compassion, a man who cares about what I think and feel, a man who wants to know *me,* and not just my body!"

He came up one step, and then another until they were on the same narrow stair, crowding her so that her back was against the plaster of the stairwell, and his big body was almost touching hers.

A dangerous light shone in his eyes, making her blood hum in her veins and her nerves dance. "Is that all I'm interested in? Your body?" he growled, a small muscle popping in his jaw.

She stared at his jaw, fascinated by that telling display of temper. He was angry and this was all so new...his temper and emotion. She'd always thought of him as supremely controlled but his tension was palpable now. He practically seethed with frustration and it made her skin tingle, particularly her lips, which suddenly felt unbearably sensitive. "Apparently so."

He stepped even closer, his eyes glittering down at her. "I wish I'd known that before I married you. It would have saved me half a billion dollars, never mind years of trouble."

"We all make mistakes," she taunted, deliberately provoking him, but unable to help herself. Drakon Xanthis's famous icy control was cracking and she wondered what would happen when it shattered completely. "Best thing you can do now is forgive yourself for making such a dreadful mistake and move forward."

Fire flashed in his eyes and he leaned in, closing the gap between them so that his broad chest just grazed the swell of her breasts and she could feel the tantalizing heat of his hips so close to hers.

"Such an interesting way to view things," he said, his head dropping, his voice deepening. "With you as my mistake."

His lips were so close now and her lower back tingled and her belly tightened, and desire coursed through her veins, making her ache everywhere.

She could feel his need, feel the desire and her mouth dried, her heart hammering harder. He was going to kiss her. And she wanted the kiss, craved his kiss, even as a little voice of reason inside her head sounded the alarm....

Stop. Wait. Think.

She had to remember...remember the past...remember what had happened last time...this wasn't just a kiss, but an inferno. If she gave in to this kiss, it'd be all over. Drakon was so dangerous for her. He did something to her. He, like his name, Drakon, Greek for dragon, was powerful and potent and destructive.

But he was also beautiful and physical and sensual and

he made her *feel*. My God, he made her feel and she wanted that intensity now. Wanted him now.

"My beautiful, expensive mistake," he murmured, his lips brushing across the shell of her ear, making her breath catch in her throat and sending hot darts of delicious sensation throughout her body, making her aware of every sensitive spot.

"Next time, don't marry the girl," she said, trying to sound brazen and cavalier, but failing miserably as just then he pushed his thigh between her legs. The heat of his hard body scalded her, and the unexpected pressure and pleasure was so intense she gasped, making her head spin.

"Would you have been happier just being my mistress?" he asked, his tongue tracing the curve of her ear even as his muscular thigh pressed up, his knee against her core, teasing her senses, making her shiver with need.

She was wet and hot, too hot, and her skin felt too tight. She wanted relief, needed relief, and it didn't help that she couldn't catch her breath. She was breathing shallowly, her chest rising and falling while her mouth dried.

"Would you have been able to let go more? Enjoyed the sex without guilt?" he added, biting her tender earlobe, his teeth sharp, even as he wedged his thigh deeper between her knees, parting her thighs wider so that she felt like a butterfly pinned against the wall.

"There was no guilt," she choked, eyes closing as he worked his thigh against her in a slow maddening circle. He was so warm and she was so wet and she knew it was wrong, but she wanted more, not less.

His teeth scraped across that hollow beneath her ear and she shuddered against him, thinking he remembered how sensitive she was, how her body responded to every little touch and bite and caress.

"Liar." He leaned in closer, his knee grinding and his hips pressing down against her hips, making her pelvis feel hot and yet hollow, and the muscles inside her womb clench. "You liked it hot. You liked it when I made you fall apart."

And it was true, she thought, her body so tight and hot and aching that she arched against him, absolutely wanton. There was no satisfaction like this, though, and she wanted satisfaction. Wanted him. Wanted him here and now. Wanted him to lift her tunic and expose her breasts and knead and roll the tight, aching nipples between his fingers. He'd made her come that way before, just by playing with her nipples, and he'd watched her face as she came, watched every flicker of emotion that crossed her face as he broke her control....

If only he'd peel her clothes off now, if only she could feel his skin on her skin, feel him in her, needing the heat and fullness of him inside her, craving the pleasure of being taken, owned, possessed—

Morgan's eyes flew open.

Owned?

Owned? My God. She *was* insane.

Visions of her months at McLean Hospital filled her head and it dragged her abruptly back to reality. She had to be smart. Couldn't destroy herself again. Never wanted to go back to McLean Hospital again.

The very memory of McLean was enough for her to put her hands on his chest and push him back, and she pushed hard, but he didn't budge and all she felt was the warm dense plane of muscle that banded his ribs, and the softness of his cashmere sweater over the dense carved muscle.

"Get off," she panted, pushing harder, putting all of her weight into the shove but Drakon was solid, immoveable. "I'm not a toy, Drakon, not here for your amusement."

His hand snaked into her hair, twisting the dark length around his fist, holding her face up to his. "Good, because I'm not amused."

"No, you're just aroused," she answered coldly, furious

with herself for responding to him with such abandon. So typical. So pathetic. No wonder her family had locked her up.

He caught one of her hands and dragged it down his body and between their hips to cup his erection. "Yes," he drawled, amber gaze burning, "so I am."

She inhaled sharply, her fingers curving around him, clasping his thick shaft as if measuring the hard length, and it was a terrible seductive pleasure, touching him like this. She remembered how he felt inside her—hot, heavy—and how the satin heat of his body would stretch her, stroke her, hitting nerve endings she hadn't even known she had.

Curiosity and desire warred with her sense of self-preservation, before overriding her common sense.

Morgan palmed the length of him, slowly, firmly running her hand down his shaft and then, as if unable to stop herself, back up again to cup the thick, rounded head. She'd never thought a man's body was beautiful before she'd met Drakon, but she loved every muscle and shadow of his body, loved the lines and the planes and the way his cock hung heavy between his muscular legs. He was such a powerfully built man, and yet the skin on his shaft was so smooth and sensitive, like silk, and the contradiction between his great, hard body and that delicate skin fascinated her.

But then he fascinated her. No, it was more than that, more than fascination. It was an obsession. She needed him so much she found it virtually impossible to live without him.

"You want me," he said. "You want me to peel your trousers and knickers off and take you here, on these steps, don't you?"

Fire surged through her veins, fire and hunger and shame. Because yes, she did want him and her orgasms were the most intense when he pushed it to the edge, making every touch into something dangerous and erotic. "You do like to dominate," she answered breathlessly.

He tugged on her hair, and it hurt a little, just as he'd intended, making her nipples harden into tight, aching buds even as she stiffened against him, her body rippling with need.

"And you do like to be dominated," he rasped in her ear.

CHAPTER SIX

SHE SHOVED AWAY from him and this time he let her go and Morgan ran the rest of the way up the stairs, racing back to her room, his voice echoing in her head. *And you like to be dominated…*.

Morgan barely made it to her bed before her legs gave out, the mocking words making her absolutely heartsick, because he wasn't completely wrong. Part of her did like it. It was sexy…hot…exciting.

But she shouldn't like it. It wasn't politically correct. She couldn't imagine her mother approving. Not that she wanted to think about her mother and sex at the same time…or even about sex in general since she wasn't going to be having sex anytime soon and God help her, she wanted to.

She wanted to be ravished. Stripped. Tied up. Taken. Tasted. Devoured—

Oh, God, she was mad, she was. What sane woman wanted to be ravished? What kind of woman ached to be tied up and taken? Tasted?

What was wrong with her?

Before Drakon she'd never had these thoughts. She'd never imagined that sex could make one feel absolutely wild. She'd never dreamed that desire could be an uncontrollable fire that made one lose all perspective…as well as one's reason….

But desire was an inferno, and she felt absolutely consumed by need now. Lying facedown on her bed, her body ached with need. Her skin burned, her senses swam. Every muscle in her body felt taut and every nerve ending far too tight. She wanted relief, craved release, and the fact that she couldn't have it made the aching emptiness worse.

Morgan buried her face in a pillow and knotted her fists and screamed. And screamed some more.

She wanted him. She wanted him, wanted him, wanted him and he could give her what she wanted, too. He'd do it. He'd do anything she wanted and yet it was wrong. They weren't together, they hadn't been together in years, and she couldn't use him to scratch an itch...no matter how powerful the itch.

And yet, oh, God, her body ached and throbbed and she felt wild...hot and tense and so very raw.

Dammit. Damn him. Damn that kiss in the stairwell. Damn this terrible incredible unforgettable chemistry.

It wasn't right to want him this much still. Wasn't fair to still feel so much, either, especially when she knew how bad he was for her, how very destructive. She couldn't blame him entirely. The doctors said the problem was hers...that she didn't have proper boundaries. She didn't have a clear or strong sense of self and the only way she'd achieve a strong, mature sense of self was by leaving Drakon....

As if it were that easy...

Just leave him. Forget him. Forget he ever existed...

And now he was downstairs, so intense and real, so physical, so sensual, so fiercely beautiful.

Morgan beat the bed with her fist, maddened by the futility of her desire. Blood drummed in her veins, need coiled tightly, hotly in her belly, and her entire body ached with emptiness. How could emptiness throb and pulse? How could emptiness burn? But it did. And she felt wild and furious and frustrated beyond reason.

If only she could go to him, and beg for him to help her, beg him to give her release. Beg for pleasure.

She'd happily crawl for him, crawl to him, if it meant that he could tame the beast inside her…that voracious hunger that made her feel too wild, too frantic, too much.

Drakon stood just inside the doorway of Morgan's suite and watched her beat her fist against the bed, her dark hair gleaming, her tunic riding high on her thighs, the soft fabric clinging to the firm, rounded curves of her hips and butt.

She had a gorgeous butt, and it made him want to spank her, restrain her, knowing it'd arouse her, make things hotter, make her wet and anxious and hungry for him.

And then he'd make love to her.

With his mouth, his tongue, his teeth, his hands, his cock. He loved the softness of her skin and the scent of her, the way she blushed, the way her tongue traveled across the bow of her upper lip and the way she'd squirm beneath him, her slim body arching, her hips grinding up to meet his, her legs opening for him.

"Undress," he said, his voice pitched so low it sounded like a growl.

Morgan swiftly sat up, eyes enormous in her face, cheeks flushed.

"Do it," he said, folding his arms across his chest.

Her lips parted in silent protest and yet he knew she was tempted, seriously tempted, because she wanted the same thing he did—excitement, pleasure, release.

"And what?" she whispered, her tongue darting to her lower lip, moistening it.

He was already hard. Now he wanted to explode. "And let me look at you. I want to see you, my beautiful wife."

"I'm not your wife."

"Oh, you are my wife. And have been my wife and will be my wife until the day the divorce is granted. Then…you'll be someone else's woman, but until then, you are mine. And you know you are. That is why you came here to me, wanting my help. You knew I'd refuse you nothing."

He saw the flicker in her eyes, that recognition of truth. "Just as you know I've never refused you anything," she whispered, her voice unsteady.

No, she hadn't, he thought, his shaft growing even harder, making him hotter, remembering how she always responded to him.

He'd known plenty of women who liked hot sex, but he'd never been with anyone as passionate as Morgan. She wasn't comfortable with her passionate nature, though, and during their six months together she'd struggled with the concept of physical pleasure, and resisted giving in to her sensual side, viewing it as a weakness, or something shameful, instead of an intimacy that brought them closer together... binding, bonding, making them one. "But I've never forced you, Morgan—"

"Not forced, no, but you have pushed me, pushed me beyond what I was comfortable doing."

"Isn't that exciting, though? To try new things...explore new things...to know and then go outside your comfort zone?"

Another flicker of emotion passed over her lovely face. She had such fine, elegant features, as well as that famous Copeland reserve, a trait shared by her equally glamorous sisters. The reserve came from the way they'd been raised... from birth they'd been privileged, and had enjoyed a luxurious lifestyle of private schools, private jets, private islands. Their money attracted attention, and men, lots and lots of men, and by the time the four Copeland girls had become women, they knew they were special. Unique. They believed they deserved better.

Drakon had been drawn to Morgan's beauty, but also her reserve. He'd viewed it as a challenge to break through her cool, haughty exterior to discover the warm woman underneath.

And once he'd touched her, she'd been more than warm. She'd burned as if consumed by a fever and during their honeymoon, those four weeks here at Villa Angelica, he'd enjoyed discovering the depths of her passion and exploring her desires, her fears and her limits.

"But everything with you was outside my comfort zone," she said, trying to hide the quiver of her lower lip. "Everything was overwhelming."

She'd said this once before to him, during the last week of their honeymoon after an erotic afternoon on a private island, and he'd been startled that her memory of lovemaking on the pristine ivory beach had been so different from what he'd felt. Returning to his yacht, which had been anchored off the island while they picnicked on the beach, he had never felt closer to her, or more committed, and he'd been shocked when she accused him of taking advantage of her. Shocked and sickened.

He was Greek—a man of surprisingly simple tastes. He valued his family, his friends and his culture, which included good food, good drink and great sex. He wouldn't apologize for enjoying sex, either, or enjoying his wife's beautiful body. What did she expect him to do? Pretend he didn't like sex? Act as though he didn't find pleasure in her warmth and softness?

Back in Athens after the honeymoon, Drakon had tried to be the husband she wanted. He stopped reaching for her quite as often, and then when he did reach for her, he changed the way he touched her, holding back to keep from overwhelming her. He knew she didn't like it when he expressed hunger, or focused too much on her pleasure, and so instead of just being with her, and enjoying her, he practiced control and distance, hoping that a less passionate husband would be more to her liking.

Instead she'd left.

And just remembering how he'd turned himself inside

out trying to please her, trying to give her what she wanted, made him angry all over again now.

He'd hated second-guessing himself back then, hated not being able to please her, hated failing as a husband.

His gaze swept over her, slowly, critically, examining her as if he owned her, and he did…at least for a few more weeks.

"Undress," he said roughly, feeling raw and so very carnal, and liking it. Enjoying it. "I want to see my wife. It doesn't seem like too much to ask for, not after giving you seven million dollars."

One of her eyebrows lifted. "At least you didn't mention the four hundred million."

"That was to your father, not to you."

"I wonder what he had to do for four hundred million."

"You think I should have asked for some sexual favors, do you?"

"You like sex a lot."

"I liked it with you a lot." He suddenly reached down, palmed his erection through his trousers, and he saw her gaze settle on his shaft, measuring the length and size.

Dark pink color stormed her cheeks and she licked her lower lip, once and again, before finding her voice. "That's obscene," she whispered.

"You did it a moment ago."

"You made me."

"You liked it. But you'll tell me you didn't. You'll tell me sex is disgusting. You'll tell me I'm disgusting, but if I touched you now, my woman, you'd be dripping wet—"

"Disgusting."

"And I'd open you and lick you and taste you and make you come." His head cocked and he shoved his hands in his trouser pockets. "When is the last time you came? How long has it been since you had an orgasm? A day? A week? A month?"

"It's none of your business."

"I did it in the shower yesterday, before you arrived. Stroked myself as I thought about you, picturing your breasts and your pale thighs and how much I enjoy being between them."

"Is there any point to this, Drakon? Or do you just wish to humiliate me?"

"Humiliate you, how? By telling you how much I want you, even now, even after you walked out on me?"

"But you don't want me, you just want to have sex with me."

"That's right. You don't believe you're attached to your body, or that your body is part of you. Instead it's a separate entity, which makes me think of a headless chicken—"

"Don't be rude."

"Then stop jumping to conclusions. Just because I like your body, doesn't mean I don't appreciate the rest of you."

"Humph!"

His eyebrows shot up, his expression mocking. "Is that the best you can do?"

She crossed her arms over her chest, her chin jerking up. "I get nowhere arguing with you."

"Very wise. Much better to just dispense with the clothing and let me have what I want." He paused, and his gaze moved slowly, suggestively over her. "And what I know you want, too. Not that you'll admit it."

Her chin lifted another notch. "And what do I want?"

"Satisfying sex without pushing the limits too far."

Dark pink color stormed her cheeks. "Without pushing the limits at all."

The corners of his mouth curled. So she did want sex. Just nice-girl sex…sweet, safe missionary-position sex. His cock throbbed at the thought. He'd like some sweet, safe-missionary sex as well. "I'll see what I can do. But first, I'd like to see you. But I'm getting bored by all the discussion. Either we're going to do this, or we're not—"

"Your shirt first."

"Excuse me?"

"You want to do this? Then we'll do this. But you're not the boss and I'm not taking orders." Her tone was defiant and her eyes flashed and she'd never been angry before when they'd played these games. She'd been shy and nervous, but also eager to please. She wasn't eager to please now. "You don't get to have all the power anymore."

"No?"

"No. I'm not your servant or slave—"

"Which is good, since I don't make love with my servants, and I don't have slaves."

"The point is, you might be able to bark orders at Bronwyn, but not at me."

"I had no idea you were so hung up on Bronwyn," he drawled, liking this new feisty Morgan. She was a very different woman from the one he'd married and that intrigued him.

"I wasn't hung up on her. You were."

"Is that how it was?"

"Yes."

"So are we going to talk about Bronwyn, or are we going to have sweet, safe missionary-position sex?"

Her lips compressed primly. "You're horrible. You know that, don't you?"

"Horribly good, and horribly hard, and horribly impatient. Now, are we, or aren't we?" he asked, sauntering toward her, relaxed, easy, his arms loose at his sides. But it was a deceptive ease, and they both knew it as the temperature in the luxurious bedroom seemed to soar and the air sparked with heat and need, the tension between them thick and hot and electric.

Closing the gap between them, Drakon could feel Morgan tense, her hands squeezing in convulsive fists, even as her eyes widened and her lips parted with each quick shallow breath.

"You're trembling," he said, "but there's no need for that. I won't eat you. Not unless you want me to."

"Drakon." Her voice sounded strangled and her cheeks were crimson, making her blue eyes darken and shimmer like the sapphire sea beyond the window.

"I hope you'll want me to. I love how you taste, and how soft you are in my mouth...so sweet. But is that too risky for you? Pushing the limits too much?"

"You love to torment me."

"Yes, I do," he agreed, circling her slowly, enjoying just looking at her, and watching the color come and go in her exquisite porcelain complexion, and listening to her soft desperate gasps of air. "But this is nothing, Morgan. I haven't even gotten started." He stopped in front of her, gazed down at her, thinking she looked very young and very uncertain and very shy, much like his virgin bride. "Now tell me, what should I do to you first?"

Morgan's heart was pounding so fast she couldn't catch her breath, and she opened her mouth, lips parting, to gulp in shallow gasps of air. She felt as if she were balancing on the edge of a volcano while little voices inside her head demanded she throw herself in.

She needed to leave, to escape the villa, to summon the helicopter and fly far, far away. Remaining here with Drakon was stupid and destructive. She might as well fling herself into that volcano...the outcome would be the same.

And yet, wasn't she already there, in the fiery pit? Because molten lava seemed to be seeping through her veins, melting her bones and muscles into mindless puddles of want and need.

She actually felt sick with need right now. But could she do this...go through with this...knowing it would be just sex, not love? Knowing Drakon wanted her body but not her heart?

"Are you crying?" he asked, his voice dropping, deepening with concern, as his hands wrapped around her arms, holding her up.

She shook her head, unable to look him in the eye.

"What's wrong?" he asked.

She swallowed hard, tried to speak, but no sound would come out. Not when her throat ached and her heart was still thundering in her chest.

He reached up to smooth a dark tendril of hair back from her face. "Have I frightened you?" His deep voice was suddenly gentle, almost painfully tender.

Hot tears scalded the back of her eyes. She bit hard into her lower lip so that it wouldn't quiver.

"I would never hurt you, Morgan," he murmured, drawing her against him, holding her in his arms, holding her securely against his chest.

She closed her eyes as the heat of his body seeped into her hands, warming her. He felt good. Too good. It was so confusing. This was confusing.

She didn't push him away, and yet she couldn't relax, waiting for the moment he'd let her go. But she didn't want him to let her go. She wanted him closer. Wanted to press her face to his chest and breathe him in. She could smell a hint of his spicy fragrance and loved that fragrance—his own scent, formulated just for him—and what it did to his skin. He smelled like heaven. Delicious and warm and good and intoxicating. He smelled like everything she wanted. He smelled like home. He *was* home. He was everything to her, but wasn't that the problem? With him, she lost herself. With him, she lost her mind.

With a strangled cry, Morgan slid a hand up across his chest, to push him back, and just like before, once she touched him, she couldn't take her hand away. She stroked across the hard plane of muscle of his chest, learning again the shape of his body and how the dense smooth pectoral muscle curved and sloped beneath her palm. God, he was beautiful. And without his shirt, his skin would feel so good against hers. She loved the way his bare chest felt against her bare breasts, loved the friction and the heat and the delicious, addictive energy—

"Can't do this," she choked, shaking her head. "We can't, we can't."

"Ssshh," he murmured, cupping her face, his thumbs stroking lightly over her cheekbones, sweeping from the curve of the bone to her earlobes. "Nothing bad will happen—"

"Everything bad will happen," she protested, shivering with pleasure from the caress. She loved the way he touched her. He made her feel beautiful, inside and out, and she struggled to remember what bad things would happen if he touched her....

"You are so beautiful," he murmured, hands slipping from her face to tangle in her hair.

"And mad, Drakon, certifiably insane—"

"That's okay."

"Drakon, I'm serious!"

"I am, too." His head dipped lower and his lips brushed hers, lightly, slowly, and she shuddered, pressed closer, a stinging sensation behind her eyes. One kiss...could it be so bad? One kiss...surely she could be forgiven that?

His lips found hers again and the kiss was surprisingly gentle, the pressure of his mouth just enough to tease her, send shivers of desire racing up and down her spine. This was all so impossible. They couldn't do this, couldn't give in to this, it's all they had and while the chemistry was intense, chemistry wasn't enough. Sex wasn't enough. She needed more. She needed a relationship, love, intimacy, commitment, but right now, she also needed this.

She'd missed him so much. Missed his skin and his scent, his warmth and his strength, and her defenses caved as his hands framed her face, and he held her face to his, deepening the kiss, drinking her in.

She could feel him and smell him and taste him now and she was lost. Nothing felt better than this. Nothing felt better than him. He wasn't just her husband, he was home and happiness—

No. No, no, no. Couldn't think that way, couldn't lose sight of reality. He wasn't home or happiness. And he'd finally agreed to let her go. After five years of wanting out, and she *did* want out, she was free.

And yet when his tongue stroked the seam of her lips, she arched and gasped, opening her mouth to him. Drakon deepened the kiss, his tongue flicking the inside of her lip, making every little nerve dance. One of his hands slid from the back of her head, down over her shoulders to her waist before settling in the small of her spine, urging her closer, shaping her against his powerful body.

She shuddered with pleasure as his tongue filled her mouth and the fingers of his hand splayed wider on her back, making her lower belly throb, ache, just like her thighs ached.

Every thrust of his tongue shot another bright arc of sensation through her, sensation that surged to the tips of her breasts, tightening them into hard, sensitive peaks, and then deep into her belly and even deeper to her innermost place, and yet it wasn't enough, not even close. Morgan dug her nails into his shoulders, pressing her breasts to his chest, practically grinding herself against his hips to feel the ridge of his erection rub against her sensitive spot at the junction of her thighs and the heat of his palm against her lower back.

It was still so electric between them, still fierce and wild, and she felt overwhelmed by desire, overwhelmed by the memory of such dizzying, maddening pleasure and the knowledge that he was here, and there could be more. And right now, she wanted more. She literally ached for him and could feel her body soften and warm for him, her body also clearly remembering that nothing in the world felt better than him in her. Him with her.

And then his hand was slipping slowly across the curve of her hip, to cup the roundness of her butt, and she nearly popped out of her skin. "Drakon," she groaned against his mouth, feeling as if he were spreading fire through her, fire and such fierce, consuming need.

She trembled as he stroked the length of her, from her hip to her breast and down again. His hands were everywhere now, pinching a nipple, stroking the cleft of her buttocks, shaping her thighs. She wanted his hand between her thighs, wanted him to touch her, fill her, wanted him more than she'd wanted anything—

Wait.

Wait.

She struggled to focus, clear her head, which was impossible with Drakon's amazing hands on her body and his mouth taking hers, promising her endless pleasure.

She had to move back, away, had to, now.

But then his hands were up, under her tunic, his skin so warm against hers, and when he unhooked her bra to cup her breasts, his thumbs grazing her tight, swollen nipples, she gave up resisting, gave up thinking and gave in to him.

He stripped off her clothes while kissing her, his hands never leaving her body as the clothes fell away, giving her no time to panic or reconsider.

Once naked, he carried her to the bed, and set her on her back in the middle of the enormous bed. The room's windows and doors were open and the sunlight spilled across the floor, splashing on the walls while the heady sweet scent of wisteria filled the room.

Morgan watched Drakon's face as he moved over her, his hard, powerful body warm, his skin a burnished gold, his strong features taut with passion. But it was his eyes that once again captivated her, and the burning intensity of his gaze. When he looked at her he made her feel extraordinary...desirable...rare...impossibly valuable. She knew he didn't feel that way about her, not anymore, but with him stretched out over her, his skin covering her, warming her, it didn't seem to matter.

She lifted her face to his, and his mouth met hers in a blistering kiss that melted everything within her. There was nothing she wouldn't give him. And as he settled his weight between her thighs, his hips pressing down against hers, she shivered with pleasure.

He was resting his weight on his forearms, but she wanted more pressure, not less, and Morgan arched up, pressing her breasts to his bare chest, loving the friction of his nipples on hers even as she opened her thighs wider, letting him settle deeper into her.

"I want you," she whispered against his mouth, her arms circling his shoulders, her hands sliding into his thick hair, fingers curling into the crisp strands at his nape. He felt good and smelled good and in this moment, everything was right in the world...at least, everything was right in her world. "I want you in me. I need you in me."

"It's been a long time."

"Too long," she said, lifting her hips, grinding up against him, not wanting any more foreplay, not wanting anything but him, and his body meshed deeply with hers.

"Patience," he answered, kissing the corner of her mouth and the line of her jaw, smoothing her hair back from her face. "There's no need to rush—"

But there was. She didn't want to wait, had enough teasing and words and thinking, had enough of everything but him. And right now she just wanted him. She reached between them, caught his hard shaft and gripped it firmly, the way she knew he liked it, and rubbed his head up and down her, the warm, rigid shaft sliding across her damp opening, making him slick, and then bringing the silken head up to her sensitive nub, drawing moisture up over her clit.

She heard him groan deep in his throat, a hoarse, guttural sound of pleasure, and it gave her a perverse thrill, knowing she could make Drakon feel something so strong that he'd groan aloud.

His hands stroked the outsides of her thighs and then down the inside and she shifted her hips, positioning him at her wet, slick core. "Do you want me?" she whispered, her lips at his ear.

"Yes," he groaned, his voice so low that it rumbled through her. "Yes, always."

And then he took control, lowering his weight, forearms pressed to the bed, and kissed her, deeply, his tongue plunging into her mouth even as he entered her body, thrusting all the way until they were one, and for a nearly a minute he remained still, kissing her, filling her, until she felt him swell inside her, stretching her, throbbing inside her, making her throb, too. Her pulse raced and her body tingled and burned, her inner muscles clenching and rippling with exquisite sensation. He was big and hard and warm and she could come like this, with her body gripping him, holding him, and Drakon knew it, knew how just being inside her could shatter her.

"Not yet," she gasped, hands stroking over his broad shoulders and down the smooth, hard, warm planes of his back, savoring the curve and hollow of every thick, sinewy muscle. Men were so beautiful compared to women, and no man was more beautiful than Drakon. "Don't let me come, not yet. I want more. I want everything."

And maybe this was just the plain old missionary position, but it felt amazing, felt hot and fierce and intense and emotional and physical and everything that was good. Sex like this was mind-blowingly good, especially with Drakon taking his time, thrusting into her in long smooth strokes that hit all the right places, that made her feel all the right things. Morgan wished it could last forever, but she was already responding, the muscles inside her womb were coiling tighter and tighter, bringing her ever closer to that point of no return. Morgan's head spun with the exquisite sensation, the tension so consuming that it was difficult to know in that moment if it was pleasure or pain, and then with one more deep thrust, Drakon sent her over the edge and her senses exploded, her body rippling and shuddering beneath his.

Drakon came while she was still climaxing and he ground out her name as he buried himself deeply within her. She could feel him come, feel the heat and liquid of him surging within her, and it hit her—they hadn't used a condom. On their honeymoon they had never used protection. Drakon wanted children and she wanted to please him and so they had never used birth control, but this was different. They were divorcing. She'd soon be single. There was absolutely no way she could cope with getting pregnant now.

"What have we done?" she cried, struggling to push him off of her. "What did we do?"

Drakon shifted his weight and allowed her to roll away from him, even as a small muscle jumped in his jaw. "I think you know what we just did."

"We shouldn't have. It was wrong."

"Doesn't feel wrong to me," he said tersely, watching her slide to the edge of the bed and search for her tunic, or something to cover up with.

She grabbed Drakon's shirt, and slipped it over her arms into the sleeves and buttoned up the front. "Well, it was. We didn't use birth control, Drakon, and we shouldn't have even thought about sex without using a condom."

"But we never used a condom."

"Because we were newlyweds. We were hoping to have

children, we both wanted a big family, but it's different now. We're separated. Divorcing. A baby would be disastrous, absolutely the worst thing possible—"

"Actually, I can think of a few things worse than a baby," he interrupted, getting off the bed and reaching for his trousers. He stepped into one leg and then the other before zipping them closed. "Like famine. Disease. Pestilence. Or someone swindling billions of dollars—"

"Obviously I didn't mean that a baby was a tragedy," she retorted, crossing her arms over her chest to hide the fact that she was trembling. Just moments ago she'd been so relaxed, so happy, and now she felt absolutely shell-shocked. How was it possible to swing from bliss to hell in thirty seconds flat? But then, wasn't that how it had always been with them?

"No, I think you did," he countered. "It's always about you, and what's good for you—"

"That's not true."

"Absolutely true. You're so caught up in what you want and need that there is no room in this relationship for two people. There certainly was never room for me."

Her eyes widened. "You can't be serious, Drakon. You're the most controlling person I've ever met. You controlled everything in our marriage, including me—"

"Do I look like I'm in control?" he demanded tautly, dark color washing the strong, hard planes of his face.

He was breathing unsteadily, and her gaze swept over him, from his piercing gaze to the high color in his cheekbones to his firm full mouth, and she thought he looked incredible. Beautiful. Powerful. Her very own mythic Greek god. But that was the problem. He was too beautiful, too powerful. She had no perspective around him. Would throw herself in the path of danger just to be close to him.

Good God. How self-destructive was that?

Before she could speak, she heard the distinctive hum of a helicopter.

"Rowan," Drakon said, crossing to the balcony and stepping outside to watch the helicopter move across the sky. "He'll have news about your father."

"Then I'd better shower and dress."

CHAPTER SEVEN

MORGAN REFUSED TO think about what had just happened in her bed, unable to go there at all, and instead focused on taking a very fast shower before drying off and changing into a simple A-line dress in white linen with blue piping that Drakon had shipped over from the Athens house with the rest of the wardrobe.

In the steamy marble bathroom, she ran a brush through her long hair before drawing it back into a sleek ponytail and headed for her door, careful to keep her gaze averted from the bed's tousled sheets and duvet.

The maid would remake the bed while she was gone, and probably change the sheets, and Morgan was glad. She didn't want to remember or reflect on what had just changed there. It shouldn't have happened. It was a terrible mistake.

She took the stairs quickly, overwhelmed by emotion— worry and hope for her father, longing for Drakon, as well as regret. Now that they'd made love once, would he expect her to tumble back into bed later tonight?

And what if he didn't want to make love again? What if that was the last time? How would she feel?

In some ways that was the worst thought of all.

It wasn't the right way to end things. Couldn't be their last time. Their last time needed to be different. Needed more, not less. Needed more emotion, more time, more skin, more love…

Love.

She still loved Drakon, didn't she? Morgan's eyes stung, knowing she always would love him, too. Saying goodbye to him would rip her heart out. She only hoped it'd be less destructive than it had been the first time. Could only hope she'd remember the pain was just grief…that the pain would eventually, one day, subside.

But she wouldn't go there, either. Not yet. She was still here with him, still feeling so alive with him. Better to stay focused on the moment, and deal with the future when it came.

Reaching the bottom stair she discovered one of Drakon's staff was waiting for her. "Mrs. Xanthis, Mr. Xanthis is waiting for you in the terrace sunroom," the maid said.

Morgan thanked her and headed down the final flight of stairs to the lower level, the terrace level.

The sunroom ran the length of the villa and had formerly been a ballroom in the nineteenth century. The ballroom's original gilt ceiling, the six sets of double glass doors and the grand Venetian glass chandeliers remained, but the grand space was filled now with gorgeous rugs and comfortable furniture places and potted palms and miniature citrus trees. It was one of the lightest, brightest rooms in the villa and almost always smelled of citrus blossoms.

Entering the former ballroom, Morgan spotted Drakon and another man standing in the middle of the enormous room, talking in front of a grouping of couches and chairs.

They both turned and looked at her as she entered the room, but Morgan only had eyes for Drakon. Just looking at him made her insides flip, and her pulse leap.

She needed him, wanted him, loved him, far too much.

Her heart raced and her stomach hurt as she crossed the ballroom, her gaze drinking in Drakon, her footsteps muffled by the plush Persian rugs scattered across the marble floor.

He looked amazing…like Drakon, but not like Drakon

in that soft gray knit shirt that hugged his broad shoulders and lovingly molded to his muscular chest, outlining every hard, sinewy muscle with a pair of jeans. In America they called shirts like the one he was wearing Henleys. They'd been work shirts, worn by farmers and firemen and lumberjacks, not tycoons and millionaires and it boggled her mind that Drakon would wear such a casual shirt, although from the look of the fabric and the cut, it wasn't an inexpensive one—but it suited him.

He looked relaxed…and warm. So warm. So absolutely not cold, or controlled. And part of her suddenly wondered, if he had ever been cold, or if she'd just come to think of him that way as they grew apart in those last few months of their marriage?

Which led to another question—had he ever been that much in control, too? Or had she turned him into something he wasn't? Her imagination making him into an intimidating and controlling man because she felt so out of control?

God, she hoped not. But there was no time to mull over the past. She'd reached Drakon's side and felt another electric jolt as his gaze met hers and held. She couldn't look away from the warmth in his amber eyes. Part of him still burned and it made her want to burn with him. Madness, she told herself, don't go there, don't lose yourself, and yet the air hummed with heat and desire.

How could she not respond to him?

How could she not want to be close to him when he was so fiercely alive?

"It's going to be all right," he murmured, his deep voice pitched so low only she could hear.

Her lovely, lovely man that made her feel like the most beautiful woman in the entire world. Her lovely, lovely man that had pushed her to the brink, and beyond, and he still didn't know…still had no idea where she'd been that first year after leaving him, or what had happened to her trying to separate herself from him.

Part of her wanted to tell him, and yet another part didn't want to give him that knowledge, or power. Because he could break her. Absolutely destroy her. And she wasn't strong enough yet to rebuild herself again…not yet. Not on top of everything else that had happened to her father and her family with the Amery scandal.

"I promise you," he added.

She heard his fierce resolve and her heart turned over. This is how she'd fallen in love with him—his strength, his focus, his determination. That and the way he smiled at her… as if she were sunshine and oxygen all rolled into one. "Yes," she murmured, aware that once upon a time he'd been everything to her…her hope, her happiness, her future. She missed those days. Missed feeling as if she belonged somewhere with someone.

There was a flicker in his eyes, and then he made the introductions. "Morgan, this is Rowan Argyros, of Dunamas. Rowan, my wife, Morgan Copeland Xanthis."

Morgan forced her attention from Drakon to the stranger and her jaw nearly dropped. *This* was Rowan Argyros? *This* was one of the founders of Dunamas Maritime Intelligence?

Her brows tugged. She couldn't mask her surprise. Argyros wasn't at all what she'd expected.

She'd imagined Drakon's intelligence expert to look like one, and she'd pictured a man in his forties, maybe early fifties, who was stocky, balding, with a square jaw and pugilistic nose.

Instead Rowan Argyros looked like a model straight off some Parisian runway. He was gorgeous. Not her type at all, but her sister Logan would bed him in a heartbeat.

Tall and broad-shouldered, Argyros was muscular without any bulk. He was very tan, and his eyes were light, a pale gray or green, hard to know exactly in the diffused light of the ballroom. His dark brown hair was sun-streaked and he wore it straight and far too long for someone in his line of work. His jaw was strong, but not the thick bulldog jaw she'd come to associate with testosterone-driven males, but more angular…elegant, the kind of face that would photograph beautifully, although today that jaw was shadowed with a day-old beard.

"Mrs. Xanthis," Rowan said, extending a hand to her.

It bothered her that he hadn't even bothered to shave for their meeting, and she wondered how this could be the man who would free her father?

Rowan Argosy looked as if he'd spent his free time hanging out on obscenely big yachts off the coast of France, not planning daring, dangerous life-saving missions.

She shook his hand firmly and let it go quickly. "Mr. Argyros," she said crisply. "I would love to know what you know about my father. Drakon said you have information."

"I do," Rowan said, looking her straight in the eye, his voice hard, his expression as cool and unfriendly as hers.

Morgan's eyebrows lifted. Nice. She liked his frosty tone, and found his coldness and aloofness reassuring. She wouldn't have trusted him at all if he'd been warm and charming. Military types…intelligence types…they weren't the touchy-feely sort. "Is he alive?"

"He is. I have some film of him taken just this morning."

"How did you get it?"

"Does it matter?"

"No." And her legs felt like Jell-O and she took a step back, sitting down heavily in one of the chairs grouped behind them. Her heart was thudding so hard and fast she thought she might be sick and she drew great gulps of air, fighting waves of nausea and intense relief. Dad was alive. That was huge. "Thank God."

For a moment there was just silence as Morgan sat with the news, overwhelmed that her father was indeed alive. After a moment, when she could trust herself to speak, she looked up at Rowan. "And he's well? He's healthy?"

He hesitated. "We don't know that. We only have his location, and evidence that he is alive."

So Dad could be sick. He probably didn't have his heart medicine with him. It'd probably been left behind on his boat. "What happens now?" she asked.

"We get your father out, take him to wherever you want him to go."

"How does that happen, though?"

"We're going to have you call your contact, the one in Somalia you've been dealing with, and you're going to ask to speak to your father. You'll tell them you need proof that he's alive and well if they are to get the six million dollars."

"They won't let me speak to him. I tried that before."

"They will," Drakon interjected, arms folded across his chest, the shirt molded to his sculpted torso, "if they think you're ready to make a drop of six million."

She looked at him. "What if they call our bluff? Wouldn't we have to be prepared to make the drop?"

"Yes. And we will. We'll give them a date, a time, coordinates for the drop. We'll tell them who is making the drop, too."

"But we're not dropping any money, are we?" she asked, glancing from him to Rowan and back again.

"No," said Rowan. "We're preparing a team right now to move in and rescue your father. But speaking to your father gives us important information, as well as buys us a little more time to put our plan in place."

She nodded, processing this. "How long until you rescue him?"

"Soon. Seventy-two hours, or less."

She looked at Rowan, startled. "That is soon."

"Once we have our plan in place, it's better to strike fast." Rowan's phone made a low vibrating noise and he reached into his pocket and checked the number. "I need to take this call," he said, walking away.

Morgan exhaled as Rowan exited through the sunroom, into the stairwell that would take him back up to the main level of the villa.

"You okay?" Drakon asked, looking down on her, after Rowan disappeared.

"Things can go wrong," she said.

"Yes. And sometimes they do. But Dunamas has an impressive track record. Far more successes than failures. I wouldn't have enlisted their help if I didn't think they'd succeed."

She hesitated. "If Rowan's team didn't succeed...people could die."

"People *will* die even if they do succeed. They're planning a raid. The pirates are heavily armed. Dunamas's team will be heavily armed. It's not going to be a peaceful handover. It'll be explosive and violent, and yet the team they're sending are professionals. They're prepared to do whatever they have to do to get him out alive."

So some of them—or all of them—could end up dying for her father?

Nauseated all over again, Morgan moved from her chair, not wanting to think of the brave, battle-tested men, men the world viewed as heroic, risking their lives for her father, who wasn't a hero.

Stomach churning, she pushed open one of the sunroom's tall arched glass doors and stepped onto the terrace, into the sunshine. She drank in a breath of fresh air, and then another. Was she being selfish, trying to save her father? Should she not do this?

Panic and guilt buffeted her as she leaned against the terrace's creamy marble balustrade and squeezed her eyes closed.

Drakon had followed her outside. "What's wrong?"

She didn't answer immediately, trying to find the right words, but what were those words? How did one make a decision like this? "Am I doing the wrong thing?" she asked. "Am I wrong, trying to save him?"

"I can't answer that for you. He's your father. Your family."

"You know I tried everything before I came to you. I asked everyone for help. No one would help me."

"Who did you approach?"

"Who didn't I?" She laughed grimly and glanced out across the terraced gardens with the roses and hedges and the pool and the view of the sea beyond. "I went to London to see Branson, and then to Los Angeles to see Logan, and then to Tori in New York, and back to London, but none of them would contribute money toward Dad's ransom. They're all in tight financial straits, and they all have reasons they couldn't give, but I think they wouldn't contribute to the ransom because they're ashamed of Dad. I think they believe I'm wasting money trying to rescue him. Mom even said he's better off where he is…that people will find it easier to forgive us—his kids—if Dad doesn't come back."

"You mean, if the pirates kill him?" Drakon asked.

She nodded.

"Your mother is probably right," he said.

She shot him a swift glance before pushing away from the railing to pace the length of the terrace. For a long minute she just walked, trying to master her emotions. "Maybe," she said, "maybe Mom is right, but I don't care. I don't care what people think of me. I don't care if they like me. I care about what's right. And while what Dad did, just blindly giving Michael the money, wasn't right, it's also not right to leave him in Somalia. And maybe the others can write him off, but I can't."

She shivered, chilled, even though the sun was shining warmly overhead. "I can't forget how he taught me to swim and ride a bike and he went to every one of my volleyball games in high school. Dad was there for everything, big and small, and maybe he was a terrible investment advisor, but he was a wonderful father. I couldn't have asked for better—" Morgan broke off, covering her mouth to stifle a sob. She couldn't help it, but she missed him, and worried about him, and there was just no way she could turn her back on him now. No way at all.

"I think you have your answer," Drakon said quietly. "You have to do this. Have to help him. Right or wrong."

They both turned at the sound of a squeaky gate. Rowan was heading up toward them from the lower garden.

"And if anybody can get your father home, it's Argyros," Drakon said.

Morgan wrinkled her nose. "He looks like a drug smuggler."

The corner of Drakon's mouth lifted. "He isn't what one expects. That's what makes him so successful."

"As long as you trust him."

"I do."

On reaching their side, Rowan announced that his office was now ready for Morgan to try to phone her pirate contact in Somalia. "We have a special line set up that will allow us to record the conversation," he said. "And my team is standing by now, to listen in on the call."

"But I can only use my phone," she answered. "And my number. They know my number—"

"We know. And we can make it appear to look like your number. Today's technology lets us do just about anything."

In the villa's dark-paneled library they attempted the call but no one answered on the other end. Morgan left a message, letting her contact know that she had six million in cash, in used bills, and was ready to make the drop but she wanted to speak to her father first. "I need to know he's alive," she said, "and then you'll have the money."

She hung up, glanced at Rowan and Drakon. "And now what?"

"We wait for a call back," Rowan said.

They had a light lunch in the library while waiting, but there was no return call. Morgan wanted to phone again but Rowan said it wasn't a good idea. "We're playing a game," he explained. "It's their game, but we're going to outplay them. They just don't know it yet."

The afternoon dragged. Morgan hated waiting as it made her restless and anxious. She wanted to hear her father's voice, and she wanted to hear it sooner than later. After a couple hours, she couldn't sit still any longer and began to walk in circles. She saw Morgan and Drakon exchange glances.

"What?" she demanded. "Am I not allowed to move out of my chair?"

Drakon smiled faintly. "Come, let's go get some exercise and fresh air."

Stretching her legs did sound nice, but Morgan didn't want to miss the call. "What if the pirate calls back and I'm not here?"

"He'll leave a message," Drakon said.

"Won't he be angry?" she asked.

Rowan shrugged. "They want your money. They'll call back."

It was close to four when Morgan and Drakon left the house to walk down to the water, and the afternoon was still bright, and warm, but already the sun was sitting lower in the sky. Morgan took a deep breath, glad to have escaped the dark cool library and be back outside.

"Thank you for getting me out of there," she said to Drakon as they crossed the lawn, heading for the stone and cement staircase that hugged the cliff and took them down to the little dock, where they used to anchor the speedboat they used to explore the coast.

"You were looking a little pale in there," Drakon said, walking next to her. "But your father's going to be all right."

"If I was pale, it's because I was thinking about what we did earlier." Her fingers knotted into fists. "Or what we shouldn't have done." She glanced up at him as he opened the second wrought-iron gate, this one at the top of the stairs.

"Which was?" he asked innocently.

She shot him a disbelieving look and his golden brown eyes sparked, the corner of his sexy mouth tugging in a slow, wicked smile and just like that the air was suddenly charged, and Morgan shivered at the sudden snap and crackle of tension and the spike of awareness. God, it was electric between them. And dangerous.

"It can't happen again," she whispered, her gaze meeting his.

"No?" he murmured, reaching out to lift a soft tendril of hair back from her cheek, but then he couldn't let it go and he let the strand slide between his fingers, before curling it loosely around his finger and thumb.

Her breath caught in her throat and she stared up at him, heart pounding, mouth drying. She loved the way he touched her and he was making her weak in the knees now. "It confuses me."

"Confuses you, how?"

The heat between them was intense. Dizzying. So much awareness, so much desire, so impossible to satisfy. She swayed on her feet and he immediately stepped between her and the edge of the stairs, pressing her up against the wall. "I can't think around you," she whispered, feeling his dazzling energy before her, and the sun warmed rock at her back.

"Thinking is overrated," he murmured, moving in closer to her, brushing his lips across her forehead.

She closed her eyes, breathing in his light clean fragrance and savoring the teasing caress. "Is it?"

"Mmm-hmm."

"Does that mean you're not going to think, either?"

She felt the corners of his mouth curve against her brow. He was smiling. And God, didn't that turn her on?

She locked her knees, her inner thighs clenching, wanting him, needing. Damn him.

"One of us should probably keep our heads," he answered, his hands cupping her face, thumbs stroking her cheekbones. "Less frantic that way."

"And I suppose you think that should be you?" she breathed, trying to resist the pleasure of his hands pushing deep into her hair, his fingers wrapping around the strands, his knuckles grazing her scalp. He was so good at turning her on, making her feel, and he was making her feel now with a little tug, a touch, and just like that, desire rushed through her…hot, consuming, intense.

"Of course," he said, leaning in to her, his mouth lightly kissing down from her brow, over her cheekbone, to the soft swell of her lips.

"Why?"

"Because no one has ever loved you the way I loved you."

Her eyes flew open and she stared into his eyes. "Don't say that."

"It's true. You know how I feel about you. You know I can not refuse you anything."

"Not true. For five years you refused to grant me the divorce."

"Because I didn't want to lose you."

"Five years is a long time to wait for someone."

"I would have waited forever for you, Morgan."

Her heart was pounding again, even harder. "That doesn't make sense, Drakon. Nothing about this…us…makes sense."

"Who said love was supposed to make sense?"

She exhaled hard, in a quick, desperate rush, and she had to blink hard to clear her vision. "Did you *really* love me?"

"How can you doubt it?"

She frowned, thinking, trying to remember. Why had she doubted it? Why had she not felt loved? How did she get from besotted bride to runaway wife?

He reached out, tipped her chin up, so he could look deeper into her eyes. "Morgan, tell me. How could you doubt me?"

"Because after our honeymoon…after we left here…I didn't feel loved…." Her voice drifted off as she struggled to piece it together. How lost she'd felt in Athens, how confused waiting for him all day, needing him so much that when he walked through the door, she didn't know if she should run to him, or hide, ashamed for feeling so empty. "But then, after a while, I didn't feel anything anymore—" She broke off, bit down into her lip, piercing the skin. "No, that's not true. I did feel something. I felt crazy, Drakon. I felt crazy living with you."

"Don't say that."

"It's true."

He stepped away from her, turned and faced the sea, then rubbed his palm across the bristles on his jaw.

Morgan watched him just long enough to see the pain in his eyes. She'd hurt him. Again.

Hating herself, hating what they did to each other, she slipped past him and continued down the stairs to the water's edge.

She had to get out of here. And she had to get out of here soon.

CHAPTER EIGHT

HE SWORE SOFTLY, and shook his head.

God, that woman was frustrating. And to think he hadn't just fallen in love with her, but he'd married her.

Married her.

Long before his wedding day, Drakon had been warned by other men that getting married changed things. He'd been warned that wives—and marriage—were a lot of work. But Drakon hadn't been daunted. He didn't mind work. He'd succeeded because he'd always worked hard, put in long hours, never expecting life to be easy.

But marriage to Morgan hadn't started out difficult. It'd been amazing initially. She'd been amazing, and everything had been easy, since Morgan had been easiness herself…joyful, uncomplicated, undemanding. And then they moved into the new villa in Ekali, the affluent Athens neighborhood, and she'd changed…expressing worries, and then doubts, and then needs which came to sound like demands.

Be home from work early.

Don't work too late.

Why aren't you ever here?

And if he were honest, he had worked long hours, really long hours, and the more Morgan pressured him to come home, the more he wanted to be at the office, and he'd told himself he was working late to provide for her, working late to ensure she had everything she needed, when deep inside he knew he was just avoiding going home to her. It wasn't that he didn't love her…but he was suddenly so aware of how she now depended on him for everything. It overwhelmed him. How could he meet all those needs? How could he manage her, and his work, and his responsibilities?

While he grew more distant, she grew more emotional, her sunny smiles fading until they were gone, replaced by a woman who looked fragile and haunted, her eyes sad, her lovely face taut, her expression stricken.

It made him angry, this change in her. Made him angry that she couldn't be like his other women…happy to shop and visit salons and spas and just enjoy being spoiled, enjoy the prestige of being Drakon Xanthis's pampered wife. It was good enough for his other women. Why not for her?

Why did Morgan want more? More to the point, what did she want from *him?*

He'd never told her—or anyone—but in his mind, she'd become like his mother. Drakon loved his mother, he was a dutiful son, but he didn't want to be around her, and that's what happened with Morgan. Morgan made him feel inadequate and he dealt with it by avoiding her.

And then one day Morgan disappeared, abruptly returning to America, and he had exploded.

How could she have just walk away from him like that? How could she give up? How *dare* she give up? He hadn't been happy all those years ago, but he hadn't walked away from her. He hadn't felt the magic, either, but he wasn't a quitter—

And then it struck him. He had quit on her. Maybe he hadn't physically left, but he'd checked out emotionally.

And only now he could see that her needs hadn't been so overwhelming. She hadn't asked for that much. But the fact that she'd asked for anything—time, tenderness, reassurance—had triggered the worst in him, and he'd reacted like the boy he'd once been, retreating, hiding, rejecting.

He'd given her money but not affection.

He'd given her toys but not his heart.

He'd given her stuff…as long as she didn't engage him, want him, need him. Don't bother him because he couldn't, wouldn't, deal with anyone else's problems—he had plenty of his own.

Ah.

And there it was. The ugly, ugly truth.

Drakon Xanthis was a selfish, shallow, stunted man. A man that looked strong on the outside but was just an angry child on the inside. And that's when he knew, that he'd wronged Morgan…badly. Cruelly. He'd taken a twenty-two-year-old woman from her home and her country and dropped her into his white marble house and told her to be silent and to not feel and to not need. To not express emotion, to not reach out, to not cry, to not talk, to not be human.

My God.

He'd done to her what his mother had done to him. Be there, Drakon, but do not need. Be present, Drakon, but do not feel….

Five years ago Drakon went in search of Morgan, seeking to right the wrongs, but she was gone. She'd vanished…completely disappeared…and his anger with himself grew. He'd loved Morgan and he'd treated her so badly. He'd taken the person who loved him, wanted him, the real him—the man, not the name, the bank account, the status—and crushed her.

He'd broken her.

He knew it. And all he'd wanted was to find her, apologize, fix everything. And he couldn't. Morgan was gone again. And Drakon was shattered. Until she came back, until he could make things right, he was a man in hell.

Now, from the top of the stairs, he watched Morgan step onto the platform down below, her brown hair gleaming in the sunlight, spilling down her back. His chest hurt, heavy and aching with suppressed emotion.

Morgan. His woman. His.

She stood on the platform, a hand shadowing her eyes as she looked out across the water. A wooden rowboat, the color of a robin's egg, was tethered to the platform and bobbed next to her. The blue rowboat, and dark sapphire sea, perfectly framed Morgan in her fitted white dress, which accented her slim curves.

She looked fresh and young standing on the platform, and when she slipped off her shoes and sat down on the pier's edge, pulling her crisp skirts high on her thigh so that she could put her bare feet in the water, he felt a fierce surge of emotion.

It had been his job to love her, cherish her and protect her. And he'd failed in all three counts.

Watching her, Drakon's chest grew tight. He'd vowed five years ago to make things right, and he hadn't made them right yet. Giving her a check and a divorce wasn't right. It was easy. Easier to let her go than to change, or struggle to save them. But he didn't want easy. He wanted Morgan. And she was worth fighting for, and she was worth changing for, and she was worth everything to him.

She was everything to him.

He'd known it the moment he'd lost her.

And now that she was here, he realized that he could not give up on her. Could not give up on them. Not because he needed to win her back, not because he needed to prove anything—for God's sake, he was Drakon Xanthis, and the world was his oyster—but because he loved *her,* Morgan Copeland.

And for the past five years, Morgan Copeland had tied him up in knots. But he was a smart man. He could figure out how to untie the knots. He could figure out how to reach her, how to make this—them—work.

It was a challenge, but he liked challenges. He'd never been afraid of tackling difficult situations. What was it that his father used to say? Problems were just opportunities in disguise?

Morgan being here was an opportunity. And Drakon would make the most of the opportunity.

"It was a mistake making love without protection," Drakon said quietly. "And I accept full responsibility should you get pregnant."

Morgan stiffened. She hadn't heard Drakon approach, but now she felt him there behind her, and her nape prickled, the hair on her arms lifted, and a shiver raced through her as she remembered how it felt being with him in her room, his skin on her skin, his mouth taking hers, his body giving her so much pleasure.

It had been so good. So intense and physical that she lost perspective. Forgot what was important. But then, hadn't that always been his effect on her?

"What does that mean?" she asked quietly, reaching up to pluck a fine strand of hair away from her eyelashes as she kept her gaze fixed on the watery horizon, where the sunlight shimmered in every direction. "That you will accept full responsibility if I get pregnant?"

"I'll assume full financial responsibility, for you and the child, and once the baby is born, I will assume full physical custody of the child—"

"What?" she choked, cutting him short as she turned to look at him where he was standing on the narrow stair landing behind her, leaning against the rock wall. "You'll take my baby?"

"Our baby," he calmly corrected, broad shoulders shifting, "and I am quite able to raise a child on my own, Morgan. I will get help, of course, but I'll be a good father—"

"You'd take the baby away from me?"

"If that would make you feel better—"

"It wouldn't."

"You said earlier that you didn't want to be a single mother."

"I don't. It wouldn't be right for the baby. But that doesn't mean you can have him or her."

He walked toward her. "But I'm ready to be a father, and you're not wanting to be a mother right now—"

"You can't say that. You don't know that. My God, Drakon! Where are you getting this from?"

"First of all, right now, as far as we know, there's no baby. And secondly, *should* you conceive, then of course I'd want to support my child—financially, emotionally, physically. I won't be an absentee father."

Her skin prickled as he stood above her. The man was pure electricity. The air practically pulsed with energy. "No, I don't want to be pregnant right now, it's not high on my to-do list at the moment, with my father being held hostage and my family in chaos, but if I was pregnant, I'd manage."

"That's not good enough. My child deserves better than that. If you are pregnant, we'll have to do the right thing for our child, which means raising him or her in a calm, stable home, without chaos."

"Then you'd be stuck with me, Drakon, because I'm not handing over my child."

"Our child."

"Which might not even exist."

"Which probably doesn't exist, because when we were newlyweds and having unprotected sex every day, twice a day, for months, you didn't get pregnant."

She bit into her lip, hating the panic rushing through here. This was just a conversation of hypotheticals. "Does that mean if I do conceive, you'd want the baby and me to live with you?"

"Yes."

It's not real, she reminded herself, don't freak out. "And we'd be divorced?"

"No."

"No?"

He shook his head. "Absolutely not. If you're pregnant, we'll stay together. If you're not, I'll have my attorney file the divorce papers. But as we won't know that for a couple more weeks, I won't have my attorney file until we know for certain."

"Awfully convenient," she muttered under her breath.

"Happily so," he answered, not rising to the bait. "This way there would be no stigma attached to the child. We're still legally married. The baby would be a result of our reconciliation."

"And if I'm not pregnant?"

"You'll be free—single—within a couple months."

Morgan didn't immediately speak. Instead she looked out across the water and listened to the waves break and felt the breeze catch and lift her hair. She might appear calm, but her thoughts were tangled and her emotions intense. "And should the unthinkable happen, should I conceive…we would all live together, as a family?"

"Yes."

She turned to look at him. "Where would we raise the baby?"

"Greece," he said firmly.

She made a rough sound, tucking a strand of hair behind her ear. "I'd prefer not to raise a child in Greece."

"Why not?"

"I don't like Greece."

"How can you not like Greece? It's beautiful and warm and so full of life."

"I found it excruciatingly isolating, and horribly boring—"

"There was no reason for you to be bored. You had money, a driver, you could have gone shopping. The sales-clerks would have loved you. They would have waited on you hand and foot."

Battling her temper, Morgan drew her feet out of the water,

wrapped her arms around bent knees. "Not all women live to shop."

"Most women do."

"You can't generalize like that. It's not true." He started to protest and she overrode him. "Obviously one or more of your past girlfriends managed to convince you that retail therapy was the answer for everything, but I'm not one of them." She rose to her feet. "Shopping when I'm lonely just makes me feel worse...wandering alone from store to store looking for something to buy...how pathetic is that?"

"It would have been better than you sitting sulking at home."

Heat rushed through her, and her cheeks suddenly burned. "Sulking? Shopping? Why in God's name did you even marry shallow, materialistic me?"

"You were young. I thought you'd change."

"I can't believe you just said that! I can't believe you think you're so perfect...that you had no blame in our failed marriage."

"So what did I do wrong?" he asked.

"You didn't talk to me."

He laughed. "*That's* my mistake?"

Her eyes blazed. "Fine, laugh, but it's true. Our marriage ended because we didn't talk to each other. It ended because we both kept everything bottled inside and I think it's time we started talking, and saying those things that aren't comfortable, but true—"

"It's not going to change anything."

"No, but at least it'll clear the air. Perhaps give us better understanding of what happened...maybe help me understand you."

"Me?" he said incredulously. "What is there to understand about me?"

"Everything! I married one person and yet I ended up with another."

He drew back, shocked. "I didn't change. Morgan, it was you. When we married, you were strong and confident, and then before I knew what happened, you turned into an angry, silent woman who only responded when I touched her. So I touched you, as often as I could, as much as I could, trying to get you back."

"Words would have worked. Words and conversation."

"I don't trust words. Don't put much stock in conversation."

"Obviously, but would it have killed you to ask me about my day, or tell me about your day—" She broke off, averting her head, unable to look at him when her heart felt so bruised and tender. What a mistake it had been…falling in love… thinking it would work. "Let's just hope I'm not pregnant," she added hoarsely. "Because I don't want to go through life like this, trying to explain myself, trying to be accepted, only to be mocked by you."

Drakon shook his head, muttering something under his breath, something with quite a few syllables and from his inflection, sounded far from flattering.

"What did you just say?" she demanded.

"Doesn't matter."

"No, it does. I want to hear this. I want to hear everything you wouldn't tell me before."

"You gave up on us so quickly, Morgan. You didn't give yourself time to adjust to married life, nor did you try to make friends."

"Maybe I did give up too soon, but you could have tried to help me adjust to Athens. Instead you dropped me off at the house and expected me to keep myself busy until you returned every night."

"I had a job to do."

"You could have made more of an effort to help me adjust. You could have taken the time to show me around, or cut your day short now and then so we could take a walk, or visit a nearby beach, or even have people over."

Drakon looked bewildered. "Have people over? For what?"

"Have dinner, visit, socialize." She could see by his expression that he still didn't get it. "Surely, you're used to entertaining…having some friends over for a barbecue or a party."

"To my house?"

"Yes."

"Never have."

"Why not?"

"My family didn't. I never did. I don't have time, nor is it something I'd want to do. I work long days, and when I go home, I want to relax, rest, focus on what I need to do the next day."

"But while you were working twelve- and fourteen-hour days, Drakon, what was I supposed to do?"

"Read a book…take language courses…learn to cook?" He shrugged, sighed, running a hand through his cropped dark hair. "Eventually we would have had children. And then, of course, you had the house."

"The *house?*" Morgan suppressed a sudden urge to throw rocks at his head. "Did you actually just say I had the *house?*"

"Yes, the house. The one I had built for you."

"You did not build that marble mausoleum for me. You bought it for me—"

"No, I bought the lot, scrapped the old house that was there and built our home for you."

"I *hated* the villa."

"What?"

Her eyebrows lifted, her lips twisting. "Yes. I hated it. It's awful. It was too white and sterile, never mind cold, modern and boxy—"

"It's a ten-million-dollar architectural masterpiece, Morgan."

"Or merely an outrageously expensive ice cube tray!"

His eyes sparked. "You disappoint me."

"Yes, so I've gathered. You work twelve-hour days while I'm home learning Greek, and how to cook, and hopefully getting pregnant." She shuddered. "What a horrendous life that would have been. Thank God I escaped when I did!"

He reached out, his fingers wrapping around her bicep to haul her against him. "Do you know how many women would be thrilled to live in that house?"

"I have no idea, although I'm sure Bronwyn would love to be one." She flung her head back to look him in the eye. "How is she, by the way? Doing well?"

"She's fine."

"I bet she is."

"What does that mean?"

"What do you think it means, Drakon?"

"I think it means you're petty and irrational when it comes to Bron. She's never been anything but polite to you—"

"Give me a break!"

"—ordering you flowers, arranging for your birthday cake," he continued, as if she'd never interrupted.

Morgan shook his hand off her arm. "How nice of her to get me flowers from you and order birthday cake for me. It makes me feel so good to know that your vice president of Southeast Asia was able to do those little things to make my birthday special since you were too busy to do it yourself."

He tensed and his jaw popped. "That's not why I didn't do it."

"No? Then why didn't you do it?" She dragged in a breath of air, holding it a moment, fighting for control, not wanting to cry now. She would not cry while discussing Bronwyn. Would not lose it now when she needed to be strong. "Because I didn't want flowers picked out by the woman who is spending all day at the office with you. I didn't want a cake ordered by her, either. She's not my friend. She's not my family. She doesn't like me and is only trying to get closer to you."

"She was doing me a favor."

"Ah. I knew it. It was about you."

"What does that mean?"

"It means, that her favor to you, was not just unnecessary, but it actually hurt me."

"That's ridiculous."

And this was why she and Drakon weren't together. This was why she'd left him, and this was why they'd never be together.

Even though part of her would always love him, they couldn't be together, because outside the bedroom, they simply didn't work. There was no real understanding, no meeting of the minds. The only time they connected, the only time they made sense, was when they were having sex. But sex was just a part of a relationship, it couldn't be the relationship.

She looked up at him, her expression fierce. "Perhaps you will permit me to give you a little advice. Maybe I can do something for the future Mrs. Xanthis. Don't let Bronwyn, or any other woman, intrude so much in your personal life. The women you work with shouldn't be allowed to overshadow the woman you live with. And should you want to send your wife flowers, or a gift, do it yourself or don't do it at all."

His eyes glittered and he looked almost pale beneath his tan. "Anything else, Morgan?"

"Yes, actually. Next time you marry, ask your bride what kind of home she wants to live in. Or better yet, include her on the design process, or take her with you when you go house hunting. That way your poor wife might actually like her cage."

"Cage?" he choked out, expression furious.

She shrugged, shoulders twisting. "It's what it felt like," she said, slipping past him to climb the stone and cement stairs that led back up to the house. And then halfway up the staircase, she paused. "But I'm not your pet, Drakon, and I won't be kept!"

And then with her skirts in her hands, she raced on up, half hoping he'd follow and end this terrible fight the only way they knew how to end things—through sex.

Because right now she wanted him and needed him, not to make her come, but to make her feel safe. Sane. Only she didn't know how to ask him for comfort, and he didn't know how to give comfort. Just raw, carnal pleasure.

But even raw, carnal pleasure would be better than nothing right now, and as she continued up toward the house, she tried not to think how good it'd feel to have him push her back against the rock wall and capture her hands in his and hold her immobile all the while kissing her senseless, kissing her until she was wet and ready for him and he could take her here, in the sun, near the sea, with the tang of salt in her nose and the sweet heady fragrance of jasmine perfuming the air, and the taste of Drakon—her husband, and her heart—on her tongue.

CHAPTER NINE

THERE WAS NO call back from the pirates and Morgan spent the rest of the afternoon in her bedroom. She didn't have to stay in her room, but she thought it safer than wandering around the villa or the extensive grounds, where she might bump into Drakon.

In her room, Morgan tried napping and she actually fell asleep, but didn't sleep long, as her mother called, waking her. It was a brief, meaningless conversation about social events and it infuriated Morgan that her mother would even ask, much less expect, Morgan to drop everything to attend a charity fund-raiser with her.

"I'm in Italy working to bring Dad home," Morgan told her mother.

"No one is going to give you the money, Morgan." Her mother paused. "And if they do, they are fools."

After hanging up, Morgan tried to fall back asleep, but she couldn't, too unsettled from the call. So she took a long bath, trying to forget the things her mother said, remaining in the tub until the water turned cold and the skin on her fingers shriveled up.

Morgan was chilled by the time she got out of the bath, and she blew her hair dry and dressed carefully for dinner, trying to fill her time, trying to stay busy so she wouldn't go find Drakon.

She wanted Drakon. She missed him. Didn't want to be

at the villa with him and yet not with him. The last time she was here, on that delicious, luxurious honeymoon, they spent almost every moment together and it didn't seem right being at the villa and not seeing him.

But then, life didn't seem right without him in it.

But finally, thankfully, she'd managed to get through the afternoon and now it was almost dinner, and time for the nightly *aperitivo.*

Morgan was the first to the living room for the Italian *aperitivo.* The pre-dinner drink was a tradition at Villa Angelica, one she and Drakon had come to enjoy during their honeymoon.

In the living room, Morgan went to the antique table that had been set up as the bar with a selection of alcohol and juices, sodas, sparkling water and tonic water and other cocktail mixes. Morgan bypassed the mixes for the pitcher of Campari. Tonight it was Campari with pomegranate. Tomorrow night it might be Campari orange. The cocktail changed every night and Morgan enjoyed sampling the different variations.

She wandered now with her cocktail to the window to watch the sunset. It would be another stunning sunset and the sky was a fiery red orange at the moment and she sipped the cocktail, basking in the warm rays of the sun reaching through the glass.

This was like a dream, she thought, one of those dreams she had when she was at McLean Hospital, when she'd dream of Drakon every night, and in her dreams they were together still, and happy...so very, very happy....

Suddenly footsteps sounded in the stairwell and Morgan turned to watch Drakon descend the final flight of stairs and step into the grand entry. Her heart turned over in her chest as she watched him. He moved with such ease, and so much grace, that he made other men look clumsy. But then, he'd always had confidence, and a physicality that other men didn't have. She'd wondered if growing up on boats, working on cargo ships as if he were a deckhand instead of the owner's son, had given him that awareness and balance.

As he crossed the hall and joined her in the living room, the enormous Venetian chandelier bathed him in light and she sucked in a breath, struck all over again by his intensity and that strong, hard face with those intensely observant eyes.

He was looking at her now. She grew warm under his inspection, remembering how much she'd wanted to go to him earlier, how much she'd craved him all afternoon.

"Hello," she said, hoping he couldn't see her blush.

"Hello," he answered, the corner of his mouth quirking as if amused.

His smile did something to her and she felt a frisson of pleasure race through her. Flustered, Morgan lifted her drink to her lips, sipped her cocktail and studied Drakon covertly over the rim of her glass. He was wearing a crisp white dress shirt open at the collar and fine trousers and he looked like the Drakon she'd married—polished, elegant, handsome— but she'd learned something new about him during the last twenty-four hours. He wasn't as controlled as she'd imagined. If anything he was a man of passion.

And that was both good and bad. Good, because he met her intensity and answered her fierce need for touch and sensation. Bad, because soon he'd be out of her life again and she couldn't imagine ever feeling this way about any other man. Couldn't imagine ever wanting any other man.

"Were you able to get a nap?" he asked, turning away to pour himself a drink.

He, too, chose the Campari cocktail and for some reason that made her happy. "I did lie down," Morgan answered, her back now to the window so she could face Drakon, "but the moment I finally fell asleep, my phone rang. It was my mother."

"Calling to get news about your father?"

"No. She just wanted to know if I'd be home to attend a fund-raiser in Greenwich with her this weekend." Morgan shook her head incredulously. "A black-tie fund-raiser! Can you imagine?"

"You used to attend events like that all the time."

"Yes, when we were socially desirable, but we're not anymore. We're hated, loathed, but Mom doesn't get it. She's trying to carry on as if everything is the same, but nothing's the same. Only Mom refuses to face facts, refuses to accept that no one wants us at their balls or parties or fund-raisers anymore." Morgan tried to laugh but couldn't quite pull it off. "Dad's being held hostage in Somalia and Mom's trying to find a date for this Saturday's symphony gala. What a horrible family you married into, Drakon!"

His amber gaze suddenly locked with hers. "I didn't marry them. I married you."

"And I'm the craziest of them all!"

He said nothing for a long moment and then he smiled, a slow, wicked smile that put an equally wicked gleam in his eye. "Is that why sex was always so much fun?"

She blushed but was saved from answering by the sudden appearance of Rowan. "Your contact from Somalia just phoned," he said, entering the living room. "He left a message. They're not going to let you speak with your father. But since you have the money ready, they want to arrange the drop, and give you instructions on where you'll find your hostage."

Morgan's smile died on her lips and she glanced at Drakon, and then back at Rowan. "Did they really say it like that?"

Rowan nodded and Morgan paled and swallowed hard. "They make my father sound like a carcass," she whispered, sickened.

"We're not dealing with sensitive people," Rowan answered.

"But don't panic," Drakon added. "I'm sure he's still alive."

She drew a quick breath and lifted her chin. "I want him out of there."

"He will be," Drakon said.

Rowan nodded. "Soon.

It took them a while to move from the living room to the dining room for dinner, but once they got there, the dining room glowed with candlelight. The dining room's antique chandelier was filled with tapers, and the iron and glass sconces on the white walls reflected onto the ceiling making every surface gleam and dance with light. But the meal was definitely subdued. Morgan was both angry and heartsick and felt impossibly distracted. Rowan barely spoke and Drakon didn't say much more than Rowan. But every now and then Morgan looked up to find Drakon watching her, his expression shuttered and impossible to read.

Perhaps if she and Drakon had been alone, she would have asked him what he was thinking, but with Rowan present, Morgan left Drakon to his own thoughts, and she tried not to dwell on her father, or his conditions in Somalia.

As Drakon said, her father would be home soon. Rowan had agreed with him.

She had to focus on that, cling to that, not allow herself to slide into panic or doubt.

Finally the dinner dishes were being cleared away and coffee was served. But sitting in silence with coffee proved even more uncomfortable than eating in silence.

"I hate them," she choked out, unable to remain silent another moment. "I hate how they've taken him and are treating him like he's nothing…nobody…just an object to be bartered."

"It is horrendous," Drakon agreed quietly.

"But it's on the rise, isn't it?" She looked up at him as she added another half teaspoon of sugar to her coffee and gave it a brisk stir. "From what I read, attacks have doubled in the last few years."

Drakon's dark head inclined. "Last year there were more hostages taken than ever before."

"Nearly twelve hundred," Morgan murmured, having done a fair amount of research on her own, trying to understand what had happened to her father. "With many being held for nine months or more. Unthinkable. But it's real. It's happening."

"At least your father will be freed," Rowan said brusquely. "There are hundreds of hostages who haven't been ransomed…that will never be ransomed."

Morgan's insides twisted. She couldn't imagine being one of the unfortunate crew who were never freed. How terrible to sit day after day, week after week, month after month waiting for a ransom that might never come. "Because someone isn't willing to pay the ransom?" she asked.

"Or able to pay it. Not all shipping companies have insurance that will pay it, and most ordinary people can't come up with millions of dollars, not even to save a loved one," Drakon answered.

Morgan put her spoon down, her eyes burning, guilt eating at her because she was able to help her father. She was able to do something and yet she felt for those who couldn't. "Fortunately, I understand the counter-piracy measures put in place this past year seem to be helping. From what I read, piracy was down during the first quarter of the year—not enough of course to give cause for celebration, but enough to know that the experts might be on to something."

"That's true," Drakon agreed. "Right now there's a concerted international effort to check piracy, and it's helping, but it certainly hasn't stopped the pirates. It's just slowed them a little."

"How do you stop them?"

"Put a stable, strong, and effective government in place.

Change their economic structure. Take out the group who is arming the pirates, and profiting from the hostage ransoms." Rowan's lips curved, his expression hard. "But if that were easy, it would have been done already. And so we do the next best thing—increase maritime intelligence and continue international cooperation on monitoring the water off the Horn of Africa."

"Until I began researching piracy I didn't realize that until recently, few countries worked together...that for the most part, most countries just focused on their own pirated vessels," Morgan answered.

Rowan shrugged. "Typical nationalistic reaction."

"How so?"

"Every country has its own navy, military intelligence and sources, so it's not easy getting everyone on the same page. Governments are protective of their military and don't want to share resources," he answered her.

Morgan frowned. "But you're military?"

"Former, yes. Just as most of us in maritime intelligence have served in one arm of the navy or another."

"Were you in the Royal Navy?" she asked.

"I've actually served in both the U.S. Navy and the Royal Navy, but at different times and in different capacities."

Morgan glanced to Drakon and then back to Rowan. "How is that possible?"

"I have dual nationalities...I was born in Northern Ireland to an Irish mother, and an American Greek father, giving me both American and British citizenship."

"Irish, too," Drakon said.

"They let you have all those passports?" Morgan asked, rather amazed.

Rowan shrugged. "If you're good at what you do."

"And you are good, I take it?"

His lips curved but the smile didn't reach his eyes. "Have

to be. There's a lot at stake—" He broke off as the sound of high heels clicking briskly on hard tiles echoed in the hallway.

They were all listening to the footsteps and Morgan stiffened, her shoulders drawing back as unease rolled through her in a huge dark wave.

Bronwyn.

Morgan went hot and then cold. But no, it couldn't be. What would Bronwyn be doing here?

And yet no one else walked that way. No one else sounded so fiercely confident in high stiletto heels.

Then there she was, appearing in the dining room doorway as if she owned Villa Angelica, as tall and blonde and statuesque as ever, dressed tonight in a formfitting red jersey knit that clung to her curves, making the most of her voluptuous body. Bronwyn, a stunning blonde with brilliant blue eyes and a dark golden tan, knew how to make an entrance.

"Hope I haven't kept you waiting," she said, smiling, as her gaze swept the dining room, before lingering on Drakon.

Morgan's stomach hurt as she saw the way Bronwyn looked at Drakon. Drakon had always said that Bronwyn was just part of his management team, a valuable employee and nothing more, but from the possessive expression on Bronwyn's face, Morgan knew that Bronwyn was fiercely attached to Drakon.

"You haven't kept us waiting," Drakon answered, rising and gesturing to a chair at the table. "Join us. Have you eaten? Would you like coffee? Something sweet?"

Bronwyn flashed Drakon a grateful smile as she moved around the dining room table to take an empty chair. "A glass of wine would be perfect. You know what I like."

Morgan ground her teeth together as she glanced from Bronwyn to Drakon and then back to Bronwyn again. How could he have invited her here, now, when they were in the middle of a crisis? How could he possibly think it was appropriate?

Bronwyn sat down and crossed one leg over the other, then gave her head a small toss, sending her long, artfully layered blond hair spilling over her shoulders down to the tops of her high full breasts. "Drakon, next time, send the helicopter for me, not a driver. I was nauseous from Sorrento on. Such a grueling drive. So many hairpin curves."

Drakon didn't respond; too busy speaking to one of the kitchen staff, requesting Bronwyn's wine.

Bronwyn turned to Rowan. "Haven't seen you in a while. How are you?"

"Busy," he answered flatly, expression hard.

"But it must be nice to be in a business that is booming," she retorted.

"Not if there are people's lives at stake," Morgan said, unable to remain silent.

Bronwyn waved her hand in a careless gesture. "Most crews on hijacked ships aren't hurt. Most are eventually released when the ransom's paid."

"Most," Morgan said, hanging on to her temper by a thread. "But that's not all, and not a cause to celebrate."

Bronwyn smiled, her long lashes dropping over her eyes, but not before Morgan caught the glittering animosity in the blue depths. "Was I celebrating? I hope not. That would be most insensitive of me, considering your father is being held hostage as we speak."

For a moment Morgan couldn't breathe. The air caught in her throat and she balled her hands into fists. "We'll have him home soon, though," she answered, struggling to sound calm. "Drakon's brought in the best to secure his release."

Bronwyn flashed Rowan an amused glance. "The best, yes, as well as the most expensive. What will the job cost Drakon this time, Rowan? Seven million? Ten? More?"

"That's none of your business, Bronwyn," Drakon said gruffly.

The Australian turned wide blue eyes on him. "You assigned me the task of improving the corporation's bottom line, which includes cutting unnecessary spending—"

"And you know perfectly well that I will pay Dunamas Maritime Intelligence from my personal account, not the corporation, so enough." Drakon's tone was cool and firm, but not cold or firm enough for Morgan.

Why did he put up with Bronwyn? Why did he allow his vice president to speak to him the way he did? He wouldn't tolerate it from anyone else, Morgan was sure of that.

"Yes, boss," Bronwyn answered, rolling her eyes even as she glanced in Morgan's direction, the exasperation in Bronwyn's eyes replaced by bruising disdain.

Interesting, Morgan thought, air catching in her throat. *Bronwyn doesn't like me, either.*

Morgan had sensed it five years ago, and had mentioned her concern to Drakon, but Drakon had brushed Morgan off, telling her not to be petty, that Bronwyn was far too professional to have any ill will toward his new wife. Morgan had felt ashamed for being petty—if that's what how she was behaving—and properly chastised, tried not to object to Bronwyn's frequent intrusions into their personal life, but it was almost impossible. Bronwyn called constantly, appeared on their doorstep at strange moments, felt perfectly comfortable drawing Drakon out of the living room and off into his study for long, private business conversations.

Morgan hated it, and had come to resent Bronwyn, all the while feeling guilty for resenting someone that Drakon viewed as so indispensible to his work.

But now Morgan knew she'd been right to object to Bronwyn's intrusiveness. Because Bronwyn meant to be intrusive. Bronwyn wanted Drakon. She'd wanted him five years ago, and she still wanted him now.

Of course, Morgan had no proof, just her female intuition and that nagging gut instinct that told her something was wrong…the same gut instinct that was telling her now that Bronwyn was still a problem.

Abruptly Morgan stood, unable to remain one more moment in the same room with Bronwyn.

"It's late and I'm still jet-lagged," Morgan said, her voice sharper than usual. "If you'll excuse me, I think I'll head to bed."

CHAPTER TEN

THE NEXT MORNING Morgan had coffee brought to her in her room and she sat on her balcony, sipping her coffee, trying to figure out how she could avoid going downstairs today. She'd slept like hell, dreaming of Bronwyn, as well as Bronwyn and Drakon frolicking in the pool, and the ballroom, and everywhere else, and the last person Morgan wanted to see was the real Bronwyn, who Morgan knew was up and about, as she could hear her voice wafting up from one of the terraces below.

Morgan glared down into her coffee as Bronwyn's laugh spiraled up again. Why was Bronwyn here? What was Drakon thinking?

"More coffee? A pastry?" a deep, distinctive male voice coming from the bedroom behind her, asked.

Morgan glanced over her shoulder, to where Drakon lounged in the doorway, looking horribly handsome and very rested. "You should knock," she said tartly, hating him for bringing Bronwyn here, to the villa, when Morgan was here feeling overwhelmed and out of control.

"I did. You didn't answer."

"Then maybe you shouldn't have come in."

"I needed to speak with you."

"But it's not polite to barge in on ladies in the morning."

"Not even if I have an invitation for an outing?"

That did give her pause, and Morgan eyed him suspiciously, excited at the idea of escaping the villa for a few hours, before realizing that she needed to be here, available, in case the pirates tried to contact her. "How can we just leave right now in the middle of everything? What if the pirates want to talk to me? Or change their demands?"

"They're not going to change their demands. They're anticipating six million dollars being delivered any day now."

He was probably right, and yet she found it hard to contemplate doing something pleasurable when her father was still in such trouble. "I wish I knew if he had his heart medicine. I wish I knew he was okay...healthy...strong. Then I'd feel better about things. But I don't know, and the not knowing is really scary."

"It's always the scariest part." His broad shoulders shifted. "But worrying doesn't change his situation, it just makes you sick, and makes it more difficult for you to cope with stress. Which is why I'm taking you out for a couple hours. Fresh air and a change of scenery will give you some perspective."

"And we could be reached if something happens?"

"Absolutely."

She hesitated. "So who would be going?"

"Just you and me, if that's all right."

Her gaze slowly swept over his face with the high cheekbones, straight nose, firm, sensual mouth, before dropping to his body. God, she loved his body...his narrow hips, his long lean, muscular torso and those sinfully broad shoulders. She glanced back up into his face, noting his arched eyebrow and his amused expression. She blushed. "Yes, that's all right."

His warm golden brown eyes, framed by those long, dense black lashes, glinted. "I'm glad."

She looked at him for a long moment, wondering what Drakon had up his sleeve, and why he'd decided to be charming today. He was reminding her of the Drakon of their courtship, the Drakon of their honeymoon—mellow, amusing, easygoing, attentive. She liked this Drakon, very much, but why was he here now? And what did he want? "When do we leave?"

"When can you be ready?"

They took the helicopter towards Naples, flying above the stunning Italian coastline, where the blue sea butted against the green swell of land, before rising up into the hills and the slopes of Mount Vesuvius, the volcano that had erupted and wiped out Pompeii.

"So beautiful," Morgan murmured, her fingers pressed against the slick helicopter window, her gaze fixed on the landscape below. "And so deceptively serene."

"Because Vesuvius is still active?"

"Isn't it considered one of the world's deadliest volcanoes?"

"Unfortunately, yes. Its Plinian eruptions aren't a good fit for the three million people living at the base, as well as up and down the slopes."

"I'd be afraid to live there."

"Scientists believe they can predict an eruption before it happens, and they do have an emergency evacuation plan.

She shivered. "I understand ancient Pompeii was beautiful."

"The villas that were on the outskirts of town would rival the finest villas today."

"I'd love to see it."

"Good. Because we're on our way there now."

Morgan clasped his arm in delight. "Really?"

"Really."

A bubble of warmth formed in her chest, rising. "I'm so glad!"

Drakon glanced down at her hand where it rested on his arm. He'd hardened the moment she touched him, it was how he always responded to her.

He drew a breath and exhaled, trying to ease some of

the tightness in his gut. "I hope you'll enjoy today," he said, grateful he could sound controlled even when he didn't feel that way. "I'm hoping you will find something in Pompeii to inspire you and your next jewelry collection."

"I don't think there will be another—"

"Yes, there will be."

"I made terrible mistakes—"

"Everyone makes mistakes, but that doesn't mean you should give up. You have a gift. You're an artist. I believe in your vision."

She looked up into his eyes, fear and hope in the blue depths. "Do you really mean that?"

"Absolutely. You will have more collections, and you will succeed."

"How can you be so certain?"

"Because I've seen what you can do, and I know you. You're truly talented, Morgan. There's no one else like you."

Drakon's car was parked at a helipad outside Pompeii, waiting for them, and the driver whisked them to the ancient city to meet a private guide who was going to take them on a behind-the-scenes tour of the ruined city.

Morgan was glad she'd worn flat leather sandals since they walked from one end of the city to another, and she listened closely to everything the guide said, captivated by his stories of first century Pompeii, a thriving city of approximately ten thousand people. She was fascinated by the buried city and its restaurants and hotels and brothels, as well as the artwork revealed…frescoes and mosaics and sculptures.

"Pompeii is the most incredible place," she said as they made their way through the extraordinary villa, House of the Faun, and back into the sunlight. "But Pompeii also breaks my heart. It was such a beautiful city, and so full of life and people and passion—and then it was all wiped out. Gone in a matter of hours."

"Are you sorry I brought you today?"

She shook her head. "No. It's amazing. All of it. The houses, the streets, the restaurants, the statues and pots and artifacts. But it hurts, too. Life is so fragile, and unpredictable. There are no guarantees. Not for anyone."

"Your life changed overnight, didn't it?"

She looked at him, suddenly wary. "You mean, with the revelation of Michael's Ponzi scheme?"

Drakon nodded and Morgan bit down into her lip. "It did," she agreed softly. "I still find it hard to believe what's happened at home. Who would have thought a year ago…even three months ago…that my father would become one of the most hated men in America? That we'd lose everything… that so many others would lose everything, too, through his, and Michael's, actions?"

They'd come to a stop next to the cordoned-off fountain with its bronze statue of a dancing faun. This beautiful solitary faun was all that was left of this once glorious, elegant garden, and she held her breath a moment, pressing a fist to her chest, as if somehow she could control the pain, ease the tenderness.

"My father was horrified when he discovered that all his clients, all his investors, had lost their money. He found out on his way to a Valentine's Day soiree—another one of those black-tie balls my mother loves—when he got the text from Michael to say that it was over. That agents from the federal government had just left his house and there would be arrests made, and that Dad should flee, rather than be indicted." Her voice faded and she struggled to continue. "At first Dad didn't believe it. None of us could believe it. And then when the shock wore off, there was anger, and shame."

Morgan worked her lip between her teeth, tasting blood but thinking nothing of it, because everything hurt now, all the time. Pain was constant. Pain and that endless, overwhelming shame. "Dad wanted to kill himself. My brother talked him out of it, telling Dad that if he was innocent, then he owed it to his family, his friends and his clients to prove his innocence, and try to recoup as much of the lost investments as he could. But then Dad vanished, and Mom said Dad would have been better off killing himself. That by disappearing, Dad had left us in a worse situation. Maybe Mom was right. Maybe Dad should have died—"

"You don't really feel that way," Drakon said brusquely. "Or you wouldn't be trying so hard to help him now."

"I guess part of me keeps hoping that if he returns, he can fix this...salvage something. Branson, you know, is determined to see all the investors paid back—"

"That's impossible."

"I know, but Branson can't escape his name. Women can marry and take a new surname. But Branson's a man. He'll be one of those hated Copelands forever."

"Someday people will forget. There will be other news that will become more urgent and compelling. There will be disasters and tragedies that will eventually cover this scandal, burying it."

Just as the volcano had buried Pompeii.

Morgan's gaze drifted slowly across the columns and walls and the sunken garden, feeling the emptiness, hearing the silence. Everything was so still here, and yet once this villa had bustled with life, with the comings and goings of the family and its household servants and pets. And all that activity and laughter and anger, all the fears and needs and dreams, ended that August day, and for hundreds of years this city lay buried beneath layers of ash and soil, grass and the development of new towns. New construction. New lives. New dreams.

"Come," Drakon said, putting his hand on her bare arm, his touch light, but steadying. "Let's walk. This place is making you sad, and I didn't bring you here to be sad. I brought you here to inspire you."

"I am inspired, and moved. Gives one perspective...and

certainly a great deal for me to be thankful for." She flashed Drakon an unsteady smile, allowing him to steer her from the garden and back to the street. "Like life. And air. And sunlight."

"Good girl. Count your blessings. Because you have many, you know. You have your health, and your creativity, and your brother and your sisters—"

"And you," she said, catching his hand, giving it a quick squeeze. "You've been here for me, and have hired Rowan to help rescue Dad. I am so grateful—"

"Please don't thank me."

"Then let me at least apologize, because I am sorry, Drakon, I am so, so sorry for what my father did, and deeply ashamed, too."

"You didn't do it, love. You aren't responsible."

"But he's my father."

"And maybe he didn't know that Amery was just depositing all that money into his own account. Maybe he had no idea. Perhaps you're right. Perhaps we wait to judge and try him, until he is back, and he can answer the charges, answer everyone's questions?"

Her heart surged, a little rush of hope, and she turned quickly to face him. "Do you really think he could be innocent? Do you think—" And then she abruptly broke off when she saw Drakon's face.

He didn't think her father was innocent. He still despised her father. Drakon was merely trying to soften the blow for her. Make her disillusionment and pain more bearable.

Her eyes burned and she looked away. "You don't have to do that," she whispered. "There's no need to say things you don't mean just to make me feel better. I'd rather hear the truth from you."

"And I'd rather protect you, *agapi mou.*"

Agapi mou. My love. Her chest squeezed, aching. "I remember when I really was your love."

"You will always be my love."

"But not the same way. It will never be the same."

"No, it won't be the same. It can't be."

He'd spoken gently, kindly, and for some reason that made it all even worse. "I hate what I did to us," she said. "Hate that I destroyed us."

"What did happen, Morgan? You were there one morning, and then gone that night. I just want to understand."

She hadn't planned on talking about what really happened, not here, not like this. "I wasn't prepared for life as a newlywed," she said, stumbling a little over the words. "I…I had unrealistic expectations of our life in Greece."

"What did you think it would be like?"

"Our honeymoon."

"But you know I had to return to work."

"Yes, but I didn't know work for you meant twelve-hour days, every day." Her hands twisted anxiously. "And I understand now, that's just how you work, and I'm not criticizing you. But I didn't understand then, how it would be, and it didn't leave much time for me. I married you because I wanted to be with you, not because I wanted your money or a villa in Greece."

"Looking back, I know now I wasn't very flexible with my hours. I regret how much I worked."

"You loved your work."

"But I loved you more, Morgan."

She'd looked into his eyes as he said it and for a moment she was lost, his amber gaze that intense, searing heat of old, and her heart felt wrenched and she fought to hold back the tears.

She couldn't cry…couldn't cry…wouldn't cry….

"So where do we go now?" she murmured, holding back the tears by smiling hard, smiling to hide her pain and how much she'd missed Drakon, and how much she'd always love Drakon. "What's next on our tour?"

"Lunch," he said lightly, smiling back at her. "I've a restaurant in mind, it's on our way home in Sorrento."

They didn't actually eat in Sorrento, but at a restaurant just outside the city, on the way to Positano. The simple one-story restaurant was tucked high into the mountain, off the beaten path, with a beamed ceiling and breathtaking views of the coast.

Normally the restaurant just served dinner, but today they'd opened for them for lunch, and Morgan and Drakon had the place to themselves.

With the expansive windows open, and course after course of the most delicious seafood and pasta arriving at their table, Morgan felt the tension easing from between her shoulders. After finishing her coffee, she leaned back in her chair. "This was really lovely, Drakon. I feel almost optimistic again. Thank you."

"I've done very little, Morgan."

"You've done everything. You've brought in Rowan and his team, and while they work to free Dad, you're keeping me occupied and encouraging me to think about life, down the road. You've shown me incredible things today, and given me ideas for future designs, and best of all, peace of mind. You're my hero…my knight in shining armor."

"So much better than a husband."

"Husbands are overrated," she teased.

"Apparently so," he answered drily.

And then reality hit her, and the memory of what had happened to them. Her smile slowly, painfully faded. "I've cost you a pretty penny, haven't I? Four hundred million here, seven million there—"

"I don't think about the money when I look at you."

"What do you think about?"

"You."

She dipped her head, and while this is what she wanted

to hear, she did feel guilty. Love shouldn't be this expensive. Love shouldn't have cost Drakon so much. "I want to pay for Dunamas's services."

"They're expensive."

"But my father isn't your responsibility, and I can't allow you to keep picking up the tab, taking hits and losses, because you got tangled up with me."

"Tangled? Is that what they call wives and weddings these days?"

"Don't try to distract me. I'm serious about paying you back. It will take me some time. I'll pay in installments, but I'll pay interest, too. It's what the banks would do. And I may be one of those entitled Copelands, but I'm not entitled to your money, and I insist on making sure you are properly compensated—"

"You're ruining my lunch."

"You've finished eating, already."

"Then you're ruining my coffee."

"You've finished that, too." She held up a finger. "And before you think of anything else I'm ruining, please know I'm immensely grateful, which is why I'm trying to make things right, as well as make them fair."

"How is it fair for me to take what little money you earn over the next ten years? I'd be ashamed to take your money."

"And you don't think I'm ashamed that I had to come back to you, with my hand out, begging for assistance?"

Frowning, he pushed his empty cup. "We should go."

She reached across the table and caught his hand in hers. "Don't be angry, Drakon. Branson's not the only one who wants to put things right. If I could, I'd pay every one of my father's investors back—"

"You're not your father, Morgan. You're not responsible."

"I *feel* responsible."

"You'll make yourself sick, obsessing about this."

"And you don't obsess about what my father did to you?"

Drakon looked down at their hands, where their fingers were laced together. "Yes, I did lose a fortune," he said after a moment, his fingers tightening on hers. "But losing you five years ago was so much worse."

"No."

"Yes." He squeezed her fingers again. "There is always more money to be made, *gynaika mou*. But there is only one of you."

The driver stopped before the villa's great iron gates, waiting for them to open to give them access to the old estate's private drive and exquisite gardens. But Morgan wasn't ready to be back at the villa with Bronwyn and Rowan and the villa staff. After so many years of not being with Drakon, it was such a joy to have him to herself.

"We'll soon find out if Rowan's heard anything," Drakon said, glancing out the window as the four-story white marble villa came into view.

"Hopefully he has," she said, feeling guilty because for the past hour she hadn't thought of her father, not once. She'd been so happy just being with Drakon that she'd forgotten why she was here in Italy on the Amalfi Coast.

"And hopefully you had a good day," he added. "I'd thought perhaps you'd be inspired by Pompeii, but it can be overwhelming, too."

"I loved it. Every minute of it."

And it was true, she thought, as the car stopped in front of the villa's entrance and the driver stepped out to come around to open their door. But it wasn't just Pompeii she loved. She loved every minute of being with him today. This was what life was supposed to feel like. This is what she'd missed so much—his warmth, his strength, his friendship, his love.

His love.

She frowned, confused, suddenly caught between two worlds—the memories of a complicated past and the changing present. In this moment, the present, anything could happen. In this moment, everything was fluid and possible.

She and Drakon were possible. Life was possible. Love was possible.

She and Drakon could make different decisions, be different people, have a different future.

Could it be a future together?

"I enjoyed today, too," Drakon said.

"I hope we can do it again."

"Visit Pompeii?"

"Not necessarily Pompeii. But another outing...another adventure. It was fun."

Drakon suddenly leaned forward and swept the back of his hand over her cheek. "It was. And good to get away from here, and all this."

Her heart ached at the gentle touch. She'd forgotten how extraordinarily tender he could be. Over the years she'd focused on his control and his aloofness, in contrast to the wild heat of their lovemaking, and she'd turned him into someone he wasn't...someone cold and hard and unreachable. But that wasn't really Drakon. Yes, he could be aloof, and hard, and cold, but that wasn't often, and only when he was angry. And he wasn't always angry. In fact, he'd never been angry during their engagement or the first couple months of their marriage. It was only later, after they'd gone to Athens and gotten stuck in that terrible battle for control, a battle that had come to include Bronwyn, that they'd both become rigid and antagonistic.

She reached up, caught his hand, pressed it to her cheek. "Promise me we'll do this again soon. Please?"

"I promise," he said, holding her gaze as the driver opened the door to the back of the car.

Drakon stepped out and Morgan was just about to follow when heavy footsteps crunched the gravel drive and Rowan appeared at their side.

"Where have you been?" Rowan demanded. "I've been trying to reach you for the past hour."

"My mobile didn't ring," Drakon answered.

"I called," Rowan said. "Repeatedly." He turned to look at Morgan, his expression apologetic. "Your father was moved from his village today and we don't know where he is at the moment. But my office is gathering intelligence now that should help us understand what happened, why and where he's being held now."

CHAPTER ELEVEN

MORGAN PACED THE living room, unable to stop moving, unable to be still.

How could her father have vanished? Where had he been taken? And why? Had he gotten sick? Had he died? What were his captors reason for moving him?

She reached the end of the living room, turned and started back again. She'd traveled this path for ten minutes now but there was no way she could sit, not when fear bubbled up in her, consuming her.

Drakon was at the opposite end of the living room, watching her, keeping her company. "Where did they take him, Drakon?" she said, stopping midstep. "Why did they move him?"

She'd asked him the same questions already, several times, as a matter of fact, but he answered just as patiently now. "As Rowan explained, high-profile hostages are often moved from one location to another to stymie rescue attempts."

"Do you think they knew we were planning something?"

"I doubt it. Rowan doesn't think so, either, but we don't know for sure. Fortunately, his office is diligently gathering intelligence now and we should know more soon. Believe me, your father is at the top of Dunamas's priority list."

"He's right," Bronwyn said, entering the living room with a brisk step, her deceptively simple knit dress, the color of ripe plums, making the most of her lush shape. "Dunamas is pulling all their sources and resources from other tasks to gather information on your father, leaving dozens of ships, countless sailors and hundreds of millions of dollars of cargo vulnerable to attack."

"That's not necessary, Bron," Drakon said, rebuking her.

"But it's true." She leaned on the back of a wing chair, her blond hair smooth and sleek and falling forward in an elegant golden shimmer. The expression in her blue eyes was mocking and she shot Drakon a challenging glance. "I know you don't like to discuss business in front of your wife, but shouldn't she know the truth? That Dunamas is dropping everything, and everyone, because Morgan Copeland's criminal father has changed village locations?"

Morgan flinched at Bronwyn's words. "Is that true? Has Dunamas pulled all its surveillance and protection from its other clients?"

"No," Drakon said flatly. "It's not true. While Dunamas has made your father a priority, it continues its surveillance and protective services for each ship, and every customer, it's been hired to protect."

"But at tremendous personal expense," Bronwyn retorted.

"That's none of your business," he answered, giving her a look that would have crushed Morgan, but Bronwyn wasn't crushed.

"Funny how different you are when she's around." Bronwyn's blue gaze met his and held.

Drakon's jaw thickened. "I'm exactly the same."

"No. You're not. Normally Drakon Xanthis rules his shipping empire with a cool head, a critical eye and shrewd sense…always fiscally conservative, and cautious when it comes to expenses and investments." Bronwyn's lips pursed. "But the moment Morgan Copeland enters the picture, smart, insightful, strategic Drakon Xanthis loses his head. Suddenly money is no object, and common sense is thrown out the window—"

"Bronwyn," he growled.

The Australian jerked her chin up, her expression a curious mixture of anger and pain. "You're just a fool for love, aren't you?"

Drakon looked away, his jaw tight, his amber gaze strangely bleak. Morgan glanced from Drakon to Bronwyn and back again, feeling the tension humming in the room, but this wasn't the sparky, sexy kind of tension that zinged between her and Drakon, but something altogether different. This tension was dark and heavy and overwhelming....

It felt like death…loss…

Why? What had happened between them? And what bound Drakon to Bronwyn, a woman Morgan disliked so very intensely.

But then on her own accord, Bronwyn walked out, pausing in the doorway to look at Drakon. "Don't be putty in her hands," she said. "You know what happens to putty."

The pressure in Morgan's chest should have eased after Bronwyn left. There should have been a subtle shift in mood, an easing of the tension, some kind of relief.

But Morgan felt no relief, and from Drakon's taut features, she knew there would be no relief.

Whatever it was that Bronwyn had just said to Drakon—and Morgan had heard her, but hadn't understood the significance, only felt the biting sarcasm—it'd hit the mark. Drakon had paled and was now ashen, his strong jaw clenched so tightly the skin along the bone had gone white.

"What just happened?" Morgan asked, her voice cracking.

Drakon didn't answer. He didn't even look at her.

She flushed as silence stretched and it became evident that he wasn't going to answer her, either.

"What was she saying, Drakon?" Morgan whispered, hating the way shame crept through her, shame and fear and that terrible green-eyed monster called jealousy, because she was jealous of Bronwyn, jealous that Bronwyn could have such a powerful effect on Drakon.

But once again Morgan's question was met with stony silence. And the silence hurt. Not merely because he wasn't talking to her, but because Bronwyn had done this to him—to *them*—again.

Again.

Morgan's hands fisted at her sides. What was Bronwyn's power? Because she certainly had something...some strange and rather frightening influence over Drakon....

Something had to have happened between Drakon and Bronwyn. Something big...

Something private and powerful...

Morgan's head pounded as she left the living room. She needed space and quiet, and headed downstairs to the sunroom, and then outside to the broad terrace beyond. But the terrace still felt too confining and Morgan kept walking, down more stairs, to the lower garden, through manicured boxwood and fanciful hedges to the old rose garden and the herb garden and then to the miniature orchard with its peekaboo views of the sea.

She walked the narrow stone path through the orchard before reaching the twisting path that followed the cliff, the path dotted with marble benches. Morgan finally sat down in one of these cool marble benches facing the sea, and drew a slow breath, trying to process everything, from her father's disappearance, to Drakon and Bronwyn's peculiar relationship, to her own relationship with Drakon. There was a lot to sort through.

She sat on the bench, just breathing in the heady, fragrant scent of wisteria and the blossoms from the citrus trees in the small orchard, when she heard someone talking.

It was Rowan approaching on the path, talking on the phone, speaking English to someone, his tone clipped, no-nonsense, and his low brusque voice was such a contrast to his appearance. He looked like sex, but talked like a soldier. And suddenly the warrior king from the film *Spartacus* came to mind.

Rowan spotted her and ended his call.

"Any news about my father?" she asked him as he stopped before her bench.

"Not yet. But don't panic."

"I'm trying not to."

"Good girl."

The sun had dropped significantly and the colors in the sky were deepening, the light blue turning to rose gold.

"It's going to be another beautiful sunset," she said. "I love the sky here, the red and orange sunsets."

"You do know its pollution, ash and smoke just scattering away the shorter-wavelength part of the light spectrum."

Morgan made a face. "That's so not romantic."

He shrugged. "As Logan will tell you, I'm not a romantic guy."

Shocked, Morgan turned all the way to look at him. "You know my sister?"

"Drakon didn't tell you?"

"No."

"Thought he had."

"How do you know her?"

"I live in L.A. Malibu."

Which made sense as Logan lived in Los Angeles, too. "How well do you know her?"

He hesitated, just a fraction too long, and Morgan realized that he *knew* her, knew her, as in the Biblical knowing. "You guys...dated?"

"Not dated, plural. One date. Met at a celebrity fund-raiser."

"What fund-raiser?" she asked, finding it impossible to imagine Rowan Argyros at a charity event.

"It's inconsequential."

But from his tone, she knew it wasn't, and Morgan fought the sudden urge to smile. There was much more to the Rowan-Logan story than what he was telling her, and Morgan eyed him with new interest, as well as appreciation, because Logan might be her fraternal twin, but Logan and Morgan were polar opposites. Morgan was quieter and shyer, and Logan was extremely confident and extroverted, as well as assertive., especially when it came to men. Morgan had married Drakon, her first love, while Logan didn't believe in love.

"How did you two get along?" she asked now, lips still twitching, amused by the idea of Logan and Rowan together. They were both so strong—it would have been an interesting date...an explosive date.

"Fine."

"I doubt that."

Rowan looked at her from beneath a cocked brow, smiling, clearly amused. "Why do you say that?"

"Because I know Logan. She's my sister. And I've met you."

"Whatever happened—or didn't happen—is between your sister and me, but I will say she talked about you that night we were together. Told me...things...about you, and your past, not knowing I was connected to Drakon."

"Did you tell her you knew Drakon?"

"No."

"Well, there you go."

He stared down at her, expression troubled. He looked as if he wanted to say something but wasn't going to.

Morgan sighed. "What is it? What's on your mind?"

"Have you told Drakon about the year following your separation? Does he know what happened?"

Morgan eyed him warily. "About what?"

"About you being...ill."

She opened her mouth, and then closed it, shaking her head instead.

"Maybe you should. Maybe it's time."

Morgan turned back to the sea, where the horizon was now a dramatic parfait of pink and orange and red, with streaks of luscious violet. So beautiful it couldn't be real. "I don't think it'd change anything...if he knew."

"I think it would change a great deal. Maybe not for you, but for him."

She shot Rowan a cynical glance, feeling impossibly raw. "How so?"

"You weren't the only one who had a hard year after you left. Drakon's world fell apart, too."

Drakon was in his room, just stepping out of the shower when he heard a knock at his door. He dried off quickly, wrapped the towel around his hips and headed to the bedroom door. Opening it, he discovered Morgan in the hall.

"You okay?" she asked, looking up at him, a shadow of concern in her eyes.

He nodded. "I was just going to dress and come find you."

"Do you mind if I come in?"

He opened the door wider, and then once she was inside, he closed the door behind him.

"You look nice," she said, her voice low and husky.

"Almost naked?"

Color swept her cheeks. "I always liked you naked. You have an amazing body."

He folded his arms across his chest and stared at her. "I can't believe you came here to compliment my body."

"No...no. But it kind of...relates...to what I was going to say."

He rocked back on his hips, trying not to feel anything, even though he was already feeling too much of everything.

But wasn't that always the way it was when it came to Morgan? He felt so much. He loved her so much.

"Can I kiss you?" she blurted breathlessly.

He frowned, caught off guard.

"Just a kiss, for courage," she said, clasping her hands, nervously. "Because I don't know how to tell you this, and I'm not sure what you'll say, but I probably should tell you. 'Cause I don't think anyone did tell you—"

He drew her to him, then, silenced her stream of words with a kiss. His kiss was fierce, and she kissed him back with desperation, with the heat and hunger that had always been there between them.

He let the kiss go on, too, drawing her close to his body, cupping the back of her head with one hand while the other slid to the small of her back and urged her even closer to his hips. Just like that he was hard and hot and eager to be inside her body, wanting to fill her, needing to lose himself in her, needing to silence the voices in his head...voices of guilt and anger, failure and shame....

But then Morgan ended the kiss and lifting her head she looked up into his eyes, her blue eyes wet, her black lashes matted. "I'm not right in the head." Her voice quavered. She tried to smile even as tears shimmered in her eyes. "I'm crazy."

"You're not crazy."

She nodded, and her lower lip quivered. "That's why you couldn't find me after I left you. I had a nervous breakdown. My family had me hospitalized."

Drakon flinched and stepped backward. "Why are you saying this?"

"It's what happened. I left you and I fell apart. I couldn't stop crying, and I couldn't eat, and I couldn't sleep, and everybody said it was this or that, but I just missed you. I wanted you."

"So why didn't you come back?"

"They wouldn't let me."

Drakon's gut churned, and his hands clenched involuntarily at his side. "*Who* wouldn't let you?"

"The doctors. The hospital. My family. They made me stay there at McLean. It's a...mental...hospital."

"I know what McLean is." Drakon looked at her in barely masked horror. "I don't understand, Morgan. You were there...why?"

"Because I was crazy."

"You *weren't* crazy!"

"They said I was." She walked away from him, moving around his room, which had been their room on their honeymoon. She touched an end table, and the foot of the bed, and then the chaise in the corner before she turned to look at him. "And I did feel crazy...but I kept thinking if I could just get to you, I'd feel better."

"So why didn't you come home to me?"

"I couldn't." She struggled to smile, but failed. "I couldn't get to you, couldn't call you or write to you. They wouldn't let me do anything until I calmed down and did all the therapy and the counseling sessions—"

"What do you mean, they wouldn't let you out? Didn't you check yourself in?"

She shook her head, and sat down on the chaise, smoothing her skirt over her knees. "No. My parents did. My mother did. My dad approved, but it was Mother who insisted. She said you would never want me back the way I was." Morgan looked up at him, eyes bright, above the pallor of her cheeks. "So I went through the treatment, but it didn't help. It didn't work. They wanted me to say I could live without you, and I couldn't."

"Why not?"

Her slim shoulders lifted and fell. "Because I couldn't."

"So why did you leave me in the first place?"

"I started falling apart in Ekali. I was fine when we first

got there, but after the first month, something happened to me. I began to cry when you were at work and I tried to hide it from you when you came home, but you must have known, because you changed, too. You became colder and distant, and maybe it wasn't you…maybe it was all me… because I needed too much from you, and God knows, my needs weren't healthy—"

"And who told you that you needs weren't healthy?" he growled, trying desperately hard to hang on to his temper. "Your parents?"

"And the doctors. And the therapists."

"Christ," he muttered under his breath, dragging a hand through his hair. "That's not true, you know," he said, looking at her. "You were young and isolated and lonely and I wasn't there for you. I know that now. I know I wasn't fair to you. I worked ridiculous hours, and expected you to be able to entertain yourself, and I owe you an apology. Actually, I owe you many, many apologies."

She managed a small, tight smile. "It's hard to remember… hard to go back…because what we had was good, so good, and then it all became so bad…." She sighed and rubbed her head. "I wish we could go back, and do it all again, and make different decisions this time."

"There's no going back, though, only going forward."

Morgan nodded. "I know, and I'm trying. And seeing Pompeii with you today made me realize that we have to go forward. We have to have hope and courage and build new lives."

He came to her, crouched before her, his hands on either side of her knees, his gaze searching hers. "I know I failed you—"

"No more than I failed you, Drakon."

"But you didn't fail me. You were perfect…you were warm and real and hopeful and sensitive."

"So why did you pull away? Why shut me out...because it felt like you did—"

"I did. I definitely shut you out, and you weren't imagining that I pulled away, because I did that, too."

"Why?"

He hesitated a moment and then drew a breath. "Because I loved you so much, and yet I was overwhelmed by feelings of inadequacy...I couldn't make you happy, I couldn't meet your needs, I couldn't be who or what you wanted, so I...pushed you away."

Her eyes searched his. "It wasn't my imagination?"

"No."

"I wasn't crazy when I left you then?"

"No."

She made a soft, hoarse sound. "So I just went crazy when I left you."

"You were never crazy, Morgan."

She smiled, sadly. "But I was. Leaving you tore me apart. I felt my heart break when I left you. Everyone kept telling me I was developing this disorder or that disorder but they didn't understand...I just needed you. I just wanted you. And they wouldn't let me have you." Tears filled her eyes. "No one believed that I could love you that deeply...but why was it wrong to love you so much? Why did it make me bad... and mad...to miss you that much?"

"They were wrong, Morgan. And I was wrong. And I know you weren't insane, because I felt the same way, too. And I couldn't get to you, either. I couldn't find you, and all I wanted was to find you and apologize, and fix things, and change things, so that we could be happy. I knew we could be happy. I just needed you home."

She reached up to knock away a tear before it could fall. "But I didn't come back."

"No. But I wouldn't give up on you, or us. I still can't give up on us." He reached out to wipe her cheek dry with his thumb. "Tell me, my love, that I haven't waited in vain. Tell me there's a place in your life for me. Give me hope, Morgan."

She just looked at him, deep into his eyes, for a long moment before leaning forward and kissing him. "Yes," she whispered against his mouth. "Yes, there's a place in my life for you. There will always be a place in my life for you. I need you, Drakon. Can't live without you, Drakon."

His mouth covered hers, and he kissed her deeply, but it wasn't enough for her. Morgan needed more, craved more, and she wrapped her arms around his neck, and opened her knees so he could move between them, his big body pressed against hers. Still kissing her, he pressed her back onto the chaise, his towel falling off as he stretched out over her, his hand sliding up her rib cage to cup her breast.

Morgan hissed a breath as his fingers rubbed her nipple, making the sensitive peak pucker and tighten. His other hand was moving down her torso, tugging up the hem of her dress, finding her bare inner thigh, his touch sending lightning forks of sensation zinging through her body, making her body heat and her core melt. She wanted him, wanted him so much, and she sucked on his tongue, desperate for him to strip her and feel his warm, bare skin on hers.

And then his phone rang on the bedside table, chiming with a unique ringtone that Morgan had never heard before.

He lifted his head, listened, frowning. "Damn."

"What?"

He shook his head and rolled away from her, leaving the chaise to pick up his phone from the table near the bed. "Damn," he muttered, reading the message. "She needs to talk to me before she returns to Athens."

Morgan didn't even need to ask who "she" was, knowing perfectly well it was Bronwyn. "Now?"

"She's leaving soon. Tonight."

"Surely she can wait a half hour?"

He didn't answer immediately, simply rolled away, his towel falling off in the process. "I won't be long."

"You really have to go now?"

"I'll be back in less than fifteen minutes."

Morgan watched him walk, without a stitch of clothing, to the closet. Dressed, Drakon Xanthis was a handsome, sophisticated man. Naked, he was absolutely beautiful.

He was beautiful now, and her mouth dried, her heart hurting as he disappeared into the closet, his body tan, skin gleaming, his muscles taut. Honed. He had those big shoulders and broad chest and lean flat abs and long strong legs, and between those legs hung his thick shaft, impressive even now, when he wasn't erect.

As the closet light came on, Morgan felt a surge of jealousy, hating that Drakon and his beautiful, hard, honed body was leaving her to go meet Bronwyn.

When he emerged a few minutes later, buckling the belt on his trousers, buttoning his shirt and tucking it into the waistband, Morgan felt almost sick.

Suddenly she felt like the young bride she'd been five years ago…uncertain, insecure, overwhelmed by her new life as Drakon Xanthis's American bride.

Drakon must have seen her fear because his brow furrowed as he gazed down at her. "There's no need to be threatened by Bronwyn. She works for me, but you're my wife."

But she'd been his wife before, and it hadn't helped her feel secure, or close to him. And while she'd been home alone for twelve, fourteen, sometimes sixteen hours a day, he'd been at the office with Bronwyn. Even if there was nothing sexual between him and Bronwyn, by virtue of being his trusted right hand, Bronwyn still got to spend time with Drakon…time Morgan would love to have. Not because Morgan couldn't be alone and needed Drakon to prop her up, but because she loved Drakon and enjoyed his company more than anyone else.

"I just don't want to feel as if I have to fight Bronwyn for you anymore," she said quietly, calmly, grateful that her voice could sound so steady when her heart was racing so fast.

"But you don't have to fight Bron for me. You never have."

And while this conversation was brutal, it was also necessary and long overdue. They should have talked about Bronwyn years ago. Morgan should have told Drakon how uncomfortable she was around her when they first married, but she hadn't, too afraid of displeasing him. And so the wound had festered, and her fear grew, until their entire relationship had become stunted and toxic.

"You love me?" she whispered.

"How can you doubt it?"

She bit down into her lip, holding back her fears, and her need to be reassured, knowing that her fears were irrational. Drakon wouldn't be here, helping her, if he didn't want to be. Drakon wouldn't have brought in Rowan to rescue her father if he didn't care about her. It was time she stopped panicking and stopped allowing her insecurities to get the upper hand. Drakon loved her. Drakon had always loved her. But he wasn't a woman…he was a man, a Greek man that had been raised to conceal vulnerabilities and avoid emotion. "I don't doubt it," she whispered. "I know you love me. Without question."

"There is no competition between you and Bron," he said roughly, his handsome, chiseled features hard.

She nodded, wanting to believe it, needing to believe it, but as he'd told her once, actions spoke louder than words. If he stayed at his office night after night until ten, making decisions, talking with Bronwyn, how was Morgan supposed to feel?

She felt a twinge of panic at the idea of returning to that life, but she had to be strong and confident. She believed in Drakon, and she had to believe that Drakon would do what was right for her…for them.

"Promise me you're not threatened by her," he said, stalking closer to her, forcing her to tilt her head back to meet his eyes.

"Promise me you won't be upset if I have to work long days, and late into the night, with her," he added.

Morgan's mouth opened, closed. She wanted to tell him she'd be fine, and she would try to be fine with it, but she couldn't promise him she'd be perfectly comfortable. She didn't know any woman who'd be perfectly comfortable with her husband being alone with a gorgeous woman night after night...day after day. Working in such close proximity created an intimacy that could lead to other things...and Morgan was sure Bronwyn did have feelings for Drakon. In fact, Morgan was sure Bronwyn was the problem here, not Drakon, but how could she tell him that?

She couldn't. But she also couldn't lie. And so with her heart racing, she swallowed convulsively. "I'm here for the long haul, Drakon. I'm here to stay. I'm playing for keeps."

His amber gaze drilled into her. "Playing for keeps," he repeated softly.

She licked her dry lips. "Yes."

"Is that a threat or a promise?"

"It's whatever you want it to be."

He laughed once, the mocking sound such a contrast to the sudden fire in his eyes. And then he was gone, walking out, leaving the door wide open behind him.

CHAPTER TWELVE

HE WASN'T GONE just a few minutes. He was gone a long time, over an hour, and Morgan returned to her room, wondering if she should dress for dinner, or if dinner would even be served tonight as it was growing late, well past the time they normally gathered in the living room for *aperitivos*.

Morgan eventually did change and go downstairs. Rowan was in the living room, having a drink.

"Can I pour you something?" he offered as she entered the candle lit living room.

"The Campari," she said, even as she tried to listen to the house, trying to hear where Drakon and Bronwyn might be.

Rowan filled her glass, handed her the cocktail. "They're outside," he said. "Or they were."

She sipped the cocktail. Campari and orange. It was tart and sweet at the same time. "Why do you say, 'were'?"

"A car arrived a half hour ago, and it just pulled away a few minutes ago." Rowan turned, nodded at the hall. "And here he is. Drakon Xanthis in the flesh." Rowan raised his glass. "I've a few calls to make. I'll have more privacy elsewhere. Cheers." And then Rowan walked out, leaving Drakon and Morgan alone.

Drakon walked past Morgan without saying a word, going to the bar where he made himself a drink. Morgan watched him wondering what had happened between him and Bronwyn.

Drakon carried his drink to the window, where he sipped it and stared out at the dark sky.

"She's gone," he said at last. "Back to Athens."

Morgan looked at his rigid back, and the set of his shoulders. "Did something happen?" she asked quietly.

"I let her go."

"What?"

"I let her go. Fired her. Terminated her employment. Whatever you want to call it."

"Why?"

"I watched her here, how she behaved around you, and I didn't like it. She has worked for me for a long time—eight years—and she was good at what she did, but I won't have any woman snubbing you, not anymore. I won't look the other way, especially if it's my employee, or a friend of mine. It's not acceptable, and you shouldn't have to endure slights and snubs...not from anyone."

Morgan heard what he was saying and appreciated everything he was saying, but there was something else happening here. Drakon was upset...angry...but Morgan didn't understand who he was upset with—Bronwyn, himself, or Morgan.

"You didn't have to fire her because of me," Morgan said, choosing her words carefully. "I meant it when I said, I was sticking around. I'm not going to let anyone scare me away. I'm not twenty-two anymore. I'm twenty-seven and I know a lot more about the world now, and a lot more about myself."

He sipped his cocktail. "I agree you've changed, but I've also changed, and Bronwyn has, too. There was a time I needed her—and she saved me, I owe her a lot, if not everything—but that was four years ago, and things are different and it's time for her to move on. It'll be better for her."

Morgan's inside flipped nervously. "How did she save you?"

He took another long drink from his crystal tumbler and then looked over his shoulder at Morgan. "If it weren't for her, I wouldn't have a company. I wouldn't have this villa. I wouldn't have anything."

"I don't understand."

"I know you don't." He sighed, shrugged, took another quick drink before continuing. "I would prefer you didn't know, and I'd promised Bron years ago I wouldn't tell you, she didn't want me to tell you. She said you wouldn't like it… you wouldn't respect me…but that's a risk I'll have to take."

Morgan sat down in one of the chairs. "Please tell me."

He walked the length of the room, and it was a long room, before dropping into a chair not far from hers. "A number of years ago, I made a mistake. Normally it wouldn't be an issue, but with the situation being what it was, the mistake was serious. It nearly bankrupted me."

He closed his eyes, shook his head, then opened them again and looked at her. "I was close to losing everything. And I mean everything. The company. The ships. The contracts. Our offices. Our homes. The cars, planes, yachts… everything…" His voice faded and for a moment there was just silence, a heavy, suffocating silence that blanketed the room. "And the worst of it was, I didn't care."

Drakon was still looking at her, but he didn't seem to see her. He seemed to be seeing something else, his expression tortured. "I didn't care," he repeated lowly, strangely detached.

Morgan had never heard him talk this way, or sound this way, and her heart thumped uncomfortably and she wasn't sure if she wanted to hear more, but there was no way she would stop him from talking.

After a long, uneasy moment Drakon continued. "I wasn't able to make good decisions during this time, and I didn't do what I should have done to protect my company, my future or my employees. I was willing to lose it all. But Bronwyn refused to just stand there, a witness, as my company and life imploded."

"So she took over," he continued. "She stepped into my empty shoes and vacant office and became me…became president and CEO and no one knew it was Bronwyn Harper forging my signature, shifting funds, slashing spending, liquidating assets." Drakon's gaze met Morgan's. "Not all of her decisions were the right ones. Some of her actions had negative consequences, but if she hadn't stepped in when she did, there would be nothing here today."

It was hard for Morgan to hear Drakon speak of Bronwyn so reverently, because Morgan wished she'd been the one who had been there for Drakon when he needed someone. "I'm glad she helped you," Morgan said huskily. "Glad she was able to help you, because I couldn't have, even if I'd wanted to."

He looked at her, amber gaze piercing. "So yes, she helped me, but she was never more than a valuable employee. She was never your rival. I never once wanted her. I have only wanted you."

"Then why fire her? If she was such a help, and you feel so grateful—"

"She wanted more than what we had." His mouth curved but the smile didn't reach his eyes. "She made it clear she wanted more, that she was in love with me, but I didn't feel that way about her. I loved you, and only you, and Bronwyn knew that."

"But she stuck around all these years…she stuck around because she had to hope she had a chance."

He shrugged. "Maybe. Probably. But she didn't. If I couldn't have you, there wouldn't have been anyone else for me. It was you or nobody."

Morgan exhaled slowly, her head spinning. "She must be heartbroken right now."

"She'll be fine. She's strong. She's smart. She'll have a better life now, away from me." Drakon drew Morgan into his arms and pressed a kiss to her temple, and then another to her cheekbone. "It's you I'm worried about."

"You don't need to worry about me."

"Rowan hasn't found your father yet."

"But he hasn't given up."

"No. And Rowan won't, not until we find your father. There is no one better than Rowan and Dunamas. They will continue looking for your father, until he is found."

"What if it takes weeks…months…years?"

"Doesn't matter. I promise you, we will never forget him, and never give up."

CHAPTER THIRTEEN

THEY ATE DINNER, just the two of them, as Rowan was nowhere to be found, and then skipping coffee and dessert, they headed upstairs to Drakon's room, where they made love, soundlessly, wordlessly, so quiet in the dark silent night.

Their lovemaking wasn't fierce and hot, or carnal and raw, but slow, careful, tender, so tender that Morgan wept after she climaxed because she'd never felt this way with Drakon before, had never made love with him like this before, their bodies so close, so connected, they'd felt like one.

Afterward, they lay side by side, his body wrapped around hers, his muscular arm holding her close to him, and still they said nothing, because there were no words, at least not the right ones. So much had happened since they'd met. So much love and yet so much loss. So much anger and pain and heartbreak...

But words right now wouldn't help, words would just get in the way, so they didn't talk, but instead lay close, filled with emotion, intense emotion that surged and ached and trembled and twisted.

Lying there in the dark, wrapped in Drakon's warmth and listening to him breathe, Morgan knew these things—she still loved him, deeply, passionately.

She also knew she wouldn't leave him. Not ever again.

But for them to have a future, they would have to talk

more, and they'd need patience, forgiveness, courage and strength.

She knew she was willing to fight for Drakon and her marriage, but there were still things she didn't understand about Drakon, things she didn't understand about the past.

And when, a half hour later, he kissed her shoulder but eased away to climb from the bed, she was filled with unease.

Turning over, she watched as he stepped into his cotton pajama pants, settling the drawstring waist low on his hips, leaving that magnificent torso bare. She watched him walk to the French door and push open the curtains. Propping an arm against the glass, he stared out at the sea, which rippled silver with moonlight.

She sat up and wrapped an arm around her knees, pressing the covers closer to her legs. "I've been thinking about what you said earlier, and how you feel so grateful to Bronwyn for saving your company...and saving you...when you made a mistake and nearly lost everything. But I know you. You don't make mistakes. What mistake did you make, that could have possibly cost you your company?"

He said nothing right away and Morgan was afraid he wouldn't speak, but then he shrugged. "I was distracted. Wasn't focused on work. And suddenly there was no money. No money to pay anybody, no money for taxes, no money at all."

"How could there be no money? Where did it go?"

Again, another long, excruciating silence. "Bad investments."

Ice filled her veins and she flashed to her father, and Michael Amery. No...he wouldn't...not a second time. She held her breath, even as her heart began to race. "You said...bad investments....plural." Morgan swallowed around the lump of panic forming in her throat. "Did you mean, investments, plural, or was there just that one horrible, huge loss to my father?"

He was silent so long that bile rose up in her throat, and she knew, she knew, there was more. She knew something else had happened, something he'd never told her. "Drakon, *agapo mou,* please, please tell me."

Drakon shifted his weight, muscles ripping across his shoulders and down his back, and then he turned toward her, the moonlight glancing briefly over his features until he'd turned his back to the window, with the light behind him, shadowing his face again. "Your father came to me asking for help after you'd left me."

Pain shot through her. Tears filled her eyes. "You gave him more money."

Drakon's lips compressed. "He was your father. He needed help."

"How much did he ask for?"

"A billion."

"Oh, my God." She pressed her hand to her mouth. "Drakon, no. You didn't…"

"What was I to do, Morgan? He was in trouble. I was his son-in-law, and I loved you. Family is family—"

"But I'd left you!"

"But I hadn't left you."

She ground her teeth together, tears blinding her, her stomach churning in bitter protest. "I can't believe this."

He laughed hollowly. "When your father came to me, telling me he was in trouble…that he had investors who needed their money back, but he didn't have the liquidity to give them their money…I thought it was my chance to win you back. But I didn't have that kind of money sitting in an account, no one has money like that, so I took loans from banks, as well as other resources, to come up with the money for your father."

"And you didn't get me back, did you?" she whispered.

For a minute there was just silence, and an almost unbearable pain, and then Drakon shook his head. "No. I gave him the money but Daniel refused to tell me where you were. Said that you'd contact me when you were ready."

"And I couldn't contact you, not at McLean." She blinked to clear her eyes. "And then what happened?"

"The economy started crashing. My creditors and lenders began to call their loans. But there was no money to give them. There was nothing I could do but file for bankruptcy, and fold. And I was fine with that, because without you, I didn't care."

"You're breaking my heart," Morgan whispered.

"I was pathetic. Bron said you'd find me pathetic—"

"Pathetic? How could I find you, who sacrificed everything for me, pathetic?" She rose up on her knees. "You were a hero. You loved me. You fought for me. You were willing to sacrifice everything for me."

He turned and looked at her, his face still shadowed but she felt his intensity. "I don't want to live without you, Morgan. I don't like life without you. And maybe that's weak—"

"Not weak," she said, leaving the bed to go to him, wrap her arms around his waist. She held him tightly, chilled by what he had told her, as well as chilled by the reality of her parents taking her to McLean and leaving her there when they knew Drakon wanted her, when they knew Drakon loved her. She didn't understand their motivations, but then, their lives were about money and appearances and Morgan knew she'd embarrassed them by coming home from Greece, heartbroken and hysterical.

He slid a hand down her back, shaping her to him. "I don't think you understand how much I loved you," he said roughly. "How much I will always love you." His voice cracked, turned hoarse. "There is no one else for me, but you. You aren't just my wife. You are my world."

"And you are mine."

"Why did you leave then?"

"I was honestly falling apart."

"Why?"

"I loved you so much, it scared me. I'd never felt for anyone what I felt for you...but the feelings were so intense, it made me feel out of control. And then when we made love... that started to do something to my head. Played games with me, made me afraid."

"Afraid? Why? How?"

"I had so little experience when I met you, and you had so much, and in bed you're...hot. Erotic. Demanding. You make everything hot and erotic, too."

"I demanded too much of you?"

"There were times I felt overwhelmed."

"Thus, your disgust."

"You never disgusted me. I shouldn't have said that. It wasn't true. I was just angry and hurt, and trying desperately hard to keep you at arm's length since I find you impossible to resist."

He stepped away from her and went to flip the light switch, turning on the small wall sconces so the room glowed with soft yellow light. "Maybe I didn't disgust you, but I must have scared you at times for you to even say such a thing."

"I never minded it being...hot...when you were relaxed with me, and spent a lot of time with me, but once we returned to Athens, I didn't see you often and then we weren't talking and it didn't feel the same. It didn't feel as warm and safe. It felt more dangerous."

"But you always came."

"Because you've got great technique." She managed an unsteady smile. "But I'd rather not come, and just be close to you, feel close to you, than have erotic sex and have you feel like a stranger."

He sat down on the side of the bed. "Come here." He smiled crookedly. "Please."

Morgan walked to him, heart thumping, and feeling painfully shy. "Yes?"

He drew her down onto the bed next to him, and kissed her, once and again, before lifting his head to look down into her eyes. "I love how sensual you are. I love your passionate nature. But I never want you to be uncomfortable with me again…in bed, or out of bed. I love you too much to hurt you or scare you or to push you away. But you have to tell me when something is too much. You have to tell me when I'm being distant or when you feel nervous or lonely or afraid."

"You want me to talk to you," she said.

"Yes. I want you to talk to me."

"That means you have to talk to me, too."

He smiled even more crookedly. "I know."

"Okay."

"But I don't want you bored…especially in bed."

"My God, Morgan, I could never be bored in bed with you."

"No?"

"No! When we're together it's not about sex…its about me showing you how much you mean to me. How much I cherish you. How much I worship you. When I touch you, Morgan, I'm telling you that nothing is more important to me than you, and that I love you with all of my heart, and all of my soul."

"Really?"

"Really." His gaze searched hers. "All I have wanted for these past five years is to have you come home. I want you home. Morgan, please come home with me—"

"Yes." She reached up, cupped his cheek, drawing his face toward hers. She kissed him, deeply, and a shiver raced through her as his tongue met hers, teasing her. "Yes. I'm staying with you, going home with you, back to Athens."

"Even though you hate that white ice cube tray?" he asked, turning his mouth into her hand and kissing her palm.

Another delicious shiver ran through her and she smiled.

"But would you mind if I added a few colorful rugs? A few paintings...some throw pillows?"

"Maybe what we really need is a new house for a fresh start—"

"No."

"Yes. I don't like the house, either."

"What?"

He laughed softly. "I hate it. It's awful. I never liked it. Not while they were building it, and not even when we moved in, but I thought you did like it, so I never told you."

"I think we have a slight communication problem," she said drily.

"You think?" he teased, pressing her backward onto the bed, and then stretching out over her, his long hard body covering hers.

"We need to work on it."

"Mmm," he agreed, kissing her throat and pushing the covers down to bare her breasts. "We're going to have to start talking more," he said, alternately kissing and licking the slope of her breast.

She sighed and arched as he latched onto one of her tight, pebbled nipples. "Okay," she gasped, desire coiling in her belly.

"Do you like this?" he asked, as he stroked down her flat belly.

"Um, yes."

"And this?" he asked, his fingers slipping between her legs.

She gasped as he caressed her most sensitive spot. "Yes. And I'm glad we're talking...but do we have to do it now?"

She felt his silent laughter as his teeth scraped her nipple. "No," he answered. "I'd much rather just concentrate on you, and making you come."

"Good."

She gasped again as his fingers slipped down, where she

was slick and wet, and then caressed up over the nub again. "Drakon?"

"Yes, *gynaika mou?*"

"Make love to me. And love me. Forever."

He shifted, bracing his weight on his arms and looked down into her eyes for an endless moment. "Always. Always, and forever, until I die."

EPILOGUE

"WILL YOU DO it, Logan? Cover for me for a few days so Drakon and I can have a brief getaway?" Morgan asked, speaking calmly into the phone, trying to sound relaxed, even though she was frustrated with Logan for dodging her calls for the past week. "You'd just be a point person for a few days, if there are any communication issues, but I doubt there will be."

"I can't drop everything and take over Dad's search just so you and Drakon can have a second honeymoon," Logan said, her voice sharp on the speakerphone. "Some of us have jobs, Morgan. Some of us must work as we don't have wealthy husbands to take care of us."

"Would you like a wealthy husband, Logan?" Drakon said, unable to remain silent in his seat across from Morgan's on his private jet. They were still on the ground, hadn't closed the doors, because Morgan had refused to take off until Logan promised she'd help. "You know it can be arranged."

"No, thank you, Drakon. I am quite capable of taking care of myself," Logan retorted crisply.

Drakon smiled. "You might actually enjoy a strong Greek husband…almost as much as he'd enjoy managing you."

"Not going to happen," Logan snapped. "But if it will help me get off this call, then yes, Morgan, I will be your contact person should something happen while you and Drakon are doing whatever you and Drakon do."

Drakon arched a brow at Morgan, and Morgan shook her

head at him, blushing. "I seriously doubt anything will happen, though. We're only going to be gone a few days…just for a long weekend—"

"I got it. You're just gone a few days. Dunamas is doing all the intelligence work and orchestrating the rescue. They'll call me if they can't reach you should there be developments." Logan paused. "Did I forget anything?"

Morgan grimaced. "No. That's pretty much it."

"Good. Now go…scram. Enjoy your trip. And try to have fun. Dad's going to be okay." Logan's voice suddenly softened. "I'll make sure he is, I promise."

Morgan hung up and looked at Drakon, who had just signaled to his flight crew that they were ready to take off. "Why am I worrying so much?"

His amber gaze met hers. "Because you deliberately withheld information from her, knowing she'd never agree to help us if she thought she'd have to deal with Rowan."

Morgan chewed on her lip. "Let's just hope she doesn't have to deal with him. Otherwise there's going to be hell to pay."

"Rowan said the exact same thing."

* * * * *

HIS DEFIANT
DESERT QUEEN

For Lee Hyat who has been there every step
of the way since reading The Italian Groom!
Thank you for being my first reader
and a most loyal and cherished friend.

PROLOGUE

SEETHING, SHEIKH MIKAEL KARIM, King of Saidia, watched the high fashion photo shoot taking place in the desert—his desert—wondering how anyone could think it was okay to enter a foreign country under a false identity and think he, or *she*, as it happened to be in this case, could get away with it.

Apparently the world was filled with fools.

Fools by the name of *Copeland*.

Jaw tight, temper barely leashed, Mikael waited for the right moment to intervene.

He'd been pushed too far, challenged directly, and he'd meet that challenge with swift retribution.

A king didn't negotiate. A king never begged, and a king refused to curry favor.

Saidia might be a small kingdom, but it was powerful. And the government of Saidia might tolerate the West, but Westerners couldn't enter Saidia, flaunt Saidia law, and think there would be no repercussions.

Jemma Copeland was a foolish woman. So like her father, thumbing her nose at the law, believing she was above it.

Perhaps Daniel Copeland had got away with his crimes. But his daughter would not be so lucky. Miss Jemma Copeland was going to pay.

CHAPTER ONE

NECESSITY HAD TAUGHT Jemma Copeland to shut out distractions.

She'd learned to ignore the things she didn't want to think about, to enable her to do what needed to be done.

So for the past two hours she'd ignored the scorching heat of the Sahara. The insistent, hollow ache in her stomach. The stigma of being a Copeland, and what it meant back home in the United States.

She'd blocked out heat, hunger, and shame, but she couldn't block out the tall, white-robed man standing just a foot behind the photographer, watching her through dark, unsmiling eyes while a half dozen robed men stood behind him.

She knew who the man was. How could she not? He'd attended her sister's wedding five years ago in Greenwich and every woman with a pulse had noticed Sheikh Mikael Karim. He was tall, he was impossibly, darkly handsome, and he was a billionaire as well as the new king of Saidia.

But Mikael Karim wasn't supposed to be on set today. He was supposed to be in Buenos Aires this week and his sudden appearance, arriving in a parade of glossy black luxury SUVs with tinted windows, had sent ripples of unease throughout the entire crew.

It was obvious he wasn't happy.

Jemma's gut told her something ugly could happen soon. She prayed she was wrong. She just wanted to get through the rest of the shoot and fly out tomorrow morning as planned.

At least he hadn't shown up yesterday. Yesterday had been

grueling, a very long day, with multiple shots in multiple locations, and the heat had been intense. But she hadn't complained. She wouldn't. She needed the job too much to be
anything but grateful for the chance to still work.

It still boggled her mind how much things had changed. Just
a year ago she had been one of America's golden girls, envied
for her beauty, her wealth, her status as an It Girl. Her family
was powerful, affluent. The Copelands had homes scattered
across the world, and she and her gorgeous, privileged sisters
were constantly photographed and discussed. But even the
powerful can fall, and the Copeland family tumbled off their
pedestal with the revelation that Daniel, her father, was the
number two man in the biggest Ponzi scheme in America in
the past century.

Overnight the Copelands became the most hated family
in America.

Now Jemma could barely make ends meet. The fallout from
her father's arrest, and the blitz of media interest surrounding
the case, had destroyed her career. The fact that she worked,
and had supported herself since she was eighteen, meant nothing to the public. She was still Daniel Copeland's daughter.
Hated. Loathed. Resented.

Ridiculed.

Today, she was lucky to get work, and her once brilliant
career now barely paid the bills. When her agency came to
her with this assignment, a three day shoot with two travel
days, meaning she'd be paid for five work days, she'd jumped
at the opportunity to come to Saidia, the independent desert
kingdom tucked underneath Southern Morocco, and nestled
between the Western Sahara and the Atlantic Ocean. She'd
continued to fight for the opportunity even when the Saidia
consulate denied her visa request.

It wasn't legal, but desperate times called for desperate
measures so she'd reapplied for a new visa as her sister, using
Morgan's passport bearing Morgan's married name, Xanthos.
This time she'd received the needed travel visa.

Yes, she was taking a huge risk, coming here under a false name, but she needed money. Without this paycheck, she wouldn't be able to pay her next month's mortgage.

So here she was, dressed in a long fox fur and thigh high boots, sweltering beneath the blazing sun.

So what if she was naked beneath the coat?

She was working. She was surviving. And one day, she'd thrive again, too.

So let them look.

Let them *all* look—the disapproving sheikh and his travel guard—because she wouldn't be crushed. She refused to be crushed. The clothes were beautiful. Life was exciting. She didn't have a care in the world.

Despite her fierce resolve, perspiration beaded beneath her full breasts and slid down her bare abdomen.

Not uncomfortable, she thought. *Sexy.*

And with sexy firmly in mind, she drew a breath, jutted her hip, and struck a bold pose.

Keith, the Australian photographer, let out an appreciative whistle. "That's beautiful, baby! More of that, please."

She felt a rush of pleasure, which was quickly dashed by the sight of Mikael Karim moving closer to Keith.

The sheikh was tall, so tall he towered over Keith, and his shoulders were broad, dwarfing the slender Australian.

Jemma had forgotten just how intensely handsome Mikael Karim was. She'd modeled in other countries and had met many different sheikhs, and most had been short, heavyset men with flirty eyes and thickening jowls.

But Sheikh Mikael Karim was young, and lean, and fierce. His white robes only accentuated the width of his shoulders as well as his height, and his angular jaw jutted, black eyebrows flat over those intense, dark eyes.

Now Sheikh Karim looked over Keith's head, his dark gaze piercing her, holding her attention. She couldn't look away. He seemed to be telling her something, warning her of something. She went hot, then cold, shivering despite the heat.

Her stomach rose, fell. An alarm sounded in her head. He was dangerous.

She tugged on the edges of the coat, pulling it closer to her body, suddenly very conscious of the fact that she was naked beneath.

Sighing with frustration, Keith lowered his camera a fraction. "You just lost all your energy. Give me sexy, baby."

Jemma glanced at the sheikh from beneath her lashes. The man oozed tension, a lethal tension that made her legs turn to jelly and the hair prickle on the back of her neck. Something was wrong. Something was very wrong.

But Keith couldn't read Sheikh Karim's expression and his irritation grew. "Come on, focus. We need to wrap this up, baby."

Keith was right. They did need to wrap this shot. And she was here to do a job. She had to deliver, or she'd never work again.

Jemma gulped a breath, squared her shoulders, and lifted her chin to the sun, feeling her long hair spill down her back as she let the heavy fur drop off her shoulder, exposing more skin.

"Nice." Keith lifted his camera, motioned for his assistant to step closer with the white reflective screen, and began snapping away. "I like that. More of that."

Jemma shook her head, letting her thick hair tease the small of her spine even as the fur fell lower on her breasts.

"Perfect," Keith crooned. "That's hot. Love it. Don't stop. You're on fire now."

Yes, she was, she thought, arching her shoulders back, breasts thrust high, the nipples now just exposed to the kiss of the sun. In Sheikh Karim's world she was probably going to burn in the flames of hell, but there was nothing she could do about it. This was her job. She had to deliver. And so she pushed all other thoughts from mind, except for giving the image they wanted.

Her shoulders twisted and the coat slid lower on her arm, the fur tickling the back of her bare thighs.

"Lovely, baby." Keith was snapping away. "So beautiful. Keep doing what you're doing. You're a goddess. Every man's dream."

She wasn't a goddess, or a dream, but she could pretend to be. She could pretend anything for a short period of time. Pretending gave her distance, allowing her to breathe, escape, escaping the reality of what was happening at home. *Home*. A sinking sensation filled her. *What a nightmare*.

Battling back the sadness, Jemma shifted, lifting her chin, thrusting her hip out, dropping the coat altogether, exposing her breasts, nipples jutting proudly.

Keith whistled softly. "Give me more."

"*No*," Sheikh Mikael Karim ground out. It was just one word, but it echoed like a crack of thunder, immediately silencing the murmur of stylists, make-up artist, and lighting assistants.

All heads turned toward the sheikh.

Jemma stared at him, her stomach churning all over again.

The sheikh's expression was beyond fierce. His lips curled, his dark eyes burned as he pushed the camera in Keith's hands down. "That's enough," he gritted. "I've had enough, from all of you." His narrowed gaze swept the tents and crew. "You are done here."

And then his head turned again and he stared straight at Jemma. "And you, Miss *Copeland*. Cover yourself, and then go inside the tent. I will be in to deal with you shortly."

She covered herself, but didn't move.

The sheikh had called her *Miss Copeland*, not Mrs. Xanthis, the name she'd used on the visa, but Copeland.

Panic flooded her veins. Her heart surged. Sheikh Karim knew who she was. He'd recognized her after all these years. The realization shocked her. He, who knew so many, remembered her.

Hands shaking, she tugged the coat closer to her body, suddenly icy cold despite the dazzling heat. "What's happening?" she whispered, even though in a dim part of her brain, she knew.

She'd been found out. Her true identity had been discovered. How, she didn't know, but she was in trouble. Grave trouble. She could feel the severity of the situation all the way down to her toes.

"I think you know," Sheikh Karim said flatly. "Now go inside the tent and wait."

Her knees knocked. She wasn't sure her legs could support her. "For what?"

"To be informed of the charges being brought against you."

"I've done nothing wrong."

His dark eyes narrowed. His jaw hardened as his gaze swept over her, from the top of her head to the boots on her feet. "You've done *everything* wrong, Miss *Copeland*. You're in serious trouble. So go to the tent, now, and if you have half a brain, you'll obey."

Jemma had more than half a brain. She actually had a very good brain. And a very good imagination, which made the walk to the tent excruciating.

What was going to happen to her? What were the official charges? And what would the punishment be?

She tried to calm herself. She focused on her breathing, and clamped down on her wild thoughts. It wouldn't help her to panic. She knew she'd entered the country illegally. She'd willingly agreed to work on a shoot that hadn't been condoned by the government. *And* she'd shown her breasts in public, which was also against Saidia's law.

And she'd done it all because she hadn't taken money from her family since she was eighteen and she wasn't about to start now.

She was an adult. A successful, capable woman. And she'd been determined to make it without going to her family begging for a handout.

In hindsight, perhaps begging for a handout would have been wiser.

In the wardrobe tent, Jemma shrugged off the heavy fur coat, and slipped a light pink cotton kimono over her shoulders, tying the sash at her waist. As she sat down at the stool before the make-up mirror, she could hear the sheikh's voice echo in her head.

You've done everything wrong...

Everything wrong...

He was right. She had done everything wrong. She prayed he'd accept her apology, allow her to make amends. She hadn't meant to insult him, or disrespect his country or his culture in any way.

Jemma straightened, hearing voices outside her tent. The voices were pitched low, speaking quickly, urgently. Male voices. A single female voice. Jemma recognized the woman as Mary Leed, *Catwalk*'s editorial director. Mary was usually unflappable but she sounded absolutely panicked now.

Jemma's heart fell all over again. Bad. This was bad.

She swallowed hard, her stomach churning, nerves threatening to get the better of her.

She shouldn't have come.

She shouldn't have taken such risks.

But what was she to do otherwise? Crumble? Shatter? End up on the streets, destitute, homeless, helpless?

No.

She wouldn't be helpless, and she wouldn't be pitied, or mocked, either.

She'd suffered enough at the hands of her father. He'd betrayed them all; his clients, his business partners, his friends, even his family. He might be selfish and ruthless and destructive, but the rest of the Copelands weren't. Copelands were good people.

Good people, she silently insisted, stretching out one leg to unzip the thigh-high boot. Her hand was trembling so badly that it made it difficult to get the zipper down. The boots were outrageous to start with. They were the stuff of fantasy, a very high heel projecting a kinky twist, just like the fashion layout itself.

They would have been smarter doing this feature in Palm Springs instead of Saidia with Saidia's strict laws of moral conduct. Saidia might be stable and tolerant, but it wasn't a democracy, nor did it cater to the wealthy Westerners like some other nations. It remained conservative and up until two generations ago, marriages weren't just arranged, they were forced.

The tribal leaders kidnapped their brides from neighboring tribes.

Unthinkable to the modern Western mind, but acceptable here.

Jemma was tugging the zipper down on the second boot when the tent flap parted and Mary entered with Sheikh Karim. Two members of the sheikh's guard stood at the entrance.

Jemma slowly sat up, and looked from Mary to the sheikh and back.

Mary's face was pale, her lips pressed thin. "We've a problem," she said.

Silence followed. Jemma curled her fingers into her lap.

Mary wouldn't meet Jemma's gaze, looking past her shoulder instead. "We're wrapping up the shoot and returning to the capitol immediately. We are facing some legal charges and fines, which we are hoping to take care of quickly so the crew and company can return to England tomorrow, or the next day." She hesitated for a long moment, before adding even more quietly, "At least most of us should be able to return to England tomorrow or the next day. Jemma, I'm afraid you won't be going with us."

Jemma started to rise, but remembered her boot and sat back down. "Why not?"

"The charges against you are different," Mary said, still avoiding Jemma's gaze. "We are in trouble for using you, but you, you're in trouble for…" Her voice faded away. She didn't finish the sentence.

She didn't have to.

Jemma knew why she was in trouble. What she didn't know was what she'd be charged with. "I'm sorry." She drew a quick, shallow breath and looked from Mary to Sheikh Karim. "I am sorry. Truly—"

"Not interested," he said curtly.

Jemma's stomach flipped. "I made a mistake—"

"A mistake is pairing a black shoe and a blue shoe. A mistake is forgetting to charge one's phone. A mistake is *not* entering the country illegally, under false pretenses, with a false identity. You had no work permit. No visa. Nothing." Sheikh Karim's voice crackled with contempt and fury. "What you did was deliberate, and a felony, Miss Copeland."

Jemma put a hand to her belly, praying she wouldn't throw up here, now. She hadn't eaten much today. She never did on days she worked, knowing she photographed better with a very flat stomach. "What can I do to make this right?"

Mary shot Sheikh Karim a stricken glance.

He shook his head, once. "There is nothing. The magazine staff must appear in court, and pay their fines. You will face a different judge, and be sentenced accordingly."

Jemma sat very still. "So I'm to be separated from everyone?"

"Yes." The sheikh gestured to Mary. "You and the rest of the crew, are to leave immediately. My men will accompany you to ensure your safety." He glanced at Jemma. "And you will come with me."

Mary nodded and left. Heart thudding, Jemma watched Mary's silent, abrupt departure then looked to Sheikh Karim.

He was angry. Very, very angry.

Three years ago she might have crumbled. Two years ago she might have cried. But that was the old Jemma, the girl who'd grown up pampered, protected by a big brother and three opinionated, but loving, sisters.

She wasn't that girl anymore. In fact, she wasn't a girl at all anymore. She'd been put to the fire and she'd come out fierce. Strong.

"So where *do* felons go, Sheikh Karim?" she asked quietly, meeting the sheikh's hard narrowed gaze.

"To prison."

"I'm going to prison?"

"If you were to go to court tomorrow, and appear before our judicial tribunal, yes. But you're not being seen by our judicial tribunal. You're being seen by my tribe's elder, and he will act as judge."

"Why a different court and judge than Mary and the magazine crew?"

"Because they are charged with crimes against Saidia. You—" he broke off, studying her lovely face in the mirror, wondering how she'd react to his news, "You are charged with crimes against the Karims, my family. Saidia's royal family. You will be escorted to a judge who is of my tribe. He will hear the charges brought against you, and then pass judgment."

She didn't say anything. Her brow creased and she looked utterly bewildered. "I don't understand. What have I done to your family?"

"You stole from my family. Shamed them."

"But I haven't. I don't even know your family."

"Your father does."

Jemma grew still. Everything seemed to slow, stop. Would the trail of devastation left by her father's action never end? She stared at Mikael suddenly afraid of what he'd say next. "But I'm not my father."

"Not physically, no, but you represent him."

"I don't."

"You do." His jaw hardened. "In Arabic society, one is always connected to one's family. You represent your family throughout your life, which is why it's so important to always bring honor to one's family. But your father stole from the

Karims, shamed the Karims, dishonoring my family, and in so doing, he dishonored all of Saidia."

She swallowed hard. "But I'm nothing like my father."

"You are his daughter, and you are here, unlawfully. It is time to right the wrong. You will make atonement for your disrespect, and your father's, too."

"I don't even have a relationship with my father. I haven't seen him in years—"

"This is not the time. We have a long trip ahead of us. I suggest you finish changing so we can get on the road."

Her fingers bent, nails pressing to the dressing table. "*Please.*"

"It's not up to me."

"But you are the king."

"And kings must insist on obedience, submission, and respect. Even from our foreign visitors."

She looked at him, seeing him, but not seeing him, too overwhelmed by his words and the implication of what he was saying to focus on any one thing. It didn't help that her pulse raced, making her head feel dizzy and light.

The grim security guard at Tagadir International Airport had warned them. Had said that His Highness Sheikh Karim was all powerful in Saidia. As king he owned this massive expanse of desert and the sand dunes rolling in every direction, and as their translator had whispered on leaving the airport, "*His Highness, Sheikh Karim, isn't just head of the country, he is the country.*"

Jemma exhaled slowly, trying to clear the fog and panic from her brain. She should have taken the warnings seriously. She should have been logical, not desperate.

Desperate was a dangerous state of mind.

Desperate fueled chaos.

What she needed to do was remain calm. Think this through. There had to be a way to reach him, reason with him. Surely he didn't make a habit of locking up American and British girls?

"I'd like to make amends," she said quietly, glancing up at Sheikh Karim from beneath her lashes, taking in his height, the width of his shoulders, and his hard, chiseled features. Nothing in his expression was kind. There was not even a hint of softness at his mouth.

"You will," he said. "You must."

She winced at the harshness in his voice. Sheikh Mikael Karim might be as handsome as any Hollywood leading man, but there was no warmth in his eyes.

He was a cold man, and she knew all too well that cold men were dangerous. Men without hearts destroyed, and if she were not very careful, and very smart, she could be ruined.

"Can I pay a fine? A penalty?"

"You're in no position to buy yourself out of trouble, Miss Copeland. Your family is bankrupt."

"I could try Drakon—"

"You're not calling anyone," he interrupted sharply. "And I won't have Drakon bailing you out. He might be your sister's ex-husband, but he was my friend from university and from what I understand, he lost virtually his entire fortune thanks to your father. I think Drakon has paid a high enough price for being associated with you Copelands. It's time you and your family stopped expecting others to clean up your messes and instead assumed responsibility for your mistakes."

"That might be, but Drakon isn't cruel. He wouldn't approve of you...of you..." Her voice failed her as she met Mikael's dark gaze. The sheikh's anger burned in his eyes, scorching her.

"Of what, Miss Copeland?" he asked softly, a hint of menace in his deep voice.

"What won't he approve of?" he persisted.

Jemma couldn't answer. Her heart beat wildly, a painful staccato that made her chest ache.

She had to be careful. She couldn't afford to alienate the sheikh. Not when she needed him and his protection.

She needed to win him over. She needed him to care. Somehow she had to get him to see her, the real her, *Jemma*. The person. The woman. Not the daughter of Daniel Copeland.

It was vital she didn't antagonize him, but reached him. Otherwise it would be far too easy for Sheikh Karim to snap his fingers and destroy her. He was that powerful, that ruthless.

Her eyes burned and her lip trembled and she bit down hard, teeth digging into her lip to keep from making a sound.

Fear washed through her but she would not crack, or cry. Would not disintegrate, either.

"He wouldn't approve of me flaunting your laws," she said lowly, fighting to maintain control, and cling to whatever dignity she had left. "He wouldn't approve of me using my sister's passport, either. He would be angry," she added, lifting her chin to meet Sheikh Karim's gaze. "And disappointed."

Mikael Karim arched a brow.

"In me," she added. "He'd be disappointed in me."

And then wrapping herself in courage, and hanging on to that fragile cloak, she removed her boot, placing it on the floor next to its mate, and turned to her dressing table to begin removing her make-up.

CHAPTER TWO

MIKAEL SAW JEMMA'S lower lip quiver before she clamped her jaw, biting down in an effort to remain silent, as she turned back to her dressing table.

He was surprised at how calm she was. He'd expected tears. Hysteria. Instead she was quiet. Thoughtful. Respectful.

He'd planned on defiance. He'd come prepared for theatrics. She'd almost gone there. Almost, but then thought better of it.

Perhaps she wasn't as silly as he'd thought.

Perhaps she might have a brain in her pretty head after all.

He was glad she wasn't going to dissolve into tears and hysteria. And glad she might be starting to understand the gravity of her situation.

But even then, he was still deeply furious with her for knowingly, willfully flaunting every international law by entering a foreign country with a false identity, and then practically stripping in public.

It wasn't done.

It wasn't acceptable.

It wouldn't even be allowed in San Francisco or New York City.

So how could she think it would be okay here?

His brow lowered as his narrowed gaze swept over her. She looked so soft and contrite now as she removed her makeup. It was an act. He was certain she was playing him. Just as her father had played his mother...before bankrupting her, breaking her.

His mother would be alive today if Daniel Copeland hadn't lied to her and stolen from her, taking not just her financial security, but her self-respect.

Thank goodness Mikael was not his mother.

He knew better than to allow himself to be manipulated by yet another Copeland con artist.

Mikael refused to pity Jemma. He didn't care if she was sorry. Had Daniel Copeland shown his mother mercy? No. Had Daniel Copeland shown any of his clients concern...compassion? *No.* So why should his daughter receive preferential treatment?

"Will I have a lawyer present?" she asked, breaking the silence.

"No," he said.

"Will I have any legal representation?"

"No."

She hesitated, brow furrowing, lips compressing, somehow even more lovely troubled than when posed on the desert sand in the fur and thigh high boots.

Yes, she was beautiful. And yes, she'd inherited her mother's famous bone structure, and yes, even in this dim, stifling tent she still glowed like a jewel—glossy dark hair, brilliant green eyes, luminous skin, pink lips—but that didn't change the fact that she was a criminal.

"Neither of us have lawyers," he added, hating that he was even aware of her beauty. He shouldn't notice, or care. He shouldn't feel any attraction at all. "There is just the case itself, presented by me, and then the judge passes the sentence."

"You represent yourself?"

"I represent my tribe, the Karim family, and the laws of this country."

She turned slowly on the stool to face him, her hands resting on her thighs, the pink kimono gaping slightly above the knotted sash, revealing the slope of her full breast. "What you're saying is that it will be you testifying against me."

He shouldn't know that her nipple was small and pink and that her belly was flat above firm, rounded hips.

Or at the very least, he shouldn't remember. He shouldn't want to remember. "I present the facts. I do not pass judgment."

"Will the *facts* be presented in English?"

"No."

"So you could say anything."

"But why would I?" he countered sharply. "You've broken numerous laws. Important laws. Laws created to protect our borders and the safety and security of my people. There is no need to add weight or severity. What you've done is quite serious. The punishment will be appropriately serious."

He saw a flash in her eyes, and he didn't know if it was anger or fear but she didn't speak. She bit down, holding back the quick retort.

Seconds ticked by, one after the other.

For almost a minute there was only silence, a tense silence weighted with all the words she refrained from speaking.

"How serious?" she finally asked.

"There will be jail time."

"How long?"

He was uncomfortable with all the questions. "Do you really want to do this now?"

"Absolutely. Far better to be prepared than to walk in blind."

"The minimum sentence is somewhere between five to ten years. The maximum, upward of twenty."

She went white, and her lips parted, but she made no sound. She simply stared at him, incredulous, before slowly turning back to face her dressing table mirror.

She was trying not to cry.

Her shoulders were straight, and her head was high but he saw the welling of tears in her eyes. He felt her shock, and sadness.

He should leave but his feet wouldn't move. His chest felt tight.

It was her own damned fault.

But he could still see her five years ago in the periwinkle blue bridesmaid dress at Morgan's wedding.

He could hear her gurgle of laughter as she'd made a toast to her big sister at the reception after.

"We will leave as soon as you're dressed," he said tersely, ignoring Jemma's pallor and the trembling of her hands where they rested on the dressing table.

"I will need five or ten minutes," she said.

"Of course." He turned to leave but from the corner of his eye he saw her lean toward the mirror to try to remove the strip of false eyelashes on her right eye, her hands still shaking so much she couldn't lift the edge.

It wasn't his problem. He didn't care if her hands shook violently or not. But he couldn't stop watching her. He couldn't help noticing that she was struggling. Tears spilled from the corners of her eyes as she battled to get the eyelashes off.

It was her fault.

He wasn't responsible for her situation.

And yet her struggle unsettled him, awakening emotions and memories he didn't want to feel.

Mikael didn't believe in feeling. Feelings were best left to others. He, on the other hand, preferred logic. Structure. Rules. Order.

He wouldn't be moved by tears. Not even the tears of a young foreign woman that he'd met many years ago at the wedding of Drakon Xanthis, his close friend from university. Just because Drakon had married Jemma's older sister, Morgan, didn't mean that Mikael had to make allowances. Why make allowances when Daniel Copeland had made none for his mother?

"Stop," he ordered, unable to watch her struggle any longer. "You're about to take out your eye."

"I have to get them off."

"Not like that."

"I can do it."

"You're making a mess of it." He crossed the distance, gestured for her to turn on her stool. "Face me, and hold still. Look down. Don't move."

Jemma held her breath as she felt his fingers against her temple. His touch was warm, his hand steady as he used the tip of his finger to lift the edge of the strip and then he slowly, carefully peeled the lashes from her lid. "One down," he said, putting the crescent of lashes in her hand. "One to go."

He made quick work on the second set.

"You've done this before," she said, as he took a step back, putting distance between them, but not enough distance. He was so big, so intimidating, that she found his nearness overwhelming.

"I haven't, but I've watched enough girlfriends put on make up to know how it's done."

She looked at him for a long moment, her gaze searching his. "And you have *no* say in the sentencing?" she asked.

"I have plenty of say," he answered. "I am the king. I can make new laws, pass laws, break laws...but breaking laws wouldn't make me a good king or a proper leader for my people. So I, too, observe the laws of Saidia, and am committed to upholding them."

"Could you ask the judge to be lenient with me?"

"I could."

"But you won't?"

He didn't answer right away, which was telling, she thought.

"Would you ask for leniency for another woman?"

His broad shoulders shifted. "It would depend on who she was, and what she'd done."

"So your relationship with her would influence your decision?"

"Absolutely."

"I see."

"As her *character* would influence my decision."

And he didn't approve of her character.

Jemma understood then that he wouldn't help her in any way. He didn't like her. He didn't approve of her. And he felt no pity or compassion because she was a Copeland and it was a Copeland, her father, who had wronged his family.

In his mind, she had so many strikes against her she wasn't worth saving.

For a moment she couldn't breathe. The pain was so sharp and hard it cut her to the quick.

It was almost like the pain when Damien ended their engagement. He'd said he'd loved her. He'd said he wanted to spend his life with her. But then when he began losing jobs, he backed away from her. Far better to lose her, than his career.

Throat aching, eyes burning, Jemma turned back to the mirror.

She reached for a brush and ran it slowly through her long dark hair, making the glossy waves ripple down her back, telling herself not to think, not to feel, and most definitely, not to cry.

"You expect your tribal elder to sentence me to prison, for at least five years?" she asked, drawing the brush through her long hair.

Silence stretched. After a long moment, Sheikh Karim answered, "I don't expect Sheikh Azizzi to give you a minimum sentence, no."

She nodded once. "Thank you for at least being honest."

And then she reached for the bottle of make-up remover and a cotton ball to remove what was left of her eye make-up.

He walked out then. Thank goodness. She'd barely kept it together there, at the end.

She was scared, so scared.

Would she really be going to prison?

Would he really allow the judge to have her locked away for years?

She couldn't believe this was happening. Had to be a bad dream. But the sweltering heat inside the tent felt far too real to be a dream.

Jemma left her make-up table and went to her purse to retrieve her phone. Mary had informed the crew this morning as they left the hotel that they'd get no signal here in the desert, and checking her phone now she saw that Mary was right. She couldn't call anyone. Couldn't alert anyone to her situation. As Jemma put her phone away, she could only pray that Mary would make some calls on her behalf once she returned to London.

Jemma changed quickly into her street clothes, a gray short linen skirt, white knit top and gray blazer.

Drawing a breath, she left the tent, stepping out into the last lingering ray of light. Two of the sheikh's men guarded the tent, but they didn't acknowledge her.

The desert glowed with amber, ruby and golden colors. The convoy of cars that had descended on the shoot two hours ago was half the number it'd been when Jemma had disappeared into the tent.

Sheikh Karim stepped from the back of one of the black vehicles. He gestured to her. "Come. We leave now."

She shouldered her purse, pretending the sheikh wasn't watching her walk toward him, pretending his guards weren't there behind her, watching her walk away from them. She pretended she was strong and calm, that nothing threatened her.

It was all she'd been doing since her father's downfall.

Pretending. Faking. Fighting.

"Ready?" Sheikh Karim asked as she reached his side.

"Yes."

"You have no suitcase, no clothes?"

"I have a few traveling pieces here, but the rest is in my suitcase." She clasped her oversized purse closer to her body. "Can we go get my luggage?"

"No."

"Will you send for it?"

"You won't need it where you are going."

Her eyes widened and her lips parted to protest but his grim expression silenced her.

He held open the door. The car was already running.

"It's time to go," he said firmly.

Swallowing, Jemma slid onto the black leather seat, terrified to leave this scorching desert, not knowing where she'd go next.

Sheikh Karim joined her on the seat, his large body filling the back of the car. Jemma scooted as far over as she could before settling her blazer over her thighs, hiding her bare skin. But even sitting near the door, he was far too close, and warm, so warm that she fixed her attention on the desert beyond the car window determined to block out everything until she was calm.

She stared hard at the landscape, imagining that she was someone else, somewhere else and it soothed her. The sun was lower in the sky and the colors were changing, darkening, deepening and it made her heart hurt. In any other situation she would've been overcome by the beauty of the sunset. As it was now, she felt bereft.

She'd come to Saidia to save what was left of her world, and instead she'd shattered it completely.

The car was moving. Her stomach lurched. She gripped the handle on the door and drew a deep breath and then another to calm herself.

It was going to be okay.
Everything would be okay.
Everything would be fine.

"It's beautiful," she whispered, blinking back tears.

He said nothing.

She blinked again, clearing her vision, determined to find her center…a place of peace, and calm. She had to keep her head. There was no other way she'd survive whatever came next if she didn't stay focused.

"Where does this elder, Sheikh Azizzi, live?" she asked, keeping her gaze fixed on a distant dune. The sun was dropping more quickly, painting the sky a wash of rose and red that reflected crimson against the sand.

"Haslam," he said.

"Is it far?"

"Two hours by car. If there is no sandstorm."

"Do you expect one?" she asked, glancing briefly in his direction.

"Not tonight, but it's not unusual as you approach the mountains. The wind races through the valley and whips the sand dunes. It's impressive if you're not trying to drive through, and maddening if you are."

He sounded so cavalier. She wondered just how dangerous a sandstorm really was. "The storm won't hurt us?"

The sheikh shrugged. "Not if we stay on the road, turn off the engine and close the vents. But I don't expect a sandstorm tonight. So far there appears to be little wind. I think it will be a quiet night in the desert."

She tried to picture the still crimson desert as a whirling sea of sand. She'd seen it in movies, but it seemed impossible now. "And so when do we see the judge?"

"Tonight."

"Tonight?" she echoed, and when he nodded, she added, "But we won't be there for hours."

"We are expected."

His answer unleashed a thousand butterflies inside her middle. "And will we know his verdict tonight?"

"Yes." Sheikh Karim's jaw hardened. "It will be a long night."

"Justice moves swiftly in Saidia," she said under her breath.

"You have no one to blame but yourself."

She flinched at his harsh tone, and held her tongue.

But the sheikh wasn't satisfied with her silence. "Why did you do it?" he demanded, his voice almost savage. "You've had a successful career. Surely you could have been happy with less?"

"I'm broke. I needed the work. I would have lost my flat."

"You'll lose it anyway, now. There is no way for you to pay bills from prison."

She hadn't thought that far. She gave her head a bemused shake. "Maybe someone will be able to—" she broke off as she saw his expression. "Yes, I know. You don't think I deserve help, but you're wrong. I'm not who you think I am. I'm not this selfish, horrible woman you make me out to be."

"Then why did you enter Saidia with your sister's passport? I can't imagine she gave her passport to you."

"She didn't."

"I didn't think so," he ground out.

Jemma bit down on the inside of her lip, chewing her lip to keep from making a sound.

"I *know* Morgan," he added ruthlessly. "Drakon was one of my best friends. And you probably don't remember, or were too young to notice, but I attended Morgan and Drakon's wedding five years ago in Greenwich. Yes, you and Morgan might both be brunettes, but you don't look anything alike. It was beyond stupid to try to pass yourself off as her."

Fatigue and fear and dread made her heartsick, and his words drilled into her, like a hammer in her head, making her headache feel worse. She pressed her fingers to her temple to ease the pain. "How did you find out I was here?"

He shot her a cool look. "You had a very chatty stylist on the shoot. She sat in a bar two nights ago drinking and talking about the layout, the models, and you. Apparently your name was mentioned oh…a dozen times. *Jemma Copeland. That Jemma Copeland. Jemma Copeland, daughter of Daniel Copeland.* In today's age of technology and social media, it just took a couple Tweets and it went viral. One minute I was in Buenos Aires, thinking everything was fine at home, and then the next I was boarding my jet to return home to deal with *you.*"

He shifted, extending his long legs out, and she sucked in an uneasy breath. He was so big, and his legs were so long, she felt positively suffocated, trapped here in the back of the car with him.

"I wish you had just let me go. We were leaving tomorrow morning anyway," she said softly. "You were out of the country. You didn't have to rush home to have me arrested."

"No. I could have allowed the police to come for you. They were going to arrest you. They wouldn't have been as polite, or patient, as I've been. They would have handcuffed you and put you in the back of an armored truck and taken you to a jail where you'd languish for a few days, maybe a week, until you were seen by our tribunal, and then you would have been sentenced to five, ten, fifteen years…or longer…in our state run prison. It wouldn't have been pleasant. It wouldn't have been nice at all." His expression was fierce, his gaze held hers, critical, condemning. "You don't realize it, but I've done you a favor. I have intervened on your behalf, and yes, you will still serve time, but it will be in a smaller place, in a private home. My assistance allows you to serve your time under house arrest rather than a large state run prison. So you can thank your stars I found out."

"I'm amazed you'd intervene since you hate the Copelands so much."

His dark gaze met hers. "So am I."

CHAPTER THREE

FOR SEVERAL MINUTES they traveled in silence.

"So why *did* you rush home from Buenos Aires since you despise the Copelands?" she asked, unable to stifle the question, genuinely curious about his motives.

He didn't answer immediately, and when he did, his answer was short, brusque. "Drakon."

She picked her next words with care. "You must know he won't approve of you locking me up, for six months or six years. I'm his sister-in-law."

"His ex-sister-in-law. Morgan and Drakon are divorced, or separated, or something of that nature."

"But he likes me. He has a soft spot for me."

Mikael's lips compressed. "Perhaps, but you're a felon. Even as protective as he is, he will still have to come to terms with the fact that you broke the law, and there are consequences. There must be consequences. Saidia cannot be lawless. Nor can I govern at whim." His head turned, and his dark eyes met hers. For a long moment there was just silence, and then he shrugged. "And at last, the Copelands will be held accountable for their crimes."

Her stomach flipped. Her heart lurched. "You want to see me suffer," she whispered.

"Your father should have accepted responsibility and answered for his actions. Instead he ran away."

"I hate what he did, Sheikh Karim. I hate that he betrayed his customers and clients...friends. His choices sicken me —"

"There was a reason your visa was denied. The refusal was a warning. The refusal should have protected you. You should not have come."

She turned her head and swiftly wiped away tears before they could fall.

No, she shouldn't have come to Saidia. She shouldn't have broken laws.

But she had.

And now she'd pay. And pay dearly.

She felt Mikael's gaze. She knew he was watching her. His close, critical scrutiny made her pulse race. She felt cornered. Trapped.

She hated the feeling. It was suffocating. Jemma's fingers wrapped around the door handle and gripped it tight. If only she could jump from the car. Fling herself into the desert. Hide. Disappear.

But of course it wouldn't work like that.

Her father had tried to evade arrest and he'd taken off in his yacht, setting across the ocean in hopes of finding some bit of paradise somewhere.

Instead his yacht had been commandeered off the coast of Africa and he'd been taken hostage and held for ransom. No one had paid. He'd been hostage for months now and the public loved it. They loved his shame and pain.

Jemma flinched and pressed her hands together, fingers lacing. She didn't like thinking about him, and especially didn't like to think of him helpless in some African coastal village.

If only he hadn't run.

If only he hadn't stolen his clients' money.

If only...

"The doors are locked," Mikael said flatly. "There is no escape."

Her eyes burned. She swallowed around the lump in her throat. "No," she murmured, "there isn't, is there?"

She turned her head away again, trembling inwardly. It had been such a bad, bad year. She still felt wrecked. Trashed. Devastated by her father's duplicity and deceit. And then heart-broken by Damien's rejection.

To have your own father destroy so many people's lives, and then to have the love of your life abruptly cast you off…

She couldn't have imagined that her life would derail so completely. One day everything was normal and then the next, absolute chaos and mayhem.

The media had converged on her immediately in London, camping outside her flat, the journalists three rows deep, each with cameras and microphones and questions they shouted at her every time she opened her front door.

"Jemma, how does it feel to know that your father is one of the biggest con artists in American history?"

"Do you or your family have any plans to pay all these bankrupt people back?"

"Where is all the money, Jemma?"

"Did your father use stolen money to pay for this flat?"

It had been difficult enduring the constant barrage of questions, but she came and went, determined to work, to keep life as normal as possible.

But within a week, the jobs disappeared.

She was no longer just Jemma, the face of Farrinelli, but that American, that Jemma *Copeland*.

Every major magazine and fashion house she'd been booked to work for had cancelled on her in quick succession.

It was bad enough that six months of work was lost, but then Damien had started losing jobs, too.

Damien couldn't get work.

Farrinelli cancelled Jemma's contract as the face of Farrinelli Fragrance. Damien didn't wait for Farrinelli to replace him too. He left Jemma, their flat, their life.

Jemma understood. She was bad for his career. Bad for business. For Damien. Farrinelli. Everyone.

Heartsick, miserable, she opened her eyes to discover Sheikh Karim watching her.

Tears filled her eyes. She was ashamed of the tears, ashamed for being weak. How could she cry or feel sorry for herself? She was better off than most people. Certainly better off than the thousands of people her father had impoverished.

But she never spoke about her father, or what he did. She didn't openly acknowledge the shame, either. There were no words for it. No way to ever make amends, either.

"Please don't think this is a challenge, nor is it meant to be disrespectful," she said quietly, swiftly dashing away tears before they could fall. "But I did not come here on a lark. I am not a rebel schoolgirl. I came to Saidia because I desperately needed the work. I had thought I'd fly in, work, fly out, and no one would be the wiser. Clearly, I was wrong, and for that, I am very sorry."

Mikael listened to the apology in silence. The apology meant nothing to him. Words were easy. They slipped from the tongue and lips with ease.

Actions, now those were difficult.

Action, and consequence, those required effort. Pain. Sweat. Sacrifice.

It crossed his mind that Jemma had no idea what was coming once they reached Haslam. Sheikh Azizzi, the judge, was not a soft touch. Sheikh Azizzi was old world, old school, and determined to preserve as much of the tribal customs as possible.

He was also Mikael's godfather and intimate with Karim family history, including Mikael's parents' drawn-out divorce, and his mother's subsequent banishment from Saidia.

Sheikh Azizzi had not been a fan of his mother, but the divorce had horrified Sheikh Azizzi and all of the country. Divorce was rare in Saidia, and in a thousand years of Karim rule, there had never been a divorce in the Karim royal family, and the drama and the endless publicity around it—the news in the international papers, not Saidia's—had alienated the Saidia public.

No, Mikael's father had not been a good king. If he hadn't died when he did, there might have been an uprising.

There *would* have been an uprising.

Which is why ever since Mikael had inherited the throne, he'd vowed to be a true leader to the Saidia people. A good king. A fair king. He'd vowed to represent his country properly, and he'd promised to protect the desert kingdom's culture, and preserve ancient Saidia customs.

Thus, the trip to Haslam to see Sheikh Azizzi.

Sheikh Azizzi was both a political and spiritual figure. He was a simple man, a village elder, but brave and wise. He and Mikael's father had grown up together, both from the same village. Sheikh Azizzi's father has served as a counselor and advisor to the royal Karim family, but Sheikh Azizzi himself did not want to serve in a royal capacity. He was a teacher, a thinker, a farmer, preferring the quiet life in ancient Haslam, a town founded hundreds of years ago at the base of the Tekti Mountains.

But when a neighboring country had sought to invade Saidia fifty some years ago, Sheikh Azizzi was one of the first to volunteer to defend his country and people. He'd spent nearly two years on the front line. Halfway through, he was wounded in battle, and yet he refused to leave his fellow soldiers, inspiring the dispirited Saidia troops to fight on.

After the war ended, Sheikh Azizzi returned home, refusing all gifts, and accolades, wanting no financial reward. He wasn't interested in being a popular figure. He didn't want attention, didn't feel he deserved the attention. What he wanted was truth, peace, and stability for all Saidia people.

"I will ask Sheikh Azizzi to be fair. I cannot ask for him to be compassionate," Mikael said suddenly, his voice deep and rough in the quiet of the car. "Compassion is too much like weakness. Compassion lacks muscle, and conviction."

"Does he know about my father, and what he did to your family?"

"Yes."

"So he won't be fair."

"Fair, according to our laws. Perhaps not fair according to yours."

For two hours the convoy of cars traveled across the wide stretch of desert, before turning southeast toward the foothills and then on to the Tekti mountain range. They traveled up a narrow winding road, through the steep mountain pass, before beginning their descent into the valley below.

Finally they were slowing, the cars leaving the main road for the walled town built at the foot of the mountains.

Jemma was very glad the cars were slowing. She needed fresh air. She needed water. She needed a chance to stretch her legs.

"Haslam," the sheikh announced.

She craned her head to get a better look at the town. Twenty-foot-tall walls surrounded it. Turrets and parapets peeked above the walls. The vehicles' headlights illuminated huge wooden gates. Slowly the massive gates opened and the convoy pulled into the village.

They drove a short way before the cars parked in front of a two-story building that looked almost identical to the buildings on either side.

Jemma frowned at the narrow house. It didn't look like a courthouse or official city building. It seemed very much like an ordinary home.

The driver came around the side of the car to open the back passenger door. "We will go in for tea and conversation, but no one here will speak English," Mikael said, adding bluntly, "and they won't understand you. Or your short skirt." He leaned from the car, spoke to the driver and the driver nodded, and disappeared.

"I'm getting you a robe," Mikael said turning back to her. "It won't help you to go before Sheikh Azizzi dressed like that. I am sure you know this already, but be quiet, polite. Respectful. You are the outsider here. You need to make a good impression."

"Sheikh Azizzi is here?"

"Yes."

"I'm meeting him *now*?"

"Yes."

Fresh panic washed through her. "I thought we were going in for tea and conversation!"

"We are. This is the judicial process. It's not in a court with many observers. It's more intimate...personal. We sit at a table, have tea, and talk. Sheikh Azizzi will either come to a decision during the discussion, or he will leave and make a decision and then return to tell us what he has chosen to do."

"And it really all rests with him?"

"Yes."

"Could you not override his decision? You are the king."

Mikael studied her impassively. "I could, but I doubt I would."

"Why?"

"He is a tribal judge, and the highest in my tribe. As Bedouin, we honor our tribal elders, and he is the most respected man from my tribe."

The driver returned with a dark blue folded cotton garment and handed it to Mikael. Mikael shook out the robe and told her to slip it over her head. "This is more conservative, and should make him feel more comfortable."

She reached up and touched her hair. "Shouldn't I have a headscarf too?"

"He knows you're American, knows your father was Daniel Copeland. No need to pretend to be someone you're not."

"But I also have no wish to further offend him."

"Then perhaps braid your hair and tie it with an elastic. But your hair is not going to protect you from judgment. Nothing will. This is fate. Karma."

Jemma swiftly braided her hair and then stepped from the car, following Mikael. *Fate. Karma*. The words rang through her head as she walked behind the sheikh toward the house.

Robed men and women lined the small dirt road, bowing

deeply. Mikael paused to greet them, speaking briefly and then waving to some children who peeked from windows upstairs before leading her to the arched door of the house. The door opened and they were ushered inside.

Candles and sconces on the wall illuminated the interior. The whitewashed walls were simple and unadorned. Dark beams covered the ceiling in the entry, but the beams had been painted cream and pale gold in the living room.

As Mikael and Jemma were taken to a low table in the living room, Jemma spotted more children peeking from behind a curtain before being drawn away.

"Sit here," Mikael instructed, pointing to a pillow on the floor in front of the low square table. "To my right. Sheikh Azizzi will sit across from me, and speak to me, but this way he can see you easily."

Jemma sank onto the pillow, curling her legs under her. "He's not going to ask me anything?"

"No. Over tea I will give him the facts. He will consider the facts and then make his decision."

"Is this how you handle all tribal crimes?"

"If it's not a violent crime, why should the sentencing be chaotic and violent?"

She smoothed the soft thin cotton fabric over her knees. "But your country has a long history of aggression. Tribal warring, kidnapped brides, forced marriages." She quickly glanced at him. "I'm not trying to be sarcastic. I ask the question sincerely. How does one balance your ideal of civility in sentencing, with what we Westerners would view as barbaric tribal customs?"

"You mean, kidnapped brides?"

Her eyes widened. "No. I was referring to arranged marriages."

He said nothing. She stared at him aghast. The seconds ticked by.

Jemma pressed her hands to her stomach, trying to calm the wild butterflies. "Do you really kidnap your brides?"

"If you are a member of one of the royal families, yes."

"You're serious?"

"Yes."

"*Why*?"

He shrugged. "It's how one protects the tribe, by forging new ties through forced marriage with other tribes."

"It's barbaric."

"It settles a score."

"You sound so cavalier about a very violent act."

"The marriage might be forced, but the sex is generally consensual." His dark gaze held hers. "One takes a bride to settle a debt, but the captive bride becomes a royal wife. The marriage must be satisfying for both."

"I sincerely doubt a forced marriage can ever be satisfying!"

"A forced marriage isn't that different from an arranged marriage, and that is also foreign to your Western way of thinking, so perhaps it's better if you do not judge."

A shadow filled the doorway and an older, robed man entered the living room.

Mikael rose, and hugged the older man. They clasped each other's arm and spoke in Arabic. After a moment both Mikael and Sheikh Azizzi sat down at the table, still deep in conversation.

Sheikh Azizzi hadn't even looked at her yet. Mikael didn't glance her way either.

Their conversation was grave. No laughter, no joking. They took turns speaking, first one, and then the other. The mood in the room was somber. Intense.

They were interrupted after fifteen minutes or so by a male servant carrying a tea tray. Sheikh Azizzi and Mikael ignored the man with the tray but Jemma was grateful to see the tea and biscuits and dried fruit arrive. She was hungry, and thirsty. She eyed the teacup placed in front of her and the plate of biscuits and fruit but didn't touch either one, waiting for a signal from Mikael, or Sheikh Azizzi. But neither glanced her way.

She longed for a sip but waited instead.

They talked for at least another fifteen minutes after the tea tray was brought in. The servant came back, carried away the now cold tea on the tray, and returned five minutes later with a fresh steaming pot.

Jemma's stomach growled. She wanted to nibble on one of the biscuits. She didn't even care what the tea tasted like. She just wanted a cup.

But she sat still, and practiced breathing as if she were in her yoga class in London. Instead of getting upset, she'd meditate.

Jemma closed her eyes, and focused on clearing her mind, and her breathing. She wouldn't think about anything, wouldn't worry…

"Drink your tea, Jemma," Mikael said abruptly.

She opened her eyes, looked at him, startled to hear him use her first name, and somewhat uneasy with his tone. It hadn't been a request. It'd been a command.

He expected her to obey.

Nervous, she reached for her tea, and sipped from the cup. The tea was lukewarm. It tasted bitter. But it wet her throat and she sipped the drink slowly, as the men continued talking.

Sheikh Azizzi was speaking now. His voice was deep and low. His delivery was measured, the pace of his words deliberate.

He's sentencing me, she thought, stomach cramping. *He's giving the judgment now.* She looked quickly at Mikael, trying to gauge his reaction.

But Mikael's expression was blank. He sipped his tea, and then again. After what felt like an endless silence, he answered. His answer wasn't very long. It didn't sound very complicated, but it did sound terse. He wasn't happy.

Jemma didn't know how she knew. She just knew.

Both men were silent. Sheikh Azizzi ate a dried apricot. They sipped more tea. There wasn't any conversation at this point.

Mikael placed his cup on the table and spoke at last. His voice was quiet, and even, but there was a firmness in his tone that hadn't been there earlier. Sheikh Azizzi replied to Mikael. A very short reply.

A small muscle pulled in Mikael Karim's jaw. His lips thinned. He spoke. It sound like a one syllable reply. A fierce one syllable reply.

She glanced from Azizzi to Mikael and back. The two men stared at each other, neither face revealing any expression. After a moment, Sheikh Azizzi murmured something and rose, exiting the room and leaving Mikael and Jemma alone.

CHAPTER FOUR

THAT DID NOT go well.

Aware that Jemma was looking at him, aware that she'd been waiting patiently, exceptionally patiently for the past hour to know her fate, Mikael finally glanced at her.

Shadows danced on the walls, stretching tall across the tiled floor. He didn't like her. Didn't admire her. Didn't feel anything positive for her.

But even in the dim lighting, he recognized her great beauty.

She wasn't merely pretty, she was stunning. Her face was all hauntingly beautiful planes and angles with her high regal brow, the prominent cheekbones, a firm chin below full, generous lips.

She was pale with fatigue and fear, and her pallor made her eyes appear even greener, as if brilliant emeralds against the ivory satin of her skin.

Sitting so close to her, he could feel her fatigue. It was clear to him she was stretched thin, perhaps even to breaking.

He told himself he didn't care, but her beauty moved him. His mother had been a beautiful woman, too, just as Mikael's father's second and third wives were both exquisite. A king could have any woman. Why shouldn't she be a rare jewel?

Jemma was a rare jewel.

But she was also a rare jewel set in a tarnished, defective setting.

He now had a choice. To save the jewel, or to toss it away? It was up to him. Sheikh Azizzi had given Mikael the decision.

"Well?" Jemma whispered, breaking the tense silence. "What did he say?"

Mikael continued to study her, his thoughts random and scattered. He didn't need her. He didn't like her. He'd never love her.

But he did desire her.

It wouldn't be difficult to bed her.

He wondered how she'd respond in bed. He wondered if she'd be sweet and hot or icy and frigid.

His gut told him she'd be hot and sweet. But first, all the Copeland taint would have to be washed away. "I am to decide your punishment for you," he said finally. "I've been given a choice of two sentences and I must pick one."

"Why?"

"Because Sheikh Azizzi knows me, and he knows I wish to do what is right, but what is right isn't always what is popular."

"I don't understand."

"I am to decide if I should follow ancient law, and tribal custom, or choose a modern punishment for you."

"And have you made up your mind?"

"No."

"What are the choices given to you?"

"Seven years house arrest here in Haslam—"

"*Seven* years?"

"Or I take you as my wife."

"That's not funny. Not even remotely funny."

"It's not a joke. It's one of the two choices presented to me. Marry you, or leave you here in Haslam to begin your house arrest." He saw her recoil and her face turn white. "I warned you that Sheikh Azizzi would not be lenient. He is not a Copeland fan either. He knows what your father did to my mother, and he wanted to send a message that Saidia will not tolerate crime or immorality."

"But seven years!" She reached for the edge of the table to steady herself. "That's…that's…so long."

"Seven years, *or* marriage," he corrected.

"No. No. Marriage isn't an option. I won't marry you. I would never marry you. I could never marry you—"

"You'd rather be locked up for seven years?"

"*Yes*. Absolutely!"

Mikael leaned back, studying her pale face and bright eyes. She was biting down, pressing her teeth into her lip. "I don't believe you."

"Not my problem."

"I'm a king. I can provide a lavish lifestyle."

"Not interested." Her eyes burned at him, hot, bright. "Seven years of house arrest is infinitely better than a lifetime with you."

He should have been offended by her response. Instead he felt vaguely amused. Women craved his attention. They fought for his affections. Ever since he'd left university, he'd enjoyed considerable female company, company he'd turned into girlfriends and mistresses.

Mikael enjoyed women. He was quite comfortable with girlfriends and mistresses. But he was not at all open to taking a wife, despite the fact that as king it was his duty to marry and produce heirs.

Something he was sure Sheikh Azizzi knew. But Sheikh Azizzi, like much of Saidia, was eager for the country's king to marry as quickly as possible.

Sheikh Azizzi also knew that nothing would pain the Copeland family more than having the youngest daughter forced into a marriage against her will.

It was fitting punishment for a family that believed itself to be above the law.

But in truth Mikael didn't want a wife. He didn't want children. He didn't want entanglements of any kind. It's why he kept mistresses. He provided for them materially and in return they'd always be available to him, without making any demands. Mikael was torn between his duty and his desires.

He studied Jemma now, trying to imagine *her* as his wife.

Without her make-up he could see purple smudges beneath

her eyes and her naturally long black eye lashes. She had a heart-shaped face. Clear green eyes. Full pink lips.

The same pink as her nipples.

His body hardened, remembering her earlier, modeling, and naked beneath the fur coat.

She had an incredible body.

He would enjoy her body. But he'd never like her. Never admire her. She wasn't a woman he wanted for anything beyond sex and pleasure.

He pictured her naked again. He'd certainly find pleasure in her curves and breasts and that private place between her legs.

"So it's house arrest," Jemma said. "Seven years. Would the sentence start tonight? Tomorrow?"

"I haven't made up my mind," he answered.

Her green eyes widened. Her lips parted and for a moment no sound came out and then she shook her head, a frantic shake that left no doubt as to her feelings. "I will not marry you. I will not!"

"It's not up to you. It's my choice."

"You can't force me."

"I can." And silently he added, *I could.*

Just like that, the idea took root.

He could marry her. He could force her to his will. He could avenge his mother's shame. He could exact revenge.

For a moment there was just silence. It was thick and heavy and he imagined she must hate it. She must find the silence stifling because she was completely powerless. She had no say. He would decide her fate. She would have to accept whatever he chose for her.

He found the thought pleasing.

He liked knowing that whatever he chose, she would have to submit.

She with the lovely eyes and soft lips and full, pink tipped breasts.

"But you do not wish to marry me," she whispered. "You hate me. You wouldn't be able to look at me or touch me."

"I could touch you," he corrected. "And I could look at you. But I wouldn't love you, no."

"Don't do that to me. Don't use me."

"Why not? Your father used my mother to bring shame on my family name."

"I'm not my father and you're not your mother and we both deserve better. We both deserve good marriages, proper marriages, marriages based on love and respect."

"That sounds quite nice except for the fact that I don't love. I won't take a wife out of love. I will take her out of duty. I will marry as it is my responsibility. A king must have heirs."

"But I want love. And by forcing me to marry you, you deprive me of love."

"Your father deprived my mother of life. I'm Arabic. A life for a life. A woman for a woman. He took her. I *should* take you."

"No."

"Saidia requires a prince. You'd give me beautiful children."

"I'd never be willing in bed, and you said even in a forced marriage, the sex is consensual."

"You'd consent."

"I wouldn't."

"You'd beg me to take you."

"Never."

The corner of his mouth lifted. "You're wrong. And I will prove you wrong, and when I do, what shall you give me in return?"

Jemma rose from the table, and went to the doorway. "I want to go. I want to go now."

"I don't think that's one of my options."

Jemma didn't know where to look. Her heart raced and her eyes burned and she felt so sick inside.

This wasn't what she'd thought would happen. This wasn't how she'd imagined this would go. Jail was bad. Seven years under house arrest boggled the mind. But *marriage*?

The idea of Sheikh Karim forcing her to marry him made everything inside her shrink, collapse.

She'd thought the last year had been horrific, being shunned as Daniel Copeland's daughter, but to be married against her will?

Her eyes stung, growing hotter and grittier. She pressed her nails into her palms, determined not to cry, even as she wondered how far she'd get if she bolted from the house and ran.

Marrying Mikael Karim would break her. It would. She'd been so lonely this past year, so deeply hurt by Damien's rejection and the constant shaming by the media, as well as endless public hatred. She couldn't face a cold marriage. She needed to live, to move, to breathe, to feel, to love…

To love.

It was tragic but she needed love. Needed to love and be loved. Needed connection and contact and warmth.

"Please," she choked, the tears she didn't want filling her eyes, "please don't marry me. Please just leave me here in Haslam. I don't want to spend seven years here, but at least in seven years I could be free and go home and marry and have children with someone who wants me, and needs me, and loves me—" She broke off as Sheikh Azizzi entered the room behind her.

The village elder was accompanied by two robed men.

Jemma pressed her hands together in prayer, pleading with Mikael. "Let me stay here. Please. *Please.*"

"And what would you do here for seven years?" he retorted, ignoring the others.

"I'd learn the language, and learn to cook and I'd find ways to occupy myself."

Mikael looked at her, his dark gaze holding for an endless moment and then he turned to Sheikh Azizzi and spoke to him. Sheikh Azizzi nodded once and the men walked out.

"It's done," Mikael said.

"What's done?"

"I've claimed you. I've made you mine."

She backed up so rapidly she bumped into the wall. "*No*."

"But I have. I told Sheikh Azizzi I've claimed you as my wife, and it's done."

"That doesn't make us married. I have to agree, I have to speak, I have to consent somehow…" Her voice trailed off. She stared at Mikael, bewildered. "Don't I?"

"No. You don't have to speak at all. It's done."

"Just like that?"

"Just like that." He rose and stalked toward her. "And like this," he added, sweeping her into his arms and carrying her out of the house, into the night.

Outside, the convoy of vehicles were gone. Villagers clustered near a kneeling camel.

"Who is that for?" Jemma choked, struggling in Mikael's arms.

He tightened his grip. "Settle down," he said shortly. "Or I'll tie you to the camel."

"You wouldn't!"

"You don't think so?" he challenged, stepping through the crowd to set her in the camel's saddle.

The leather saddle was wide and hard and Jemma struggled to climb back off but Mikael had taken a leather strip from a pouch on the camel and was swiftly tying her hands together at the wrist, and then binding her wrists to the saddle's pommel.

The crowd cheered as he tethered her in place.

"Why are they cheering?" she asked, face burning, anger rolling through her as she strained to free herself.

"They know I've taken you as my wife. They know you aren't happy. They know you are ashamed. It pleases them."

"My shame pleases them?"

"Your shame and struggles are part of your atonement. *That* pleases them."

"I don't like your culture."

"And I do not like yours." He scooted her forward in the saddle, and then took a seat behind her, his big body filling the space, pressing tightly against her. "Now lean back a little."

"No."

"You'll be more comfortable."

"I can assure you, I would not be comfortable leaning against you."

"We are going to be traveling for several hours."

She shook her head, lips compressed as she fought tears. "I hate you," she whispered.

"I wouldn't have it any other way." He gave a tug on the reigns and the camel lurched to its feet.

The villagers cheered again and Mikael lifted a hand, and then they were off, heading for the gates and the desert beyond.

CHAPTER FIVE

THEY RODE FOR what felt like hours through an immense desert of undulating dunes beneath a three quarter moon. The moon's bright light illuminated the desert, painting the dunes a ghostly white.

Jemma tried to hold herself stiff and straight to avoid touching Sheikh Karim but it was impossible as time wore on, just as it was impossible to ignore his warmth stealing into her body.

A half hour into the journey she broke the silence. "Where are we going?"

"My Kasbah. My home," he said. "One of my homes," he corrected.

"Why this one?"

"It is where all Karims spend their honeymoon."

She didn't know what to say to that. She didn't know what to think, or feel. So much had happened in the past few hours that she felt numb and overwhelmed.

Part of her brain whispered she was in trouble, and yet another part hadn't accepted any of this.

It didn't make sense, this forced marriage. She kept thinking any moment she'd wake up and discover it a strange dream.

Her captor was big and solid, his chest muscular, his arms strong, biceps taut as he held her steady in the saddle, his broad back protecting her from the cold.

He struck her as powerful but not brutal. Fierce and yet not insensitive.

In a different situation she might even like him. In a different situation she might like the spicy exotic fragrance he wore. In a different situation she might find him darkly beautiful.

But it wasn't a different situation. There was no way she could find him attractive, or appealing. She wasn't attracted to him, or the hard planes of his chest, or even aware of the way his muscular thighs cradled her, pinning her between his hips and the saddle's pommel.

They lapsed back into a silence neither tried to break. But an hour later, Mikael, shifted, drawing her closer to him. "There," he said. "My home."

Jemma stared hard into the dark, but could see nothing. "Where?"

"Straight in front of us."

But there was nothing in front of them. Just sand. "I don't see—"

"Watch."

The brilliant moonlight rippled across the desert, bathing all in ghostly white.

And then little by little the desert revealed a long wall, and then a bit later she was able to see shapes behind the wall. The shapes became shadowy clay buildings.

In the middle of the night, in the glow of moonlight, it looked like a lost world. As if they'd traveled back in time.

She sucked in a nervous breath as they approached massive wooden gates cut into the towering clay walls. Two enormous gas lanterns hung on either side of the dark wooden gate, and Mikael shouted out in Arabic as they reached them, and just like that, the gates split, and slowly opened, revealing square turrets and towers within.

Robed people poured into the courtyard as the gates were shut and locked behind them.

They were lining up before the first building with its immense keyhole doorway, bowing repeatedly.

"What's happening?" she whispered.

"We're being welcomed by my people. They have heard I've brought home my bride."

The camel stopped moving. Robed men moved forward. Mikael threw the reins and one of the men took it, and commanded the camel to kneel.

Sheikh Karim jumped off the camel, and then turned to look at her. His gaze held hers, his expression fierce. "What we have just done is life changing. But we've made a commitment, and we shall honor that commitment."

Then he swung her into his arms and carried her through the tall door of his Kasbah, into a soaring entrance hall, its high white plaster ceiling inset with blue and gold mosaic tile.

He set her on her feet, and added, "Welcome, my wife, to your new home."

A slender robed female servant led Jemma through the Kasbah's labyrinth of empty halls. The maid was silent. Jemma was grateful for the silence, exhausted from the long day and hours of travel. The last time she'd glanced at her watch it had been just after midnight, and that had to be at least an hour ago now.

The silent maid led Jemma down one hallway to another, until they reached a white high ceilinged room with walls covered in delicate ivory latticework. The bed's silk coverlet was also white and stitched with threads of the palest gold and silver, while silver and white silk curtains hung on either side of the tall French doors which opened to a courtyard of ivory stone and planters filled with palms, gardenias and white hibiscus.

The room wasn't huge but it was opulent, elegant, and blissfully serene, an inviting, soothing oasis after a grueling and frightening day.

"Tea? Refreshment, Your Highness?" the maid asked in polite, accented English.

Your Highness?

Jemma glanced behind her, expecting Mikael to be there. But no one stood behind Jemma. The room was empty.

And then it hit her. The maid was speaking to her. They

all knew she'd married Mikael, then. They all knew she was his bride…

Would he come to her tonight? Did he expect to consummate the marriage tonight?

Jemma sank down on one of the white sofas in the sitting area, no longer sure her legs would support her.

"No, thank you," she said. "I'm fine. I think I just want to sleep."

"Shall I draw you a bath before I leave?"

Still dazed, Jemma nodded. "Yes, please."

A few minutes later the maid had gone and steam wafted from the bathroom, fragrant with lilacs and verbena.

Jemma entered the grand white marble and tiled bathroom with the gleaming gold fixtures, the sunken tub illuminated by a multitude of dazzling crystal chandeliers above.

Awed by the grandeur, she stripped off her dusty robe and gritty clothes and slid into the water for a soak.

The hot scented bath felt so good after the jarring camel ride that Jemma was reluctant to leave the bath until the water began to cool. By the time she finally pulled the plug, she could barely keep her eyes open another moment.

Wrapped in an enormous plush white towel she returned to her bedroom, not at all sure what she'd wear to sleep in, and there on the oversized bed was a simple white cotton nightgown with lace trim at the shoulders and hem.

Jemma slipped the nightgown over her head, gave her long hair another quick towel-dry and then climbed beneath the soft smooth cotton coverlet, desperate to sleep. She didn't even remember trying to fall asleep. She was out within minutes of turning off her bedside lamp.

She was still sleeping deeply when woken by a firm, insistent knock on the outer door.

Opening her eyes, she frowned at the dimly lit room, confused by what she saw. It took her a moment to figure out where she was. Sheikh Karim's Kasbah.

And then she remembered—she'd married him.

Or so he'd said. She didn't feel married. She didn't feel anything at all but sleepy and numb.

Jemma slid her legs from the bed and slipped on the white robe she'd seen draped over a chair before she answered the outer door.

It was Mikael.

"Good afternoon," he said.

She tucked a tangled strand of hair behind her ear. "Afternoon?"

"It's after two."

"Is it? I can't believe it."

"I've ordered coffee to be sent to you, and then you're to join me for a late lunch in the east pavilion. Don't be late." He turned and walked toward the door, but Jemma followed.

"That sounds rather rude, Sheikh Karim," she said, following after him. "Is that how you speak to all your women?"

He glanced at her. "I'm accustomed to being in charge."

"That's fine, but you don't need to be quite so aggressive. A little kindness and courtesy can go a long way."

"I thought I was being kind and courteous by sending coffee to you."

"Yes, but then you ruined it by ordering me to join you, tacking on a warning not to be late. It would have been much nicer if you'd simply asked me to join you in thirty minutes."

"Kings do not ask, Jemma. They command."

"I'm sorry, but I didn't marry a king. I married a man. That is, if we are truly married…"

"We are married. Quite married. As married as one can be in Saidia," he said, cutting her off, and walking back toward her. "But if it takes our consummating the marriage to feel married, then so be it. Tonight I will take you to my bed and there won't be any question in your mind afterwards."

"That's not what I want!"

"How do you know? You've never been in my bed. I think once you are there, you'll like it very much." And then he was gone.

* * *

The next half hour seemed endless to Jemma. He was planning on consummating the marriage tonight?

But she didn't even know him.

She couldn't imagine having sex with him.

He couldn't be serious.

And yet here she was, in the Kasbah, being waited on hand and foot, so she didn't doubt him anymore. He wasn't a man who made jokes. He meant what he said, which meant…

He intended to bed her tonight.

Jemma's clothes from last night had been washed and dried and returned to her. She dressed in the short skirt and blouse, and then slipped her feet into her high wedges. Her hair was wild, a thick tangle of waves from falling asleep with it still wet, and she subdued the waves as best as she could, pulling the long mass into a ponytail and then adding some fat silver bangles to her wrist and simple silver hoops to her ears. Not very fancy but it was the best she could do.

And then the maid knocked on the door. She'd returned to escort Jemma to lunch, leading her through the maze of hallways and halls to a door that led outside to a beautiful walled garden shaded by palms with a tiled fountain in the center of the courtyard.

Mikael was already there, waiting for her.

"I recognize those clothes," he said.

"It's all I have with me."

"I had some gowns put in your wardrobe."

"I didn't see them," she answered, aware that she hadn't looked, either.

He was silent a moment, studying her. "We need to talk, but you also need to eat, so we shall sit, and eat, and talk and hopefully become better acquainted so this wedding night will be more…comfortable…for you."

She made a soft sound of protest. "I don't think eating and talking will make anything about tonight comfortable. I can't believe this is real. Can't believe any of this is happening. I didn't say any vows. I didn't agree to anything."

"You didn't have to. I claimed you and that was all that was needed. My word is law."

"That makes for a very quick and convenient ceremony."

"The ceremony might be quick, but the honeymoon isn't. We will stay together here for sixteen days before we return to my palace in the capitol."

"You don't even like me. How can you contemplate bedding me?"

His lips quirked. It was as close to a smile as she had ever seen from him. "You are not an unattractive woman, Jemma. And I'm sure you are quite aware that a man can desire a woman without engaging one's emotions."

"So when you bed me tonight, it will be without tenderness or passion."

"If you are worried about the act itself, you needn't be. I am a skillful lover. I will take my time and be sure to satisfy your needs. It wouldn't be a proper honeymoon if I didn't."

A proper honeymoon.

A proper honeymoon was the trip to Bali with Damien. They'd already booked their air and hotels when he'd broken it off. She'd planned a wedding that hadn't taken place. And now she was married without a wedding and trapped here for a honeymoon she didn't want.

Her eyes burned. Her throat ached. Jemma blinked and looked away, across the courtyard, to the splashing fountain. The water danced and trickled and it amazed her that the water could be so light and tinkling when her heart felt so heavy and broken.

"I don't want to be pleasured," she whispered, reaching up to brush away a tear before it could fall. "I don't want any of this."

"You will become less resistant to the idea as time goes on."

She choked on a hysterical laugh as she glanced at him. "You think?"

He shrugged. "I imagine for you, being from a Western culture, this is terribly strange, but it is not as strange for me. I hadn't ever expected to marry for love. I've known all along that my bride would be from a different tribe. I just didn't expect it to be...yours."

"The despised Copelands."

"Fortunately, you are no longer a Copeland, but a Karim. You've left your family and are now a member of mine. You have a new name. A new start. And new responsibilities. I think it will be good for you." He gestured to the table in the shade. "We can talk more, as we eat. Sit—" he broke off, even as her eyebrows arched.

His lips curved grimly. He gave her a slight bow. "Forgive me," he drawled, not sounding the least bit apologetic. "Let *us* sit. We should try to be comfortable."

She didn't like his tone, and she hated the situation. Nothing about this was right. She would have gladly picked jail or house arrest over being trapped with him. "I can't eat. I'm too upset."

"Then I shall eat, and you can watch, because I am hungry."

"And you wonder why I'm not excited about this honeymoon."

"Yes, I do wonder. By choosing you as my first wife, I've made you a queen. You are wealthy beyond measure. That should please you to no end."

"I've had money. I don't care about money. I care about kindness, and decency. Strength. Compassion. Integrity."

"I have all that, too, so you're in luck. Now, let's eat."

"You are not compassionate."

"I am, for those requiring compassion. But you, my queen, do not need my compassion. You are doing an excellent job feeling sorry for yourself already."

She exhaled in a quick rush. "You lack sensitivity, Sheikh Karim."

"Possibly, as well as patience. Particularly when I am hungry." His dark gaze met hers and held. "But you are only making this more difficult for yourself. Fighting me, fighting the marriage, fighting to accept that we are married and that this marriage is real. I take our vows very seriously."

"What vows? I said none!"

"I claimed you, I've married you," he said, "and so it is done. Now sit. Before I carry you to the table myself."

Reluctantly, unwillingly, Jemma took a seat at the low table inside the shaded pavilion kept cool by overhead fans.

She hadn't thought she could eat, but the first course of chilled soup settled her stomach and she was able to eat some of the grilled meat and vegetables in the second and third courses. She felt better with food, calmer and less jittery. But even then, she was in shock. She thought she'd be in shock for quite some time.

There wasn't much conversation during the meal, which was fine with her. Instead Mikael studied her from across the table as if he were a scientist and she an animal he was observing.

He was the animal, though.

Maybe not an animal. But he was the one that was untamed and unpredictable. The very air around him seemed to snap and crackle with energy and tension, making the soft afternoon light dangerous, mysterious, while her heart raced and her pulse drummed, too thick and quick in her veins.

"Saidia is nothing like your country. Saidia is still essentially tribal in culture," Mikael said, as the last of the dishes were cleared away and he rinsed his fingers in a bowl of hot scented water and dried them on a soft cloth before sending the bowl and towel away. "I expect it will take you time to adjust to our culture, but you must keep an open mind. Our customs will be foreign to you but there is a reason for everything, and value to everything we do."

"And that includes kidnapping one's bride?"

"Most definitely."

"I don't see how kidnapping a woman can ever be justified. Women are not objects, not property."

"Only princes and kings, members of the royal family, kidnap a young woman for marriage."

"That's even worse."

He shook his head. "The custom of kidnapping one's bride goes back a thousand years. It helps protect one's family and society by strengthening tribal relations, forging bonds between rival tribes, protecting one's women and children from nomad tribes that might seek to prey on vulnerable tribes."

"I'm sorry. I still can't wrap my head around the custom."

"Many of Saidia's young people joke about the ancient customs when attending university, but if you asked them if forced marriages and arranged marriages should be banned, not one of them would vote to have them outlawed. It's part of our history. It's a big part of our cultural identity."

"So not all Saidia citizens have an arranged marriage?"

"About half of our young people in the urban areas choose a love marriage. If you move away from the big cities, nearly everyone prefers arranged marriages."

"Why the difference?"

He shrugged. "In the desert, people strongly identify with their tribe and tribal customs. You don't have the influence of technology. Towns are remote. Travel is difficult and change is viewed with suspicion. When you come to Haslam or the other desert communities south of the Takti Mountains, it's like traveling back in time. Haslam isn't the city capitol. The desert isn't urban. And I, as the king, must be sensitive to the new and old faces of my country. I can't alienate the youth in the city, but I must also respect the youth in the desert."

"They don't both want the same thing?"

"They don't want the same thing, nor do they understand each other. It's been a struggle for us, in terms of keeping Saidia connected. When our students are ten, we try to encourage the children to do an exchange; children from the desert leaving home to spend a week in the city with a host family, and the children in the city to go to the desert for a week. It used to be mandated but that became problematic. We still want children to participate, but our city children are bored by the desert and the lack of entertainment, and the children from the desert are overwhelmed by the city noise, pollution, and frenetic activity."

"So what do you do?"

"Try to respect both aspects of the Saidia culture, and be careful not to alienate either."

"It's a balancing act," she said.

"Absolutely." He studied her a long moment, his gaze slowly sweeping from her face down to her shoulders and then breasts. "I don't want to see you in those clothes anymore. I have provided you with a wardrobe, a more suitable wardrobe for the climate, the Kasbah, and our honeymoon."

Jemma had just begun to relax, forgetting her own situation having been pleasantly distracted by the discussion, but suddenly reality came crashing back. She tensed, flushed, angered as well as frustrated. "Is that a request or a command, Your Highness?"

"Both."

"It can't be both. It's either one or the other."

He gave his dark head a shake. "There you go again, making it difficult. You don't need to resist so much."

"Oh, I do. I most certainly do. I'm not a doll, or a mindless puppet. I'm an adult, a woman, and very independent. I've been on my own, and paying my own bills, since I was eighteen. I value my independence, too."

"I appreciate spirit, but there is a difference between spark, stubbornness and plain stupidity." He lifted his hand to stop her before she could speak. "And no, I'm not saying you are stupid. But right now you're stubborn. If the stubbornness continues too much longer, then yes, you've moved into stupidity."

Her cheeks burned. Her temper blazed. "I could say the same for you. You are equally stubborn in your refusal to see me for who I am."

"I see exactly who you are."

"A criminal Copeland!"

"No." He leaned forward, his dark gaze boring into her. "My wife."

Something in his words and fierce, intense gaze stripped her of speech and the ability to think.

For a moment she simply sat there, dazed, and breathless.

"You *are* going to experience culture shock," he said firmly, "but I fully expect you to adjust. We will be here until you adjust. So instead of arguing with me about everything, I think it is time you tried to be more open minded about this, us, and marriage to a Saidia king."

"I'm trying."

"No, I don't think you are, not yet. But I have all day. We have all day. We have all night. We have weeks, actually."

Her lips pressed firm. She glanced away, studying the exotic pink and blue mosaic tile work on the inside of the pavilion. The tiles were beautiful, the colors gorgeous, and unabashedly romantic. The remote Kasbah would have been extremely romantic if she were here, with someone else. Someone like Damien.

She still loved him.

Or maybe, she still loved who she thought he had been. Loving, strong, protective.

Turned out he wasn't so loving. Or protective. His strength was an illusion…all beautiful body and muscle but no core. No spine. No backbone, at least not when it was needed.

"You're not going to cry, are you?" Mikael asked, a hint of roughness in his deep voice.

She shook her head hard. "No."

"You're looking very sad at the moment. Thoroughly crushed. Don't tell me that twelve hours of marriage to me has broken you already."

Jemma jerked her chin up. "Not crushed, or broken. Nor will I be. I won't give any man that kind of power over me."

"Not even that pretty model ex-boyfriend of yours?"

Jemma stifled a gasp. So Mikael had done his research then, and discovered her humiliation at the hands of Damien. She lifted her chin defiantly.

"Especially not him."

"Mmm." But Mikael didn't sound as if he believed her.

"Damien hurt me, but he didn't break me. And my father hurt me, but he didn't break me. And you, Sheikh Karim, might intimidate me, and bully me, but you will not break me, either."

"I do not bully you."

"Oh yes, you do. At least, you try to."

He leaned farther back into the pillows surrounding the low table. The corner of his mouth curved. "You really aren't afraid of me?"

"Why should I be afraid? You're Drakon's friend. You came to his wedding. You saved me from seven years of jail."

He must have heard the ironic note in her voice because the corners of his mouth quirked, and that faint lift of his lips made her heart suddenly do a strange double thump.

The man was extremely intimidating, and yet when he smiled, even this faint half-smile, he became dangerously attractive.

"Ah, yes, I saved you from jail. And you, my queen, are so very grateful."

She didn't miss his sarcasm. "I would have been more grateful if you'd put me on a plane back to London. That would have been nice."

"Indeed, it would have been. But terribly weak on my part. A man must have morals, and principles, and a king even more so."

She stood up and paced restlessly around the pavilion. She knew he watched her. She glanced at him and saw the same, faint smile playing at his lips, eyes gleaming. He seemed amused or entertained. Maybe both. "You're in a good mood," she said, facing him from across the pavilion.

"Would you prefer it if I were in a bad mood?"

Jemma didn't need to think about that one too much. "No, but surely you didn't anticipate taking a Copeland daughter for your wife?"

"That is correct. But you are easy to look at, and I am quite certain, a pleasure to hold."

"That sounds terribly shallow."

His broad shoulders shifted. "It's not a love match. I don't have to like you, or love you. I just need you, as my first wife, to be good, obedient and fertile."

She stiffened and looked at him askance. *First wife*? There would be others? "Multiple wives, Your Highness?"

"Traditional Islamic law allows men four wives, but a man must be able to treat them equally. And not all men choose to have multiple wives. It's really an individual decision."

She couldn't help laughing. It struck her as terribly wrong, and yet also, terribly funny. This wasn't her life. This couldn't be happening. He might as well have plucked her from the photo shoot and locked her in his harem. "Do you intend to take more wives?"

"I haven't thought that far, but my father had four wives. My grandfather, his father, just had two."

But two wives was still one too many.

She shot him a swift glance, trying to decide if he was joking. She hoped he was. Or hoped he'd come to his senses and let her return home. "I thought the practice of polygamy had been outlawed in modern Arab countries," she said, leaning against one of the columns supporting the pavilion arches.

"Tunisia did, yes," he agreed, "But most other countries have focused on reform. In Iraq, a man can take a second wife if he obtains permission from the government, while Morocco and Lebanon have added a clause in the premarital contract, allowing a woman to divorce her husband if he takes a second wife without her consent."

"Were your father's wives happy?"

He reached for a bite of mango from the platter of dried and fresh fruit. "Most of them. He was an excellent provider. But my father was also good to them. Respectful. Tried to please them. Refused to beat them."

Jemma's jaw dropped. "And that constitutes a good husband?"

His dark eyes met hers across the table. He arched a brow. "Don't you think so?"

"No."

"Marriage in Saidia is a duty. It's our duty to have children. It is through marriage we gain family, and family is our most cherished institution. Family is everything here. You protect your family at all costs." He paused for a half second. "Which is how your father failed you. He refused to protect you."

CHAPTER SIX

MIKAEL STUDIED JEMMA as she leaned against the column, her face turned away from him, giving him just her profile.

The late afternoon sun dappled her with light and shadows. He was too far away to see the freckles across the bridge of her nose but he imagined them there, as well as the soft pink of her lips.

Looking at her from across the pavilion made him remember her working yesterday, posing for that Australian photographer. She'd been so fierce and determined as the sun beat down on her, baking her inside the fur and thigh-high boots. But she hadn't complained, nor had she as they'd traveled by camel to the Kasbah late last night, her slim warm body against his chest and thighs. He'd felt protective of her last night as they'd crossed the desert. He'd been aware of the dangers in the desert, but even more aware of her.

Last night she'd stirred now and then, restless, and probably uncomfortable, but she hadn't uttered a word. He'd respected her for that.

He had wished she wouldn't wiggle though, as each time she shifted in his arms, her back had rubbed against his chest, and her small, firm backside had pressed against his groin.

He had tried not to think about her firm backside, her rounded hips or her full soft breasts, which he'd seen in all their glory earlier.

And now she was his wife. His bride.

The villagers of Haslam had been happy for him. His people wanted him settled. They wanted him to have children. They wanted to know that there was an heir, and a spare, and then another dozen more. They were also glad he'd taken a bride, following tradition. Tradition was still so very important in Saidia.

Mikael's gaze followed the play of sunlight and shadows over her body. She looked lithe and lovely in her clothes. He was looking forward to getting her out of them. He wondered what she'd be like in bed.

"Do you really hate him?" he asked, reaching for a date and rolling it between his fingers.

"My father?" she asked, clarifying his question.

"Yes."

Her shoulders twisted and she looked away, turning her head so that he could see just the curve of her ear and the line of her smooth jaw. "He did terrible things," she whispered.

Mikael said nothing.

Jemma drew a deep breath, her chest aching, her heart blistered. "But no, I don't hate him. I hate what he did to us. I hate what he did to those who trusted him. But he's my father, the only father I've ever known, and years ago, when I was little, he was like a king. Handsome, and charming and powerful, but also fun. For my fifth birthday, he brought the circus to me. We had a whole circus set up in our front yard with a big top tent, and acrobats and clowns and everything. He organized that. He made it happen." She sighed. "My parents divorced just before I turned six. I didn't see him very much after that."

"So he was a good father when you were little?"

"In a young child's eyes, yes. But during the divorce the battle lines were drawn and I, due to my age, went to Mother. All of us went with Mother, except Morgan, who chose to live with our father."

"Do you know why your parents divorced?"

Jemma hesitated. "I think he wasn't faithful."

"Was the divorce quite bitter?"

"Not as acrimonious as it could have been. They divided up kids and property and went on with their lives."

"But neither married again."

"No. Mother was too upset—she'd loved my father—and he didn't want to lose any more assets."

"This is why love marriages are dangerous. Far better to go in with a contract and no romantic illusions, than enter the marriage with impossible hopes and dreams of a fairy tale relationship that can't exist."

"But in an arranged marriage there is no love."

"Love isn't necessary for a good marriage. In fact, love would just make things more difficult."

"How shall I fulfill…my duties…without love?"

For a moment he was baffled, and then amused. Her point of view was so peculiarly Western. As if only those who had a romantic relationship could find satisfaction in bed. "Love isn't necessary for physical pleasure."

Jemma saw him rise from the cushions and walk around the table. She swallowed hard as he approached her, not knowing where to look, or what to do. Her heart was pounding and her brain felt scrambled.

"Marriage isn't all bad," he added quietly, circling her. "Our marriage will honor you. You are my queen. The first lady in my land. There will be no more public scorn. No more shaming. You will be protected."

His voice was a deep, low rumble, the pitch husky and strangely seductive. Jemma turned her head, watched his mouth. His firm lips suddenly fascinated her. "Until you take your next wife," she said, feeling almost breathless.

"Would you feel differently if you were my only wife?" he asked, reaching out to lift a dark strand of hair from her eyelashes and tuck it carefully behind her ear, his fingertips then caressing the curve of her ear before falling away.

His skin had been so warm, and his touch had been light,

fleeting, and yet she'd felt it all the way through her, a ripple of pleasure.

Aware that she'd never survive, not if she remained this close, Jemma moved away, crossing to the far end of the pavilion where the light was even more dappled. "Are you saying I would be your only wife?" she asked.

"I never planned on taking more than one wife," he answered.

"If you hoped to reassure me, you're not succeeding."

"Do you need reassurance? Is that what this is about?" He was moving toward her again, walking slowly, confidently, relaxed and yet still somehow regal.

Jemma's heart hammered harder as he closed the distance. She didn't feel safe. She didn't feel comfortable or in control.

He didn't stop walking until he was directly in front of her, less than a foot away. "There is always anxiety on a honeymoon," he added, his voice dropping, his tone soothing. "It is natural to feel fear…even reluctance. But you will soon realize there is nothing to be afraid of. You will discover you can trust me. That you are safe with me. Safe to explore your fantasies."

"No!" Her voice spiked as she put a hand out to stop him, unable to imagine exploring any fantasies with him. This was so overwhelming. "This is too much, moving too fast."

She pushed past him to leave the pavilion and step into the sun. She felt his gaze follow her. "You need to give me time," she insisted. "You need to let me come to terms with everything."

"You've had the day."

She spun around. "No, it's not even been a full day. I was asleep until just a couple hours ago. You're not being fair. I need time. Time to accept the changes. Time to accept this new future."

"You will have that time, but you do not need to spend it alone. I think it is essential we spend time together, forming a relationship, and creating the foundation for our future."

She made a soft sound of protest. "How do you expect us

to have a relationship when there is no give or take? When you make the demands and insist on compliance? How can we have anything when you have all the power and control?"

"My power will never be used to hurt you. My power protects you, just as it protected you on the shoot, and then again in Haslam."

"You say you will protect me, but you forget what I'm sacrificing…my independence, my career, my friends, my hopes, my dreams." She shook her head. "But how do I know you will truly protect me? How do I know I can trust you when you use your power to subjugate my will?"

He looked at her, eyebrows lifted. "Because I've given you my word. My word is law."

"In Saidia, maybe. But I'm not Arab or Bedouin. I'm American. And my father said many things, but as we both know, he meant none of them. Damien said more things, promising me love and safety and security, and he didn't mean them, either. So no, I don't trust you. But that's because I don't trust men. How can I? Why should you be any different?"

He didn't speak, but this time he was listening. Carefully. Closely.

"You want a good wife," she said breathlessly. "Well, I want a good husband. I want a kind husband. You say you have integrity and strength. How do I know that? You must allow me to discover the truth myself. You need to allow me to develop trust. And that will take time. You must give me time to prove you are indeed a good man, a strong man, not a liar or a cheat." She pressed her lips together to stop them from trembling. "I understand that my family owes your family something. But I think you owe *me* something."

"You will have my wealth, and more riches than you can imagine."

"I don't want riches! Money doesn't buy happiness." Her fist went to her chest. "And I want happiness. This last year has been awful. Damien didn't break me, but he broke my heart. He hurt me so badly and I'm not ready for more pain."

"So what do you want?"

"Hope," she whispered. "I want hope."

"I don't understand."

"I want to believe that if this…marriage…is not good for me, if you are not good for me, you will set me free."

He said nothing. She could tell she'd surprised him. Caught him off guard.

"I cannot spend my life here in Saidia an unhappy hostage. I can't imagine you'd want such a woman for your wife, either. For that matter, I can't imagine your mother would want you to make your wife so terribly unhappy."

"Do you know anything of my mother?" he asked, his voice sharp.

She shook her head. "No."

"Then maybe it's time you learned who I am, and where I've come from. Follow me."

Jemma trailed after Mikael as he exited the courtyard. They traveled through a maze of hallways. Every time she was sure he'd turn right, he turned left. When she anticipated him turning left, he went right. The Kasbah halls seemed to be circular. It made no sense to her.

Finally he stopped in a spacious hall topped with a skylight and opened the tall door. "This is my personal wing," he said. "It includes a bedroom, office and living room, so I can work when here, should I need to."

She followed him through the tall door into a handsome living room. Wooden panels had been pulled back from the trio of windows and sunlight flooded the room, making the pair of low sapphire velvet couches glow and the gold painted walls shimmer.

They continued through the living room into another room, this one also bright with natural light as one entire wall was made of glass doors.

The room itself was sparsely furnished, the buff stone walls unpainted, and the plush carpet beneath her feet intricately woven of pale gold, faded blue, and a coral pink.

A low couch was on one side of the room while an enormous dark wood desk inlaid with pearl dominated the other side, positioned to face glass doors with the view of a spacious, but Spartan courtyard.

He crossed the floor to the desk, opened a drawer, and drew out a small jeweled picture frame. He held the frame out to her. "This is my mother at twenty-three, just two years younger than you are now."

She took the frame from him. The woman was young and blonde and very beautiful. She had straight bangs and high, elegant cheekbones. Her long hair hid one shoulder and her blue eyes were smiling, laughing, up at the camera.

"She's...so fair," Jemma said, brows tugging as she studied the laughing beautiful girl with straight white-blonde hair.

"She was American."

Jemma's head jerked up. Her gaze met his.

He nodded once. "Your mother was descended from a Mayflower family. So was my mother. She was American as apple pie."

Jemma felt a lump grow in her throat. She looked back down at the photo, noting the girl's swimsuit and cover up and the blue of the sea behind her. "Where was this taken?"

"The Cote d'Azur. My father met her when she was on holiday with friends in Nice. My father swept her off her feet. They were married within months of meeting."

"She's so beautiful."

"She was young and romantic and in love with my father... as well as in love with the idea of becoming Saidia's queen."

Jemma handed the framed photo to him. He put it back in the drawer. "My father betrayed her trust," he said quietly. "And then your father betrayed her trust. Which is why I promise you, I will not betray you. I am a man of my word. And if I vow to provide for you properly, I will. Over time our marriage will hopefully heal the rift between families and countries. It won't be immediate. It might not even happen in our generation, but I hope that it will be better for our children." He studied her, expression fierce, resolute. "We begin our journey as husband and wife tonight, by sharing our first meal together in the Bridal Palace."

Jemma's throat ached. She felt close to tears. "Would your mother approve of what you're doing?"

"Leave her out of this."

"How can I?" she choked. "You don't!"

"One day you will understand the importance of honor. One day when we have our children—"

"No!"

"That is fair. You are right. I will save the talk of children for later. Instead let us focus on tonight, and how we shall retreat to the Bridal Palace, for the first of our eight nights. For the next eight nights, I will pleasure you."

"And what happens after that eighth night?" Jemma asked tartly. "Do you disappear into your suite? Return to Buenos Aires? What happens then?"

"You are in control for the next eight nights. You get to pick a different pleasure each evening, or the same pleasure, or…no pleasure."

She frowned, not understanding.

He saw her expression, correctly reading her confusion. "According to Saidia law, the first eight nights are the groom's. The next eight nights are the bride's. The Saidia bride doesn't have to take her husband into her room, or her bed, for any of the next eight nights, unless she wants to. What happens during the second eight nights is entirely her choice."

"What is the point of that?" Jemma asked.

"It was to teach a randy bridegroom not to be selfish in bed, and provide an incentive for the groom to be patient and tender with his new bride, pleasuring her so thoroughly that she'll hunger for her husband's touch."

Jemma's cheeks were on fire again. Heat coursed through her, her skin prickled, suddenly almost too sensitive.

Mikael's dark eyes met hers. "And I assure you, I intend to

please you so thoroughly you'll beg me to return to your bed for every night of your eight nights."

She drew a slow breath, head spinning. Everything inside of her felt tight, tense.

"I have never heard of any honeymoon being so purely… carnal and erotic."

"It might sound like that, until you remember that most royal brides brought here were innocent virgins, carried here against their will. As I told you, it was customary for the royal groom to kidnap a bride from one of the rival desert tribes. The honeymoon was his chance to win his bride's affection, and loyalty, before he took her home with him. But, if he couldn't win her affections by the end of the sixteen days, then she could leave him without repercussions or shame."

That last bit caught Jemma's attention. "She could choose to go home?"

"If he couldn't make her happy in their sixteen days together." He reached out, stroked the sweep of her cheekbone, making her skin tingle. "I will please you," he said, quietly, decisively. "I promise to satisfy you completely."

She stared at him, wide-eyed, heart pounding. She'd loved Damien and she'd been quite sure Damien had loved her, but he'd never been overly concerned with pleasing her. Pleasuring her.

She couldn't quite get her head around the idea that Mikael was promising to satisfy her completely.

Sexually.

Fulfilling her every fantasy.

"You are making a lot of promises," she said unevenly, her mouth drying.

"They are promises I fully intend to keep."

"I worry that you are…unrealistic."

His hard expression softened. Amusement glimmered in his eyes. "I worry that your expectations are too low." His lips curved faintly. "Perhaps it's time I show you the Kasbah? This is no ordinary desert palace. Its outer walls hide a secret palace."

"A secret palace?" She looked at him, intrigued. "What does that mean? That there's a palace within the palace?"

"Yes. That is exactly what I do mean. Would you like to see? I can take you on a tour of the Bridal Palace now if you're interested."

The Bridal Palace? Was that its real name? Her eyebrows arched. "I'm very interested."

He smiled. "Good. We will start the tour with the rooms near your suite."

CHAPTER SEVEN

THEY LEFT HIS rooms, and walked through the maze of halls and corridors with Mikael giving her the history of the palace as they returned to her wing. "This Kasbah is known in Saidia as the Bridal Palace. For hundreds of years this is where the king of Saidia brought his new bride after the wedding ceremony. It is where the royal couple honeymoons, and where the king or prince would introduce his virgin bride to the pleasures of the marriage bed."

Mikael pointed down one hall, which led to the entrance of the Kasbah. "The bride would arrive, and pass through the same entrance you passed through last night, and then be escorted by her new maids to this wing. On arrival, the bride would be bathed, massaged with fragrant oils, then robed and taken to the first chamber, the white chamber—a room hidden off your room—which historically has been called the Chamber of Innocence. In the Chamber of Innocence, the groom claims his bride, consummating the marriage. In the morning, the bride is transferred to a different suite.

"Here," he added, walking down another hall to a different corridor and taking a turn to the right. "This is the Emerald Chamber." He opened the only door in the corridor and stepped back to let her have a look. "This is where the bride and groom spend their second day."

Jemma carefully moved past him to glance around the room. The walls were glazed green, the floor was laid with green and white tiles. The bed was gold with green silk covers and a dozen gold lanterns hung from the ceiling.

"There's a courtyard attached," he said. "The garden is fantastic, and the pool looks like a secret grotto."

They stepped out of the room, into the hall. They walked in a circular pattern, continuing right, down another hall to another door. "The Amethyst Room," he said, and it was a room of purple and gold, even more luxurious and exotic than the Emerald Chamber.

"There are eight rooms like these," Mikael said. "In this section of the Kasbah, the rooms have all been laid out in the shape of a large octagon, with a shared garden in the center. Some of the rooms also have a private courtyard, too. Each of the rooms are significant because they represent a different sensual pleasure."

He'd just opened a door to the Ruby Chamber but she didn't even look inside. She stared at Mikael, stunned, and fascinated. "Seriously?"

He nodded. "Each suite has a pleasure attached, and it varies from a form of sex, to a particular position."

Jemma blushed, suddenly very warm. "You're making this up."

"Not at all. Each night for eight consecutive nights, the groom takes his bride to a new room, initiating her into new carnal delights, teaching her, pleasuring her, as well as ensuring she knows how to pleasure him."

Her face burned, hot. It was almost as if a fire had been lit inside of her and she didn't know if it was the things he was saying, or his tone, but his words created erotic pictures in her head, pictures that were so intimate and real that she could scarcely breathe.

He led her around to each of the eight suites, and she marveled at each. The Bridal Palace was beyond fantasy. It was magical. Jemma felt as if she'd entered another world. A world she couldn't have imagined existed anywhere. And yet it did. *Here.*

The exotic perfection was almost too much to take in, each suite more spectacular than the last, the rooms splashed with jeweled color—violet, sapphire, gold, ruby, turquoise, emerald, and silver. The chambers were connected by tall columned corridors, the white and gold tiles shimmering at all hours of the day, while in the very center was a luxurious walled garden featuring pools, fountains, and exotic red, gold and ivory mosaic tiled pavilions.

She'd thought her courtyard was lovely, but the Bridal Palace's secret courtyard was so lavish and sensual it stole her breath, and made her heart hurt.

She didn't know why the Bridal Palace's sensual beauty created pain. She was certain it'd been designed to delight.

"You're very quiet," the sheikh said, turning to look at her.

She passed a small waterfall that tumbled and splashed into a deep bathing pool. "I'm in awe," she said, thinking this was the kind of place you wanted to be on your honeymoon. The low beds covered with the softest cotton and banked with silk cushions. The fragrant garden both hid and revealed the various gleaming pools.

This was a place for passion. Pleasure. Here anything seemed possible...

"I've never seen anything like this before," she added, voice unsteady. "It takes my breath away. These rooms, the gardens, they're pure fantasy. I feel like I'm in a dream."

"I think that's the point," he said, leading her from the central courtyard, through a room shimmering with silver, to the outside hall. "The fantasy element is to help both bride and groom overcome their inhibitions. Here, everything is possible."

The door shut behind them and they were suddenly back in an ordinary hall, in an ordinary world.

She looked at the closed door, amazed by what they'd just left behind. "The rooms...your story...it's a fairy tale for adults."

"But it's not a fairy tale, or a story. It's real. Part of Saidia's culture and tradition. This is where every Saidia king has brought his bride for eight hundred years."

"Your parents came here?"

He nodded. "My father brought my mother here. And now I've brought you."

Jemma's mouth opened, closed. She couldn't think of a single thing to say. It was all too incredible...the exotic beauty, as well as the seductive nature of the Kasbah. Everything in this palace was hedonistic. Indulgent. And he was using the promise of pleasure to cast a spell over her.

"Tonight is the first of our sixteen nights here. For the next eight nights, I shall pick the pleasure, and then on the ninth night, it becomes your choice."

He was walking her back to her suite now, and Jemma was glad he was leading. She felt dazed. Lost. Caught up in the most impossible dream.

"Not tonight," she said as they reached her door. "I'm not ready."

"A kidnapped bride is never ready," he said, and yet he was smiling to soften his words. "I also am not insensitive to the strangeness of our situation. I understand you have fears, and misgivings, but I believe it is better to begin sooner than later. You will be less anxious once we know each other."

"But shouldn't that happen before physical intimacy?"

"The physical intimacy will bind us together. It is the act of physical love that distinguishes the relationship, separating us from others."

Jemma pressed her hands together, fingers locking. "One more day. *Please*."

"But you had one day already. We had today."

"I slept most of it away!"

"Which should mean you are rested and refreshed for tonight." They'd reached the entrance to her suite of rooms. He gestured to her door. "Inside your room you will find several presents from me. You will receive more later. For the next eight days and nights I will shower you with gifts, jewels, and my undivided attention. I think you shall soon discover that these eight days and nights will be everything you ever dreamed...and more."

His gaze met hers and held, even as his words echoed in her head, making her nerves dance.

Everything you ever dreamed...and more.

Just like that the night crackled, the air hot and heavy, sultry in the exotic pavilion.

Mikael was so close that he made the hair on her nape rise and her skin prickle. All she could think about was the sheikh stretching his big powerful body out over hers. Blood rushed to her cheeks and she fought to control her breathing.

"You are awfully confident, Your Highness."

"We are married. Don't you think it's time you used my given name?"

"I do not feel married."

"That will change soon."

Jemma disappeared into her room, pulse racing. She turned from the door and nearly tripped over the mountain of trunks stacked just inside the entrance to her sitting room.

The young maid was standing next to the trunks, smiling. "For you," she said. "From His Highness."

Jemma backed away from the trunks, panicked by the tower of gifts.

She didn't want presents. Didn't want to be showered with expensive gifts and jewels.

She wanted the life she had in London. She wanted her friends. Wanted her work. She wanted her own identity and freedom.

The maid watched Jemma, her dark eyes bright, expression cheerful and excited. "Shall I start your bath, Your Highness? We have much to do to prepare."

Jemma shook her head, feeling anything but excited. She couldn't do this. Couldn't go through with this. She wasn't the kind of woman who just gave up, who just gave in. She was not meant to be Mikael's queen. Her future was not here in Saidia, nor did she have any desire to bear the children that would heal the rift between families and countries.

"It is a very big day," the maid added carefully, her confident expression slipping, revealing the first hint of concern. "Much to do. Much tradition."

Jemma sat down on the edge of one of her low white sofas, her hands folding in her lap. "These are not my traditions."

The maid knelt next to Jemma. "Your Highness, do not be frightened. His Highness, Sheikh Karim, is a very good and powerful man. He is very fair. A man of his word. If he tells you something, it is so."

"I think you would say that about all Saidia kings."

"No. I would not say that about the last king, Sheikh Karim's father. The old king was not a good man. He made his first wife very sad. I think His Highness, Sheikh Karim, saw much as a boy. I think he saw things a child should not see. This is why he is different from his father. He has worked very hard to be a good king. The people love him. He honors and respects Saidia people, and Saidia tradition." The maid smiled. "The king will be good to you. You will be happy. I am already happy for you." Her hand indicated the trunks. "Already he has sent many gifts. He tries to show you already he is pleased with you. That you bring him honor."

Jemma shook her head. "He's trying to buy me."

The maid frowned. "Buy you? Like a camel?"

"Yes. But I'm not a thing to be bought."

"His Highness does not buy you. His Highness honors you. Gifts show respect. In Saidia, gifts are good things." She smiled more brightly. "Maybe now you look at your gifts, and then we get ready for tonight."

Jemma struggled to smile. "You open the trunks for me. Show me what is inside."

For the next several minutes, all the maid did was unpack the trunks, starting with the largest leather trunk on the bottom of the stack.

The biggest trunk was filled with clothes. Kaftans, skirts, sarongs, tunics, slinky evening gowns. The medium trunk contained shoes and heels and elegant jeweled sandals. The small trunk held jewelry and accessories.

There was one last trunk, but this one wasn't leather, but silver. The silver box's gleaming surface was embossed with elegant scrollwork and a jeweled handle. Jemma carefully unfastened the latches. Inside the silver box was a white garment bag, white shoes and a small, delicate white silk pouch.

"This is for tonight," the maid said, unzipping the garment bag to remove a long white satin gown that looked like something from a Hollywood movie. "Your bridal gown."

"My wedding gown?" Jemma corrected, thinking maybe she'd misunderstood the girl's English.

"No. The honeymoon gown. For pleasure." The maid smiled, her cheeks pink. "Tonight is the first night. You go to him in white. You meet him in the Chamber of Innocence."

"How do you know all this?"

"I come from the same tribe as Sheikh Karim. My mother and grandmother served the new Karim brides. And now I serve you. It is my job to prepare you for the king's pleasure."

Jemma was neither a virgin nor an innocent and yet she blushed, furiously, feeling ridiculously embarrassed, and shy. "I'm not sure about this."

"You don't need to worry. His Highness will know everything. He will teach you."

Jemma flushed again, her cheeks burning, trying not to feel mortified. The maid must think she was a timid virgin.

"Do you want to try it on?" the maid asking, admiring the long white satin gown.

"No." Jemma turned away from the gown, the fabric soft and begging to be touched, focusing instead on the remaining wedding night gifts and accessories. White satin shoes. Delicate white satin undergarments. And of course, the white silk pouch.

Curious, Jemma loosened the silver strings and emptied

the pouch into her hand. Glittering diamond and pearl earrings spilled into her palm. A small card slid out last, landing on top of the stunning diamond drop earrings.

My first gift to you. Please wear them tonight. I think they will look magnificent on you.

Jemma read the card twice, and then slowly exhaled, her heart hammering.

Was this really happening? Would she really go to him tonight, dressed like a virgin sacrifice, dazzling in diamonds and white?

Jemma slipped the earrings back into the silk pouch, and then placed the pouch and shoes inside the silver trunk before closing the lid and fastening it shut.

Yesterday afternoon she'd been in the middle of a photo shoot when Mikael arrived. She'd known nothing about him, and very little about Saidia, and yet now she was his wife, and being prepared for his bed.

She still couldn't wrap her head around it.

Jemma sat back on her heels and looked at the young maid. "Have you ever heard of a royal groom not satisfying his bride? Have you ever heard your mother or grandmother mention a kidnapped bride returning to her family? Has it happened in Saidia history before?"

The maid nodded. "Yes."

"A long, long time ago, or more recently?"

"During my great-great-grandmother's time, I think. Many, many years ago. And…" The maid chewed her lip, looking unsure of herself. "Maybe my mother's time."

Jemma frowned. "Your mother served my husband's mother."

"Yes."

"Mikael's mother was unhappy?"

"Not at first. Not during the honeymoon, but later."

"Why?"

She shrugged. "I do not know. My mother would never say."

The maid left to start Jemma's bath, and rather than argue with the maid about privacy, Jemma stripped her clothes off and spent the next half hour soaking in the deep marble tub, lost in thought.

The Kasbah was a palace within a palace, and Mikael descended from a line of royal men who'd been taught that it was necessary to know how to please a woman in bed, and even his *duty* to give his woman pleasure. But not just pleasure. He was expected to make her fall in love with him. She needed to want to stay in Saidia. She needed to be happy. And if, during the honeymoon, the Saidia groom couldn't make his bride happy, she could leave him after sixteen days.

The history fascinated Jemma. But it wasn't just history. They were facts. And the facts gave her pause.

If a Saidia man couldn't please his wife, he had to let her go.

Did that mean Mikael would let her go if he couldn't please her?

Out of the bath, the maid set to work rubbing exotic fragrant oils into Jemma's skin, and Jemma provided no resistance, lost in thought.

She'd been brought here as Mikael's first wife. But perhaps now she could force him to free her following their honeymoon. If she wasn't happy after eight days, she'd refuse him the next eight and demand to be allowed to return to her tribe.

While the oil dried, Jemma walked around the courtyard in her cotton kimono, letting the sun's warmth help her skin absorb the oil.

She knelt by the pool in the courtyard, and gazed down into the clear blue water, the bottom of the pool covered in cobalt blue tiles. Her face reflected back at her, her dark hair pulled back from her face, her expression appeared surprisingly serene in the water. Her calmness belied her resolve.

She would leave here.

She would not be charmed.

She would not fall in love.

She would not give him children.

What she'd give him were eight days and nights, and during those days and nights he'd have access to her body. But he'd never have her heart.

The maid fetched Jemma from the courtyard to do her hair.

Jemma's stomach churned as she sat at the silver dressing table, while the maid combed and twisted her hair into place, roping in strands of pearls and clusters of diamonds until Jemma's long dark hair was a glittering, jeweled work of art.

Was Mikael aware that he'd given her a way out? Did he know that she understood her freedom could be won?

But first she'd have to surrender to Mikael for eight days, and eight nights.

Could she do it?

Could she give herself to him totally? Handing over her body, her will, her need for control?

"Shall I help you with your dress now?" the maid asked, Jemma's hairstyle complete.

"No," Jemma said suddenly. She couldn't finish dressing, couldn't slip into the white satin gown, not until she'd seen Mikael. She needed to speak to him. She needed his promise that he'd honor Saidia tradition. "I need to go see His Highness, now. Will you please take me to him?"

The maid opened her mouth as if to protest and then nodded. "Yes, Your Highness. Please, follow me."

The maid knew the palace corridors and they walked swiftly from her wing to his.

The maid knocked on the outer door of Mikael's suite and then stepped back, discretely disappearing into the shadows.

Jemma drew a deep breath as she waited for the outer door to open. It did, and Mikael's valet gestured for Jemma to enter the king's suite.

Jemma glanced up into Mikael's central hall with the soaring ceiling topped by a skylight. She remembered the skylight and the second floor lined with balconies, reminding her of the New Orleans French Quarter.

"Looking for me?" Mikael's deep voice sounded behind her.

Jemma turned, blushing as she spotted Mikael in nothing but a snug white towel wrapped securely around his waist, revealing broad shoulders and muscular torso.

"Yes," she said, forcing her gaze from his impressive body up to his face. His black hair was damp, and glossy, his jaw freshly shaven. His gaze met hers and held.

Handsome, she thought, dazzled by the play of golden light over his bronze features. He was too handsome for his own good. No wonder he was arrogant.

"What can I do for you?" Mikael asked as his valet disappeared.

"We need to talk."

"And I thought you'd come to thank me for my gifts," he answered, smiling faintly.

"They are…lovely," she said hesitantly. "So yes, thank you. But—"

"But you want something else?" he interrupted.

She flushed. "Yes. You could say that."

His eyes, fringed by those endless lashes, narrowed. His gaze swept over her and even from across the courtyard she felt the heat in his eyes, felt the possession.

"What is it?" he asked.

Jemma grew hot. Her pulse quickened. She'd walked quickly the entire way from her room but it didn't explain this new heat in her veins. This was his fault. When he looked at her, he made her head light, made her feel ridiculously dizzy and weak. "I want something that isn't a physical gift."

"You don't care for jewels and clothes?"

"They're fine, but not my favorite gifts."

"I thought every woman loved jewelry and exquisite clothes."

"I am sorry to disappoint you."

He circled her slowly. "You don't disappoint me. You in

trigue me. I'm intrigued right now. What it is that you want so badly you'd race to my room just an hour before we are to disappear into the Chamber of Innocence?"

Mikael watched color sweep Jemma's cheeks. She was beautiful in the pink kimono robe, and she sounded breathless and all he could think of was peeling the thin fabric from her shoulders and kissing the pale skin at her collarbone.

She had a beautiful body. He wanted her body. He wanted her.

"Would you care to sit?" he asked her.

"No. I think I'm better standing."

"Does what you need to say require courage?" he asked, wondering if she knew how beautiful she was. He doubted it. She was surprisingly modest. She had no airs or attitude. Someone in her family had done a good job raising her.

"It depends on how you'll take it," she answered.

"Then perhaps let's not talk now. Tonight is special. Tonight is about pleasure."

"Tonight cannot happen without us speaking, Your Highness."

He sighed, an exaggerated sigh. The sigh was purely for show. He was playing with her, enjoying her fire. "*Laeela*, I confess I'm not pleased with the direction our relationship is taking. We do a lot of talking. Or more accurately, you do a lot of talking, and I seem to be doing a great deal of listening."

"You're wrong, Your Highness. You actually never listen."

"I'm sure that's not right. It seems like you talk a great deal."

"That's maybe because you're not used to a woman who has a brain and wants to use it."

"I see." It required effort not to give in to the smile. "That might explain it, but I'm wondering if talking now will maybe interfere with our pleasure tonight? Perhaps we should wait and talk later."

"Most men probably never want to talk, Your Highness, but we must."

"Fine. You talk, and I will listen, provided there is no more of this Your Highness when we are in private. You're my wife, about to come to my bed. I understand you must call me Your Highness in public, but we are alone at the moment, and my name is Mikael."

She blinked and wet her lips, her face awash in rosy color, her eyes a brilliant green in her lovely face, flashing fire.

"Now, what is it you had to say?" he added, reaching out to touch her pink cheek.

She just looked at him with wide green eyes and he savored the moment. "What is it?" he persisted. "Tell me."

She drew a quick breath. "I want you to make me a promise."

She was negotiating with him. Interesting. "Yes?"

"I want you, as the king and leader of the Saidia people, to promise me that you will honor Saidia tradition, and the custom of your tribe."

He could see from the tilt of her chin that she expected him to fight her. She expected a problem. She was preparing to battle.

"I always try to honor Saidia tradition," he said.

"Then promise to honor this tradition."

"Perhaps you need to tell me what it is, first."

She looked into his eyes and then away. She seemed to struggle to find the right words, and then she shrugged, and blurted, "If you cannot make me happy in the first eight days and nights of our honeymoon, I want you to promise to send me home, to my family. My people."

She'd shocked him. For a moment he could think of nothing to say.

"During the tour you explained why the honeymoon is so important," she continued. "It made sense to me, and it made me respect your culture more. I am grateful you come from a culture that believes a woman should be happy, because I, too, believe a woman should be happy. I believe all women should be happy, just as I believe all women should have a say in their marriage, and future." She drew another quick breath. "*I need* to have a say in my future. I need my voice heard. You must give me my voice back."

"But you have your voice. I hear you quite plainly."

"Then give me a gift I will cherish, the gift of your word. Promise me I will be free to return home if you cannot make me happy."

"You doubt me?"

"I won't if you promise me I can trust you."

"I've told you my word is law."

"Then say to me, 'Jemma, if you aren't happy in eight days, I will put you on a plane, and send you back to London.'" Her green eyes held his. "That is all you have to do, and I will believe you, but I need a promise from you, or it is impossible to give you my body, or my heart, if I'm afraid, or full of fear and doubt."

He said nothing.

"Mikael," she added more softly, persuasively, "I need to know that I can trust you. I need to believe you will take care of me. Your promise is the gift of dignity and honor. Your promise means I feel safe and respected, and that gives us the basis for a future. Otherwise, we have nothing. And how can you build a future on nothing?"

She was like a queen, he thought, watching her. Beautiful and regal. Proud, slender, strong. With her dark hair and stunning green eyes, she could easily be one of the great Egyptian queens. Cleopatra. Nefertiti. Ankhesenamun.

If they had met under different circumstances, he would have made her his lover or mistress. He would have enjoyed spoiling her with gifts. He liked to spoil his woman, liked to please her. But he didn't love. He didn't want to love. Love complicated relationships. Love wasn't rational.

He was determined to be rational. He was determined to be a good king.

She reached toward him, her hand outstretched. "Mikael, I need to know you have not just your best interest at heart, but mine, too."

He stiffened. "As king I have all my people's best interests at heart."

"As my *husband,* you must have mine, too."

"I do."

Her hand lightly settled on his chest. "Then promise me, and I can meet you tonight with calm, and confidence, and *hope*."

He glanced down at her hand where it rested so lightly on his chest, just above his heart.

He captured her hand in his, holding her small fist to his chest. His thumb swept her wrist. He could feel the wild staccato of her pulse. She was afraid. He didn't like her fear. "You've no need to be afraid."

"That is not the same thing as a promise."

"You are still getting to know me, but you will discover I am a man of my word. I do not make rash promises, nor do I break my commitments."

She bit her lip and looked at him from beneath her long dark lashes. "So what does that mean?"

"It means I have eight days to make you happy."

He could see her bite down harder, her pink lip turning white in the center, where her teeth pressed into the tender flesh.

He both envied and pitied the spot.

Once she was completely his, he would suck and lick that poor lip to make amends. His body hardened in anticipation. He would very much like to suck and lick all of her. He would like to feel her tighten beneath him, and then shatter. "But I also understand your mistrust of men. Your father abandoned you, and then your fiancé did the same. You've been surrounded by men who only think of themselves, making rash promises, which is why I can safely give you my word that I *will* make you happy."

"And yet, if you cannot, you will let me return to London?"

His dark gaze raked her, appreciating the jut of breasts and swell of hips beneath the thin kimono. "Yes."

CHAPTER EIGHT

BACK IN HER room, Jemma couldn't look at herself as she stepped into the beautiful fitted white satin gown. It was too soft and sensual to be a wedding gown, and yet the slinky satin somehow managed to give the impression of a long and Western style bridal gown. The wedding night without the traditional wedding ceremony.

She sucked in a nervous breath as the maid fastened the dozens of tiny hooks in the back of the long dress, and then with shaking hands, she attached the diamond and pearl earrings to her earlobes.

She couldn't believe how her stomach flip-flopped as she stepped into her white-beaded silk shoes. Designer shoes. They fit like a glove.

Jemma glanced at herself in the dressing table mirror. She looked like a bride dressed for the bedroom.

And wasn't that exactly what she was? She was being prepared for her husband's bed. Oiled and scented and bejeweled for his pleasure.

But earlier, in his room, when he'd taken her hand, she hadn't felt fear. She'd actually liked the way his touch made her feel. He was strong and warm and it was such a small thing, this linking of fingers, and yet significant. Touch was powerful. His touch was surprisingly comforting.

And now she was curious about tonight. But not afraid.

Mikael arrived at Jemma's suite of rooms at eight o'clock and he watched her cross the sitting room floor, as she moved toward him, her head high, her eyes wide, the large diamond teardrops swinging from her earlobes, the brilliant cuts in the stone casting tiny dancing lights in every direction. Her gown molded to her body, the delicate straps and cups of the dress revealing smooth shoulders and the swell of her breasts before hugging her flat tummy and the lush curve of her hips and butt.

His narrowed gaze slid over her tall, slender body, appreciating how the satin caressed her, and yet he could also see her without the luscious satin, remembering that stunning glimpse of her when she'd dropped the fur coat during the shoot, and how the full shape of her breasts had been revealed.

The impact of her physical beauty had shocked him. He'd had such a visceral reaction there on the sand dune. He'd been furious—outraged—but he'd also felt a wave of pure possession.

Mine, he'd thought.

He'd wanted to cover her. Take her away from everyone. He'd told himself it was duty, responsibility, a response to a wrong.

Now he wondered if it was more than that.

Mine.

He held out his hand to her. She gave him her hand. It was shaking. He took her hand, his fingers lacing with hers.

He lifted her hand to his mouth, just as he had earlier, but this time he kissed the back of each finger. "Eight days and nights."

"And it all starts now?"

"Yes."

He swung her into his arms then and carried her down the connecting halls until they reached the entrance to the Bridal Palace.

"We are here," he said, pushing the door open and carrying her inside to a room that glowed with hundreds of white candles.

Jemma spotted the bed, surrounded by more candles, and looked the other way. "Are we going to bed now?"

"No." His deep voice sounded amused. "I'm starving. Haven't eaten since our late lunch. Wouldn't you prefer a bite to eat first?" he asked, setting her on her feet.

"Yes," she said quickly. "Please."

Mikael took her hand and led her past the dozens of candles illuminating the immense bed, to the opposite side of the room, where a door opened to a private courtyard fantastically transformed into a tropical garden with a manmade grotto and splashing waterfall. Dozens of candles lined the walkway, and more candles outlined the steps to the grotto and door.

It was warm in the garden, and fragrant with orchids and lilies and Mikael pulled her close to his side as he led her along the narrow path lined with candles, down an even more narrow stone staircase to a secret room inside the grotto where a table had been set for them among a sea of pale blue silk cushions.

The grotto was made entirely of stone and illuminated with a dozen blue glass lanterns that hung from the pale ivory stone ceiling. Water lapped in a small pool while above them came the sound of rushing water tumbling through over the waterfall.

"This is unbelievable." Jemma breathed, taking a seat among the cushions, very aware of Mikael as he sat down next to her.

He'd come to her tonight not in traditional Saidia robe and head covering, but in black trousers and an elegant dress shirt and once seated at the table, he proceeded to roll the sleeves of his shirt back on his muscular forearms, and then open the shirt another button at the collar, revealing a hint of bronzed skin just below his throat.

"That's better," he said.

She swallowed hard. He'd shocked her earlier in the towel, but it was just as shocking to see him now in Western clothes. He didn't look like a sheikh. He just looked gorgeous.

He looked at her. "You don't think so?"

"No, you look…quite…good," she murmured, thinking good was a total understatement. He looked fantastic.

"Quite good," he repeated, lips curving slightly. "I will take that as a compliment coming from you."

"I'm sure you are complimented all the time. You must know you are very beautiful for a man."

He laughed then. It was the first time she'd ever heard him laugh, really laugh, and the flash of his straight white teeth against his bronzed skin, and the crinkle of his eyes made her heart race.

"I don't get complimented very often," he said.

"No? Why not?"

"I think people might be afraid to pay me compliments."

She arched a brow. "What do you do? Chop off heads?"

"No. But I have a reputation for being no-nonsense."

"I'm sorry to hear that."

His teeth flashed again but he said nothing else, and for the next hour staff came and went, bearing platters of food until the low table was covered. Chicken with tomatoes and honey. Lamb cutlets, tangy beef, coconut rice, a tagine of yam, carrots and prunes.

After the past several days of stress, Jemma was glad to just relax, and eat, and sip her wine. Mikael was his most charming tonight. During dinner he told her stories, amusing stories. "You said earlier you're not a fan of jewels and clothes," he said, leaning against the cushions. "So what do you like? Art? Antiques? Cars?"

"Books." She could see she'd surprised him. "I love to read."

"Fiction?"

"Fiction, non-fiction, everything. Although when I was a girl, I only wanted to read romances. My mother was convinced I'd run off and join the circus or something equally risky and foolish."

"What will she think when she discovers you've married me?"

"She'll be horrified."

He didn't seem to like that. "Why?"

"Because our cultures are too different and she'd be worried that I'd be trapped in a life where I couldn't be myself, and the lack of freedom would make me desperately unhappy."

"That's quite specific."

"Morgan's short, unhappy marriage made quite an impression on all of us."

"And yet the day of her wedding she seemed ecstatic."

"Exactly. But Morgan was so infatuated with Drakon that she didn't ask any hard questions about what her life would be like in Athens, and their marriage was a shock for her. She ended up bitterly unhappy as a new bride in a new city and their relationship quickly fell apart." Jemma smoothed a wrinkle from her satin skirt. "Mother had warned her that life in Greece, as the wife of a Greek shipping tycoon wouldn't be easy, not for an independent American girl who is accustomed to making decisions for herself. And so I'm quite sure my mother would be even more upset if I turned around and married a Saidia sheikh."

Mikael said nothing for a long moment. "Even if it improves your situation?"

It was Jemma's turn to fall silent.

"I'm aware your brother is the only Copeland who has any financial assets left," Mikael added. "And the only reason he does, is because he lives in Europe, and his assets couldn't be seized, but your government will go after him. What he hasn't yet lost due to scandal, will soon be taken by your government."

"Maybe it won't happen," she said, not really believing it herself.

He gave her a skeptical look. "Isn't that the same thing you said about your mother's home? And didn't the government just take that?"

Jemma drew a short breath. It had been one thing losing

the house on St. Bart's and the lodge in Sun Valley, but it was
painful losing one's childhood home. Jemma had lived in the
Greenwich house from the time she was six until she'd left
for London. And maybe she didn't live at home any longer,
but it was still her home. It was where she liked to picture her
mother, where they all came together to celebrate Christmas
or a special occasion.

The government shouldn't have taken the house a month
ago. It was her mother's, from the divorce. But apparently
her father's name was on the title, too, and that was all they
needed to seize it.

"It's not been easy for my mother, no," Jemma said roughly,
unable to look at him, the pain fresh and sharp all over again.
"But she's lucky she has a few friends who have stood by her.
She's relying on their kindness now."

Jemma didn't tell the entire truth.

Yes, a few friends had stood by her mother. But the rest had
dropped her. The majority had dropped her. Just like most of
Jemma's friends had disappeared, too. It happened to her sisters as well. She had no idea if her brother, Branson, was abandoned. He'd never talked about it, even though he, too, lived in
London. But then, Branson never revealed anything personal.
He'd always been private and self-contained, so self-contained,
that Jemma hadn't been comfortable going to her brother this
year and asking for help, or a loan, or even a friendly ear. Instead she'd struggled to handle it all—the shame from her father's duplicity, and the pain of being rejected by the man she
loved more than life itself.

She felt Mikael's fingers on her cheek. She stiffened and
drew back, then realized he'd touched her because he was wiping away tears. Her tears.

She hadn't even realized she was crying.

"I'm sorry," she whispered, turning away to hide her face.

He turned her face back to him and gently swept his thumb
across her right cheek, and then her left. His expression was
troubled. Brooding. "Do you cry for your mother?"

"Yes."

"Just your mother? Or, perhaps you are also still hurting from that spineless Englishman who calls himself a model?"

She made a soft, rough sound. "He's a great model."

"But a lousy man."

She smiled despite herself, and then her smile faded. "My sister Logan said he did me a favor. She said it was better that I find out who he is now, before we married, instead of after."

"Your sister is right." His thumb slid across her cheekbone, and then down, along her smooth jaw, his attention fixed now on her mouth. He was going to kiss her. She was sure of it, she could tell by the expression in his eyes, and the way the air sparked and crackled around them, tense, and electric.

She felt raw and emotional. Confused. Everything was changing; the energy between them was different. He'd been so harsh and cold in the beginning but he was different now. He seemed as if he might care.

His head dipped. Her tummy flipped. Her pulse raced. His mouth almost touched hers, but didn't. His breath caressed her lips. "I am sorry that spineless Englishman hurt you. I am also sorry that I add to your pain."

Her heart squeezed. She struggled to catch her breath, feeling bruised.

"But I will make you happy, *laeela*. I promise."

She stared into his eyes, lost, dazzled.

"You will enjoy being my wife." He stroked her cheek again. "You will have riches beyond compare."

Jemma exhaled hard, and sat back, the magic gone.

He didn't understand her. He didn't understand that what she wanted, *needed*, had nothing to do with wealth. "Money does not buy happiness. I've no desire for riches, or wealth. I've had both, and money can buy things, but not what my heart needs."

"What about your body?"

"My *body*?"

His dark eyes gleamed. "What about what your body needs?"

"I don't understand."

"Who worships your body?"

Without wanting to, she thought of Damien. They'd had a good relationship, and great sex, but she wouldn't say Damien ever worshipped her body. She'd never had a boyfriend who'd worshipped her body, and had begun to think after conversations with her girlfriends, that few men did. "No man worships a woman's body."

"I fully intend to worship your body."

"This is incredibly uncomfortable. Perhaps it's time we discussed your body."

Mikael grinned. Like his laugh earlier, it was the first time she'd really seen him smile, a real smile and his teeth flashed again, and a tiny dimple appeared on the right side of his mouth. It was astonishing. Not just because he'd smiled, but because of what it did to his face. The smile transformed his hard, fierce features. He looked so approachable, so appealing.

She sucked in a breath, dazzled. "You shouldn't do that, you know."

A hint of a smile lingered at the corners of his mouth. "Do what?"

"Smile."

"Why not?"

"It makes you seem almost human."

"I *am* almost human."

"I had no idea," she retorted, trying to ignore the thumping of her heart and the way he made desire coil inside her.

He smiled again, and his expression was so warm and playful that she suddenly wanted more of him.

Wanted him closer. Wanted him kinder. Wanted him to be good to her.

"I like how fierce you get," he said.

"You deliberately provoke me."

The dimple deepened at the corner of his mouth. "Maybe."

In that moment she saw who he might have been had his life turned out differently. Or perhaps, this is how he might have been with her from the start, had she not been Jemma Copeland.

Maybe he really was warm and sexy, charming and engaging. Maybe.

"And my body is very fine," he said, the smile still lingering in his eyes. "I appreciate your concern."

Suddenly, she very much wanted to know more about him, who he was, and how he lived. Did he have lots of women in his life? Was he the kind of man who serial dated or did he prefer having a long-term relationship?

"Tell me about your body," she said, trying to sound offhand. "Does it see a lot of action?"

"I don't think that's appropriate."

"I'm not asking you to divulge names or numbers. I just want to know you. I'm curious about you. It's the sort of thing a woman wants to know about her man." She held his gaze. "So, are you a player?"

"I used to be a player. I'm not anymore. I haven't been for a couple years."

"Why?"

"Age? Maturity? I just know that around thirty I started to get tired of the chase, and would have just one relationship at a time. How about you?"

"I like having a boyfriend, but don't need to be in a relationship. I'm picky. I would rather be with no one than just anyone."

"A woman with high standards."

"A woman that prefers books to casual sex."

"You might just be the perfect kidnapped bride."

There was silence for a minute and Jemma felt a thousand different things.

But then from the first time she'd met Mikael, he'd made her feel a lot. And here, in this…pleasure palace…she'd begun to feel the whisper of a craving for something. She wasn't sure what it was she wanted, but her dreams last night had stirred something within her and all day she'd felt a restlessness and an ache.

Like a craving for sensation.

Staring into his eyes, she was teased by the possibility. Teased by the suggestion of pleasure. It would feel so good to feel good again. To feel like a woman again. To feel close to someone again.

"If you've finished your dinner," Mikael said rising. "It's time to come with me."

They climbed the stairs from the grotto's secret room to the courtyard of fragrant white lilies and vines clinging to rock. White candles still glimmered against the walls and outlined the walkway. But now in the middle of the courtyard, between the waterfall and door to the Chamber of Innocence stood a narrow table covered in crisp white sheets.

Jemma looked at Mikael, uncertain. "What is that?"

"A massage table. I'm going to give you a massage," he said. "You'll lie there, face down—"

"Why?"

"Most massages start with the back."

"Yes, but why are you giving me the massage?"

"I think you'd enjoy it. And it would help you relax. I want you to relax. I want you to realize that everything that will happen here in the Bridal Palace will feel good. I will never do anything you don't want. And if I do something that does make you uncomfortable, all you have to do is speak up." He drew the top sheet back on the table. "Any questions?"

Jemma tugged on her dress. "Do I wear this?"

"No. You'll take that off—everything off—and then lie down between the sheets, naked."

He'd turned around to give her privacy while she disrobed, but she was on the massage table now, tucked between the sheets.

He looked down at her on the table, her dark glossy hair tumbling over one shoulder.

The massage was for her, not him. He wanted her now. He wanted her naked in his bed now. But she wasn't ready, and he'd meant it when he told her that she had to be comfortable. She had to want him before anything would happen between them.

He placed his hands over the sheet covering her back, letting her feel the pressure of his hands, letting his hands warm her.

After a moment he smoothed his hands over the sheet covering her back.

She felt good. Warm, solid but smooth.

This wasn't going to be a sexual massage. He'd told her that before they started. It was to show her he could be trusted. He wouldn't hurt her, or force her to do anything she didn't want to do.

This massage was simply to help break the ice.

Develop awareness. Create ease between them. Stir the senses, too, so that she'd be comfortable with him physically. You couldn't impose desire. It must come from within.

He concentrated on learning the shape of her back through the sheet, the sheet protecting her, giving her a sense of safety. He had told her that at any point she could stop the massage. If at any point she felt uncomfortable or threatened, she just needed to speak up and the massage would end. But he didn't expect her to stop it.

Moving from her shoulders down, he ran his palms from her spine out, smoothing tension away, relaxing the muscles, letting her continue to warm, encouraging her to breathe more deeply.

After several minutes he drew the sheet down, folded it low on her hips, leaving her lovely back exposed. His eyes followed the line of her body, the narrowing of her waist to the soft swell of her hips. The sheet rested on her bottom, hiding the cleft of her cheeks, but again, he knew it was there. He wanted to see it. Touch it. Touch her.

And he would touch her, but not there, not today.

He drew her long hair into his fist, and quickly braided it, before draping the braid over her shoulder, leaving her back bare.

As he stepped away to reach for the oil he could see her profile. Her eyes were closed, her full lips softly parted. Her pale skin gleamed, and his gaze dropped to the side of her soft breast, and then lower to the gentle curve of hip.

He hardened. He'd wanted her for hours. He felt as if he lived in a constant state of arousal around her.

He'd desired many women, and knew how to pleasure his women, but this one made him ache.

Or maybe it was the fact that he couldn't have her, not today, or tomorrow, or even the day after that made him hurt.

Pouring warm oil into his hands, Mikael rubbed his palms together, spreading the oil, thinning it, and yet the slippery texture was so sensual that he wasn't sure he could do this. It was to tease her, but he was teasing himself and he hated it.

He placed his hands in the middle of her back, where he'd rested them a few moments ago when the sheet still covered her, and then he began to stroke her back, with smooth, firm deliberate strokes to relax her.

She was tense but he was patient, and as he worked on her back, he focused on the satin texture of her skin, the supple muscle beneath the skin, and the long elegant lines of her—shoulder, upper arm, spine, hip, thigh to calf.

For the next two hours he rubbed and kneaded, massaging every muscle group, working on her back, and then massaging her front, her arms, shoulders and the upper planes of her chest. Aware of the stiff peaks of her nipples beneath the loosely draped sheet his own body tightened in response. He wanted her.

He would wait until she gave herself to him. Would wait until she asked—no, begged—for release.

His hands stopped moving. He leaned over her, whispered that he was done, and told her to hold the sheet.

She did, and he scooped her up, carrying her into the Chamber of Innocence where he laid her in the big bed.

"Good night," he said, smoothing the hair back from her forehead. "Sleep well. I will see you in the morning."

He'd carried her into the bedroom and then left her.

Jemma rolled over onto her tummy, and pressed her face into the pillow, her body aching.

She ached for more. Ached to be filled, satisfied.

Hopefully she wouldn't have to lie here like this tomorrow night feeling so…tense. Frustrated. It wasn't a good feeling. Hopefully tomorrow it would be different. Hopefully tomorrow she'd sleep contented. Because wasn't that the sheikh's promise? He was to fulfill her needs, give her pleasure?

Yes, the massage had been nice.

She'd very much enjoyed being rubbed and stroked with warm fragrant oils.

And he'd been a great masseuse, the best she'd ever had. He'd been extremely thorough, taking his time, making the massage last for hours. But that was the trouble.

The massage was supposed to be the start of something. A preliminary to foreplay. She'd expected more. The feel of his fingers working knotted muscles, made her imagine his fingers doing other things…

She'd lay on the massage table knowing that soon he'd touch her, and it wouldn't be just relaxing, but exciting. Stimulating.

She couldn't help daydreaming during the massage, couldn't help fantasizing.

She'd entertained the fantasies, too, because surely she'd need them for the next thing. Sex.

But there had been no next thing.

Just the deliciously long massage by a man who obviously had quite a bit of expertise, and then a good-night.

Most cordial of him. If she'd gone to a spa she'd expect him to be waiting on the other side of the door with a lovely chilled glass of lemon water for hydration purposes. But she wasn't at a spa. She'd expected the massage to…deliver…

It hadn't.

The sheikh knew exactly what he was doing.

Turning her on, leaving her high and dry, leaving her wanting more.

Jemma would have something to say to Mikael Karim in the morning.

CHAPTER NINE

IT TOOK HER a long time to fall asleep the night before, and when she woke in the morning, it took her a long time to want to leave her bed.

The massage hadn't just stirred her body, it'd somehow stirred her emotions. She woke up feeling unsettled. Undone.

Mikael had promised her that he'd make her happy in their eight days together, but she felt far less comfortable and optimistic now than she had yesterday before he'd carried her across the threshold of the Chamber of Innocence.

But maybe it was this room, she thought, her gaze sweeping the white marble chamber. It was too formal and too cold.

Too lonely, too.

She hadn't imagined that the eight nights of pleasure would start with her sleeping alone. She understood why he'd done it—he was trying to put her at ease—but it was isolating here in this room. The cold marble and silk panels might appeal to someone else, but not to her.

She grabbed her pillow and hugged it. She suddenly missed her family very much and that was saying something because Jemma had been independent for years.

When she'd moved to London at eighteen, her sister Victoria had teased her, saying Jemma would never last in London, and predicted that she would be back within a matter of weeks.

Victoria was wrong. Jemma had never returned, and it had actually been surprisingly easy to leave her family. Maybe it was because as the youngest, she'd grown up watching the others move on and move out. By the time she'd reached her teens, it was just her, and her mom, and her mom was ready for freedom, too.

And London had been a good fit. Once Jemma had moved there, she'd found it easy to embrace her new life, seizing every opportunity, taking every decent job, whether home or abroad. She liked to travel, was comfortable in hotel rooms, didn't mind the long hours, either. Being the youngest, and having to learn to entertain herself, proved beneficial. Jemma was self-reliant. She told herself she needed nothing, and no one.

But that wasn't true, either.

Of course she needed people. She needed good people, loving people, people who wouldn't abandon her the moment things got difficult.

A knock sounded on her door and it opened to reveal Mikael, dressed in casual khaki trousers and a white linen shirt, with a scrap of hot orange fabric in his hands.

"For you," he said, carrying the sheer tunic to her where she lay in bed.

She blinked at him, this new him, still finding it difficult to reconcile the intimidating sheikh with this very sexy man who looked as if he'd be incredibly comfortable without anything on.

Her hands shook as she unfolded the tunic. The neckline was again jeweled and bundled in the center was a tiny blood-orange bikini.

"We're swimming?" she asked, lifting the bikini top, and noting that the silky cups looked very small.

"Only if you feel like it. We're having breakfast outside in the center courtyard, next to the pool. It's already hot today. You might want to swim." He gazed down at her. "You don't have to wear the suit, either. I wasn't sure how comfortable you'd feel swimming naked."

Heat rushed to her face. She grabbed the tiny bikini. "I'll wear the suit, thank you."

* * *

It was a very lazy, self-indulgent day. Jemma felt as if she were on holiday at a luxurious resort. She'd been in and out of the pool a couple times to cool off, but now she stretched out on a plush lounge chair, sunbathing, while Mikael lay on a lounge chair next to her, reading.

She couldn't help sneaking glances at him every now and then, astonished to see him in swim trunks. Astonished by his abs, and his long muscular legs, and the thick biceps. He was nothing like the sheikh she'd met three days ago. He seemed nothing like a sheikh at all.

She looked past him to the pool that sparkled in the sun. She could see one of the staff walking toward them with a tray of fresh chilled towels and more lemon flavored ice water, along with little cups of something.

The little cups contained sorbet, a delicious pineapple sorbet that Jemma ate with a tiny spoon. Mikael didn't eat his. But he sat up to watch her lick the melting sorbet from her spoon.

"You make me hungry," he said, his dark gaze hooded, his deep voice husky.

She blushed and pretended she didn't understand, but it was impossible not to understand what he meant when he stared at her mouth as if it were edible.

"You have a sorbet here," she said. "It's melting quickly, though."

"Perhaps I'll just pour it on you and lick it off."

A wave of heat hit her. She suddenly felt scorching hot. "You wouldn't."

"Don't tempt me."

She sucked the tiny bit of fresh pineapple from the tip of the spoon, assessing. "Where would you pour it?"

"You play with fire, *laeela*."

She squinted up at the sun. "It is hot out."

"Very hot," he agreed, his deep voice now a rumble.

Her tongue flicked at her upper lip, sweeping the sticky juice off. "Maybe you should get into the pool and cool off."

"Maybe you should stop eating your ice as if you were desperate to have sex." He saw her expression and shrugged. "Just a bit of friendly advice."

"You're trying to help me, are you?"

"Protect you."

She sucked hard on the little spoon before looking at him, winged eyebrow arching. "From whom?"

"Maybe from what," he replied, his dark gaze now sweeping her as if he could eat all of her from head to toe.

It was thrilling. Her pulse quickened and Jemma felt a little frisson of excitement race through her. "Which is...?"

"Ravishment."

"Ah." She swallowed hard, and pressed her thighs and knees together, suddenly finding it very hard to breathe normally.

She couldn't remember the last time being ravished sounded appealing. In fact, being ravished had never sounded appealing until now.

It was time something exciting happened. She'd sat here all morning in her tiny blood-orange bikini and wanted his attention. Now that she had it, she wasn't ready to lose it.

"Would it hurt?" she asked. "Being ravished?"

He considered her, his dark gaze raking her. "No," he said at length. "It'd feel very, very good."

Jemma squeezed her knees tighter. "How do I know? You've never even kissed me."

His eyes lit. His hard features shifted, his jaw growing harder even as his mouth curved. He looked dangerous and gorgeous.

She wanted him to pounce on her, devour her.

"Do you want me to kiss you?" he asked, his eyes so dark and hot and intense that she felt like the sorbet, melting into a puddle of sweet sticky juice.

She was almost twitching in her lounge chair. She felt so turned on and strung out at the same time. "Yes. But only if you kiss really, really well."

* * *

Mikeal hadn't planned on liking his new bride. He hadn't even wanted to like her. But she was growing on him. She was by turns smart, funny and fierce, and stunning whether in a formal gown, or a swimsuit by the pool.

She looked incredible right now, as a matter of fact, with her hair still damp from her last swim, her skin flushed and golden from the sun, her amazing body barely covered in that swimsuit which was the color of his desert at sunset.

He'd wanted her all morning but her provocative words threatened to push him over the edge.

She was such a tease. He liked it, though. He liked her fire, wanted to taste her fire. Flame it. Make her burn.

"If you're such a great kisser, why haven't you kissed me?" she asked, tossing her head, sending damp strands of hair over her shoulder to cling to the swell of her breast.

Desire and hunger shot through him. He ached. He hurt. But he would take this so slow that she would be the one begging for him.

His gaze swept over her, admiring the fullness of her breasts, her flat belly, and the bright silky fabric just barely covering her there, between her thighs.

His body tightened with arousal.

"If I start kissing you," he answered, his voice so deep it was almost a growl, "you wouldn't want me to stop."

"You're so conceited," she said, nose in the air, but squirming at the same time.

"I'm honest."

Her cheeks darkened to a dusty pink. "To me, it sounds like a boast. You talk a lot but do very little."

He loved that he could arouse her so easily. He could feel her humming now, wanting, needing. "You love to challenge me," he drawled.

"I was just saying—"

He snapped his fingers, interrupting her, and then pointed to his chair. "Come here."

Her green eyes darkened, widened. She swallowed hard.

"Come, big talker," he said. "Let's see how brave you really are."

And just like that, her courage failed. She ducked her head, bit her lip, uncertain and shy.

He hid his smile. He'd expected as much.

She was a tease. One of those good girls who wanted to be bad.

He stood up, crossed to her chair, and tugged her to her feet. Her green eyes flashed again, worry, excitement, uncertainty.

He held her by the wrist, led her into the red and ivory pavilion behind them, and drew the silk curtains closed, hiding them.

"Sit," he ordered.

She sat down on one of the low couches that wrapped the wall. He sat down next to her.

"What are we doing?" she whispered.

"Whatever we feel like doing," he answered, his head dipping, dropping low, his mouth so close she could feel the warmth of his breath against her skin.

Jemma held her breath, waiting for the kiss. She felt as if she'd been waiting forever for this moment. But he was taking his time, his lips lightly brushing across her cheek toward her ear.

She turned her head toward him, wanting his mouth on her mouth but his lips were exploring the high curve of her cheekbone, his lips a caress across her sensitive skin. Hot darts of pleasure shot through her. His mouth felt good on her. He smelled good, too. She wanted more of him, not less.

Jemma turned her mouth to his again, inhaling his scent, relishing the rich spicy fragrance of his skin. He'd shaved earlier, this morning, and his jaw was smooth and firm, his mouth full and so very sensual.

Promising pleasure.

Unable to resist, Jemma put her lips to his, and waited. Waited to see what he would do. Waited to see what would happen next.

If he intended to seduce her, she would let him do the work. She was in the mood to be seduced, too. Ready for pleasure, sensation, satisfaction. Exquisite satisfaction.

His hand moved to her chin, fingers trailing across her jaw in a leisurely exploration, and yet every little brush of his fingers made her insides tighten and squirm and her breasts, already aching, feel excruciatingly sensitive.

She wanted him to touch her there, on her nipples, and touch lower, between her thighs. She sighed, growing impatient.

"You're not happy?" he asked, against her mouth.

She squirmed as his fingers played with her earlobe, lightly circling the soft tender skin again and again, making her senses swim and her head spin. "This is a bit frustrating," she answered. "I think it's time you just kissed me."

His lips brushed hers again. "But I am kissing you."

"No," she said, arching as he found the hollow beneath her ear and did something delicious to it, so delicious that she clenched inwardly, craving his hard body filling her, warming her, satisfying her. "A proper kiss," she insisted, no longer caring that she was supposed to resist him. Somehow reality no longer mattered, not when need licked at her veins and Jemma felt starved for sensation.

She reached up to clasp his face, her hands learning the shape of his jaw, the hard angles and planes as she pressed her lips to his, deepening the kiss, focused only on the heat between them.

He drew back after a moment, his eyes almost black in the dark pavilion interior. "Maybe we should stop. I don't want to force you."

"I don't think you're forcing me," she said, giving her head a slight shake, as if to clear her head of the heat and need and intense physical craving to be touched. *Taken*.

She throbbed and pulsed in places that shouldn't throb and pulse. "If anything, I feel as if I'm forcing you."

The corner of his mouth lifted. "I'm not being forced. Trust me."

She stroked her hand over the warm hard plane of his face.

Such a beautiful face. He was using his good looks against her. His charm, too. "You're too good at this."

His laughter was a deep rumble in his chest. "That's better than being bad at this."

"You're making it impossible for me to resist you."

"But you can. All you have to do is say stop, and we are done. I will never force you to do anything."

Then his mouth traveled down her neck, over her collarbone, down her chest, to the swell of her breasts. He lips teased the underside of the breast through the fabric of her bikini, finding nerves in every place he touched. She shivered, gasping as his mouth settled over her taut nibble, sucking the tip through the fabric.

She arched as he sucked harder, the pressure of his mouth making her inner thighs clench together with need.

She was the one to tug the fabric away from her breasts, exposing her nipple, and she was the one to draw his head back down, so his lips covered her bare breast.

She sighed at the feel of his mouth on her hot skin. His lips were warm, the tip of his tongue cool, but once he took the tight bud of her nipple in his mouth, it was his mouth that felt hot, wet, and she gasped, arching into him, her hips lifting, grinding, her body on fire.

She wanted him to take her now. She wanted his hands between her thighs, peeling her bikini bottoms off, wanted him to part her knees and thrust deep into her body, filling her, making the maddening ache inside of her go away.

But he didn't go lower, his hands stayed at her breasts, his mouth fastened to her nipple, sucking and licking, drawing hard on her, whipping her to a frenzy. Throbbing, she rolled away from him, and sat up, stunned that he'd brought her to the verge of an orgasm. She would have climaxed, too, if she hadn't stopped him.

She could barely look at him, excruciatingly shy. The sensations inside her were still so intense. How could she climax without him even touching her between her legs?

Mikael turned her face to him. "Did I scare you?" he asked quietly, his dark eyes searching hers.

She shook her head, but there were tears in her eyes. Her emotions felt wild.

"What then?"

"You're just very good at all…that."

He stroked her cheek with his thumb. "It was too much."

Her eyes burned. Her throat squeezed. "I don't know you." His touch was soothing. It eased some of the tension within her, but not enough. "I don't know you," she repeated. "And for me to feel this way, physically, I think I should."

Jemma always found a way to surprise him.

But it wasn't her words that surprised him now, as much as her emotion. He felt her confusion. She didn't understand what she was feeling.

She wasn't who he thought she was. She was nothing like her father. And her softness and sweetness reminded him of his mother.

Suddenly, he wondered what his mother had been like, as a girl, before she'd married his father. She must have been daring and adventuresome. She was American, after all, and she'd married his father, a sheikh, and although she'd loved the exoticism of her husband's culture, she'd apparently never assimilated into the culture, and Mikael's father hadn't helped her adapt, either. He'd left her to fit in. Left her to sort it out for herself.

A mistake.

But then, their entire marriage had been a mistake. Even he had been a mistake.

His mother had said as much, too.

His chest grew tight, the air bottled inside his lungs.

He did not want his future to be like his past. He did not want his children to grow up with such terrible unhappiness.

He lifted Jemma's hand, kissed her palm, her wrist, feeling the flutter of her pulse against his lips. Her skin felt soft and warm. She was soft and warm and he felt the strongest urge to protect her.

"I have a gift for you," he said, leaning back on the cushions.

"I don't need gifts," she answered, still unsettled, still reserved. "In fact, material things just leave me cold."

"So how can I spoil you?"

"I don't want to be spoiled."

"What can I give you then?"

She studied him for a long moment. "I want to know about you. Tell me something about you."

"Me?"

"Rather than presents, every day tell me something new about *you*."

"Showering you in jewels would be easier."

"Exactly." She looked at him, her expression almost fierce. "So if you want to give me something meaningful, give me part of you. Let me know you. That would be a true gift...one *this* bride would treasure."

He smiled faintly. "What shall I tell you? What would you like to know?"

"Tell me more about your mom," she said promptly. "And your dad."

"That's not a very pleasant subject."

"Parents and divorces never are."

"So why would you want to know about them?"

"Because they're important people in our lives. Our parents shape us. For good, and for bad." Her gaze met his. "Were you closer to one than the other?"

He sighed. He didn't want to talk about this, he didn't, but he liked her lying here next to him. She felt good here, and he wanted her to stay. "I don't remember being close to my father," he said after a moment. "But I'm sure he doted on me. Saidia parents tend to spoil their children, especially their sons."

"And your mother?"

"Adored me." It was uncomfortable talking about his mother. "She was a good mother. But then they divorced."

"Do you know why they divorced?"

He looked at her. "Do you know why your parents divorced?"

"My dad was having an affair."

Mikael hated the heaviness in his chest. He reached out and touched a strand of her hair, tugging on it lightly. "My father wanted to take a second wife," he confessed.

"So they divorced?"

"Eventually."

"What does that mean?" Jemma asked, turning onto her side.

"It means it took her nearly five years to successfully divorce him. My father didn't want the divorce, so he contested it."

"He loved her," Jemma said.

"I don't think he loved her. But he didn't want her to shame him. He was the king. How could his wife leave him?"

Jemma was silent a long moment. "Your mother loved him. She didn't want to share him?"

"I don't remember love. I remember fighting. Years of fighting." And crying. Years of crying. But not the tears of Saidia women. His mother only cried quietly, late at night, when she thought no one was listening.

But he had listened. He had heard her weeping. And he had never done anything about it.

Jemma put her hand on his chest, her palm warm against his skin. "She had to know when she married your father that he might take another wife."

"She said he promised her that he would never take another wife. She said he had it added to their wedding contract. But it wasn't there. My father said my mother never added a clause, and that she knew all along there would be other wives. That she was only the first." He hesitated, trying not to remember too much of those years, and how awful it'd been with the endless fighting, and then his mother crying late at night when the servants were asleep. "By the time the divorce was final, he'd taken three more wives."

Mikael looked away from the sympathy in Jemma's eyes,

uncomfortable with it. He focused on the ceiling of the pavilion, and the whirring of the fan blades. "I was eleven when the divorce was finalized."

Her fingers curled against his chest. "Did you go live with her?"

"No. I stayed with my father."

"You wanted to?"

"I didn't have a choice. I had to stay with my father." He glanced at her. "In Saidia, like many Arab countries, mothers do not retain custody of the children in a divorce. The children usually go to the father, or the closest male relative, and the sons always remain with the father."

She rolled closer to him, both hands against his chest now. "But you saw your mom sometimes?"

"No."

"Never?"

"She was expelled from Saidia." He reached out and caught her hair again, playing with the strand. "I wouldn't see her again for almost twenty years. In fact not until just a few months before your sister Morgan's wedding."

"What?"

He let go of the strand. "I couldn't see her after she left, and then, I wouldn't see her."

Jemma just stared at him, eyes wide, her expression shocked. "You punished her for the divorce."

He shrugged. "I had a hard time forgiving her for divorcing my father. Because yes, she knew that by divorcing my father, she'd lose me. He made it clear he wouldn't let me leave with her. But she divorced him anyway. She chose to leave Saidia and leave me behind." Mikael abruptly pulled away, rolling from the low cushions to stand up, and offered her his hand. "It's hot. We talked. I think it's time to cool off with a swim."

They swam and splashed for a half hour until their lunch was brought to them. They sat in their wet swimsuits beneath the shade of a palm tree eating lunch.

As Jemma nibbled on her salad she watched Mikael from beneath her lashes.

She was still processing everything he'd told her in the pavilion about his parents' marriage and divorce. Knowing that his mother was an American made it worse as Jemma found it so easy to identify with the woman, and how she must have felt in this Arab country with her powerful royal husband. And yet, even though his mother was an American and unhappy here, how could she leave her child behind?

How could she adore her son but then walk away from him?

"Do you look like your father?" she asked Mikael as they finished their meal.

Mikael ran his hand through his short black hair. "I wish I hadn't told you about the divorce."

"Why?"

"I'm not comfortable with it. Or proud of my father. Or myself. Or of any of the decisions made."

Jemma understood, more than he knew. She'd wanted to go live with her mother when her parents divorced, but she hadn't wanted to lose her father. And for years after the divorce, she'd still looked forward to seeing him, and she'd cherished the gifts he'd sent in the early years after the divorce—the dolls, the pretty clothes, the hot pink bike for her twelfth birthday—but then her parents quarreled again when she was thirteen, and all contact stopped. Her father disappeared from her life completely.

She hated him, and yet she loved him. She missed him and needed him. She went to London to start over, to get away from her past and herself, and she thought she had. Until the news broke that he'd stolen hundreds of millions of dollars of his clients' money.

Jemma looked at Mikael. "I sometimes think that if my parents hadn't divorced, and my father had been more involved in our lives, he would have made different choices. I think that if maybe we'd stayed close, he would have realized how much we loved him and needed him."

Mikael's expression was incredulous. "You blame yourself?"

"I try to understand what happened."

"He was selfish."

She flinched. "You're right."

"He was the worst sort of man because he pretended to care, pretended to understand what vulnerable people needed, and then he destroyed them."

Jemma closed her eyes.

"Who befriends older women and then robs them?" he demanded.

Eyes closed, she shook her head.

"Your father told my mother to refinance her house and give him the money to invest, promising her amazing returns, but didn't invest any of it. He just put it into his own account. He drained her account for himself." Mikael's voice vibrated with contempt and fury. "It disgusts me." He drew a rough breath. "We should not talk about this."

She nodded, sick, flattened.

Silence stretched, heavy and suffocating.

Mikael left his chair and paced the length of the pool. Jemma's eyes burned and she had to work very hard not to cry.

She was so ashamed. She felt raw and exposed. In the Arab world, she represented her family. She was an extension of her family, an extension of her father. Here in Saidia his shame attached to her. His shame would always taint her.

Silently Jemma left the pool, returning to the Chamber of Innocence to shower in the white marble bath, and shampoo her hair to wash the chlorine out. As she worked the suds in, she gritted her teeth, holding all the emotion in.

She wasn't sad. She wasn't scared. She wasn't lonely. She wasn't miserable in any way.

No, miserable would be living in Connecticut, trying to find a place to stay, wondering who might take her in, if maybe one of her mother's few remaining friends might allow her to crash on a couch or in a guest bedroom.

Rinsing her hair, she lifted her face to the spray. It was so hard to believe that her family had once had everything. Hard to believe they'd been placed on a pedestal. Their beautiful, lavish lifestyle had been envied and much discussed. Magazines featured their Caribbean home, their sprawling shingle house in Connecticut, the log cabin in Sun Valley. They had money for trips, money for clothes, money for dinners out.

Jemma turned the shower off, wrung the excess water from her hair wondering if any of it had been real.

Had any of it been their money to spend?

How long had her father taken advantage of his clients?

Bundled in a towel, she left the bathroom, crawled into the white and silver bed and pulled the soft Egyptian sheet all the way over her, to the top of her head.

It was hard being a Copeland. Hard living with so much shame. Work had been the only thing that kept her going, especially after Damien walked away from her. Work gave her something to do, something to think about. Working allowed her—even if briefly—to be someone else.

Now she just needed to get home and back to work. Work was still the answer. She simply had to get through these next seven days. And seven nights.

Jemma drew a big breath for courage, aware that the night would soon be here.

CHAPTER TEN

SHE WAS TO dress for dinner.

That's what the card attached to the garment bag instructed: *Dress for dinner. I will collect you at nine.*

Jemma unzipped the bag, and pushed away tissue to discover a sumptuous silk gown the color of ripe peaches. Ornate gold beading wrapped the hem and the long sleeve of the asymmetrical gown. The gown gathered over one shoulder creating a full flowing sleeve, while leaving the other shoulder and arm bare.

It was beautiful. Exotic. A dress for a desert princess.

There was a jewelry box in the bottom of the garment bag containing gold chandelier earrings studded with diamonds and pearls. They looked old, and very valuable.

She lifted an earring, holding it to her ear and looked in the mirror. The delicate gold and diamond earring was stunning against her dark loose hair. She'd wear her hair down tonight, dress like a desert princess. She hoped Mikael would not be angry this evening. The morning had been fun. He'd been a great companion. For a couple hours she'd forgotten why she was here.

He arrived at her door promptly at nine. Jemma had been ready for almost an hour. Opening the door she discovered he was dressed in his traditional robe again and she felt a stab of disappointment, preferring him in Western clothes. She felt more comfortable when he looked familiar, and not like the foreign sheikh he was.

"You look stunning," he said.

She smiled, hiding her nervousness. "Thank you."

"Do you know what we are doing for dinner?" he asked, leading her from the room, and down the outer corridor.

"No."

He smiled down at her. "Good."

He escorted her all the way to the front of the Kasbah, and out through the grand wooden doors. A car and driver waited for them.

The driver opened the back door of the black sedan. Jemma glanced at Mikael before climbing in. But he said nothing and his expression gave nothing away.

With Mikael seated next to her, the driver left the walled Kasbah. Soon they were driving through the desert, the car flying down the ribbon of asphalt. Moonlight bathed the miles of undulating sand.

Mikael pointed to the landscape beyond the tinted window. "This, my queen, is all yours."

She looked out the window, at the vast desert, and then back at Mikael, struggling to keep a straight face. "It is truly lovely sand."

"Are you making fun of my desert?"

"Absolutely not."

"Good." His eyes gleamed. "Because I value every single grain in this desert."

She smiled, and he smiled back and then his smile faded. He reached out and lightly touched the ornate gold chandelier dangling from her lobe. "These look beautiful on you."

"They are exquisite," she agreed.

"But you said you do not value jewels."

She looked at him warily. "Not as much as some women, no."

"But you value...*talking*."

He sounded so pained that her lips curved and her heart turned over. "Sharing," she explained.

"How do you feel about apologies?"

She lifted her brows. "In my experience, women love them. Men tend to hate them."

He smiled faintly. "That seems true in my experience as well." He hesitated. "And as difficult as it is for me to say I'm sorry, I owe you an apology. I was curt with you earlier, at the pool, and I focused my anger on you, when it's your father I am angry with."

She shifted uncomfortably. "You don't have to apologize. Every word you said was true. Your mother was treated terribly—"

"Yes," he interrupted quietly. "But that doesn't excuse how I spoke to you. And it doesn't make my behavior acceptable. You were reaching out to me, and sharing your experiences, and your feelings, and I lashed out, hurtfully. I am sorry for that. I take no pride in my faults, and as you have seen, I've many."

For a long moment Jemma could think of nothing to say. It was hard to speak when her eyes burned and her throat ached. She was surprised, and touched, by his honesty, never mind the humility. "Of course I forgive you. We all have things that hurt us."

His dark head inclined. "I am sensitive with regards to my mother, because my father mistreated her, and then I mistreated her, too."

"You were just a boy at the time of their divorce."

His features tightened. "I hated her for getting the divorce." The words were said bluntly, sharply. "Was her pride so important? Was her pride more important than me? She knew when the divorce was finalized, she'd leave the country, without me." He extended his legs as much as he could. "I'd be lying if I said that I understand now. Because I don't. Maybe I won't ever. But it was terrible then, being eleven, and knowing my mother chose to leave me."

Jemma reached to him, put her hand on his arm. "Perhaps she didn't think she'd really lose you. Maybe she thought things would turn out differently."

"How?"

"Maybe she thought your father would back down, change his mind, not move forward and marry a second wife. Or maybe she had worked out some sort of alternative custody arrangement. Maybe your father had agreed to share you...or even grant her custody while you were a child." Jemma leaned toward him, the delicate gold and diamond earring tinkling. "If your father had deceived her about the marriage contract, who knows what he might have said to her? Or promised her?"

He glanced at her. "But I didn't know that as a boy. I didn't know he was to blame. That he was the one who'd lied. So I blamed her."

"You were angry with her."

"I hated her."

"And then as an adult you learned the truth."

"Yes." His lips curved but the smile didn't reach his eyes. "And I hated him."

"You told him that?"

"No, not then."

"But you did go to your mother? You tried to make amends?"

He sat still, expression blank. "I waited a long time. I waited too long. If I'd gone to her earlier, and tried to help her earlier, she might not have relied so much on others. On outsiders."

"Like my father."

He nodded. "I should have been there for her sooner." His expression turned mocking. "You can see why I don't like talking about the past. I was not a good person. I was a very destructive person, and that is why I'm so driven to redeem the Karims and restore honor to our family and Saidia. I cannot let my mother's death be in vain."

"I think you judge yourself too harshly," she said gently.

"Power is never to be abused."

"I have yet to see you abuse your power. If anything, you appear determined to be fair, even if your idea of justice is very different from how we, in the West, would view it."

"Then perhaps I have begun to make amends." He smiled at

her, but his smile failed to light his dark eyes, then he glanced out the window, and nodded. "See those lights in the distance? That's where we are having dinner tonight, my queen."

Jemma gazed out at the swathe of darkness with the pin-pricks of light. "Is that a restaurant?"

"No." Amusement warmed his voice. "Not a restaurant. At least not the way you'd think of it. But it is where we're eating."

CHAPTER ELEVEN

JEMMA WAS SPEECHLESS as Mikael escorted her into the tent. Plush crimson carpets covered the sand. Rustic copper lanterns hung from the tent's wooden poles. More lanterns and candles glowed on low tables. From the fire pit outside the tent she caught a whiff of roasted lamb. As if on cue, her stomach growled.

Mikael looked at her. "Ready to eat?"

"Starving," she admitted.

"You're in luck. Our first course is ready."

The grilled vegetables and meat were served with a couscous flavored with slivered almonds and currants. They scooped up the couscous and meat with chunks of warm sesame bread and Mikael was fascinating company, as always.

Jemma welcomed his stories about Saidia's history and tribal lore, understanding now why he'd worn his robes tonight. This was his desert. His world.

Just then the evening breeze played with the sheer silk panels lining the tent, parting the material, giving her a glimpse of the white moon and the deep purple black sky.

The night sky was so bright and the stars dazzled. The sky never looked like this in London or New York. But in the vastness of the desert, with darkness stretching in every direction, the sky literally glowed with light.

"Beautiful night," Mikael said, following her gaze.

She nodded. "Amazing. I feel like I'm in a fairy tale."

He hesitated a moment. "I think after the honeymoon, we

should go visit your mother. I don't want her to worry about you. She has enough worries already."

"You'd let me travel with you?"

"With me, and without me. Marriage isn't a prison, and I'd never keep you from your family, or opportunities, provided you were able to fulfill your duties as my wife and queen." He paused, studying her. "I have a house in London. It's large, and comfortable. Well located. It needs you. Someone to fill it with people and parties."

Jemma looked away, emotion making her chest ache. "Now you're just teasing me. Tempting me with possibilities that are…impossible."

"How so?"

"You shouldn't dangle things before me. Or opportunities. I'm strong, but not that strong. If I stayed here, it shouldn't be for things." She turned to look at him again, her gaze locking with his. "It should be for the right reasons. It should be for you."

For a moment there was just silence. And then Mikael leaned forward, captured her face in his hands and kissed her lightly on the lips before releasing her.

Jemma's heart turned over. Her lips tingled. She nearly pressed her fingers to her mouth to stop the throbbing.

"Next time I see Sheikh Azizzi I must thank him," Mikael said, his deep voice pitched even lower. "I was angry with him in Haslam. I was angry that he'd try to saddle me with you, but obviously he knew something I didn't."

"Saddle doesn't sound very complimentary."

"You weren't happy about it, either."

No, that was true. She was shocked, angry, desperate. But happy? No.

But she almost felt happy right now. For the first time in months and months she felt calm. She felt content. She felt as if she could breathe.

Which is why she had to be careful. She needed to keep her guard up. It was vital she not let Mikael get too much closer.

While they'd talked a servant had removed the dishes, replacing the platters and bowls with trays of delicate biscuits and dried fruits.

"You really like London?" Mikael asked her, taking one of the dates stuffed with cheese and rolling it between his fingers. "It was never a culture shock?"

"I liked it from the start. No one paid me any attention. I felt free there." She selected one of the flaky almond cookies and broke it in half. "It's different now. I'm known, and more alone than ever."

"You're lonely?"

She nodded. "Yes. I miss what I had. Not the things, but the friends, the activities, the energy. I used to wake up every day, excited to see what the day would bring. Now I just get by. Push through."

"Once we return to Ketama, once everyone knows of our marriage, you will discover that doors presently closed to you, will open. As my wife, you will be welcome everywhere. As my wife, no one would dare to shame you, or exclude you."

Jemma popped half the cookie in her mouth and chewed, but her mouth had gone dry, and the cookie tasted like sawdust. "I don't want to be accepted because people are afraid of alienating you. I want to be accepted because people like me." Her eyes suddenly burned and she took a sip from her golden goblet. "It hurts to be scorned."

"Which is why you need my protection. I do not want you to suffer more than you have."

His gaze met hers and held. His dark eyes burned into her. She felt her pulse quicken, and butterflies flit wildly in her middle, her body humming with awareness.

Mikael would be a protective husband. He would probably be generous to a fault. He'd already showered her with gifts and trinkets, and was good at paying her compliments.

She wondered what marriage to him would be like. Not the honeymoon part, but the *ever after* part.

What kind of husband would he be?

Would he have expectations for his wife's behavior? Rules for the relationship? What would he not permit, or tolerate?

Mikael's eyes met hers, and held. "You have something on your mind."

"You can read me too easily. Have you always been so attentive to women?"

"No. Never." He leaned over and refilled her goblet. "I'm usually accused of being insensitive and self-absorbed."

"Are you different with me?"

"It would seem so."

"Because I am your wife?"

"Because I can't help but pay you attention. You command it."

"I *command* it. Interesting."

"You are a queen now. You are in a position of significance."

"Careful. The power might go to my head." But she was laughing as she said it, and from his lazy smile, she knew he was amused. "Do you enjoy your power?"

He thought about the question for a moment and then nodded. "Sheikhs are allowed to be as demanding as they like. It is the benefit of being royal. But power carries responsibility to provide for one's family, and people, and protect them as well. This is where my father failed. This is where I cannot fail."

"I do not think you will. You have the right mindset. You are focused on the right goals."

"I am less focused now that you are here," he admitted. "With you here I find I only want to think about you."

"It is your honeymoon."

"*Our* honeymoon," he corrected, reaching out to stroke her cheek, and then press his thumb to her lips.

Heat raced through her, followed by a frisson of sensation that made her breasts tingle and her legs quiver. She felt so aware of him and the awareness was a bittersweet tension, her body humming in response. She ached inside, at the place where her thighs joined, and she hated wanting…needing…

Jemma squeezed her thighs together, denying the need, and

struggling to ignore the way her skin tingled, sending fresh darts of sensation from her breasts to her belly.

His gaze met hers and held, and he couldn't know what she was thinking or feeling, but she blushed anyway, heat racing through her, making her hot and cold.

She was attracted to him. She was responding to him. It crossed her mind that she just might be in over her head.

"Yes, *laeela*?" he asked, reclining against the cushions. "What are you thinking?"

She shouldn't have agreed to this. She shouldn't have played this game. It was a game she could lose. "You...your government," she stuttered, thinking she could never admit that sex was on her brain. Sex, seduction, sensual lovemaking...no, better to keep the conversation away from the personal.

"Our government?" he repeated, eyes crinkling. "Politics intrigue you?"

No, but you intrigue me. You make me wonder about everything I do not yet know. Instead she crossed her legs and tried to calm herself. "Did you inherit your power?"

"Yes."

"Because you were first born, of the first wife?"

"Yes."

"Do you have brothers and sisters?"

"Yes. Many."

Interesting. "Are any of them in a government position?"

"There are three that have inherited significant tribal power and wealth, but so far these half brothers prefer to avoid work and responsibility."

"They are the sons of your father's second wife?"

"She had three boys in quick succession. They are handsome, popular, and quite headstrong."

"You like them?"

"I love them." He hesitated, smiling wryly. "And I imagine I will like them even better once they begin to grow up."

She grimaced. "It's easy to be self-indulgent when you're given everything. I grew up in a wealthy family, surrounded by peers from equally wealthy families. It's not the real world. As difficult as it's been this past year, I'm glad to be living in the real world. I know now who my true friends are. I know what matters."

"I hope one day my brothers discover what's true, and real."

"Perhaps they need an incentive to mature. Perhaps it's too easy for them…being young, handsome, and wealthy."

"They do have it too easy. Nothing is worse than a spoiled, billionaire prince."

"Were you ever like that? A spoiled, billionaire prince?"

"It was different for me. I've always known I would be king. And I've always been conscious that I was the son from the bad first wife, the American wife. I've tried hard to do the right thing, to avoid additional scrutiny and criticism."

She studied him, still warm, still so fascinated by this man and how he made her feel things and want things. But she had to be careful. She needed to remain in control. "We don't hear much about Saidia in the news in the US."

"That's because we try to stay out of the news, and we are a stable country. Historically, the Karims have gone to great lengths to ensure our people's happiness."

"So people are happy?"

"Yes. We have excellent schools and health care. Girls are actively encouraged to attend school, even pursue higher education. Marriage is forbidden under the age of eighteen, without parental consent." His dark eyes glowed. "Does that answer all of your questions? Or is there something else you'd like to know?"

The gleam in his eye was dangerous. It made her pulse leap, and her stomach lurch. Just like that, she felt him…near her, around her, as if they were connected. One. Which was ludicrous. She barely knew him and they weren't touching. He was reclining four or five feet away.

And yet her skin tingled and her insides felt strange, her nerve endings wound too tightly.

The desert wasn't safe. Not with Mikael in it.

"And what are you thinking of now?" he asked, his deep voice pitched low, making her think of dark sensual things that she shouldn't be thinking, not when alone with him.

"What is your seduction plan?" she asked. "What's supposed to happen tonight?"

He didn't smile, but she could have sworn he was laughing at her.

"What do you think is going to happen?"

She hated it when he answered her question with another question. "No idea. That's why I asked."

"I have an idea of how I think the evening will go," he said, watching her with that lazy interest, which she knew now wasn't lazy at all.

He was paying close attention to her, listening attentively to everything she said, observing everything she did.

He, too, was aware of the energy between them. Something was happening. She felt the heat and tension, the prickling awareness. It was sexual. And tangible. Her gown which had been so comfortable earlier now felt hot and tight, constricting.

"You are impossible," she whispered, breathless. He made her breathless.

Did he know the effect he had on her? Did he know that he made her curious? Weak?

She felt weak now, and hot, so hot, as tiny tongues of desire made her nipples tighten inside the delicate fabric of her dress.

"Yesterday was touch," he said. "I gave you a massage."

"Yes," she agreed. "It was an incredible massage, too."

"Today…what have we done so far?"

"Kissed," she whispered.

"Exactly. Today I can only kiss you."

"Oh." She tried to stifle the stab of disappointment.

"Fortunately, there are many different ways I can kiss you."

He stood up and walked around the perimeter of the tent, dropping the heavy panels, making the soft sheer silk curtains flutter in as the outside covers fell. "Different places I can kiss you."

Jemma held her breath as he continued to walk around the tent, closing them off from the night, and his staff, tying the cords on the inner panels, sealing them into a private world.

Soon the tent was a cocoon, and darker, with the loss of moonlight.

Mikael reached for a lantern and moved it, hanging it a little behind her. "Different places you might want me to kiss you." He moved another lamp, bringing it closer to the table next to her. "The lamps are so I can see you," he said. "I want to see you."

Her insides wobbled. She bit down on the inside of her lip to hide her flurry of nerves.

"I want to see you as I make you come," he added.

Her lips parted, shocked. She sat up taller, her hands going to her knees.

She shouldn't like it when he talked to her like this, but she did. He was untamed. "You think I'm joking?" he asked.

She didn't know how to answer, wasn't sure what to do or say, so she simply looked at him, chewing on the inside of her lip, nervous. Anxious. Excited.

This was his night. His game. He held the power.

"I have waited all afternoon for this," he said, prowling around her again, dark eyes burning, emphasizing the high hard lines of his cheekbones, jaw and chin. "Waited to see you naked. Waited to taste your skin."

A funny pang pinched her heart. She struggled to breathe.

He was frightening, arrogant, headstrong.

He was also overwhelmingly powerful, physical, and sexual.

She'd never met another man like him and she shouldn't be drawn to him, but she was.

For some reason she responded to him, to his edges and complexity. She was intrigued by his harsh justice, as well as his sensual nature.

She craved the sensual side of him. She wanted the sensation and pleasure of being bedded by him. She wanted to sleep with him. Wanted him naked against her, wanted his bare hands on her breasts and his mouth on her body. Wanted to be pinned beneath him and feel him thrust hard and deep, burying his body inside hers.

He moved in front of her, crouching before her, and tilted her chin up to look into her eyes. "I want you," he said, his deep voice velvety soft. "But I want your pleasure more."

And then he kissed her, deeply, the kiss so slow and so erotic that it immediately torched her senses, making her head spin.

He pressed her back against the soft carpet, and stretched out over her. She could still feel the press of his arousal through his robes. He was long and thick and hard.

His hand found her breast through her thin gown, his fingers rubbing and pinching and kneading her taut nipple. She trembled and sighed as he focused on one breast, and then the other.

She was hot and wet and aching for more.

Jemma pressed her thighs together, craving satisfaction.

"Don't come," he murmured against her mouth. "Relax. Let me enjoy your beautiful body."

"You're turning me on," she answered.

He shifted his weight, his hips grinding against hers.

The head of his arousal pressed against her pubic bone. His warmth made her want to open to him. She wanted him inside her, not on her. "This is torture," she whispered.

"Good torture," he said, drawing away, and placing a kiss on her chin, and then her neck, and he kissed his way down to her breastbone, and then lower, over the fabric of her gown covering her belly and then lower still, kissing the V of her thighs, his breath heating her skin, making the silk gown warm and damp. Making her warmer, damper.

She groaned as his teeth lightly nipped her. "Please," she whispered. "Be nice."

"I'm being very nice," he said.

And then he shifted his weight off her completely, and he reached for the hem of her gown.

Her heart slammed into her rib cage as he pushed her skirt

up, and carefully tugged her lace panties down, sliding them off her ankles, over each of her jeweled shoes. Then he parted her thighs, pushing them wide, and settled between them to kiss the inside of her knee, and then continued kissing her inner thigh, slowly working his way to her most intimate place.

Jemma gasped as his warm mouth settled on her, his tongue sliding up and down, stroking her.

She shuddered with pleasure, overwhelmed by the intense sensation. His mouth and touch made her feel so many different and disorienting emotions and sensations, filling her head with pictures and colors, all intense and vivid, electric and erotic.

The eroticism exposed her. The eroticism challenged her.

Who was she? What was she? What was true?

Jemma cried out as his tongue pushed deeper, his mouth cool where she felt so warm, his tongue circling provocatively across her taut, sensitive nub. At the sound of her cry, his hands pushed her thighs wider, his thumbs pressing against her bottom, holding her open.

It was shocking. Shocking because it was *him*, doing this to *her*.

She'd been raised to think for herself, raised to be independent, successful, and her brain told her she shouldn't enjoy this…being handled, managed, seduced. But her body liked it, and she was beginning to realize there was another side of her, a side she found rather frightening.

It was darkly sensual, and wanton. Illicit, too.

It was almost like an erotic dream…sexy, and sensual, and intense…

So intense, especially when he sucked and there was no holding back. The tension and pressure grew, electric sensation shooting through her. She couldn't resist it, couldn't resist him. With a cry she climaxed, shattering from his expert tongue and the intimate kiss.

For a moment after, Jemma didn't know who she was, or where she was. For a moment, she was just part of the night and the diamond studded sky. She felt endless, and open and free.

And then little by little she returned to herself, and him.

Opening her eyes, she looked at him, unsure as to what his reaction would be.

His dark eyes were hooded, his expression watchful. But protective. Maybe even a little possessive.

"Say something," she whispered.

"You're beautiful."

Her cheeks burned. "I don't even know how...or why...." She licked her upper lip, her mouth dry, her heart hammering. "Or what happened."

"I do." He crouched next to her, lifting a strand of hair from her warm, flushed face. "I wanted you to feel good. Did I make you feel good?"

"Yes."

"Then I feel good."

CHAPTER TWELVE

AN HOUR AND a half later, back at the Kasbah, Jemma lay in the center of the enormous bronze jeweled bed in the Topaz Chamber, and watched the blades of the fan turn overhead, hearing but not listening to the hum of the fan, seeing the orange silk panels at the window stir. The cool air felt good against her heated skin.

The soft whir of the fan's blades and the caress of cool air soothed her.

She was panicking. But there was no need to panic. Everything would be okay. Nothing terrible had happened, nothing life changing. He'd kissed her. Touched her. Brought her to an orgasm. It wasn't the end of the world, and it was not as if she hadn't ever indulged in oral sex before. Damien hadn't loved to do it, but that didn't mean she couldn't enjoy it.

And yet it was all so confusing. Her feelings. Her desire. And that rush of guilty pleasure, after he'd brought her to a climax.

Why had she felt guilty? Why should she feel bad for feeling pleasure? Was it because his lovemaking lacked love? Was it because his lovemaking had been so erotic?

She wished she knew. She wished she understood. She wished she wasn't alone now, in the bed, feeling this way.

Mikael had said he'd return soon. He'd told her after he escorted her back to the chamber, that he needed to make a phone call, and promised to come back as soon as he could, but it'd been an hour. She was still waiting.

"What's wrong?" Mikael's voice sounded in the doorway. She sat up quickly, startled, and yet also relieved.

"You're back," she said, drawing the sheet closer to her breasts. She'd changed from the evening gown into the peach satin nightgown with the gold straps that had been left out for her.

"Yes. Disappointed?" he drawled.

"No. I'm glad."

"Are you?"

She nodded, feeling strangely undone. Her throat ached. She swallowed around the lump. "I…missed…you."

He turned on a small golden lantern in the corner; the soft light illuminated the wide gold and orange stripes on the walls, this room as exotic as the tent earlier in the desert.

He'd showered and changed into black silk pajama pants and a black robe that he'd left open over his bare chest. His skin gleamed, gold. "I was gone longer than I intended," he said, reaching into the pocket of his robe. "But I've come bearing gifts."

"You know how I feel about presents," she said, as he took a seat next to her on the bed.

"Yes, but you should know by now how much I like giving them." He drew a wide jeweled gold cuff from the pocket of the robe, the thick cuff inlaid with pink diamonds, rubies, and topaz and fastened the bangle around her wrist

She glanced down at the heavy gold bangle, thickly studded with jewels. It had to be worth hundreds of thousands of dollars. "Are these all real gems?"

"Yes."

"It's old."

"At least one hundred and fifty years."

The ornate bracelet on her wrist slid forward, exquisite pink and ruby stones catching the light, casting prisms on the wall. A jeweled bed. A jeweled wrist. But jewels wouldn't keep her here. Jewels sparkled but they couldn't keep her warm. They wouldn't make her feel needed, loved. And that was what she wanted most. Love.

"Thank you," she said, giving her hand another light shake, admiring the enormous stones in the thick gold, using the time to divert his attention so he wouldn't see the tears in her eyes.

Things were becoming more complicated. She'd begun to feel things and if she wasn't careful, she'd make a mistake. A terrible mistake. And enough mistakes had been made.

"My pleasure," he answered.

She glanced up at him, hoping he wouldn't see her chaotic emotions. "Did you just return to give me this?"

"No." He took off his robe, and tossed it onto a low chair in the corner. "I forgot something."

"You did?"

"Yes. You." He went to the gold lantern and turned off the light before returning to the bed. "Scoot over. And don't worry. You can relax. You are safe. Nothing is happening tonight. I just want to sleep near my beautiful wife."

In bed, he drew her close to him, his arm loose around her waist, his hand resting on her hip.

For a moment she couldn't breathe. For a moment she waited, wondering if panic would hit. If she'd become nervous or uncomfortable.

If she'd dislike being held by him, held close to him.

None of those things happened.

He felt good. He felt warm. She felt safe.

Jemma woke up alone.

She told herself she didn't mind. Told herself she was glad. She needed space. She liked her independence. But it'd felt good having Mikael near her last night. She'd slept deeply for a change and she woke rested, and anxious to see him.

But Mikael didn't put in an appearance that morning. Instead there was a purple bikini and delicate violet silk cover-up waiting for her, along with a note telling her that tonight she'd sleep in the Amethyst Chamber.

Jemma changed into the pretty purple bikini and slipped the delicate silk cover up over her head, letting the light fabric settle against her tummy and thighs.

Purple was a good color for her. It flattered her skin. She wondered if Mikael would have a gift made from amethyst gems for her tonight. A necklace, a ring, or possibly earrings. She didn't want it, or need it, but it gave her something to think about, rather than her emotions.

She missed Mikael.

She didn't want to be alone.

But she had breakfast outside and then paced the courtyard, swimming when she grew too hot.

Lunch came and went, with her again eating by herself inside one of the air conditioned pavilions, needing the shade.

It was a long day waiting. She grew restless and angry. She peeled off the filmy violet cover up and swam again, and then stretched facedown on a lounge chair, the high desert temperature drying her purple suit almost instantly.

She buried her face in the crook of her arm, telling herself to relax, and calm down. She was getting herself worked up over nothing. Mikael would join her when he could. He'd be there as soon as he could manage it. There was no reason to feel so desperate, or lonely...

And then he was there.

Just like that.

His shadow stretched over her lounge chair, blocking the sun, and she turned over onto her back and looked up at him.

He gazed down at her with dark, smoky eyes. He was dressed in his robes. She suspected he'd had business earlier. But she didn't ask and he didn't tell her.

She raised a hand to shield her eyes and she let her gaze wander over him, up over his chest, to his neck, his hard jaw, the chiseled cheek and then to his eyes. He had ridiculously beautiful eyes. She'd kill for his lashes. It would save her a fortune in eyeliner and mascara.

"You smile." Mikael's deep husky voice vibrated between them, coloring the air, filling the space around them.

Heat danced through her, little sparklers lighting nerve endings beneath her skin. She flexed her feet, feeling her toes curl.

Amazing how little it took for him to turn her on.

Just a long glance from his dark eyes.

A word from his lips.

A certain pitch in his voice.

That's all it took and everything within her melted, wanting. Wanting him and what he did to her, and what he could make her feel.

Jemma drew a slow breath, and then exhaled just as slowly, trying to calm the frantic beating of her heart. "You have the longest, darkest eyelashes," she said, hating the slightly breathless note in her voice, knowing he'd notice. He always did. "I should steal them. You don't need them. I'm the model, not you."

The edge of his mouth lifted. He sat down on the edge of her lounge chair, his hand settling on her knees and then sliding up a couple inches on her thigh. "No Saidian queen has ever held a job."

"Are you saying I can't work if I am your queen?"

"You *are* my queen, and I haven't made any decisions with regard to your career. Although truthfully, it would be very unusual in Saidia, and would probably create a great deal of controversy, if you did continue working."

"So we know what that means."

He tapped the tip of her nose. "We don't know what that means, Miss Smarty Pants." He moved his hand to her thigh, his palm warm against her skin. "Would you miss modeling?"

"I would miss working."

"But not modeling specifically?"

She shrugged, and struggled to focus, which wasn't easy with the warmth of his hand stealing into her thigh. "I enjoyed my job until recently…when everyone dropped me."

"Could you be happy doing other things?"

He'd begun to draw invisible circles on her thigh, setting the nerve endings on fire.

"Such as?" she asked, her voice growing husky.

"Making public appearances. Talking to girls and advocating literacy. Making love to me. Having babies."

Every word he spoke was accompanied by another swoop of his finger across her bare skin, flaming the nerve endings all the while moving closer to her tiny purple bikini bottoms.

She was tempted to press her knees together to stop his fingers and yet she loved his touch, wanted more, wanted him to strip the bottoms off of her and part her thighs and settle between them again, and put his mouth on her, using his tongue and fingers to trace the shape of her soft folds and the tight sensitive clit—

"You're distracted," Mikael said, leaning in to kiss her, even as his palm slid over her thigh to her hip.

She shivered at the caress and the brush of his lips over hers. He pushed her heavy damp hair from her face and kissed her again, more deeply.

She sighed, as he lifted his head. She wanted more, not less. "Maybe a little," she agreed. "Where have you been?"

"I had some business to attend to."

"Out here?" she asked glancing around. "In the middle of the desert?"

"There is technology." He dipped his head, kissed her again, another tingling, soul-stirring kiss that made shivers race through her.

She reached up to touch his face. "When can I use your technology?"

"When the honeymoon is over."

"Is this tradition, or your rule?"

"Both. I want you to myself, and tradition says I have eight days to do just that…keep you hidden from the world during my attempt to win your heart."

"Are you trying to win my heart?" she asked, as his hand

stroked up her waist to brush the curve of her breast. "Or win my body?"

"I think I've already done that."

"You sound so sure of yourself," she said, gasping as his hand slipped beneath the fabric of her bikini top to cup her breast.

"I am." His head dropped and he kissed her again, even as he kneaded her breast and teased her sensitive nipple.

Desire surged through her, a hot, insatiable current that scalded her skin and made her melt on the inside. She leaned into his hand, her body aching, straining for more contact.

"You're starting it again," she whispered against his mouth. "You're wreaking havoc on my defenses."

His dark gaze held hers, the irises dark, mysterious. "You don't need defenses against me."

"Oh, I absolutely do. If I lose control, all bets are off."

"If you lose control, you're still safe with me." He kissed her again, and then caressed her lower lip, and the hollow beneath. "You will always be safe with me."

"I don't know, because this feels pretty dangerous."

He smiled a wicked smile which made her breath catch and her pulse race, making her heart pound and hum with the rest of her body.

His dark gaze settled on her mouth, and the quiver of her lower lip. "Good. Because this is desire."

The quiver of her lip intensified, along with the reckless rhythm of her heart. Blood drummed through her veins, warming her, making her skin hot and sensitive.

"And desire is important," he added, drawing his fingertip from her lower lip, down the middle of her chin, and lower still, down her neck to the base of her throat, and then on to her breastbone. It was such a light stroke, but slow, and long, and he lit every nerve ending he touched. "Desire makes us feel alive."

"It's so sexual."

"Mmm," he murmured, the corner of his mouth curving, and yet it wasn't a smile. It looked like hunger. "Is that a problem?"

She shivered, and would have looked away if he hadn't caught her chin, and forced her gaze to meet his. Her mouth dried. She licked her lips, blood roaring in her ears. "Sex without emotion is empty," she said.

"Is it? Even when you have this intense chemistry?" he asked, stroking the curve of her breasts, avoiding the taut, straining nipple. "How can this be empty?"

Her thoughts slowed, became tangled, her senses taking over, smothering reason. Was this empty? Was this connection bad?

Mikael's fingertip drew slow, lazy circles down the slope of her breast to the valley between, and then down across her flat belly to gently press against her through the material of her bikini bottoms.

She sighed as her head lit up with color and lights and pleasure.

"We enjoy each other," he added, tracing her softness, his knuckle brushing against her where she was so very sensitive. "We've been affectionate. We both feel a strong physical connection. What is missing?"

Love.

She wanted more than sex, more than pleasure. She wanted love. But it was so hard to say when he was touching her so intimately, making her head spin, and her senses pop and explode.

It was hard to focus, even harder for her to speak. "A relationship can't just be about sex," she said. "And I want more than pleasure."

"You don't think pleasure can lead to more?" His fingers slipped beneath the material to caress her intimately. She was hot and slick and he teased her, making her gasp and squeeze her thighs together to ignore what was happening inside of her.

"Can't pleasure generate love?" he persisted, before leaning over her and kissing one taut nipple through her top.

"I don't…think…so," she said, sucking in a breath as he

sucked her, drawing on her hard enough to create sharp pinches of sensation, the pleasure so intense it was almost like pain.

As he worked her breast he pressed his fingers into her, stroking her deep and rhythmically, matching the draw on her nipple.

Fire streaked from her breast to her womb. She felt her inner muscles clench him, her body already so hot and wet she knew she wouldn't last, knew she couldn't hold back. He had magic in his hands, and he knew just how to touch her, just how to seduce her. He could make her his slave with just a kiss and a touch...

"But you don't know for sure," he said, stroking deep, creating a maddening friction. His dark eyes sparked. "Pleasure happens in the mind. Love happens there, too." He leaned close, his lips grazing hers. "Why can't one lead to the other?"

She leaned in to the kiss, kissing him with desperation and hunger, as the tease of desire became a fierce consuming need. She hummed with tension. It coiled inside of her, throbbing, insisting, making her feel wild for release. "I need you," she choked. "Need you to make love to me."

"I am," he said, as his fingers pressed deep.

She bucked against his hand, frantic, and frustrated. "Not like this. I want you, your body, your skin, in bed, on me." She'd go mad if she didn't have him soon. "Let's go inside," she whispered, licking her lip, her mouth dry, heart hammering. "Now."

"And what shall we do there?" he asked.

She gave her head a shake, dizzy, dazed. "Everything."

The corner of his mouth lifted. "This is only day three, *laeela*. We're to draw the pleasure out...make you wait."

"I waited all day for you!" she protested.

"Pleasure can't be rushed."

"Oh, I think it can. You've already made me half mad." She sat up, and pulled him forward to kiss him deeply, drawing his breath into her, opening her mouth to him, welcoming the tip of his tongue, sucking on the tip even as he thrust his fingers into her. She was so close to shattering, so close that she was afraid he'd stop, and walk away, and leave her aching. "I need you," she whispered against his mouth, frantic for him, frantic for release.

"You have me," he answered, his hands where she needed them, his mouth on hers, his tongue answering hers.

Her fingers curled into his crisp hair. Her nails pressed against his scalp. She leaned into him, pressing her breasts to his chest, letting her hips move, grinding against his hand. She was wanton but he felt good and tasted good and right now, she felt alive, and hungry for life, which was so different from how she'd felt this past year.

To go from dead to life...

To feel beautiful, and powerful...

He brought her to a climax, and she cried out as she shattered against him. She tipped her head against his, panting in release.

She should be horrified. Instead she felt strong. Hopeful. Jemma opened her eyes, looked into his. "What have you done to me?" she whispered.

"I'm just making sure you're satisfied," he said, kissing her.

"I'm satisfied," she said, still breathless. "But what about you?"

"I'm good."

"Yes," she agreed. "You are." And he did feel good. He felt solid and real and permanent in the best sort of way. "Can we now go to the bedroom?"

He kissed her again, and smoothed her hair back from her face. "I wish I could. Unfortunately, I have another conference call and this one is going to take a while. The staff knows to serve you dinner when you're hungry. Don't wait for me."

"Not again!"

"I know it's frustrating but it's important. Trust me." His dark eyes held hers, searching hers. "Do you believe me?"

She sighed, and nodded, because she did believe him. She couldn't imagine him lying to her. Not now. Not ever. "Yes."

"Just know that I will come to you tonight in the Amethyst Chamber, as soon as I can."

"I don't want to go there without you."

"But I will be there, *laeela*. I promise. Soon."

She ate dinner alone in the Amethyst Chamber, the walls painted a deep plum, and then stenciled in gold. The low wooden bed was framed with long embroidered silk curtains in shades of purple and plum, with violet hued pillows and a silk coverlet decorating the bed.

She didn't belong here, she thought, finishing her dinner, and returning the dishes to the tray by the door.

She didn't belong in Saidia and she didn't belong in Mikael's life. When she was with him, he distracted her from reality, making her forget what was true and important.

Like her work, and her family.

Like getting back to London and to those who did love her.

It was good to be away from him this evening. It was good to have time to herself, to find herself, and most of all, to remember how she'd come to be here, at the Bridal Palace, in the first place.

She'd been forced here. She'd been forced into this marriage. And she'd been forced to surrender to Sheikh Karim.

She had to remember that. Had to remember the facts, and reality, next time Mikael showed up, and touched her, and kissed her and made her want nothing but him.

She fell asleep, with the light on, determined to be strong when he arrived. She would resist him this time. She wouldn't melt for him. She wouldn't ache or need or shatter in his hands. Not anymore. Never again.

As her eyes closed she counted the days and nights she'd been here. Tonight was the third night. That meant there were just five more and then she'd be free.

Jemma woke up, blinked. It was morning. She looked around, pushing her long hair back from her face, and tugging the strap of her filmy purple nightgown back up onto her shoulder.

She was alone.

Good.

Good, she silently insisted. She'd gone to bed alone so it shouldn't surprise her that she was the only person in the bed, but she'd dreamed about Mikael all night, dreamed of Mikael kissing her, making love to her, and it'd felt so real. She woke up feeling as if he had been there, with her.

But he wasn't. It was a figment of her imagination. A dream.

She stretched her arm out across the empty bed, suddenly terribly homesick.

Day four, she told herself. Just four more days, and four more nights, and she'd be home.

The thought should have pleased her, reassured her, instead her heart fell, and her eyes burned. She missed Mikael. She shouldn't miss him. She should hate him.

The wooden door to the en suite bath creaked. Jemma sat up, startled.

Mikael appeared in the doorway, wearing nothing but loose cotton pajama pants that hung deliciously low on his hip bones. He raked a hand through his dark hair, making muscles ripple in his arms and chest.

She stared at his lean flat abdomen, each muscle hard and distinct.

"You're awake," he said, walking toward her and giving her the most devastatingly wicked smile.

Her heart lurched. "Where did you come from?"

"The bathroom."

Her heart did another funny little tumble. Just looking at him made her feel a pang. She didn't understand why he did that to her. She frowned. "How?"

"I walked."

She made a face, rolling her eyes. "Yes, but when?"

"Just a few minutes ago."

Her mouth dried. Her pulse was doing crazy, wild things. "But you weren't here. I fell asleep waiting for you."

"You might have fallen asleep before I arrived, but I did

come to you last night. I slept with you last night. I promised you I'd be here, and I am." He drew back the covers and slid in next to her. "You don't remember last night?"

"No." She frowned. "Did we...do...things?"

He reached across the bed for her, dragged her toward him, tangling her bare legs in the covers. "No. Regretfully not. I just held you. And spent the night with an endless hard-on."

She laughed as he pulled her under him but her laughter died as he lowered his powerful body onto hers. He was hard now. His length pressed against her belly.

"It's back," she whispered breathlessly.

"That's because it never went away." He dipped his head and kissed the side of her neck.

She sighed and arched against him. His hips ground against hers. She pressed her hips up, rubbing against the tip of his thick shaft, wanting it, wanting him.

"You want me," he said, his voice a rasp in her ear.

She nodded as his mouth covered hers, and she wrapped her legs around his hips. She did want him. All of him. And not just the things he did to her, but the things he made her feel. "Yes," she said, because she needed this, needed to feel. It had been a year of so much sadness and confusion that she needed to feel something warm and good again.

Mikael was making her feel very warm and good.

"What shall I do to you?" he murmured, kissing her jaw, and then her chin, before brushing her mouth with his.

She reached up, and wound her arms around his neck, drawing his head down. "Everything."

They kissed for hours, kissing until they were both panting and damp and tangled in sheets. Jemma wanted more, but she also loved this, the intense need, the desire, the fierce pleasure of just wanting and being wanted.

Her body ached and throbbed, even as her heart ached and throbbed. And as Mikael kissed her, touched her, his hands lighting her on fire and keeping the flames burning, glowing, she began to think that this might not just be lust anymore.

This wasn't about sex, either. It was more than sex. More than desire. Something else was stirring to life but what it was, she didn't know, and wasn't ready to face. Wasn't sure she could.

"I have news for you," he murmured against her mouth, his hands tangled in her hair. He kissed her once more. "We should talk."

Jemma went still. "What is it?"

"Your mother." He shifted his weight and moved away from her, rolling onto his back. He grabbed a pillow and placed it under his head. "And she's not sick, so you don't need to look at me like that."

"Like what?" Jemma demanded, sitting up, and tugging her sheer nightgown down, hoping she was adequately covered.

"Like something terrible has happened to her. Nothing terrible has happened. What's happened is good."

"What's happened?"

"It isn't good for your mother to have so much stress. A woman of her age needs to have her own home. I think she will do better if she has her own place again."

"Of course she would. We would all like that for her. But it's a dream at this point."

"There's a turn of the century shore colonial in Keofferam in Old Greenwich that I think would suit her. It has a big wraparound porch, and a small caretaker's apartment over a detached garage for a housekeeper or nurse, should your mother one day require one. It's recently been renovated so your mother wouldn't have to do anything."

"Yes, that all sounds very lovely, but you can't buy property in that area for less than two million, and a home such as the one you describe would easily be upward of three million—"

"Almost four," he agreed, "but it's in pristine condition and has the high ceilings and elegant formal rooms she would enjoy."

Jemma reached for a pillow and drew it to her chest. "You sound as if you know her."

"I did meet her at your sister's wedding, but you forget, your mother and mine were very similar in background. It's not difficult to imagine the kind of home she would be comfortable in, so I can tell you now that the house is in escrow, and I've been assured it will close at the end of today, as the wired funds have already reached the bank. I had my Realtor purchase the house in your mother's maiden name, which apparently is her legal name again. No one can take it from her."

Jemma stared at him. "I don't understand."

"I think she's suffered enough, don't you?"

Jemma struggled to speak around the lump filling her throat. "But you hate the Copelands."

"I hate your father, but your mother shouldn't be punished for his crimes." He hesitated. "Nor should you. So I did what I thought was best. It is my gift to you—"

"It's too much. I can't accept—"

"You don't have to. The gift is in your mother's name. There's nothing you can do about it."

"She won't accept it."

"She has."

"What?"

"I have been communicating with your brother, Branson. He has assisted me with a few financial details."

"He would never do that!"

Mikael sat up, muscles tightening across his chest, rippling down the length of his bare, lean torso. "You don't think a son wants his mother safe? Protected?"

"I know Branson. He wouldn't allow you to do such a thing."

"He would, if he understood we had done it together."

Jemma grew still. "You told him about…us?"

"I told him you were here with me, and that I intended to make you my queen."

"And he was okay with that?"

Mikael nodded and lay back down, arms folding behind his head. "Better than okay. He was very pleased for both of us and offered to throw us a party in London, as soon as we could visit. I told him we'd be there soon, probably before the end of the month."

She squeezed the pillow tighter. "You sound so smug."

"You should be happy I helped her, not angry."

"You can't do these things, though."

"Why not? I am your husband. It's my duty to provide for you and your family."

"A family you hate."

"Things have changed. You are my wife, and my family now, and I seek to honor you, and your family—"

"But what happens when I leave here in four days? What happens when you send me back? You promised you would, if I wasn't happy—"

"Are you unhappy?"

Her mouth opened but no sound came out. Was she unhappy?

It was strange to be asked that question now, so bluntly, because no, she wasn't unhappy. She was actually happier than she'd been in months, maybe even years.

"That's not the point," she said, sliding off the bed to pace the room.

"It's not?"

"No." She paced back toward him, confused, frustrated, no longer sure of anything.

"Then what is the point? Because I thought I had eight days to prove to you that I could make you happy, and I am making you happy, so what is the problem?"

She threw out her hands. "This!" she cried, gesturing at the purple walls with gold stencil. "This," she added, plucking at the silk nightgown. "This," she said, pointing to the bed, where he lay so supremely confident and comfortable, looking every bit a king. "None of this is real. None of this is my real life. It's just a dream. It's surreal. It's not going to last!"

"Says who?" he asked tersely, revealing the first hint of impatience.

"Me!"

"And you are an expert on reality? You, with the model for a boyfriend and the plan to enter Saidia on a stolen passport?"

"It wasn't stolen, it was my sister's, and you're hateful to throw Damien in my face. You know I loved him, and you know he hurt me. And you're just jealous because you can bombard me with expensive gifts but you know deep down, you'll never be able to buy my love."

Jemma walked out, pushing through the doors to the central courtyard, and then on to the other side, through a door to the Chamber of Innocence. She grabbed an ivory robe from the bathroom, wrapped it around her, and then walked out, leaving the Bridal Palace in search of her own wing. Her rooms, the ones she'd been brought to on arriving at the Kasbah.

She was done with this stupid honeymoon game. Done being kept locked up like a kidnapped bride. She wanted out. She wanted to go home.

"Where do you think you're going?" Mikael's deep voice rang out behind her. "We're not done, *laeela*."

"I am."

"It doesn't work that way."

"Maybe not for you!"

"Or you," he retorted, scooping her up into his arms and dropping her over his shoulder. "You owe me eight days and nights, and we're only halfway through. I get four more, and I will take all four."

"I don't want to do this anymore!"

"Too bad." He was carrying her back the way she'd just come, walking swiftly, his arm anchored across the back of her legs, holding her in place. "This isn't a game. You don't get to run away when you're tired or your feelings are hurt. This is real, you and me. This is reality."

He'd kicked open a door down the hall and then kicked it closed behind him. The room was dark and yet he knew where he was going, crossing the floor with long sure strides to drop her unceremoniously on the bed.

She scrambled into a sitting position. "Get out."

"That's not happening."

"I want to be alone."

"That's not happening, either." He untied the sash at her waist, peeled the robe off her shoulders and reached for the hem of her nightgown.

She slapped at his hands. "Don't touch me!"

"That, my dear wife, *is* happening."

CHAPTER THIRTEEN

MIKAEL REACHED PAST Jemma and turned on the small glass lamp on the bedside table, flooding the room with soft ruby light. The bed beneath Jemma gleamed with luxurious red satin, while the large jeweled mirror on the ceiling reflected the silk-covered walls and the decadent satin sheets.

With an irritated flick, he yanked the hem of Jemma's violet nightgown up, pulling it over her head and then tossing the scrap of violet silk onto the floor, before kicking off his own pajama bottoms. "We don't need these anymore," he said flatly, "now that we're in the Crimson Chamber."

Jemma scrambled back on the bed. "You've lost your mind."

"Maybe. Or maybe I've lost all patience. I'm not sure which right now," he said, grabbing her ankle and pulling her back toward him.

Jemma sprawled back on the bed, her long dark hair spilling across the crimson satin, her green eyes flashing. She'd never looked more beautiful. He would have her now. No more games. She was his. He'd chosen her. Married her. She was his queen.

He stretched out over her, and settled his weight between her thighs, his arousal pressing against her core.

She was hot, wet and his length rubbed against her slick heat. It would be so easy to thrust into her, and take her.

So easy to prove to her how much she wanted him.

He knew she craved him physically.

He knew he could make her scream and climax. He could draw out the orgasm and make it last for hours, too.

But that wasn't the point. His expertise as a lover wasn't in question. His future as a husband was. His father might have failed as a husband, but Mikael wouldn't.

Mikael dropped his head, and kissed her neck just above her collarbone, and then kissed higher on her neck, at the spot beneath her ear. He kissed the hollow and then the earlobe. He caught her earlobe in his teeth, his teeth lightly scraping, his breath lightly blowing in her ear.

He felt her nipples pucker and harden against his chest. He released her wrists and stroked her arms, moving in toward her ribs to cup the sides of her breasts, her skin soft and warm and then he stroked out again until his hands covered hers, his fingers linking with hers.

He kissed the side of her jaw, kissed the pulse beating frantically in the hollow beneath her ear and then he covered her mouth with his and kissed her, deeply, his tongue thrusting into her mouth, probing, possessing.

Her thighs parted wider for him. Her hips arched, her body rocking up against him.

"You aren't really angry because I helped your mother," he said, lifting his head to look down into her face. The paleness in her face was gone. Her cheeks flushed pink. She wanted him. "You're angry because you're afraid. You're angry because you're afraid these gifts—particularly this gift to your mother—will trap you in Saidia, with me."

Her eyes widened and she bit down into her lower lip.

He was right. That was her fear.

His chest grew tight. He felt an unaccountable pang, the pang eerily reminiscent of the ache and loss he'd felt after his mother left Saidia all those years ago. "*Laeela*, I made you a promise. You give me eight days and nights, and I will not keep you here against your will—"

"It's not you I'm afraid of," she interrupted. "It's me. I believe you will let me go. I believe you will put me on a plane should I request it. But I'm afraid that I might not request it, might not insist on it, and then everything that is uniquely me and mine, everything that I have worked so hard for all these years, will be gone."

"But if you remain here, you gain a new identity and a new life."

"As *your* wife. But I won't be anyone without you, and I vowed years ago to never be dependent on a man, much less a powerful man, and here in Saidia, I will be completely dependent on you."

"Is that such a bad thing if the powerful man is a just man?"

Her eyes turned liquid and she swallowed hard. "You already make my heart ache."

"I think we would make a good team, *laeela*."

She struggled to smile. "Maybe you should just make love to me."

He dipped his head, kissed her lips. "Good idea. So what do you want, my beautiful bride? How can I please you today?"

"You," she said. "I just want you."

Jemma saw heat flare in Mikael's eyes and felt him harden against her.

She rocked her hips up, savoring the sensation of him against her. He was hard and warm, so warm, and she couldn't remember ever wanting anyone like this. "Make love to me, Mikael," she added, wrapping her arms around his neck and sinking her fingers into his crisp hair. "I need you."

His mouth covered hers, his tongue parting her lips to take her mouth even as he thrust smoothly, deeply into her body, filling her, stretching her.

He felt unbelievable.

She felt unbelievable.

Jemma's eyes burned and her chest ached, emotion bubbling up inside of her. Her arms slid down around his shoulders to hold him tighter. He was big and powerful and yet he fit her, and felt perfect to her.

Mikael kissed her, drawing her tongue into his mouth, sucking the tip even as he buried himself deeper into her body. She welcomed his weight and the fullness that stole her breath, and then he began to move. His lean sculpted hips dipped and he pressed deeper, then withdrew, only to stroke deep into her again.

She sighed and arched as he hit a spot inside her that tingled with pleasure. "More," she said, pressing up against him as he drove into her.

"I don't want to hurt you."

"It doesn't hurt. It feels so good." And it was true. It felt delicious everywhere. She felt delicious. Everything inside her was warm and sweet and bright. She felt like sunshine and honey, orange and spice and each stroke made her sigh a little deeper, and press against him a little harder.

"Don't stop," she whispered, meeting each of his thrusts, needing the friction, feeling the tension build. Each stroke of his body made her nerve endings tense, tighten, tingle.

He drove into her faster, increasing the rhythm. She loved the rhythm, the deep hard thrusts, the slickness of their bodies together, the warmth of his chest against hers. She could smell the scent of him, and them together, and it smelled right, felt right, more right than anything she'd ever felt before.

It didn't make sense, but then, none of this made sense and maybe passion never did.

The teasing tension within her quickened, sharpened, becoming bigger, and more powerful.

She panted and strained against him, wanting to come, not sure she could come and then he slipped his hand between them, stroking her even as he thrust hard into her wet tight body.

She wasn't prepared for the intensity of the orgasm and she screamed his name as he continued to stroke her, pushing her over the edge, her control shattering, her body climaxing, convulsively tightening around him.

He tensed, strained, his big powerful body arching as he buried himself deep inside her. She was still convulsing around him, her body squeezing him. With a guttural cry, he pulled out, making sure he spilled his seed into the sheets and not her.

She rolled over on the bed, on to her back, eyes closed, still struggling to catch her breath. He followed, lying on his side, next to her, his hand settling low on her hip.

She floated, feeling blissfully relaxed, and yet also very aware of Mikael at her side. She could feel the pressure of his hand, the warmth of his skin, smell his masculine spicy scent, practically hear his steady heartbeat. He was more real to her right now than she was.

He'd become her world in four days. It was exactly as she'd feared.

Jemma opened her eyes to find Mikael looking at her, his dark eyes so beautiful but so impossible to read. "Yes?" she whispered, dazzled, dazed.

"How do you feel?"

She let out a soft laugh and she turned to him, moving into his arms to rest her face on his chest. She could hear his heartbeat, smell his scent.

He smelled good. He felt good. He felt perfect, really.

"Good," she said softly, smiling unsteadily, because her emotions were bubbling up high and fast. "Very, very good."

They slept for an hour like that and Jemma woke first, sleepily stirring but couldn't move as Mikael's arms were around her and his muscular thigh was tucked between hers.

She lifted her head, looked down at him. He was still asleep, his thick black lashes beautiful onyx crescents against the gold of his cheek.

He looked different asleep. Younger. Boyish. Just a man, not a sheikh.

She put her head back down and nestled closer, liking the weight of his arm, the texture of his skin. He felt right. Perfect.

Did other women feel this way after making love? She'd had sex before but it hadn't felt like this. Like something important had happened. Something significant.

Even now she felt the rippling of emotion, like aftershocks. Something inside her felt aware, awake. Stirred.

Was this love? It couldn't be. She had to be feeling merely the side effect of seduction, and passion, all the result of his expert lovemaking.

If that was the case, then why did her very heartbeat seem to repeat his name? *Mik-ael. Mik-ael. Mik-ael.*

A moment later, he shifted, rolling on to his back, carrying her on top of him. His hand tangled in her long hair, and he parted her thighs, pushing her down against his hips. He was hard again, his erection rubbing against her. "Are you too sore to let me love you again?" he asked, his deep voice as husky and smoky as his dark eyes.

"No."

He lifted her, drawing her down on him, and with his hands on her hips, he helped her ride him, slow and deep, and then faster as the pleasure built.

After they both came, she tumbled forward onto his chest, and he held her. Her eyes closed. She listened to the thud of his heart and breathed him in.

He felt so good. He made her feel safe. *Happy.*

She was happy. This was the best place she'd been in months, emotionally, physically. In years.

Silence stretched between them, silence and a tingling awareness that everything had changed.

Mikael breathed in, out, and she traveled with his breath, his chest lifting her, carrying her.

That's how it'd been when they were joined. She'd felt lifted, carried, supported.

It had been so intimate, and yet it wasn't just sex. It felt like so much more, maybe because it had been so intense, and so physical, it'd demanded all of her, and she'd surrendered.

Making love to him, she gave herself up to him, offering him everything—her body, her mind, her emotions…her heart.

Why her heart? It made no sense. Jemma protected her heart. She'd learned it was necessary for survival. And yet in one morning of lovemaking, she'd dropped her defenses, lost her boundaries and become someone else. Or something else.

Changed.

There was that word again. She couldn't help going back to it. Changed. Altered. Shattered.

Confused.

How could sex do that? How could sensation be so powerful? She didn't understand and yet everything inside her felt open. Her heart felt open.

She pressed her palm to his chest, savoring the steady thud of his heart. "Did you really buy my mother a house?" she asked huskily.

His fingers played with her hair, twisting the long strands. "I will go check and see if the escrow has closed. I expect it will have."

"And then it will be hers?"

"And hers alone," he agreed.

Jemma hesitated. "Even if I leave here in four days?"

"No one can take it from her."

Jemma was profoundly moved, but also troubled. "I don't know what to say. I know I should thank you—"

"You don't need to thank me. I didn't buy it for you. I did it for her."

"You don't even know her."

"I met her at Morgan's wedding. She was kind to me. I liked her. She reminded me of my mother."

Mikael left her to check on the status of the house and Jemma showered and dressed, slipping into the long ruby beaded skirt and matching ruby top laid out on the bed. Breakfast was served in the courtyard. She'd just sat down and had her first coffee when Mikael returned.

"Escrow closed. The paperwork has been signed. The house is hers," he said, taking the chair opposite Jemma's.

"Thank you," Jemma said. "Thank you for caring for her. Thank you for wanting the best for her."

"I do for her what I should have done for my mother." His brow furrowed, and his voice dropped, cracking. "I was not good to my mother. I failed her, and I will carry that pain, and that shame, with me forever."

She reached across the table, and covered his hand with hers. "How did you fail her? What did you do?"

"Nothing. That is what I did. Absolutely nothing."

"I don't understand."

"When I explain, you'll be appalled. And you should be. My behavior was selfish and it still disgusts me, but it's too late to fix things. Too late to make amends."

Jemma winced at his sharp tone, his voice laced with self-loathing and scorn. "Explain to me."

"I was twenty-two when I learned the truth about my father and mother, that my father had lied to her, and had destroyed their wedding contract so he could take another wife. I was furious with my father," he said, "but I'd lost my mother years ago, when I was just a boy, eleven, and I was terrified of losing my father, too. He had so many other children, so many other sons he could admire and love, and so I pretended I didn't know the truth about the divorce. I pretended that I didn't know who my father was—a liar, a cheat—and I acted as if my father was this wonderful man."

"You were his son," she said. "You were showing him respect."

"My father had turned his back on my mother. I understood he expected me to do the same. And so I did, even when she came to me on my twenty-fifth birthday, asking for help. She was nervous about her future. She wanted financial assistance, and advice. She was worried she wasn't managing her money well. She was worried she'd run out if she didn't have the right investments."

"Did you help her?"

"No."

"No?"

His jaw tightened. "I took her to coffee and told her I couldn't help her, that she'd created this situation by leaving my father. I told her there was nothing I could do." Mikael averted his face, staring off across the courtyard, his features set. "She didn't cry. She didn't beg. She just folded up her papers and slipped them back into her purse, then kissed me, and left."

Jemma's eyes burned. "You were young."

"I wasn't young. I was angry." He turned to look at her, expression fierce. "I wanted to punish her for leaving me all those years ago, for leaving me with a father who barely remembered me because he had so many wives and sons and daughters, all clamoring for his attention. So I rejected her, wanting her to hurt as I had hurt."

Silence stretched.

He drew a deep, rough breath. "I never did help her with her investments, even though I had degrees in finance and economics. Even though I worked in London as an institutional investor until I was nearly thirty." Mikael shifted restlessly. "I knew money. I knew how to make money. And I could have aided her, protected her, but I didn't. So she went to your father and trusted him, and we all know how that turned out."

"But she didn't go to my father until after Morgan's wedding. At least, that's what I thought you said."

"Yes. But she went to him because she'd made some bad investments earlier, and your father promised he could do impossible things with what capital she had left. He could get her an incredible return on her investment with him, and so she gave him everything. Everything. And he stole it all."

Jemma winced, sickened all over again by her father's betrayal. "That's on his head, not yours."

Mikael turned his head, looked at her from beneath his dense black lashes. "My mother should have died of old age, comfortable in her American home. But she lost her home, along with her nest egg. Heartbroken, and terrified, she took her life. Hung herself in the hall of her home the day she was to be evicted."

Jemma stared at him, aghast. "She killed herself?"

He nodded. His jaw worked, and he ran a hand down his throat, as if trying to find the words. "She was just fifty-four," he said when he could finally speak again. "But she'd lost her home…again. She knew she couldn't go to my father. She was afraid to come to me. We were still rebuilding our relationship and she was afraid I'd be disappointed in her, so she panicked. She did what she thought was the best answer for all."

"I'm so sorry."

"I still have that last note, the note she left, saying she was sorry, and begging me to forgive her for being stupid and weak."

He turned his head abruptly but not before Jemma saw the suffering in his eyes.

For several moments there was just silence, an endless, impossible silence heavy with grief.

Jemma reached out and placed her hand over his. "People make mistakes," she whispered.

"It's my fault she died," he said. "At first I blamed my father, and your father, but I am the one responsible for this. I did this to her. I rejected her. Refused her. I left her no hope—"

"Would you have helped her if she came to you about her house, Mikael?" she interrupted, leaving her seat and moving around the table to kneel before him. "If she'd told you her situation, that she had nowhere to go, and no way to pay her bills, would you have taken care of her?"

"*Yes*."

"Are you sure? Or is that what you say now?"

He stiffened, shoulders squaring. His dark eyes burned down at her. "You don't think I would?"

"*I* know you would," she said, taking his hands, holding them tightly. "But do you? That's the important question. Because until you believe you would have helped her, you won't be able to forgive…you, her, or your father."

CHAPTER FOURTEEN

MIKAEL WAS DONE talking. He'd said far more than he'd intended to say but he was glad he'd told Jemma the truth. Glad she knew now who he was, and what he was. Better for her to know on the fourth day than the eighth. Better to give her all the facts up front, instead of blindsiding her at the end.

He rose from the table, drew her up to her feet. "I cannot think anymore, or talk anymore. I am talked out. I need diversion. What about you?"

"What do you have in mind?"

"You'll see."

She followed him back into the Crimson Chamber. The satin sheets had been changed, and freshly made, the bed lined with stacks of ruby-hued pillows.

A bright white light shone from the ceiling, onto a screen attached to the far wall.

He saw Jemma glance up at the light, and then saw the moment she realized it was actually a projector. "Is that what I think it is?" she asked, turning to him.

"Do you like movies?"

"Yes."

"I do, too. I thought maybe you could use a break from the pool and the sun and would enjoy a good film."

"I'd love it. But only if you stay with me. Otherwise I wouldn't enjoy it at all."

Jemma loved their afternoon at the movies in the Crimson Chamber. The dark red walls and rich burgundy and ruby pillows and cushions made the room feel like an elegant, and exotic, movie theatre. Staff brought them food during a break between the two films, a break Jemma laughingly called the "intermission," and then curled back up in Mikael's arms when the second film began.

He had to leave at the end of the second movie to check in with his staff. He kissed her before he left and promised to meet her for dinner in the courtyard. They were to dine outside tonight, inside the pink and turquoise tiled pavilion. "We'll go to the Turquoise Chamber tonight. You'll enjoy tonight," he told her, kissing her again.

"I've enjoyed every night," she answered truthfully, smiling up at him.

She arrived in the courtyard that evening before he did, dressed in the filmy turquoise kaftan that had been laid out for her.

The kaftan was long, reaching her ankles and it swished as she walked, clinging to her stomach, hips and thighs.

Jemma wandered around the grand courtyard, admiring the large blue tiled pool lit by blue and pink lights, and pausing to smell the sweet fragrant lilies and roses that grew in clusters in enormous glazed pots.

She was glad she'd arrived in the courtyard before Mikael. She enjoyed having this moment to herself, liked the excitement bubbling within her, and the sense of anticipation.

She'd enjoyed this afternoon with Mikael. She'd found it hard to concentrate on the movies, though, with him there, at her side. She'd wanted him to make love to her, but he hadn't. He'd held her, and kissed her several times, but he'd otherwise shown admirable restraint.

She, on the other hand, wanted to be touched. She'd curled at his side, pretending to watch the movie when all she really wanted was touch. She was beginning to feel addicted to pleasure. Or was she addicted to him? She didn't know, wasn't sure how she could know.

Jemma felt a tingle down her spine. She wasn't alone anymore. She knew Mikael had arrived even before she turned to see him.

Slowly she faced him. He was standing at the far end of the pool, watching her. "That color suits you," he said.

Suddenly the courtyard hummed with energy. She felt the same electric surge in her veins, her heart racing, too.

He was wearing black trousers and a white linen shirt and he looked handsome and virile and confident.

Her husband. Her king.

She smiled, amused by the thought, but the thought took hold. He might very well be a good husband for her. He seemed to be a good king.

A servant appeared with a tray of cocktails and together Jemma and Mikael walked around the courtyard, with Mikael pointing out various plants that had significance, whether due to age, or relationship to the Kasbah.

"The date palms were for a great-grandmother, and the citrus trees were for my grandmother. The trees are replaced every ten to fifteen years, depending on their maturity and fruit production. My mother loved pink roses, so those were for her." Mikael smiled at her. "What shall we plant in your honor? What is your favorite flower?"

She shook her head. "I think it's all perfect just the way it is. I wouldn't change anything."

"You don't want to be immortalized in the Bridal Palace's garden?" he asked.

She knew he was teasing her. She could see it in his eyes and the quirk of his mouth and she felt a bubble of warmth inside her.

She was happy.

That's why she felt different…why everything seemed different. The happiness explained the bright sparks in her head and in her eyes. The happiness made her tingle, and her insides fizz.

It wasn't the desert heat temperatures heating her, warm-

ing her, but happiness. And she was happy because of him.
Happy because she cared about him. And cared maybe more
than she should.

They made love in the Turquoise Chamber and fell asleep tangled together, skin damp, limbs intertwined.

Jemma woke first, it was early.

Day five, she thought. She would be here for only three
more days.

She counted the nights in her head, remembering the colors...

White the first night in the Chamber of Innocence, and
then Topaz, Amethyst, Ruby or Crimson, and then last night
was Turquoise.

Where would they go tonight? To the Emerald Chamber?
Sapphire?

Did it even matter?

She had to leave. Had to return to London. Didn't she?

Confused by her conflicting thoughts, Jemma quietly left
the bed and stepped outside to the courtyard. It was still early.
The sun was just rising and the temperature felt cool, the early
morning painted the palest pink and yellow.

Jemma's maid appeared in the courtyard with coffee and
a tray of breakfast pastries. Jemma refused the pastries but
sipped the coffee in a chair near the tranquil pool, listening
to the chirp of birds nesting high above in the palm fronds.

Mikael appeared in the doorway a half hour later. He'd
showered and dressed and was wearing his robes. "I need to
go to Ketama," he said, approaching her to drop a kiss on the
top of her head. "I will be back tonight. I wouldn't leave if I
didn't have to."

She tipped her face up to him, frowning at the amount of
time he'd be traveling, first by camel, and then by car. "Won't
it take you all day to get there?"

He kissed her again, this time on her brow. "I have a helicopter here. The pilot's ready. If we leave now, I'll be back this evening."

"And you have to go?"

"Yes," he said, sounding very decisive.

"Be careful," she said.

He kissed her one last time, this time on the lips. "Always."

It seemed as if it would be a long day with Mikael gone, but Jemma's maid led her to the Emerald Chamber, with the wall of antique leather-bound books.

Jemma studied the spines, delighted to discover that many were in English, and many were written by her favorite English authors. Charles Dickens, Thomas Hardy, Jane Austen, the Bronte sisters, E.M. Forster, and more.

Jemma selected *Mansfield Park* by Jane Austen and curled up in bed to read. She read the afternoon away and was still reading when the maid appeared to help Jemma dress for dinner.

"Is His Highness back?" Jemma asked, reluctantly putting the book down.

The maid shook her head. "No."

"Then why do I need to dress for dinner? Can't I have dinner here, in bed?"

Jemma finished the novel over dessert and promptly began *Sense and Sensibility* but ended up falling asleep over it.

She was still asleep, holding the novel, when Mikael arrived at midnight.

He stood over the bed for a moment watching her before carefully plucking the book from her hand, drawing the covers up to her shoulder, and turning the lamp out next to the bed.

He showered in the marble bathroom and then after drying off, joined her in bed. He was naked. But then, so was she.

Jemma woke up in the night and reached out to her side, relieved and delighted to discover Mikael there.

She moved toward him, and he opened his arms to her, drawing her close.

She pressed her face to his warm chest, breathing in his scent. He was back and he felt good and smelled good and she lifted her face to his, offering her lips. He kissed her, taking her mouth and then rolling her onto her back, to thrust deep inside her.

She wrapped her legs around his hips, taking all of him, wanting to hold him as close as possible, aware that things were changing. She was changing.

She...loved...him.

She loved him.

All of a sudden it made sense. She was happy because she was in love.

They fell back asleep and then woke up sometime in the morning to make love again. This time Jemma didn't fall back asleep but slipped from bed to head to the bathroom to shower.

Mikael watched Jemma cross the bedroom, naked, her beautiful body so familiar to him now.

Maybe that's why his chest felt heavy and tight as he watched her disappear into the bathroom.

Maybe that's why sex had felt different last night and this morning.

Maybe it's because she was familiar to him. Important to him.

But she was different, too, he thought. She hadn't merely been in his arms, but with him...in him...which didn't make sense, as it was his body filling hers, but somehow she'd gotten inside of him. He had felt *her*, feeling her not just with his body but his heart.

The emotions and sensations had made the sex more intense.

She'd felt so alive beneath him, so fierce and fragile, so beautiful that he couldn't get close enough to her, and he'd tried, God knew he'd tried.

Slow, deep strokes, hands holding her down, and still so he could kiss her, ravish her, draw her all the way into him.

And it hadn't been enough. He couldn't get enough. Even after one, two orgasms…hers, his.

Before, when he'd pleasured her, he'd wanted to blow her mind, enslave her through passion, make her yield to him. Belong to him. If she was going to be his, she should be happy with him.

But today it'd been something else.

There had been more heat than ever before but the heat wasn't about skin or erotic zones. It wasn't about the orgasm, either.

It was her. Wanting her. Holding her. Being with her.

And he could have sworn she'd been into him. Not the act. Not the friction and tension, not the positions, either.

Somehow the game of seduction had changed and become something more. More real, more honest, more raw. Suddenly, the stakes seemed higher than ever. Could he make Jemma happy? Could he keep her here with him in Saidia?

And if he could, was it fair to her? Or to those in her family?

Mikael threw back the covers, and headed for the bathroom where he could hear Jemma showering.

Hot steam filled the white marble bath, thick fragrant clouds hanging in the air.

He could just make her out through the wisps, her long hair piled high on her head, her hands on her breasts, spreading the bath gel across her lovely pale skin. He hardened, wanting her, craving her again.

He should be sated by now. He should have had his fill.

How many times did a man need a woman?

And yet watching her dark head dip, as she looked down her long, slim torso, to the suds running from her breasts to her belly, his body tightened, his arousal surging upright.

He couldn't stay away. He needed her. Again. He'd have her, too.

Mikael pushed open the glass door to the sunken shower, steam rising, embracing him.

Jemma turned toward him, startled, her lips parting in surprise.

Her eyes, those lips, her face…

Hunger raced through him. Hunger and the need to have her, hold her, keep her. He reached for her, and pushing her back against the wet marble wall, pressed his chest to hers, feeling the slippery film of soap suds between them, skin slick, enticing.

He rubbed his chest across her soft breasts and felt her nipples pebble. He inhaled sharply, as something wrenched in his chest.

This was new, this need. He didn't understand it. Didn't understand this desire. It was bigger than before, fiercer, wild in a way that baffled him, knocking him off balance.

Sex did not confuse him.

Women did not confuse him.

But he was confused now.

Confused by Jemma with the green eyes and soft lips and sweetness that pierced his heart and made him want to please her and protect her, keeping her safe, keeping her from harm's way.

With the water coursing down she lifted her face to his and he couldn't resist her lips. His head dropped, his mouth slanting across hers, hands framing her face.

Beautiful Jemma.

Beautiful woman.

Beautiful heart.

His chest burned. His eyes stung. He leaned in, crowding her, trying to take the upper hand. He was the master here. He was in control. He would prove this was just sex.

He broke off the kiss and turned her around, pressing her breasts to the warm slick marble even as he pulled her bottom toward him. His hand reached between her legs, finding her softness, and heat. He pushed up against her bottom, stroking her, feeling her legs quiver as his body strained against her.

She was so hot, so wet. He wanted to bury himself in her,

wanted to have her surround him, hot and tight, but he was too rough right now, and he couldn't hurt her. Couldn't force her. She'd given him so much earlier, it would be wrong to just take her now—

"I'm waiting," she said, her voice husky, her hips rocking against him. "Stop teasing me. You know I want you."

The sex was hot and Jemma left the shower satisfied, but Mikael did not.

That wasn't right, taking her like that. But was bringing her to the Kasbah in the first place right? He'd kidnapped a foreign woman. Forced her to marry him.

He toweled off slowly, guilt beginning to eat at him, even as a little voice in his head whispered, *you are wrong. This is wrong.*

He didn't like the little voice, didn't want the little voice. The voice represented the past, and weakness. But Karims must be strong. Karims must be above the law.

Mikael spent several hours at his desk on phone calls and in meetings before changing into comfortable clothes to meet Jemma for dinner in the grand courtyard. The pavilions and pools had been lit with sapphire and pink lights.

Jemma wore a long deep blue kaftan with silver and gold embroidery. The inky color of her dress made her green eyes even more brilliant. He sat across from her at dinner to see her, but the table between them meant he couldn't touch her too easily.

Instead he watched her face and her eyes as she talked during their meal. Her green eyes shimmered when she laughed. She laughed easily, her expression dancing.

She was so warm. And good. She deserved good things, and good people.

He was not a good person.

Powerful, yes. Wealthy, exceptionally so. But good? No.

During dessert and coffee he remembered he had a gift for her, and he pulled the velvet box from the pocket in his robe.

"For you," he said, handing her the box.

She looked up at him, dark winged eyebrows lifting higher. "You have to stop."

"Never."

She laughed, eyes dancing. "Fine. I tried. I won't fight you anymore because a gift now and then is rather nice." Then she opened the box, lifted the stunning sapphire earrings out, jaw dropping in awe. "Oh," she whispered, giving one earring a slight shake. "These, my husband, are absolutely stunning."

Mikael's lips curved, and yet on the inside he grew very still. *My husband*, she'd said. Not sarcastically, or angrily. But kindly. Warmly.

It made his chest tighten and ache. He tried very hard to be a good king, but that didn't make him deserving of a woman like Jemma.

"Be careful," he said to her, leaning across the table and kissing her gently. "Be careful of wolves in sheep's clothing."

She smiled into his eyes as her hand reached up to cup his face. "I know of no sheep. Just wolves. And hawks. And scary desert scorpions and snakes."

He stared into her eyes an extra moment, taking her in, feeling the impact of her beauty and warmth. "I could very well be one of those poisonous scorpions or snakes."

"You could." She rubbed his jaw, fingernails scratching lightly along his stubble before sitting back. "But I don't think so. I've seen who you are. You're a man determined to restore honor to your country, and preserve tradition. You are protective of women, just look at how you've treated me, and provided for my mother."

"Because I failed to provide for mine."

"You're making amends."

"Too late, though, for her."

He rose abruptly from the table, unable to sit another moment, and extended his hand to her. "Come with me."

He led her to the enormous bed in the Sapphire Chamber, and stripped her of her gown and delicate silk bra and thong before kissing her and making love to her. The lovemaking was slow, sensual, lasting for hours.

Satiated, Jemma remained in Mikael's arms. He held her closely and Jemma sighed, feeling secure.

He felt right to her. Being with him felt good. The humiliation and shame of the past year couldn't hurt her when she was in his arms. Damien's rejection no longer mattered. Damien wasn't anything but a lousy model, a spineless man. She smiled to herself, feeling safe…content…loved.

Mikael had somehow made her feel whole again, and strong.

Saidia wasn't home, but Mikael could be. And while he hadn't said words of love, he'd given her something else. His commitment. His promise.

She trusted his word. She cherished his vows because he was a man of his word, and a man who took his commitments seriously.

This, she thought, wrapping her arms over his, this is what she needed. This is who she wanted. This was her future.

In the morning, Jemma woke slowly, feeling deliciously lazy, and deeply rested. Eyes still closed, she let herself breathe and float. At least, it felt as if she were floating. Everything inside her was warmth and light. Easy.

The world was good.

Life was better.

Her lashes fluttered, a butterfly kiss, and she opened her eyes, and saw Mikael lying next to her. She smiled with pleasure. She loved sleeping with him, loved having him there with her all night.

She was quite attracted to this man.

"Good morning, *laeela*," Mikael said, eyes still closed, his voice deep and husky with sleep.

"You're awake," she said, pleased.

"No. I'm still sleeping," he said, his voice still with that lovely gravelly growl she found enormously sexy. "My eyes are shut."

"Then how did you know I was awake?" she asked, amused, propping her head on her hand.

"I could feel you watching me."

"Then you are awake."

He sighed. His beautiful dark eyes opened, and he looked at her, black eyebrow lifting. "*Now* I am."

She grinned. "Hi."

He sighed again, heavily, but his eyes glinted. "Hello."

Jemma laughed softly. He was acting put out but he wasn't really. "How did you sleep?" she asked him.

"Well. And you?"

"Exceedingly well."

"You like our fresh desert air."

"No, I like you. Being held by you." She felt bold, but she didn't care. How could she be shy around him when he made her feel so beautiful and strong? "That's three nights you've stayed with me, all through the night."

"I am committed to your pleasure."

"You most certainly are," she agreed, hiding her smile as she studied his hard, handsome features. Such a striking face. All strong lines and edges and then that soft curve of lip… lower, upper. He was so nice to look at. "I appreciate your commitment."

A deep groove formed next to his mouth. His lips quirked. "You are shameless."

"You've only yourself to blame, Your Highness. You've made me shameless."

He reached out to brush long strands of hair from her brow, gently pushing them back from her face, his thumb easing across her forehead in a soft caress. "Have I? How?"

Just that light touch sent shivers through her, and darts of pleasure to her breasts and between her thighs. Senses stirred, she exhaled slowly, carefully, her thoughts tangling. It was hard to think when Mikael touched her. "How can I feel shame when everything we do together makes me feel wonderful, and powerful?"

"Sex makes you feel powerful?"

She frowned. It didn't sound right, not phrased like that. "I'm sure great sex makes lots of people feel powerful, but I wasn't referring to sex in general, but sex with you." She frowned again. Because that didn't sound right, either. She wasn't having sex with Mikael. She was making love with Mikael. She was loving Mikael.

She was most definitely *in love* with Mikael. She wished she could tell him. Wished she knew how to tell him that the pleasure she felt with him wasn't merely sexual. It wasn't just physical. Her pleasure was in her heart, and soul.

She looked into his eyes, and she flashed back to that first day on the desert dunes when she'd been melting inside the fur coat and high boots. He'd had the same intense expression in his dark eyes and she'd been afraid...

Now she was afraid again, but for a different reason. She couldn't imagine being happy without him.

"Kiss me," she whispered, reaching up to his face, placing her hand against his hard, high cheekbone as she pressed her lips to his. "Possess me. Remind me that I'm your wife and queen."

His wife and queen.

Mikael stared blindly out through the glass doors, seeing nothing of his courtyard, and seeing only Jemma's face.

He, who was so good at creating order, structure, and discipline, hadn't planned on falling in love with her. He hadn't planned on wanting her, or needing her, not the way he wanted her and needed her.

He'd married her out of duty and responsibility but suddenly his marriage was one of love. Trust. *Respect.*

He'd known he was growing fond of her these past few days. He'd known he was getting attached, too. It hadn't troubled him. At least, he hadn't let it trouble him. He would only allow himself to think of one thing—doing what was right for Saidia. But now he felt a wash of shame. This was wrong chaining her here, to him. He couldn't trap her in Saidia. He couldn't do it to her. She deserved so much better than this.

Jemma was in her sapphire room, sitting on the floor, painting her toenails when Mikael entered a half hour later.

He didn't knock. But then, he hadn't knocked on the door in days, taking it for granted that her room was his. That she was his. He was right. It hadn't even taken eight days to fall in love with him. She'd given him her heart far earlier…maybe even that first day they'd met, when she'd been modeling on the sand dunes.

He silently watched her paint her pinky toe a foamy mint green. She glanced up at him, smiling. "I remember how much you like the color green."

"I don't remember that at all."

"You said you loved my eyes."

"Yes, your eyes. Not green toenails."

Jemma laughed and dipped the brush into the bottle for more polish. "Are you sure that's what you said? I worry about your memory."

"I worry about you and facts."

She grinned, happy. Ridiculously happy. Everything inside her bubbled up warm, and hopeful. Her heart felt good. Mikael made her feel good. And safe. *Loved*. He might not say the words the way she wanted to hear them, but she felt his love in his actions. She felt his affection and love in the way he touched her, and the warmth and passion with which he kissed her. She saw it in the amusement in his eyes as they talked, teasing, bantering. The fact that he would banter with her, and laugh with her, said it all.

Lips curving, she added a second coat to the pinky toe, before capping the bottle of polish and setting it aside. She tipped her head back to look up into his beautiful face, with those dark, mysterious and oh so sexy eyes. "What can I do for you this beautiful day, my love?"

The hint of amusement died from his eyes, his expression

shuttering, his jaw hardening. It was a subtle shift. Someone else might not have picked up on the change, but she did. Jemma had spent so much time studying him these past eight days that even the narrowing of his eyes didn't go unnoticed.

"There is nothing you need to do. It's all been done," he said.

"It can't *all* be done," she said, noting the change, but trying to tease him. "The Kama Sutra refers to hundreds of positions, and we've only tried—" she scrunched her eyes closed, as if thinking very hard "Four or five?"

"I think you've practiced plenty."

She feigned shock. "You're sick of sex?"

His smile was crooked. "No, but I think we need to get out. Go and do something. I've a picnic packed. Get your suit. We're heading to the beach."

"Camels to the beach? Now that would be interesting."

His mouth quirked, reluctantly amused. "We'll take the helicopter to Truka, and then my car to the beach town of Tagadir."

In the helicopter, on the way to Truka, Mikael explained that the Karim family owned miles of a beautiful private beach in the ancient resort town of Tagadir. There had once been an elegant nineteenth century villa in Tagadir, but the villa had been torn down by Mikael's father who planned to build a new one, but the new one was never constructed. However, the beach was still there, with its soft white sand and beautiful warm water.

They reached the entrance to the Karim estate just after noon, passing through tall black, wrought iron gates. The long driveway toward the water was bordered with blooming hibiscus hedges in pinks and bright corals, but on reaching the end of the drive, right where one would expect to see a grand building, there was nothing but the ruins of a cement foundation, with stone steps leading down to the beach.

The driver delivered the picnic basket and blankets to the beach and then returned to the car. Jemma stood on the last step and surveyed the private cove. A small, but elegant stone pavilion rose from the sand. Otherwise there was nothing. The beach truly was lovely, and private.

After lunch, Mikael and Jemma swam. They dried out on their blanket and then returned to the water to cool off when the sun became too fierce. Mikael was back on the blanket now, watching Jemma float and splash.

Her skin glowed golden after these past few days lounging at the Kasbah pool. The touch of gold in her skin brought out the green of her eyes. In her white bikini she was beyond stunning.

He watched as she waded in, stepping from the surf to wring the water from her long dark hair.

He loved looking at her and talking to her and making love to her. He loved her company and enjoyed her laughter. The laughter was good, and needed. He had a tendency to be silent and stern but she brought out a more playful side in him. He hadn't always been hard.

Loving Jemma had opened him up, softened his heart.

He needed to send her home, back to her family, back to those who loved her and wanted what was best for her like her mother, and Branson, her brother, and the sisters who all adored Jemma.

Mikael wasn't sure that Jemma would understand. He hoped she wouldn't take his decision as a rejection. He wasn't rejecting her, but protecting her.

This was the time he could return her to her people, without shame or stigma. After the eight days and nights, before the official sixteen days of honeymoon ended.

He couldn't wait, either. He didn't want her to become too attached. He didn't want her to confuse lust and love. She was dazzled by pleasure, seduced by endorphins and chemicals. Orgasm tricked women's brains, flooding them with chemicals that made them attach…feel…need.

There was a reason Saidia men made love to their captive brides for eight days without ceasing. The sex, the pleasure, it was a drug. The frequent and intense orgasms helped the woman bond to her man so by the end of the honeymoon, the bride didn't want to leave her groom. The bride had become attached, even addicted to her groom, craving his scent, his touch, his feel, and each coupling would reinforce the attachment, and aid in procreation.

Mikael knew all this. Jemma didn't.

It was time he told her.

She dashed across the hot sand to join him on the blanket. She was laughing as she tumbled down onto the blanket, dripping water on him, making him wet.

"Wicked girl," he said, reaching for her.

She wrinkled her nose at him, making fun of him. His chest grew hot and tight. He had to have her, needed to touch her. He slid his hand into the long damp strands of her hair, the sea making her hair gritty, and he rolled her onto her back, and settled over her, kissing her, drinking her in.

He could taste the salt water on her lips and the cool ocean on her breath and it heated his blood, making him hungry. He deepened the kiss, his tongue parting her lips. Mikael teased her tongue, stroking it, stroking her mouth, delving into it until he felt her shudder and arch against him.

He shifted, and leaned back on the blanket, and drew her on top of him, settling her slim hips between his thighs, so that his arousal pressed thickly against her.

Jemma sighed against his mouth, and he felt her yield to him, her body softening, shaping to his, her lovely full breasts crushed to his chest, her nipples peaked, hard, and he reached around to cup her bottom. She sighed again as he palmed her buttocks, his fingers kneading the smooth muscle. She groaned deep in her throat as he pressed her down against him, rubbing her pelvis against him, feeling her softness cup him. He nearly groaned, too.

She felt so good. He stroked her hips, her rounded bottom, her inner thighs, all while driving his tongue into her, an insistent rhythm that made her writhe helplessly against him, her body trembling in anticipation.

She strained to get even closer, her breath coming faster.

His hands slid up her thighs, until his fingers brushed the fabric of her bikini bottoms. She was hot, wet, and her heat scorched him. He rubbed across her, feeling her softness through the fabric, finding her sensitive spot.

Her eyes widened and she panted. He loved the way she did that…gasp, shudder, pant. She was so beautiful and sensual. He loved that she could forget her inhibitions and lose herself in him. In them.

He caressed her between her thighs again and again, feeling her grow hotter, wetter. She jerked, nerve endings exquisitely sensitized, and flung her head back, her eyes emerald, cheeks flushed. With her dark hair still wet and the halo of sun above them, she looked like a goddess from the sea and he had to have her, now.

He rolled her over onto her back, and tugged her damp bikini bottoms off of her. His thighs parted hers and he sank into the cradle of her hips, nudging her soft folds, eager to be inside her. His tip stroked her smooth, secret places, her creamy heat calling to him, drawing him in.

Mikael entered her with a thrust, slipping deeply inside her tight body.

He loved her the way he knew she liked to be loved—deep, slow, hard—and with his body he tried to say all the things he'd never be able to say in words.

That she mattered too much.

That she was too valuable.

That she deserved so much more than he could give.

CHAPTER FIFTEEN

JEMMA LAY IN his arms on the blanket in the sand, resting comfortably, happily. There was no place she'd rather be than here, in his arms, against his chest. "What day is this?" she asked, lifting her chin, to look at him.

"I think I've lost count," he said, smoothing her hair back from her brow.

She lifted a brow. "Really? I don't believe that for a minute."

"So what day is it?"

"Day eight. The last day and night of your half of our honeymoon."

She waited for him to say something. He didn't.

"Tonight you are still in control," she added, blushing a little. "But tomorrow I take over. Tomorrow I'm in charge for the next eight days and nights."

She smiled into his eyes, waiting impatiently for him to say something, something warm and sexy. Something encouraging. Something.

But he didn't speak. He just looked at her, his dark eyes somber, expression grave.

Her heart did a funny double beat. Nervous and uncomfortable, she chewed the inside of her lower lip. "You've gone awfully quiet," she murmured.

His jaw shifted, his lids dropping, hooding his eyes. "I have been thinking a great deal about tonight."

"So have I. I think it's time you let me pleasure you."

"I don't think there is going to be a tonight."

Jemma froze. Blinked.

"There is just…today," he added quietly.

For a second she couldn't breathe. She couldn't think. Couldn't do anything at all.

"I married you so you wouldn't have to remain in Haslam under house arrest for seven years. But the eight days are up. I have fulfilled my responsibility as a groom, and I can now return you to London, without losing face."

She still couldn't take it all in. She took his words apart, bit by bit, processing them. Digesting them.

He didn't want an eighth night. He didn't want to be married to her. He intended to put her on a plane for London.

She licked her lips, her mouth dry. Parched. "I'm confused," she whispered.

"I did what needed to be done," he said carefully, after an endless moment, a moment where the silence cut, wounded.

Jemma slowly pulled away, and then scooted away, and sat up. She crossed her legs, hiding herself. "You never intended to keep me as your wife?"

"It's not feasible. Nor realistic. My mother wasn't happy in Saidia. You wouldn't be happy here, not long term. You'd be better marrying an American or a European man. Someone Western with Western thought processes and beliefs."

"So all this time…these eight days and the past seven nights…what was it about? Just sex?"

He shrugged. "Please."

"But you said pleasure could lead to more. You said pleasure could lead to love."

"I was wrong."

She looked at him, then away, trying to ignore the panic in her head and the sickening rush of hurt and pain through her veins.

This wasn't happening, not now. She'd fallen in love with him and she'd given herself to him.

"Why?" she whispered, staring out at the white sandy beach

and the sea beyond. "Why do this to me? Why go through all the motions and seduce me and pleasure me and pretend to care? Pretend to want me?"

"I do care about you. I never had to pretend to want you. I still want you. I still desire you. But I've realized I care too much about you, to trap you here in Saidia. You need more than this desert and my palaces. You need the world you grew up in."

"This isn't about me," she said, interrupting him. "This is about your mother. It's about her relationship with your father, not about you and me." Jemma drew a rough, unsteady breath. "I am not your mother. I am not sheltered. I am not a naive young American girl thinking she's being swept off by Valentino. I've experienced hard things and known tremendous pressure, and public criticism, and personal shame. So don't think for me, and don't make decisions for me, at least, not without consulting me, because, Mikael, I know what I want and need, and I want and need *you*."

"You don't know me."

"I don't know who you were in the past. I never knew you as a boy or a young man, but I know who you are now. You're smart, courageous, honest. *Brave*. You have strong morals and values, and a fierce desire to do the right thing. I love that about you. In fact, I love you."

"You don't love me. You love the pleasure, you love the sensation."

"That's ridiculous!"

"It's not. I've seduced you with pleasure. I bonded you to me with all the hormones from sex and orgasm."

"Stop talking," she said, springing to her feet. "Your words are killing me. They're poisonous. Toxic. Just get rid of me now. Drop me off at the airport. But don't say another awful, hateful word."

He rose, towering over her. "You're being irrational."

"I am? Really? You spent eight days seducing me. Eight days making love to me in every conceivable position, showering me with gifts, assuring me that as your wife I'd be protected, safe, *secure*. Well, your idea of security is very different from mine, Sheikh Karim!"

"I'm sending you home to protect you."

"From what? *Whom*? The paparazzi? The media? The bloodthirsty public? Who are you protecting me from?"

"Me," he ground out, his voice low and hoarse.

She flung her head back, stared into his eyes, furious. "Maybe it's time you let go of the past, and your self-loathing and hatred. Maybe it's time to forgive. Because you are so determined to be fair to your country and your people but, Mikael Karim, you are not fair to yourself, and you're screwing up royally right now. You had me. You had my heart. And you've just thrown it all away."

They didn't speak on the walk back to the car.

They didn't speak, either, as the car traveled the long private driveway lined with hibiscus and palms to the enormous black and gold iron gates that marked the entrance to the Karim family's private beach.

The gates opened and then closed behind them. Jemma turned her head as if to get a last look at the brilliant blue coastline before it disappeared and swiftly wiped away a tear. The sun shone down on the water, and the ocean sparkled. She turned back to face the front, and wiped away another tear, seeing how the red gold sand stretched before them, reminding her of the Kasbah and the Bridal Palace and how Jemma and Mikael had spent the past eight days there.

All the experiences. The sensation. The pleasure. The emotion.

The car picked up speed on the empty highway. There was so little traffic in this part of Saidia that the driver could fly down the black ribbon of asphalt. He did, too.

Mikael stared out the window, lost in thought, and Jemma left him to his thoughts.

One minute all was quiet and the next they were smashed

sideways, slammed off the road in a screech of screaming brakes, screeching metal and shattering glass.

The impact knocked Mikael's car sideways, and the two cars, hit again, and once more, before the red sports car went sailing overhead to land off the road in the sand.

The heavy black sedan spun the opposite direction, until it finally crashed on the other side.

For a moment inside the car there was no sound.

Mikael shook his head, dazed.

"Jemma?" Mikael's hard voice cut through the stillness as he turned toward her.

She lay crumpled against the door, her face turned away from him.

"Jemma," he repeated more urgently, reaching for her, touching the side of her face. It was wet. He looked at his hand. It was covered in blood.

She was flown by helicopter to the royal hospital in Ketama. Mikael traveled with her, holding her hand. Mikael's chauffeur walked away with cuts and bruises like Mikael, while the driver of the other car didn't need a helicopter. He'd died at the scene.

Jemma spent hours in surgery as the doctors set bones and dealt with internal bleeding. She then spent the next few days heavily sedated.

Mikael refused to leave her side. Fortunately, he was the king, and this was the royal hospital named after the Karim family, so no one dared to tell him to leave her, either.

The doctors and specialists had all said she'd be okay. She was simply sedated to help reduce the swelling. She would mend better, and be in less pain, if she were sedated, and resting.

Mikael wanted her to rest, but he needed to know that she was okay.

So for three days he slept next to her bed. Nurses brought

coffee to him. His valet brought him clean clothes daily. Mikael used Jemma's hospital room shower when needed.

He struggled with that last day, the beach trip to Tagadir, her reaction when he told her he was sending her away, and then the silent car ride before the sports car slammed into them.

Was the accident karma?

Was this his fault, again?

He leaned over the bed, gently stroked her cheek, the bit of cheek he could reach between all the bandages. The shattered window had cut her head badly. They'd picked glass out for hours before finally getting the side of her head stitched and stapled closed.

He'd been furious that they shaved part of her hair, but the doctors insisted they had to. Now he just wanted to see her eyes open. He wanted to hear her voice. He needed to apologize and tell her he loved her and it wasn't lack of love that made him send her away, but the need to protect her, and do the right thing for her.

She didn't understand how much she meant to him. She was laughter and light and life.

She was his soul mate.

His other half, his better half. Yes, his queen.

That afternoon on the beach, she'd said hard things to him, but she'd also spoken the truth.

Mikael's battle wasn't with her. His battle was with himself.

He didn't like himself. Didn't love himself. Couldn't imagine her, her of all people, loving him.

And so he was sending her back to a world he wasn't part of, sending her to people who were more deserving.

Mikael closed his eyes, his fist pressed to his forehead, pushing against the thoughts and recriminations, as well as the memories tormenting him.

He should have been a better son to his mother. He should have denounced his father once he realized his father had lied, that his father had broken his promise to his mother. He should have given his mother the assistance, advice, and support she'd needed.

But he hadn't. And she'd died alone, in terrible emotional pain. And he couldn't forgive himself for his part in her suffering.

How could he?

He squeezed his fist tighter, pressed harder against his forehead, disgusted. Heartsick.

She'd be alive now if he'd given her help. She'd be alive if he'd acted when he should have. It would have been easy. Asking forgiveness was not that complicated. It was simply a matter of pride.

His eyes burned and he squeezed them shut, trying to hold the burning tears back. *Forgive me*, he thought, sending a silent prayer up to his mother.

And not that he deserved any help, or protection, but Jemma did. Jemma deserved so much, and maybe his mother could pull a few strings up there. Maybe his mother could do something on Jemma's behalf.

Help her, Mother. Help my Jemma. Help her heal, if you can.

And then gently, carefully he lifted Jemma's hands to his lips, pressed a kiss to her skin.

He didn't know how long he sat there, holding her hands, his lips pressed to her skin, but he wouldn't let her go. He refused to let her go. He needed her.

He loved her.

He couldn't be the man he wanted to be without her.

She had to survive and forgive him. She had to survive to be his friend, his lover, his companion. She had to survive so he could make things right with her.

"Forgive me, *laeela*," he whispered, exhausted by the vigil by her side, but not wanting to be anywhere else, either. He wouldn't leave her. Not now. Not ever.

Her eyes fluttered. Mikael sat forward. He stroked her brow, where her delicate, dark eyebrows arched. "Forgive me," he repeated. "I need you to come back. I need you with me."

"Forgive…" Jemma whispered, her eyes fluttering again, and slowly opening. Her brows tugged. Her gaze was unfocused. "Mikael?"

"You're awake."

"Where am I?"

"Ketama. The royal hospital."

"Why?"

"There was an accident." He stood, and gazed down intently into her eyes. "You were hurt."

It seemed hard for her to focus, but otherwise her eyes looked the same, clear and cool and green.

She blinked, and licked her lips, her mouth dry. "Do you have any water?"

"I'll ring the nurse." He pushed the button on the side of the bed. "Do you hurt?"

"A little. Not bad." She frowned. "I don't remember an accident."

"That's all right. You don't need to. It was bad. It's a miracle you're here."

She was silent a long moment. "What day is it?"

"Monday."

"No, what day? Of the eight days?"

He leaned over, kissed her gently on the cheek. "Day eleven, or twelve. I forget. It's been a blur."

"Oh." And then her expression changed, her brows knitting, tightening. "You're sending me home. You don't want me."

"Let's not talk about that right now."

"You don't love me."

"Jemma. *Laeela*," he said roughly, sounding agonized.

She turned her face away from him, closed her eyes. "It's fine. I want to go home. I want to go now."

A knot filled his throat. His chest ached with bottled emotion. "You can't go anywhere until you're better."

She tried to sit up. She winced at the effort.

"Lie down, be still—"

"I won't have you making decisions for me," she interrupted hoarsely. "I won't have you commanding me or dictating to me, because you're just like the others. You're just the same, making promises you never intended to keep—"

"That's not true," he interrupted fiercely, before lowering his voice. "I love you. I do. I don't know how it happened, but it happened. I didn't want a love match, but love found me anyway in you, and the only reason I was sending you home was to give you your freedom and future back."

"But my future is with you! My home is with you. And you, you—" She broke off and squeezed her eyes closed even as tears seeped beneath her lashes. "You don't even care."

"I care," he said, leaning over her, and kissing her carefully on the forehead, between bandages. "I care so much that I only want what's best for you, and I am not sure Saidia is best for you. It wasn't good for my mother. She was lonely here."

"But I'm not your mother," Jemma answered, opening her eyes. "And you're not your father. We can have our own marriage, and we can do it all differently. We can do it right. But you have to believe that, too. You have to fight for us, too."

"I'm fighting," he murmured, stroking her cheek gently, tenderly. She was all bruises, scrapes and stitches and more beautiful than any woman in the world. "I'm fighting for us, fighting for you. I haven't been able to leave your side, afraid that if I left, you'd disappear."

She struggled to smile even as tears fell, slipping from the corners of her eyes. "I'm here."

He smiled down at her, and caught a tear before it slid into her hair. "Yes, you are, my wife, my heart, my queen."

Jemma's lower lip trembled. "You can't ever threaten to send me away again."

"I won't. Not ever. We are going to make this work, and we will have hard days and arguments and hurt feelings, but

I promise you, I am here for you and with you. You and I are meant to be together."

"Not because it's your duty," she whispered.

He smiled. "No, it's not because of duty. We are together because you are my love, and the queen of my heart."

* * * * *

HER SINFUL
SECRET

CHAPTER ONE

"LOGAN, WE'VE GOT a crowd outside. *Logan.* Are you listening?"

Frustrated by yet another interruption, Logan Copeland tore her gaze from her script, yanked off her headset and glared up at her usually very capable assistant, Joe Lopez. She'd come to think of him as a genius and a blessing, but he wasn't much of either at the moment. *"Joe."*

"We've got a problem."

"Another one?" she asked incredulously. They were down to less than twenty-four hours now before tomorrow night's huge gala fund-raiser, the biggest of Logan's career, and nothing was going right in the tech rehearsal for the fashion show that would happen during the gala, and nothing would go right if Logan continued to be interrupted.

"We honestly don't have time for this. *I* don't have time for this. And if you want to run the show tomorrow on your own, that's fine—"

"I don't," he interrupted, expression grim. "But this is big, and I can't manage this one without you."

"Why not? And why does everything have to be a big problem right now?" she retorted, aware that every interruption was costing more time with the crew, which cost more money, which meant less money for the charity. "If this isn't life or death, you need to deal with it, and let me get one good run-through in before—"

"The media has descended. Full-on, out of control paparazzi stakeout. Here."

Logan's expression brightened. "But, Joe, that's great news. The PR team is succeeding. I heard they were the best. How is that a problem?"

"Logan, they're not here because of tomorrow's Hollywood Ball. They're not interested in the Gala or doing good. They're here for *you*."

Logan suddenly found it hard to breathe. She pressed the clipboard to her chest, headset dangling from her fingers. "For the press conference about the Ball," she said firmly, but then at the end her voice quavered, and the fear and doubt was there.

"No." Joe shoved his hands into his jeans pockets. He was a smart, young, artistic twentysomething just a couple years out of college, and he'd been invaluable to Logan since coming to work for her two years ago, a little over a year after her whole world had imploded due to the scandal surrounding her father, Daniel Copeland. Lots of people had wanted nothing to do with Logan after news broke that her father was the worst of the worst, a world-class swindler and thief preying on not just the wealthy, but the working class, too, leaving all of his clients nearly bankrupt, or worse.

Joe had grown up in a tough Los Angeles neighborhood marked with gang violence, so the Copeland scandal hadn't been an issue for him. He wanted a job. Logan needed an assistant. The relationship worked.

He, like everyone, knew what her father had done, but unlike most people, he knew the terrible price Logan had paid. In most business and social circles she was still persona non grata. The only place she could work was in the nonprofit sector. "They are here to see *you*," he repeated. "It's to do with your dad."

She stilled. Her gaze met Joe's.

His dark brown gaze revealed worry, and sympathy. His voice dropped lower. "Logan, something's happened."

The tightness was back in her chest, the weight so heavy she couldn't think or breathe.

"Have you checked messages on your phone?" he added. "I am sure you'll have gotten calls and texts. Check your phone."

But Logan, normally fierce and focused, couldn't move. She stood rooted to the spot, her body icy cold. "Was he freed?" she whispered. "Did the kidnappers—"

"Check your phone," a deep, rough, impatient male voice echoed, this one most definitely not Joe's.

Logan turned swiftly, eyes widening as her gaze locked with Rowan Argyros's. His green gaze was icy and contemptuous and so very dismissive.

She lifted her chin, her press of lips hiding her anger and rush of panic. If Rowan Argyros—her biggest regret, and worst mistake—was here, it could only mean one thing, because he wouldn't be here by choice. He'd made it brutally clear three years ago what he thought of her.

But she didn't want to think about that night, or the day after, or the weeks and months after that…

Better to keep from thinking at all, because Rowan would use it against her. More ammunition. And the last thing a former military commander needs is more ammunition.

He didn't look military standing before her. Nor had he looked remotely authoritative the night she met him at the bachelor auction fund-raiser to benefit children in war-torn countries in need of prosthetics. He'd been a bachelor. She'd helped organize the event. Women were bidding like mad. He would go for a fortune. She didn't have a fortune, but when he looked at her where she stood off to the side, watching, she felt everything in her shift and heat. Her face burned. She burned and his light green gaze remained on her, as the bidding went up and up and up.

She bought him. Correction: she bought *one night* with him.

And it only costs thousands and thousands of dollars.

The remorse had hit her the moment the auctioneer had shouted victoriously, "Sold to Logan Lane!"

The intense remorse made her nauseous. She couldn't believe what she'd done. She'd filled an entire credit card, maxing it out in a flash for one night with a stranger.

She didn't even know then what Dunamas Maritime was. Insurance for yachts? Ship builder? Cargo exporter?

He knew that, too, from his faint mocking smile. He knew why she'd bought him.

She'd bought him for his intense male energy. She'd bought his confidence and the fact that of all the attractive men being auctioned, he was by far the most primal. The most sexual.

She'd bought him because he was tall and broad shouldered and had a face that rivaled the most beautiful male models in the world.

She'd bought him because she couldn't resist him. But she hadn't been the only one. The bidding had been fierce and competitive, and no wonder. He was gorgeous with his deep tan, and long, dark hair—*sun-streaked* hair—and his light arresting eyes framed by black lashes. There was something so very compelling about him that you couldn't look away. And so she didn't. She watched him… and wanted him. Like every other woman at the charity event.

They'd all looked and wanted. And many had bid, but

she was the one who'd bid the longest, and bid the highest, and when the heart-pounding bidding frenzy was over, she came out the victor.

The winner.

And so, from across the room that night, he looked at her, his mysterious light hazel eyes holding hers, the corner of his mouth lifting, acknowledging her victory. Looking back she recognized the smile for what it was—mockery.

He'd dared her to bid, and she had, proving how weak she was. Proving to him how easily manipulated.

By morning he would hate her, scorning her weakness. Scorning her name.

But that hadn't happened yet. That wouldn't happen until he'd taken her again and again, making her scream his name as she climaxed once, twice and then, after a short sleep, two more times before he walked out the door the next morning.

The sex had been hot, so hot and so intense and so deeply satisfying. With anyone else it might have felt dirty, but it hadn't been with him. It'd just felt real. And right.

But she did feel dirty, later, once he'd discovered she wasn't Logan Lane, but Logan Lane Copeland, and the shaming began.

It was bad enough being hated by all of America, but to be branded a slut by your very first lover? A man that wasn't just any man, but one of the best friends of your twin sister's new husband?

Of all the people to sleep with…of all the men to fall for…why did it have to be Rowan Argyros with his passionate Irish Greek heritage and ruthless nature? There was a reason he'd risen through the military. He was a risk taker with nerves of steel. A man who seized opportunities and smashed resistance.

She knew, because he'd seized her and smashed her.

Logan exhaled now, blocking the past with its soul-crushing memories. She hated the past. It was only in the last year she'd come to terms with the present and accepted that there could be a future. A good one. If she could forgive herself…and him.

Not Rowan—she'd never forgive Rowan. It was her father she needed to forgive. And she was trying, she was.

"My father," she said now, her gaze sliding across Rowan—still so tall and intimidating, still so sinfully good-looking—and then away, but not before she realized his long hair was gone. Shorn. He looked even harder now than before. "Is…he…?"

Rowan hesitated for just a fraction of a second, and yet his expression didn't soften. "Yes."

She willed herself not to move, or tremble. She firmed her voice so it wouldn't quaver. "How?"

He hesitated yet again, and she knew that he knew every detail. He was a maritime antipiracy specialist, based out of Naples, with offices in Athens and London as well as a large country estate in Ireland. He hadn't told her any of that. Her sister Morgan and her husband Drakon Xanthis had, after their wedding.

"Does it matter?" he asked quietly, coolly.

"Of course it matters," she retorted, hating him even more. Hating him for taking her virginity and mocking her afterward for enjoying his body and touch and for leaving her to deal with the aftermath on her own, as if he hadn't been the one in that big bed with her…

His silence made her fear the worst. Her heart hammered. Her stomach fell. She wished she was hearing this from Morgan or Jemma, or her older brother, Bronson. They would all have broken the news differently. "Did they…did they…?"

And then she couldn't wait for the words, the confirmation that her father, kidnapped and held hostage off the coast of Africa, had been killed, possibly executed. It was all too sickening and her legs wobbled and her head spun, her body hot, then cold and then very cold.

She tried to look for Joe, the very best assistant one could ever hope for, but all she saw was Rowan and he was staring her down with those pale hazel-green eyes.

"Don't," he growled, his deep, rough voice now sounding far away, as if he was standing at the far end of a tunnel.

Maybe he was.

She couldn't see him well. Things were cloudy at the edges. He was cloudy, and she blinked, almost amused that Rowan could think he could still dictate to her, once again telling her body what to do...

"You're not doing this now," he snapped.

But she did. Her world went dark.

Swearing, Rowan dove to catch Logan before she crashed to the ballroom floor, but he was too far away and couldn't break her fall. Her head slammed on the edge on the stage as she went down.

He was there to scoop her up and he swore again, this time at himself, for not reaching her more quickly, and then at useless Joe, for not catching her, either.

She was still out cold as he settled her into his arms, her slender body ridiculously light. He shifted her so that her head fell back against his biceps, and his narrowed gaze raked her pale face, noting the blood pooling at the cut on her temple, and beginning to trickle into her thick honey-colored hair. She was going to have a nasty bruise, and probably one hell of a headache, later.

She was also still impossibly beautiful. High cheekbones, full lips, the elegant brow and nose of a Greek goddess.

But beauty had never been her issue. If she'd just been a pretty face, he could forgive himself for their night together, but she wasn't just a beautiful girl, she was Logan *Copeland*, one of the scandalous Copelands, and as amoral as they came.

It was bad enough being bought at a charity auction but to be paid for with embezzled funds?

"Grab her things," he told the man hovering at Logan's side. He wouldn't be surprised if Joe was Logan's lover. A boy toy—

He broke off, unable to continue the thought. He didn't like the thought. But then, he didn't like anything about being here today.

He didn't have to be the one doing this. He could have sent one of his men. Every one of his special ops team at Dunamas Intelligence had come from an elite military background: US Navy SEALs, British Special Forces, Russia's Alpha Group, France's National Gendarmerie Intervention Group, Spain's Naval Special Warfare Force. Rowan hadn't just interviewed and hired each, he'd then trained them personally for intelligence work and rescue operations.

Any one of his men could do what he was doing. He should have sent anyone but himself.

But Rowan wasn't about to let anyone else near her. He told himself it was to protect them—she was a siren after all—but with her in his arms, he knew it was far more personal and far more primal than that.

He didn't want any man near her because even three years later, her body belonged to him.

Logan struggled to open her eyes. Her head hurt. Her thoughts kept scattering. She was being carried up and up. They were moving, climbing, but climbing what? She could hear breathing as well as the sound of heavy, even thudding close to her ear. She was warm. The arms holding her were warm. She battled to open her eyes, needing to focus, wanting to remember.

She stared hard at the face above her, noting the jaw, a very strong, angular jaw with a hint of dark beard. He had a slash of cheekbone and a firm mouth. And then he looked down at her, and the sardonic hazel-green depths sent a shiver through her.

Rowan.

And then it started to come back. Joe saying there was a problem. Something with her father and then Rowan appearing…

She stiffened. "Put me down."

He ignored her, and just kept climbing stairs.

Panic shot through her. "What's happening? Why are you carrying me?"

She wiggled to free herself.

His grip grew tighter. "Because you fainted, and you're bleeding."

"I didn't."

"You did. You smacked your head on the edge of the stage when you fainted, probably have a concussion."

"I'm fine now," she said, struggling once again. "You can put me down. Now. Thank you."

"You won't be able to make it up the stairs, and we've got to get out of here, so don't fight me, because I'm not putting you down," he said shortly, kicking the door to the roof open. "And if you don't like being carried, then next time don't be clumsy. Faint somewhere soft."

"Where's Joe? I need Joe!"

"I'm sure you do," Rowan gritted as they stepped into

the dazzling California sunshine. "Don't worry, he's following with your things."

"My things? But why?"

"I'll fill you in once we're in the air. But enough chatter for now." His cool gaze dropped and swept from her face down her neck to the swell of her breasts. "You're not as light as you like to think you are."

But before she could react, they were at the helicopter and the pilot was jumping out and opening the door. Rowan was putting her in the helicopter in one of the passenger seats but she turned in his arms, leaning past to find Joe.

"Logan," Joe said, trying to reach her.

Rowan kept his arm up, blocking Joe from getting too close. "Put her things down," Rowan directed, "and step back."

But Logan grabbed Joe's sleeve. "Handle things at home, Joe. Please?"

Joe's dark eyes met hers and held. "Where are you going? When will you be back?"

"She'll call you," Rowan said drily. "Now say goodbye."

"Tomorrow's event," Logan said.

Joe nodded. "We'll make it work. I'll make it work. Don't worry."

And then Rowan was climbing into the helicopter and the pilot began lifting off, forcing Joe to run backward to escape the intense wind from the churning blades.

"Nice boy," Rowan said, shutting the door as Joe scrambled to safety. "Definitely on the young side, but so much more trainable before twenty-five."

Logan shot him a furious glance. "He's not my boyfriend."

"Your lover, whatever." He shrugged. "It's not for me to judge what you do with your father's money—"

"I don't have a penny of my father's money."

"I'm sorry. It wasn't his money. His embezzled billions."

She ground her jaw tight and looked away, chest aching, eyes burning, mouth tasting like acid. She hated him…she hated him so much…

And then he leaned over and checked her seat belt, giving it a tug, making the harness shoulder straps pull tight on her chest.

She inhaled sharply, and his fingers slid beneath the wide harness strap, knuckles against the swell of her breasts.

"Too tight?" he asked, his gaze meeting hers, even as her nipples tightened.

"With your fingers in there, yes," she choked, flushing, her body now hot all over. The linen and cotton fabric of her cream dress thin enough to let her feel everything.

He eased his hand out, but not before he managed to rub up against a pebbled peak.

And just like that memory exploded within her—his mouth on her breast, alternately sucking and tonguing the taut tip until he made her come just from working her nipple.

Her response had whetted his appetite. Not content with just the one orgasm, he devoted himself to exploring her body and teaching her all the different ways she could climax. It had been shocking but exciting. She'd been overwhelmed by the pleasure but also just by being with him. He'd felt so good to her. She'd felt so safe with him. Nothing he did seemed wrong because she'd trusted him—

Logan bit into her bottom lip hard to stop the train of thought. Couldn't go there, wouldn't go there, not now, not when her head ached and the helicopter soared straight up, leaving the top of the old Park Plaza Hotel building so quickly that her stomach fell, a nauseating reminder that she still wasn't feeling 100 percent.

She put a hand up to her temple and felt a sticky patch of blood. She glanced down at the damp crimson streaking her fingers, rubbed them, trying not to throw up. "I know you specialize in rescue and intelligence, but isn't the helicopter getaway a bit much?"

Rowan thrust a white handkerchief into her hands.

She took it, wiping the blood from her fingers, hoping she hadn't gotten any on her dress. This was a new dress, a rare splurge for her these days. As she rubbed her knuckles clean she could feel him watching her. He wasn't amused. She wasn't surprised. He didn't have a sense of humor three years ago. Why should he have one now?

"I just meant, it's a little Hollywood even for you," she added, continuing to scrub at her skin, feeling a perverse pleasure in poking at him, knowing he'd hate anything to do with Hollywood. Rowan Argyros might look like a high-fashion model, but she'd come to learn after their—encounter—that he was hardcore military, with the unique distinction of having served once in both the US Navy and the Royal Navy before retiring to form his own private maritime protection agency, a company her brother-in-law had invested heavily in, wanting the very best protection for his Greek shipping company, Xanthis Shipping.

Even more bruising was the knowledge that Morgan and Drakon were such good friends with Rowan. They both spoke of him in such glowing terms. It didn't seem fair that Rowan could forgive Morgan for being a Copeland, but not her.

"Look down," Rowan said tersely, gesturing to the streets below. The huge hotel, built in 1925 in a neo-Gothic style, filled the corners of Wilshire, Park View, and West Sixth Street. "That mob scene is for you."

Still gripping the handkerchief, she leaned toward the window which made her head throb. A large crowd pressed up against the entrance to the building, swarming the front steps, completely surrounding the front, with more bodies covering the back.

It *was* a mob scene. They were lying in wait for her. "Why didn't they go in?" she asked.

"I chained the front door. Hopefully your Joe will find the key, or he'll be in there a while."

Logan reached for her purse and slipped the handkerchief inside and then removed her phone. "Where did you put the key? Joe can't stay in there—"

"That's right. You've left him with instructions to manage things at home." He watched her from beneath heavy lids. "What a good boy."

She ignored him to shoot a quick text to Joe.

Rowan swiped the phone from her hands before she could hit Send.

She nearly kicked him. "Why are you so hateful?"

"Come on, babe, a little late now to play the victim."

Logan turned her head away to stare out the window, emotions so chaotic and hot she could barely see straight. "So where are you taking me?"

"To a safe spot. Away from the media."

"Good. If it's a safe spot, you won't be there." She swallowed hard, and crossed her arms over her chest. "And my father. He's really dead?"

"Yes."

She turned her head to look at him. Rowan's cool green gaze locked with hers, expression mocking. "If it makes you feel better," he added, lip curling, "it was natural causes."

Blood rushed to her cheeks and her face burned. Good God, he was even worse than she remembered. How could that be possible? "Of course it makes me feel better."

"Because you are such a dutiful daughter."

"Don't pretend you cared for him," she snapped.

"I didn't. He deserved everything he got, and more."

She hated Rowan. Hated, hated, hated him. Almost as much as she wanted to hate her father, who'd betrayed them all—and she didn't just mean the Copeland family, but his hundreds of clients. They'd trusted him and he'd robbed them blind. And then instead of facing prosecution, instead of accepting responsibility for his crimes, he'd fled the country, setting sail in a private yacht, a yacht which was later stormed off the coast of Africa—he was taken prisoner. Her father was held captive for months, and as time dragged on, the kidnappers' demands increased, the ransom increased. Only Morgan was willing to come up with money for the ransom...but that was another story.

And yet, even as much as she struggled with her father's crimes and how he'd shamed them and broken their hearts, she still didn't want him suffering. She didn't want him in pain. Maybe she didn't hate him as much as she thought she did. "So he wasn't murdered. There was no torture," she said, her mouth dry.

"Not at the end."

"But he was tortured."

His eyes met hers. "Shall we just say it wasn't a picnic?"

For a long moment she held her breath, heart thumping hard as she looked into his eyes and saw far more than she wanted to see.

And then she closed her eyes because she could see something else.

The future.

Her father was now dead and so he would never be prosecuted for his crimes, but the world still seethed. They demanded blood. With Daniel Copeland gone, they'd go after his five children. And while she could handle the scrutiny and hate—it was all she'd been dealing with since his

Ponzi scheme had been exposed—her daughter was little more than a baby. Just two and a quarter years old, she had no defenses against the cruelty of strangers.

"I need to go home," she choked. "I need to go home now."

Rowan had been watching the emotions flit across her face—it was a stunning face, too. He'd never met any woman as beautiful. But it wasn't just her bone structure that made her so attractive, it was the whole package. The long, thick honey hair, the wide-set blue eyes, the sweep of her brows, the dark pink lips above a resolute chin.

And then the body...

She had such a body.

He'd worshipped those curves and planes, and had imagined, that night three years ago, that maybe, just maybe, he'd found the one.

It's why he became so angry later, when he discovered who she was, because he'd felt things he'd never felt. He'd felt a tenderness and a connection that was so far out of his normal realm of emotions. What had started out as sex had become personal. Emotional. By morning he wasn't doing things to her, he was making love with her.

And then it all changed when he discovered the pile of mail on her kitchen counter. The bills. The magazine subscriptions.

Logan Copeland.

Logan Copeland.

Logan Lane Copeland.

It had blindsided him. That rarely happened. Stunned and then furious, he turned on her.

Many times he'd regretted the way he'd handled the discovery of her true identity. He regretted virtually everything about that night and the next morning, from the intense lovemaking to the harsh words he'd spoken. But over the years the thing he found himself regretting the most was the intimacy.

She'd been more than tits and ass.

She'd meant something to him. He'd wanted more with her. He imagined—albeit briefly—that there could be more, and it had been a tantalizing glimpse at a future he hadn't thought he would ever have. But then he saw it and realized that he wanted it. He wanted a home and a wife and children. He wanted the normalcy he'd never had.

And then it was morning and he was trying to figure out the coffee situation, and instead he was dealing with a liar-deceiver situation.

He wasn't in love. He wasn't falling in love. He'd been played.

And he'd gone ballistic. No, he didn't touch her—he'd never touch a woman in anger—but he'd said things to her that were vile and hurtful, things about how she was no better than her lying, crooked, greedy father and how it disgusted him that she'd bought him with money that her father had embezzled.

He didn't like remembering that morning, and he didn't like being responsible for her now, but he could protect her during the media frenzy, and he'd promised his friend and her brother-in-law, Drakon, that he would.

"There's no going home," he said tersely. "Your place must be a zoo. You'll be staying with me until the funeral."

Her blue eyes flashed as they met his. "I'm not staying with you."

"Things should calm down after the funeral. There will be another big story, another world crisis, people will tire of the Copelands," he said as if she'd never spoken.

"I have a job. I have clients. I have commitments—"

"Joe can handle them. Right?"

"Those clients hired me, not a twenty-four-year-old."

"I did think he looked young."

She lifted her chin, and her long hair tumbled over her shoulder, and her jaw firmed. "He's my assistant, Rowan. Not my lover."

"You don't live together?"

"No."

"Then why would you tell him to manage things at home?"

Her mouth opened, closed. "I work from home. I don't have an outside office."

"Yet he was genuinely worried about you."

She gave him a pitying look before turning to look out the window. "Most people are good people, Rowan. Most people have hearts."

Implying he didn't have one.

She wasn't far off.

His lips curved faintly, somewhat amused. Maybe if he was a teacher or a minister his lack of emotions would be a problem. But in his line of work, emotions just got in the way.

"The tin woodsman was always my favorite character," he said, referencing L. Frank Baum's *The Wonderful Wizard of Oz*.

"Of course he was," she retorted, keeping her gaze averted. "Except he had the decency and wisdom to want one."

CHAPTER TWO

"SO WHERE ARE we going?" she asked as the minutes slid by and they continued east over the city. Los Angeles was an enormous sprawl, but she recognized key landmarks and saw that they were approaching the Ontario airport.

He was slouching in his seat, legs outstretched, looking at her from beneath his lashes, not at all interested in the scenery. "One of my places."

He acted as if he was so casual. There was nothing careless or casual about Rowan Argyros. The man was lethal. She'd heard some of the stories from Morgan after her night with Rowan, and he was considered one of the most dangerous men on the planet.

And she had to pick him to be her first lover.

Genius move on her part.

Although to be fair, he'd never touched her with anything but sensitivity and expertise. His hands had made her feel more beautiful than she'd ever felt in her entire life. His caress had stirred her to the core. It would have been easy to imagine that he cared for her when he'd loved her so completely…

But he hadn't loved her. He'd pleasured her because she'd *paid* him to, giving her a twenty-thousand-dollar lay.

She swallowed around the lump filling her throat. Her eyes felt hot and gritty as she focused on the distant flight tower. She didn't want to remember. She hated remembering, and she might have been able to forget if it hadn't been for the one complication...

Not a small complication, either.

So she regretted the sex but not the mistake. Jax wasn't a mistake. Jax was her world and her heart and the reason Logan could battle through the constant public scrutiny and shame. Twice she'd had to close her Twitter account due to Twitter trolls. She'd refused to shut down her Instagram, forcing herself to ignore the daily onslaught of scorn and hate.

She'd get through this. Eventually. The haters of the world didn't matter. Jax mattered, and only Jax.

"So which home are we going to?" she asked, trying to match his careless, casual tone, trying to hide her concern and growing panic. Jax's sitter left between five and six every day. Even if Joe went to the house to relieve the sitter, he was merely buying Logan a couple of hours. Joe had never babysat Jax for more than an hour or two before. Joe was a good guy, but he couldn't care for the two-year-old overnight. Knowing Joe, he'd try, too, but Logan was a mama bear. No one came between her and her little girl.

"Does it matter?" he asked, pulling sunglasses from the pocket of his jacket.

So very James Bond. Her lip curled. He noticed.

"What's wrong now?" he asked.

She glanced away from him and crossed her legs, aware that she could feel the weight of his inspection even from behind his sunglasses. "Morgan told me how much you love your little games." She looked back at him, eyebrow arching. "You must be feeling very powerful now, what with the daring helicopter rescue and clandestine moves."

"I do like your sister," he answered. "She's good for Drakon. And he for her."

Logan couldn't argue with that. Her sister had nearly lost her mind when separated from her husband. Thank God they'd worked it out.

"Hard to believe you and Morgan are twins," he added. "You're nothing alike."

"Morgan chose to live with Dad. I didn't."

"And your baby sister, Jemma, she just chose to move out, even though she was still a teenager."

Logan swung her leg, the gold buckle on her strappy wedge sandal catching the light. "You're not a fan of my family, so I'm not entirely sure why we're having this conversation."

"Fine. Let's not talk about your family." His voice dropped, deepening, going almost velvet soft. "Let's talk about us."

Let's talk about us.

Her entire body went weak. She stopped swinging her leg, her limbs suddenly weighted even as her pulse did a crazy double beat.

Us. Right.

She couldn't see his eyes, but she could tell from the lift of his lips that he was enjoying himself. He was having fun, the same way a cat played with its prey before killing it.

She could be nervous, show fear, try to resist him—it was what he wanted. Or, she could just play along and not give him the satisfaction he craved.

Which, to her way of thinking, was infinitely better.

She smiled at him. He had no idea who he was dealing with. She wasn't the Logan Lane he'd bedded three years ago. He'd made sure of that. "Oh, that would be fun. I love talking about old times." She stared boldly into the dark sunglasses, letting him get a taste of who she'd become. "Good times. Right, babe?"

For a moment he gave her no response and then the corners of his mouth lifted even higher. A real smile. Maybe even a laugh, with the easy smile showing off very white, very straight teeth. The smile changed his face, making him younger and freer and sexy. Unforgivably sexy. Unforgivably since everything inside her was responding.

Not fair.

She hated him.

And yet she'd never met anyone with his control and heat and ability to own a room…and not just any room, but a massive ballroom…as if he were the only man in the entire place. As if he were the only man on the face of the earth. As if he'd been made just to light her up and turn her inside out.

Her heart raced and her pulse felt like sin in her veins. She was growing hot, flushing, needing…and she pressed her thighs tighter.

No, no, no.

"We were good," he said, still smiling at her, and yet his lazy drawl hinted at something so much more dangerous than anger.

Lethal man.

She'd wanted him that night and the fascination was back, slamming into her with the same force of a two-ton truck.

Something in her just wanted him.

Something in her recognized something in him and it shouldn't happen. There was no reason for someone like Rowan to be her type…

"It was you," she said, feeling generous. And what harm could there be in the truth? Because he was good—very, very good—and he was making her feel the same hot bright need that she'd felt during the bachelor auction. And it'd been forever since she'd felt anything sexual, her hunger smashed beneath layers of motherhood and maternal devotion. "You have quite the skill set."

"Years of practice, love."

"I commend your dedication to your craft."

His dark head inclined. "I tried to give you value for your twenty grand."

She didn't like that jab. But she could keep up. He and the rest of the haters had taught her how to wrap herself in a Teflon armor and just deflect, deflect, deflect. "Rest assured, you did. Now, if I knew then what I know now, I might have given you a few pointers, but I was so green. Talk about inexperienced. Talk about *embarrassing*. A twenty-four-year-old virgin." She shuddered and gently pushed back a long tendril of hair that had fallen forward. "Thankfully you handled the old hymen like the champ you are."

He wasn't smiling anymore.

Everything felt different. The very air was charged, seething...pulsing...

She gave him an innocent look. "Did I say something wrong?"

Rowan drew off his sunglasses and leaned toward her. "Say that again."

"The part about the hymen? Or the part where I wished I'd given you a few pointers?"

His green eyes were no longer cool. They burned and they were fixed intently on her, laser beams of loathing.

She'd finally gotten a rise out of him. She had to work very hard to hide her victorious smile. "But surely you knew I was a virgin," she added gently. "The blood on white sheets...?"

"It wasn't blood. It was spotting."

She shrugged carelessly. "You probably assumed it was just from...vigorous...thrusting."

His eyes glowed and his square jaw turned to granite. "You weren't a virgin."

"I was. And don't you feel honored that I picked you to be my first?" She glanced down at her hands, checking her nails. She must have chipped one earlier, when she fainted and fell. She rubbed a finger across the jagged edge and continued conversationally. "You set the bar very high, you know. Not just for what happened in the bedroom, but after."

He said nothing and so she looked up from her nails and stared into his eyes. "I can't help but wonder, if I hadn't climaxed during each of the...sessions...would you still have called me a whore?" She let the question float between them for a moment before adding, "Was it the fact that I enjoyed myself...that I took pleasure...that made me a whore? Because it was a very fast transition from virgin to whore—"

"Virgins don't spend twenty grand to get laid," he said curtly, cutting her short.

"No? Not even if they want to get laid by the best?"

He'd stopped smiling a long time ago. He had a reputation for being able to handle any situation but Logan was giving him a run for his money.

If it were any woman but Logan Copeland, he'd be impressed and maybe amused. Hell, he'd been amused at the start, intrigued by the way she'd thrown it down, and given it right back at him, but then it had all taken a rapid shift, right around the time she'd mentioned her virginity, and he didn't know how to fight back.

She'd been a virgin?

He didn't do virgins. He didn't take a woman's virginity. And yet he'd done her...quite thoroughly.

Dammit.

"You're taking my words out of context," he said tightly, trying to contain his frustration. "I didn't call you a whore—"

"Oh, you did. You called me a *Copeland* whore."

He winced inwardly, still able to hear the words ringing too loud in the kitchen of her Santa Monica bungalow. He could still see how she'd gone white and the way her blue eyes had revealed shock and then anguish.

She'd turned away and walked out, but he'd followed, hurling more insults, each a deliberate hit.

He despised the Copelands even before the father's Ponzi scheme was exposed. The Copelands were one of the most entitled families in America. The daughters were fixtures on the social scene, ridiculously famous simply because they were wealthy and beautiful.

Rowan grew up poor and everything he had, he personally had worked for.

He had no time for spoiled rich girls.

How could shallow, entitled women like that respect themselves?

Worse, how could America adore them? How could America reward them by filling their tabloids with their pictures and antics? Who cared where they shopped or which designer they wore?

Who cared where they vacationed?

Who cared who they screwed?

He didn't. Not until he'd realized he'd screwed one of them senseless.

But it hadn't been a screw. That was the thing. It had been so much more.

Rowan's jaw worked. His fingers curled into fists. "I regret those words," he said stiffly. "I would take them back, if I could."

"Is that your version of an apology?"

It had been, yes, but her mocking tone made it clear it wasn't good enough. That he wasn't good enough.

Rowan wasn't sure whether to be offended or amused.

And then he questioned why he'd even be offended. He'd never cared before what a woman thought of him.

He'd be a fool to care what a Copeland thought of him.

"It is what it is," he said, the helicopter dipping, dropping. They'd reached the Ontario airport. His private jet waited at the terminal.

Her head turned. She was looking down at the airport, too. "Why here? Do you have a place in Palm Springs?"

"If I did, we'd be flying into Palm Springs."

"I find it hard to believe you have a place in Ontario."

"I don't." He left it at that, and then they were touching down, lowering onto the tarmac.

Rowan popped the door open and stepped out. He reached for Logan but she drew back and climbed out without his assistance.

She started for the terminal but he caught her elbow and steered her in the other direction, away from the building and toward the sleek white-and-green pin-striped jet.

She froze when she realized what was happening. *"No."*

He couldn't do this again, not now. "We don't have time. I refuse to refile the flight plan."

"I'm not leaving Los Angeles. I *can't*."

"Don't make me carry you."

She broke free and ran back a step. "I'll scream."

He gestured to the empty tarmac. "And what good will that do you? Who will hear you? This is the executive terminal. The only people around are my people."

She reached up to capture her hair in one hand, keeping it from blowing in her face. "You don't understand. I can't go. I can't leave her."

"What are you talking about?"

"Jax." Her voice broke. "I've never been away from her before, not overnight. I can't leave her now."

"Jax?" he repeated impatiently. "What is that? Your cat?"

"No. My baby. My daughter."

"Your *daughter*?" he ground out.

She nodded, heart hammering. She felt sick to her stomach and so very scared. She'd forced herself to reach out to Rowan when she'd discovered she was pregnant, but he'd been even more hateful when she called him.

"How did you get my number?" he demanded.

"Drakon."

"He shouldn't have given it to you."

"I told him it was important."

He laughed—a cold, scornful sound that cut all the way to her soul.

"Babe, in case you didn't get the message, it's over. I've nothing more for you. Now, pull yourself together and get on with your life."

And so she had.

She didn't tell him about the baby. She didn't tell him he was having a daughter, and whatever qualms she had about keeping the information to herself were eventually erased by the memory of his coldness and hatefulness.

Her father had broken her heart, shaming her with his greed and selfishness, but Rowan was a close second. He was despicable. Like her father, the worst of the worst.

Thank goodness he wasn't in Jax's life. Logan couldn't even imagine the kind of father he'd be. Far better to raise Jax on her own than have Jax growing up with a father who couldn't, wouldn't, love her.

And now, facing Rowan on the tarmac, Logan knew she'd made the right decision. Rowan might be a military hero—deadly in battle, formidable in a combat zone—but he was insensitive to the point of abusive and she'd never allow him near her daughter.

"You're a *mother*?" he said.

She heard the bewildered note in his voice and liked it. She'd shocked him. Good. "Yes."

His brow furrowed. "Where is she now?"

"At home." Logan glanced at her watch. "Her sitter will leave at five. I need to be back by then."

"You won't be. You're not going back."

"And what about Jax? We'll just leave her in a crib until you decide you'll return me?"

His jaw worked, the small muscle near his ear pulling tight. "Drakon never mentioned a baby."

Her heart did a double beat and her stomach heaved. "They don't know."

"What?"

"No one knows."

"How can that be?"

"It might surprise you, but we don't do big family reunions anymore."

He folded his arms across his chest. "Who is her father?"

She laughed coolly. "I don't think that's any of your business, do you?"

He sighed. "What I meant is, can't her father take her while you're gone?"

"No."

"I think you need to ask—"

"No."

"Not a good relationship?"

She felt her lip curl. This would be funny if one enjoyed dark comedy. "An understatement if I ever heard one."

"Can her sitter keep her?"

"*No.*" The very idea of anyone *keeping* Jax made

Logan's heart constrict. "I've never been away from her for a night. She's a toddler…a baby…" Her voice faded and she dug her nails into her palms, waiting for Rowan to say something.

He didn't. He stared at her hard.

She couldn't read what he was thinking, but there was definitely something going on in that head, she could see it in his eyes, feel it in his tension. "I need to get home to her." Her voice sounded rough. She battled to maintain control. "Especially if there are paparazzi at the house. I don't want them doing anything—trying anything. I don't want her scared."

"Logan, I can't let you anywhere near the house. I'm sorry." He held up his hand when she started to protest. "I'll get her. But you must promise to stay here. No taking off. No running away. No frantic phone calls to anyone. Stay put on my plane and wait."

She glanced toward the white jet and spotted his staff waiting by the base of the stairs.

He followed her gaze. "My staff will make sure you're comfortable. As long as you stay here with them you won't be in any danger."

Stiffening, Logan turned back to face him. "Why would I be in danger? It's just the paparazzi."

"Bronson was shot late last night in London." Rowan's voice was clipped. "He's in ICU now, but the specialists believe he should make a full recovery—"

"Wait. What? Why didn't you say something earlier?" Bronson was the oldest of the five Copelands and the only son. "What happened?"

"Authorities are investigating now, but the prevailing theory is that Bronson was targeted because of your father. The deputy chief constable recommended that all members of your family be provided with additional security.

My team has already located Victoria and is taking her to a safe location. Your mother is with Jemma already. And now we have you."

Logan felt the blood drain from her head. Fear made her legs shake. "Please go get Jax. Hurry."

"Give me your phone."

"I won't call anyone—"

"That's not why I want your phone. I'm taking it so I can be you and make sure Joe understands what I need him to do."

"You're involving Joe?" she asked, handing him the phone.

"You trust him, don't you?"

She nodded. "The password is zero, three, three, one."

Rowan started for the helicopter and then turned around. "Didn't we meet March 31?"

She went hot all over. "That's not why it's my password." She heard her defensive tone and hated it.

"Never said it was. But it does make it easy for me to remember your code." And then he signaled the pilot to start up the chopper and the blades began whirling and he was climbing in and the helicopter was lifting off even before Rowan had shut the door.

CHAPTER THREE

ROWAN WAS GONE for two hours and twenty-odd minutes, and during those long two plus hours, Logan couldn't let herself think about anything...

Not Bronson, who'd been hurt. Or her family who were all being guarded zealously to protect them from a nut job.

She couldn't think about her daughter or how frightened she must be.

She couldn't think about her huge event taking place tomorrow and how she now wouldn't be there to see it through.

She couldn't think about anything because once she started thinking, her imagination went wild and every scenario made her heartsick.

Every fear pummeled her, making her increasingly nauseous.

But of all her fears, Jax was the most consuming. She loved her brother and sisters but they were adults, and it sounded as if they now had a security team protecting them. But Jax...her baby...?

Logan exhaled slowly, struggling to keep it together. Rowan *had* to be successful. And there was no reason he wouldn't be. He was the world's leading expert in hostage and crisis situations and removing a toddler from a Santa Monica bungalow was not a crisis situation. But that didn't mean her heart didn't race and her stomach didn't heave and she didn't feel frantic, aware that all kinds of things could go wrong.

But Rowan being successful meant that he would be with Jax, and this terrified her. The haters and shamers had hardened her to the nonstop barbs and insults, but Jax was her weakness. Jax made her vulnerable. And maybe that's because Jax herself was so vulnerable.

A light from the cockpit drew her attention and she glanced up, noting the three men up front—two pilots and the male flight attendant.

They were an interesting-looking flight crew bearing very little resemblance to the pleasant, professional, middle-aged crew you'd find on a commercial plane. These three were lean, muscular and weathered. They looked so fit and so tan that it made her think they'd only recently retired from active duty with the military. As they spoke to each other in low voices, she tried to listen in, but it was impossible to eavesdrop from where she sat.

Abruptly the three men turned and looked at her and then the male flight attendant was heading her way.

"Did you need something, Miss Copeland?" he asked crisply. He didn't look American, but he didn't have an accent. He was an enigma, like the rest of the crew.

"Is there any water?"

"I'll bring you a bottle. Would you like a meal? Are you hungry?"

She shook her head. "I don't think I could eat. Just water."

But once she had the bottle of water, she just held it between her hands, too nervous to drink more than a mouthful.

The minutes dragged by, slowly turning into hours. She

wished someone would give her an update. She wished she knew *something*.

But just when she didn't think she could handle another minute of silence and worry, the distinctive sound of a helicopter could be heard.

She prayed it was Rowan returning—

The thought stopped her short. Just hours ago such a prayer would have struck her as ludicrous. But he'd gone after her baby and she was grateful for that.

Who would have ever thought she'd pray to see him again?

As the helicopter touched down the flight crew stood at the entrance of the jet as if prepared for battle.

Logan arched her brows. Rowan was serious about personal safety, wasn't he?

But then the helicopter was down and the door was opening. Rowan was the first to step out and he was holding Jax, and as he crossed the tarmac, Joe Lopez was close behind carrying two suitcases.

What was Joe doing? Had he insisted on accompanying Jax to be sure she was safe? Or had Rowan wanted Joe along in case Jax got scared?

Either way Logan was delighted when the men stepped onto the plane with the baby.

Jax squealed when she saw Logan. "Momma!"

Logan opened her arms and Rowan handed the child over. "Hello, sweet girl," Logan whispered, kissing her daughter's soft cheek again and again. "How's my baby girl?"

Jax turned her head to kiss Logan back. "I love Momma."

"And Momma loves you. What did you think of the helicopter?" Logan asked her, giving her a little squeeze. "Was it noisy?"

Jax nodded and clapped her hands to her head. "Don't like ear things. Bad."

Rowan met Logan's gaze over Jax's head. "Not a fan of the headset."

"Not surprised. She has a mind of her own," Logan said.

"She does like Joe, though. She insisted on sitting on his lap during the flight. He's good with her, too," Rowan said.

Logan glanced back toward the galley where the flight attendant was taking the two suitcases from her assistant. "It was nice of him to come. Or did you make him?"

"I didn't make Joe do anything. He is apparently very devoted to you—"

"Don't start again."

"Just saying, he's here because he insisted."

"I appreciate it. He's been awesome with her since the beginning." Logan frowned at the size of the two suitcases. "How long are we going to be gone?"

"Your buddy Joe did the packing. Apparently you girls need a lot when you travel."

Logan's eyes met Rowan's. She gave her head a slight shake, her expression mocking. "You sound a little jealous of him, you know."

"Me, *jealous*, of that…kid? Right." Rowan made a scornful sound and turned away as Joe approached Logan.

"You all right?" Joe asked Logan even as he handed Jax a sippy cup with water.

Logan nodded and shot Rowan's retreating back a disapproving look. "I hope he wasn't rude to you," she said to Joe. "If he was, don't take it personally. He's that way with everyone."

Joe smiled and shrugged. "I've met worse."

Logan gave him a look.

His smile broadened. "He doesn't bother me. And he was actually pretty sweet with Jax—"

"Don't say it. Don't want to hear it." Logan cut him short. "So is he going to send you back in the helicopter or are you having to grab a cab back? If you need a cab, just put it on my account. I won't have you paying for something like that. It'll be ridiculously expensive."

"I'll grab a rental car and drop it off at LAX." Joe hesitated a moment. "Are you going to be okay?"

Logan kissed the top of Jax's head and nodded. "Need tomorrow's event to go off without a hitch—"

"It will. The fund-raiser will be huge, and the fashion show will be wonderful. But you're the one I'm worried about."

"Don't. I'm fine. And my company…it's everything. It's my reputation. My livelihood. It's how I provide for Jax—" She broke off, overwhelmed by stress and the weight of her reality. Her reality was harsh. People didn't give her the same benefit of the doubt they gave others. She didn't get second chances or opportunities…no, she had to fight tooth and nail for every job, forced to prove herself over and over again.

"I'll handle it," Joe said quietly, his deep voice firm.

"Thank you."

And then he kissed Jax on the top of her head and he left.

Rowan didn't seem to even notice that Joe had gone and it burned Logan up, how arrogant and callous Rowan was. Joe had been a huge help and Rowan didn't thank him or care.

Why couldn't Logan fall for someone like Joe…someone smart and kind and caring? Someone with *emotions*?

And then as if able to read Logan's mind, Rowan was returning. "We need to go." He nodded at the toddler. "Are you going to hold her for takeoff, or do you want me to buckle her car seat into a chair next to you?"

"Which is safer?" Logan asked.

"Car seat," he answered promptly.

"Then let's do that."

"Has she ever been on a plane before?"

Logan shook her head. "We don't...go out...much." And seeing his expression she added, "We don't need the attention."

"Have things been that difficult?"

"You've no idea." And then she laughed because it was all she could do. The haters and shamers would not win. They wouldn't. She'd make sure of that, just as she'd make sure her daughter would grow up with a spine and become a woman with courage and strength.

Rowan glanced at his watch. They'd been flying four hours but still had a good four to five hours to go. He was glad that the toddler finally slept, though. Earlier she'd cried for nearly an hour when she couldn't have her blanket. Joe had brought the blanket when they met up at the Santa Monica airport. The blanket was either in a seat or on the floor of the helicopter or perhaps it got dropped on the tarmac during the transfer to the plane. Either way, the baby was inconsolable and Logan walked with Jax, up and down the short aisle, patting her little girl's back until Jax had finally cried herself to sleep on Logan's shoulder.

Now Logan herself was asleep in one of the leather chairs in a reclined position, the little girl still on her chest, the child's two miniature ponytails brushing Logan's chin.

Seeing Logan with the child made him uncomfortable.

He didn't like the ambivalence, either. He didn't like *any* ambivalence, preferring life tidy, organized, categorized into boxes that could be graded and stacked.

He'd put Logan into a box. He'd graded the box and labeled it, stacking it in the corner of his mind with other bad and difficult memories. After he'd left her, after their night together, he'd been troubled for weeks…months. It had angered him that he couldn't forget her, angered him that he didn't have more control over his emotions. He shouldn't care about her. He shouldn't worry about her. And yet he did.

He worried constantly.

He worried that someone, somewhere would hurt her.

He worried about her physical safety. He worried about her emotional well-being. He'd been so hard on her. He'd been ruthless, just the way he was with his men, and in his world. But she wasn't a man, and she wasn't conditioned to handle what he'd dished out.

He'd come so close, so many times to apologizing.

He'd come so close to saying he was wrong.

But he didn't. He feared opening a door that couldn't be shut. There was no point bonding with a woman who wasn't to be trusted. Trust was everything in his world, and she'd lied to him once—Logan Lane, indeed—so why wouldn't she lie again?

Maybe the trust issue would be less crucial if he had a different job. Maybe if his work wasn't so sensitive he could be less vigilant…but his work was sensitive, and countless people depended on him to keep them safe, and alive.

Just as Jax depended on her mother to keep her safe.

He wanted to hate Logan. Wanted to despise her. But watching her sleep with Jax stirred his protective instinct.

At two years old, Jax was still more baby than girl, her wispy blond hair a shade lighter than her mother's. They both had long dark eyelashes and the same mouth, full and pink with a rosebud for an upper lip.

Sleeping, Jax was a vision of innocence.

Sleeping, Logan was a picture of maternal devotion.

Together they made his chest ache.

Rowan didn't want his chest to ache. He didn't want to care in any way, but it was difficult to separate himself when he kept running numbers in his head.

March 31 plus forty weeks meant a December birthday. Jax had a December birthday. December 22 to be precise. He knew because Joe had located Jax's birth certificate at the house and put it in a file for Rowan. You couldn't just whisk a baby out of a country without any legal documentation. If they were flying on a commercial plane, he'd have to go through government channels, which would have required a passport.

But since they weren't flying on a private plane, his pilot had submitted a manifest — which had included Logan Copeland. The manifest had not included the baby as he hadn't known there was a baby until just hours ago.

The baby could potentially be an issue, but as Rowan had diplomatic immunity, he wasn't too worried for himself.

Logan was another matter. She could definitely find herself in hot water should various governments discover she'd smuggled a baby out of one country and into another.

Fortunately they would be landing on Rowan's private airstrip on his private property, so there shouldn't be guards or officers inspecting his jet, or interrogating his guests.

But if they did…what would he say about Jax?

The child born exactly forty weeks after March 31.

Aware that she was being studied, Logan opened her eyes. Rowan sat watching her in a leather chair opposite hers.

He wasn't smiling.

She just held his cool green gaze, her heart sinking. She didn't want to panic and yet there was something very quiet, and very thoughtful, in his expression and it made her imagine that he could see things he couldn't see and know things he couldn't possibly know.

He couldn't possibly know that Jax was his.

He couldn't possibly imagine that she would have slept only with him. Her one and only lover in twenty-seven years. That didn't happen anymore. Women didn't wait for true love…

And so she arched a brow, matching his cool expression, doing what she did best—*deflect, deflect, deflect*. "Was I snoring?"

"No."

"Was my mouth open, catching flies?"

"I want a DNA test."

The words were so quietly spoken that it took Logan a moment to process them. He wanted a DNA test. He did suspect…

Deflect, deflect, deflect. "That's awfully presumptuous, don't you think?"

"You said you were a virgin. You made a big fuss earlier about how I manhandled your hymen—"

"I did not say that."

"—which makes me doubt you were out getting laid by someone else in the following five to seven days."

"Your math is excellent. I commend you. Not just a skilled lover, but also a true statistician, except for the fact that Jax wasn't due for another month. She arrived early."

"Your sweet girl was almost nine pounds, my love. She wasn't early."

Logan's stomach heaved. He knew how much Jax weighed. He knew her birth date. What else did he know?

"She's not yours," she repeated stubbornly.

"No, she hasn't been, but she should be, shouldn't she?"

Logan held her breath.

"We'll test tomorrow, after we land."

"You're not going to poke her with a needle—"

"We'll do a saliva swab. Painless."

"Rowan."

"Yes, Logan?"

Logan's heart was beating so fast she was afraid it'd wake Jax. "You don't even like children. You don't want them. And you despise girls—"

"Is this what you've been telling yourself the past three years? Is this your justification for keeping Jax from me?"

You called me a whore. You said the worst, most despicable things to me.

And yes, those words hurt, but that wasn't why she didn't tell him. "I tried," she said, her voice quiet but thankfully steady.

"And when was that?"

"When I called you. Remember that? I phoned to tell you, and instead of a 'How are you? Everything okay?' you demanded to know how I got your number." She stared Rowan down, her gaze unwavering. "Even when I told you that Drakon had given it to me because it was important, you were hateful. You mocked me, saying you'd given me all you could."

Her voice was no longer quiet and calm. It vibrated with emotion, coloring the air between them. "After you hung up, I cried myself sick, and then eventually I pulled myself together and was glad. *Glad* you wanted nothing to do with me, glad you wanted nothing to do with us, glad that my daughter wouldn't have to grow up as I did, with a selfish, uncaring father."

For a long moment Rowan said nothing. He just studied her from his seat, his big, lean, powerful body relaxed, his expression thoughtful. He seemed as if he didn't have a care in the world, which put her on high alert. This was

Rowan at his most dangerous, and she suspected what made him so dangerous was that he cared.

He cared a great deal.

Finally he shifted and sighed. "There are so many things I could say."

Logan's heart raced and her stomach rolled and heaved. "Why don't you say them?"

"Because we are still hours away from Galway—"

"Galway?" she interrupted.

"—and I don't feel like arguing all the way to Ireland."

She blinked at him, taken aback. "We can't leave the US. I don't have a passport with me, and Jax doesn't even have one yet."

Rowan shrugged, unconcerned. "We're landing on a private airstrip. There won't be any customs or immigration officers on our arrival."

"And what about when we return? Don't you think it will be problematic then?"

"Could be. But Joe packed your passport when he packed for you, and he sent along Jax's birth certificate, so we do have that."

That's how Rowan knew Jax's birth date. That's how he knew what he knew. But how did Joe know where to find her legal documents? She'd never told him...

Logan watched the slow drumming of Rowan's fingers on his hard thigh, mesmerized by the bronze of his skin and the tantalizing movement of strong fingers, the drumming steady, rhythmic.

The man had good hands. They'd felt so good on her. His touch had a sensitivity and expertise that was so different from his reputation as an elite fighter...warrior...

He'd made her feel things she didn't think she could feel, but no more. Hope and beauty—

No. Couldn't go there again, couldn't remember, couldn't

let herself fantasize that what had been was anything but sex. He'd made it clear she was just a lay. Sweat and re-lease…exercise.

Her eyes burned and she swallowed hard, disgusted with herself for still letting his callous words upset her, hurt her. She shouldn't care. She shouldn't.

And yet she did.

Maybe if the sex hadn't been so good she could play this game. Maybe if she hadn't felt hope and joy, and maybe if he hadn't made her feel beautiful… Things she hadn't felt in so long. So many people had been hateful about her father. The world had become ugly and hostile, and then Rowan had been the opposite. He'd been light and heat and emotion and she couldn't help feeling connected to him. Bonded.

And then he discovered the Copeland part of her name, having missed that the night before…

Logan exhaled slowly, head light and spinning, dizzy from holding her breath too long. "I can't do this with you," she said lowly, her hand reaching up to adjust Jax on her chest. "Not with her here."

"What do you think we're going to do?"

"Fight. Be hateful." Her voice sounded strained to her own ears. "But Jax shouldn't be part of that. It's not fair to her, or good for her—"

"I've no desire to hurt my daughter," he interrupted. "And I don't need a damn DNA test to confirm it. We'll have it done so we can correct her birth certificate, but I don't need it to prove anything. She's obviously mine."

"Ours," she whispered, and it killed her to do it, killed her to say it but Jax had to be protected, no matter the cost. "Obviously ours."

The corner of Rowan's mouth lifted and his expression turned rueful. "I suppose it's a good thing that your father died. In time we will even view his passing as a blessing because it brought us all together. You, me and our daughter."

There was nothing frightening in his tone. If anything he sounded…amused. But Rowan's sense of humor was nothing like hers, and her heart lurched.

"So what is the next step?" he asked, smiling faintly, green eyes gleaming. "A wedding at the castle? And do we do it before or after your father's funeral?"

Thank God she was sitting. Thank God for armrests. Thank God Jax stirred then and let out a whimper, saving Logan from having to answer.

Jax whimpered once more and stretched, flinging out small arms in an attempt to get more comfortable.

Logan wanted to whimper, too.

This was crazy, so crazy.

Rowan was crazy.

"I think we do it before," he added reflectively. "It will give everyone something to celebrate. Yes, there will be sadness over your father's life being cut short—he was such a good man, so devoted to his family and community—but then everyone will be able to rejoice over our happy and surprising news. We're not just newlyweds, but proud parents of a two-year-old girl."

"You hate my father, and you hate me—"

"That's the past," he said gently, cutting her short. "It's time to leave the past in the past and concentrate on the future. And you're going to be my wife and we'll have more children—"

"You're having a really good time with this, aren't you?"

His broad shoulders shifted. "I'm trying to be positive, yes."

"I don't think you're trying to be positive as much as sadistic," she retorted, fighting panic because she didn't think Rowan was teasing. He seemed quite serious, which was terrifying as Rowan's entire career was based on his ability to play dirty. "We're not marrying. There won't be more children. There is no relationship. There has never been a relationship. So don't start throwing your weight around because I won't put up with it."

He had the audacity to laugh. "No? What will you do? Call Joe?"

Her cheeks burned. "You have such a problem with him. If I didn't know you better, I'd say you were jealous."

"I don't even know where to begin with that statement… so many ways I could run with it." He smiled at her, a charming smile that made her want to leap from her chair and run.

"Joe," he said politely, "works for *me*."

When her lips parted he held up a hand to stop her.

"He's worked for me since the day you hired him. He didn't attend USC. He never studied art, communications or design. And he's not twenty-four. He's thirty-one, and before he came to work for Dunamas, he was a member of Delta Force."

Logan couldn't wrap her head around what Rowan was telling her. Joe was not a military guy. Joe was young and sweet and hardworking…

But Rowan misunderstood her baffled expression. "First Special Forces Operational Detachment Delta," he said.

"I don't need an explanation for the abbreviation Delta Force. I need to understand how someone I hired from a pool of candidates worked for you."

"They all worked for me."

"No."

"How many résumés and cover letters did you get?"

"Six. No, five. One withdrew hers."

"How many did you interview?"

"Four."

"How many in person?"

"The top three."

"Trish Stevens, Jimmy Gagnier and Joe Lopez. Trish wanted too much money. Jimmy made you uncomfortable because he knew about your family. And Joe was just so dang grateful to have a job." The corner of his mouth quirked but he wasn't smiling. "And you believed him because you wanted—needed—to believe him."

"But I called his references…" Her voice faded as she heard herself and realized how foolish she sounded. She stared hard at a point just past Rowan's shoulder, willing her eyes to stop stinging, willing the awful lump in her throat to stop aching.

She'd trusted Joe.

She'd trusted him with her work and her family and her life…

"I thought he was a good person," she whispered, feeling impossibly betrayed.

"He is. He would have died for you. No questions asked."

"I'm sure that must have cost you a pretty penny."

"Joe did protect you," Rowan said. "And he wasn't a spy—"

"I don't believe that for a minute."

"If he was a spy, he would have told me about the baby. He never did." Rowan's voice deepened, hardened. "His job was to protect you, and he did. He was so devoted to you that he also protected you, and Jax, from me."

Logan had nothing to say to that. She stared at Rowan, stunned, because theoretically, if Joe was employed by Rowan, he probably should have told Rowan he was protecting a woman and a baby…

"Yes," Rowan said. "He took his job as your security

detail very, very seriously. He never once mentioned anything about a pregnancy or a baby or that he spent lots of
time working from your home."

She almost laughed, feeling slightly hysterical. "Do you
have any idea the things I had him do? The errands after
work? The trips to the dry cleaner? He even helped feed
Jax dinners when I was working away at my computer…"
Logan swallowed hard. "I thought he loved her. And maybe
it wasn't love, but I thought he really did care about us."

For several minutes there was just silence and then
Rowan made a low, rough sound. "He did," Rowan said
shortly. "For two years Joe protected you and your secret.
He shouldn't have, though. That was a critical error on his
part. I've fired him. He'll find it difficult getting another
high-level security job." And then Rowan walked away,
heading to the galley.

Logan watched his back, the sting of tears prickling her
eyes. She didn't think it was possible, but her very bad day
had just gotten worse.

CHAPTER FOUR

ROWAN WAS POURING HIMSELF a neat shot of whiskey when Logan appeared in the narrow kitchen galley.

She stood in the doorway, arms crossed over her chest. She was so much thinner than she'd been three years ago. He'd known she worked hard, but he hadn't expected her to look quite so stressed. If he'd known she was pregnant... if he'd known there was a child...

He threw back the shot and looked at her. "Yes, love?"

"I'm not your love."

His fingers itched to pour another drink but he never had more than one. At least, never more than one in a twelve-hour span. He couldn't afford to lose his head. Ever.

But he had lost it once. He'd lost it March 31 three years ago to *her*. The evidence of that was curled up in a chair, hair in two tiny ponytails. They'd used protection the night of the bachelor auction. He knew he'd used protection. Clearly it hadn't been the right protection, or enough.

"Have you heard anything about Bronson? Is he stable or still in critical condition?"

"Bronson will remain in ICU for another few days, but he's been stabilized. The decision to keep him in ICU is for his protection. It's easier to secure the ICU unit than another floor."

"And Victoria? Where is she is right now? Who exactly has her?"

"By now your sister should be with Drakon and Morgan—"

"Oh, that's going to go over beautifully."

"Why?"

"They don't get along. At all."

"Drakon and Victoria?"

"Morgan and Victoria." She frowned. "I wouldn't leave Victoria there. She should go to Jemma. They're close. Victoria will be far happier there."

"It's too late for that. What's done is done and hopefully your sisters will realize that this isn't the time to bicker."

Her eyebrows rose. "They don't bicker. They've had a massive falling out, over my father. It's painful for everyone."

"Then I wish Drakon well because it's his problem now." Rowan leaned back against the narrow galley counter, the stainless steel cool against his back. He allowed his gaze to slide over Logan's slender frame, studying her intently. "Why didn't you get an abortion?"

If his question shocked her, she gave no indication. "It wasn't the right choice for me," she answered, her voice firm and clear.

She was good, he thought. She sounded so grounded and smart and reasonable, which just provoked him even more.

He gripped the counter's edge tightly. It was that or grab her by the shoulder and drag her into his arms. His kiss wouldn't be kind.

He was not feeling kind.

It was difficult to feel kind when his cock throbbed in his trousers and his body felt hard and hungry.

He remembered the smell of her and the taste of her

and how soft and warm and wet she'd been as he'd kissed
her there, between her legs, and made her body tighten
and break with pleasure. And then he'd thrust in, burying
himself hard, and she'd groaned and stiffened and he'd
thought that had been pleasure, too.

Now he knew he'd taken her virginity ruthlessly. Not
knowing…

Not knowing the first damn thing about her.

A Copeland. A virgin. A society princess dethroned.

"Don't fire Joe," she said, breaking the tense silence.
Her voice was husky. He heard the pleading note, and it
made him even angrier. Why did it bother him that she
was pleading for Joe? Was it because he worried that she
cared for him? Or was it because he wanted her to plead
for him…

She'd begged him three years ago, begged for his hands
and his mouth, begged to be touched and taken, and he'd
obliged.

Now look at them. Parents of a tiny girl.

He wouldn't ignore his responsibilities. He wouldn't
punish the girl the way he'd been punished when his father knocked his mother up.

His father who drank too much and let his fists fly. His
mother who drank too much and forgot to come home.

Not that he blamed her. Home was not a nice place
to be.

"Please," Logan started again. "Please don't—"

"Joe doesn't need you begging for his job," Rowan said
curtly, unable to bear hearing her plead any longer. It was
far too reminiscent of a childhood he hated. It was far too
reminiscent of a person he didn't want to be. "He knew
what he was doing. He made his own choices—"

"For Jax."

"For you," he corrected. "I know he cared for you. I

know he developed…feelings…for you. I know when his attachment became more than just a strong sense of duty."

"And yet you left him on the job."

Rowan really wanted another drink, craving the burn and the heat in his veins because maybe then he wouldn't want to push her up against the galley wall and put his hands into her hair and take her soft mouth and make her whimper for him.

He felt like an animal.

He didn't want to be an animal.

His work usually kept him focused but right now he had none. Just her and her wide, searching blue eyes and that dark pink mouth that demanded to be kissed.

"No," he ground out, knuckles tight as he gripped the stainless counter harder. "I didn't *leave* him on the job. I relieved him months ago. Back before the Christmas holidays. He refused to step down. He refused to abandon you."

Her lips curved, tremulous. "Unlike you?"

If she'd been icy and mocking he could have ignored the jab. If she'd shown her veneer, he would have let her be. But her unsteady words coupled with the tremble of her lip made his chest squeeze, the air bottled within.

He'd hurt her, because he'd meant to hurt her.

He was very good at what he did.

Rowan reached for her wrist, his fingers circling her slender bones and he pulled her toward him. She stiffened but didn't fight him. If anything she'd gone very still.

"Let me see your head," he said gruffly, bringing her hips almost to his. He lifted a heavy wave of honey-colored hair from her forehead to inspect her temple.

With one hand still in her hair, he tipped her head, tilting this way and that to get a proper look. It didn't look too bad. She must have cleaned the wound while he'd gone to pick up Jax. The cut was scabbing, and he saw the start of a dark bruise. The bruise would be uglier tomorrow, but all in all, she was healing.

"I'm sorry I didn't catch you," he said, his deep voice still rough. They might not be on good terms but he didn't like that all he did was bring her pain. "You went down hard."

"I've survived far worse," she answered, her smile full of bravado, but the bold smile didn't reach her blue eyes, and in those blue eyes fringed by thick black lashes there was a world of hurt and shadows. Far too many shadows.

He tipped her head farther back to look into her eyes, trying to see where she'd been and all that had happened in the past three years and then he felt a stab of regret, and blame.

He'd left her out there, hanging.

He'd left her, just as she'd said.

He, who protected strangers, hadn't protected *her*.

His head dropped, his mouth covering hers. It was a kiss to comfort her, a kiss to apologize for being such an ass, and yet the moment his mouth touched hers he forgot everything but how warm she was and how good she felt against him. Her mouth was so very soft and warm, too, and her chest rose and fell with her quick gasp, the swell of her breasts pressing against his chest.

He had not been celibate for the past three years. He liked women and enjoyed sex, and he'd found pleasure with a number of women but Logan didn't feel like just any woman—she was different. She felt like his. But he didn't want to explore that thought, not when he wanted to explore her, and he slid a hand down the length of her back, soothing her even as he coaxed her closer, heat in his veins, hunger making him hard.

He wasn't going to force her, though. She could push

him away at any moment. He'd let her go the moment she said no, the moment she put a hand to his chest and pressed him back.

And then her hand moved to his chest, and her fingers grabbed at his shirt, and she tugged on the shirt, tugging him toward her.

The heat in his veins became a fire.

He deepened the kiss, his tongue tracing the seam of her lips until she opened her mouth. His tongue flicked over her lower lip and then found the tip of hers and teased that, and then the inside of her upper lip, teasing the delicate swollen skin until he felt her nails dig into his chest, her slender frame shuddering. He captured her hip, holding her close, wanting nothing more than to bury himself in her and make her cry his name again...

She wasn't like any other woman. He'd never met another woman he wanted this much.

The kiss became electric, so hot he felt as if he was going to explode. He didn't want to want her like this. He didn't want to want anyone like this. He didn't want his control tested, didn't want to feel as if he couldn't get enough, that he'd never have enough, that what he missed, needed, wanted was right here in this woman—

He broke off the kiss and stepped back. He was breathing hard, his shaft throbbing but that was nothing compared to what was happening in his chest, within his heart.

She was not the right one for him.

She couldn't be.

He didn't like spoiled, entitled society girls, and he didn't respect women who'd never had to work for anything...

"One of us should be with Jax," he said curtly. "Make sure she's safe in case there's turbulence."

"I was just on my way back to her," Logan replied turning around and walking away, but not before he saw the flush in her cheeks and the ripe plumpness of her pink lips.

He nearly grabbed her again, wanting to finish what he'd started.

Instead he let her go, body aching, mind conflicted.

There was no love lost between them. They couldn't even carry on a civil conversation but that didn't matter if he took her to bed. They didn't have to like each other. In fact, it might even be better if they didn't like each other. It didn't matter with them. The sex would still be hot.

Logan returned to her seat and carefully scooped Jax back into her arms and sat down with her daughter, not because Jax needed to be held but because Logan needed Jax for safety. Security.

Rowan's kiss had shaken her to the core.

Her heart still pounded, her body flooded with wants and needs that could destroy her. Rowan was not good for her. Rowan was danger...

She swallowed hard and closed her eyes, determined to clamp down on her emotions, determined to slow her pulse.

She didn't want him. She couldn't want him. She couldn't forget what happened last time, and she wasn't even talking about the blisteringly hot sex, but the emptiness afterward. The sex hadn't just been sex. It hadn't felt like sweat and exercise...release...it'd felt transformative.

It'd been...bliss.

And then he'd walked out of her Santa Monica house, door slamming behind him, and her heart had shattered into a thousand pieces. Never mind what he'd done to her self-respect.

She couldn't be turned on now. She couldn't be so stupid as to imagine that he'd be different, that the lovemaking would be safer or that the aftermath would be less destructive.

He was fire. And when he touched her, she blistered and living with burns wasn't her idea of a calm, centered, happy life.

She needed a calm, centered, happy life. It was the only way to provide for Jax. The only way to raise Jax in a healthy home.

Rowan Argyros might be seduction on two legs, but he wasn't the daddy she wanted for Jax, or the partner she needed—and then suddenly he was back, dropping into the leather seat across from hers and extending his legs, his dark head tipping back, his eyes closing, hiding his intense green eyes.

But even with his eyes closed the air felt charged. Magnetic.

She glared at him, hating how her pulse jumped and raced and her body grew hot all over again just because he was close.

Without even opening his eyes he said, "We still have a good four plus hours to go. I'd sleep if I were you. You'll feel better—"

"This is not my first international trip," she said curtly, cutting him off. Of course he'd think she was staring at him. And yes, she was, but that was beside the point.

The edge of his mouth lifted. "Suit yourself."

"Yes, I will."

The corner lifted higher.

Her stomach tightened. Her pulse raced. She pressed her lips into a thin, hard line, trying to hold back all the angry words she wanted to hurl at him.

He brought out the worst in her. He did. She needed to get away from him, and the sooner the better. But how?

She wasn't dealing with an ordinary man. If she set

aside her personal feelings for a moment, she'd admit that
he was extraordinary in every way, but that was the problem. With Rowan she couldn't set aside her personal feelings. With Rowan it was nothing but personal.

The night he'd spent with her had changed her forever.
His touch was so profound that he might as well have taken
a hammer and chisel to her heart, carving his name into
the very marrow of her being.

Even now she could feel him as if his hand was on hers.

As if his chest was pressed to hers.

She could feel him because just the smell, touch, taste
of him made her burn. She wanted him still. She wanted
more.

But more would break her. More would crack her all
the way open, draining her until there was nothing left of
Logan Copeland.

But maybe that's what he wanted. Maybe he wanted
to destroy her.

If so, he was off to a good start.

Logan woke to the sound of murmured voices. Opening her
eyes she spotted Rowan standing across the aisle with Jax
in his arms. They were facing a big screen and watching
a Disney movie featuring fish, and Rowan was discussing the cartoon with her. Jax had her finger in her mouth
and seemed more fascinated by Rowan than the huge blue
tang searching for her parents.

Jax was already a petite little girl and tucked against
Rowan's chest, in his muscular arms, she looked impossibly small.

Logan swallowed around the lump filling her throat.
Jax was her world. Her center. Her sunshine. And Logan
didn't want to share her, and she most definitely didn't
want to share her with someone who didn't deserve her.

Just like that, she heard another voice in her head.

It was her mother's voice, raised, emotional. *He doesn't deserve us...he doesn't deserve any of us...*

She must have shifted, or maybe she made a sound, because suddenly Rowan was turning and looking at her. "You were out," he said.

"How long?"

"Long enough for us to watch a movie." And right on cue the film's credits rolled.

"Dory," Jax said to Logan, pointing to the enormous flat screen.

Logan smiled at her daughter. "You love Dory, don't you?"

Jax nodded and, popping her finger back into her mouth, looked at Rowan. "Dory can't 'member."

Rowan nodded. "But she still found a way to be successful. That's what's important. Never give up." And then his gaze met Logan's over Jax's head. "A good lesson for all of us, I think."

Logan left her seat and reached for her daughter. "I'll take her. See if we can find a snack—"

"She ate while you were sleeping," he answered, handing her back. "She likes chicken. And she couldn't get enough cantaloupe."

And then he was walking away, and Logan gave Jax a little cuddle and kiss, even as her heart pounded, aware that everything in her life had changed. There were men you could escape. There were men you could forget. But Rowan Argyros was neither.

They landed just before noon on a long, narrow runway that sliced an emerald green field in two. The touchdown was so smooth it felt like they'd landed on glass. Logan kissed the top of Jax's head. Her daughter had been awake for the past several hours and she was relaxed and content at the moment, quietly sucking on her thumb. Logan had worked hard to discourage the habit but she let it go now as it probably helped Jax's ears adjust to the change in pressure.

The jet slowed steadily and then did a smooth turn on the landing strip, and began a long taxi back the way they'd just come.

Logan returned her attention to the emerald expanse beyond. It was misty outside, the windows covered with fine water droplets. Now that they were on the ground she could see that the fields were actually a vast lawn, and the green lawns gradually rolled up to a hill dominated by a large gray castle with a tall square stone tower and smaller towers at different corners.

As they taxied, they headed closer to the castle, and different features came into view. The big square tower's parapet. The tall Gothic windows. The arches above the narrow windows. There were no trees or shrubs to soften the starkness of the castle. Instead it just rose up from a sea of green, and it didn't strike Logan as a particularly friendly castle. Maybe it was the dark sky and drizzly rain, but the forbidding exterior made her think it was a fortress, not a home, and the last thing she wanted was to be locked up. Trapped.

"Who lives there?" she asked uneasily, hoping against hope that this was not the Irish estate Morgan had talked about. Morgan and Drakon had visited Rowan's Irish estate a year or so ago and she'd made it sound palatial. This was not palatial.

"I do." Rowan shifted in his chair, legs extended, hands folded on his lean flat stomach. "When here."

She glanced out the rain-splattered window and sucked on the inside of her lip, trying to maintain her calm because as impressive as the castle was, it lacked warmth. She couldn't find anything inviting about such a massive building. "I can see why you don't spend that much time in Ireland."

"I'm here quite often, and I am very fond of the place. I gather you don't like it?"

"It's stark." She hesitated, before adding, "And very gray."

"There's a lot of stone," he agreed. "But it's sturdy. The oldest towers are over six hundred years old. The newer sections are two hundred years. But when I bought it, I refurbished the interior and you'll find it quite comfortable." His smile was crooked. "I love my mother's country but I must have a little too much of my father's Greek blood, or maybe I'm just getting older, but I don't like being cold."

Her gaze met his and there was something mocking in his eyes, but it wasn't unkind as much as challenging. He seemed to be daring her to say something, daring her to disagree, but looking at him there was nothing old or weak about him. He was powerful from the top of his head to the intense gold of his eyes, to the tips of his toes.

"I somehow don't think the cold bothers you all that much," she answered. "At least, I remember your saying three years ago that you trunk it when you surf in California. Even in winter."

He shrugged carelessly and yet there was a flicker of heat in his eyes, as if surprised that she'd remembered. But of course she remembered. That was the problem. She remembered *everything*.

"I don't like wetsuits." Rowan's deep voice rumbled in his chest and his head was turned, his gaze fixed on the drizzly landscape beyond the window. "Not even here, when I'm surfing in Wales or Scotland."

The jet had rolled to a stop. The flight attendant was at

the door. Logan glanced at him and then at Rowan who'd also unfastened his seat belt and was rising.

"Are there good waves in the UK?" she asked.

"One of my favorite breaks is in Scotland. Thurso East. I like Fresh in Pembrokeshire, too." He gazed down at her for a moment, a faint smile playing at his lips and yet the smile didn't touch his eyes. Those were a cool green, a much cooler green than the emerald lawns outside, and then he extended a hand to her. "Fresh can be dangerous, though. The reef break is heavy and significant, and then there is the army firing range above. It's not for beginners."

"And you like that it's frightening."

"I'd call it exhilarating." His lips curved ever so slightly, his expression almost mocking. "Just as I am finding you exhilarating. I had no idea I had a family. Everything is changing. *Fáilte abhaile*," he said in Gaelic. "Welcome home."

She'd had three plus years to get over him. Three years to grow a thick skin...an armor...and yet he'd dismantled her defenses with just a few words, a careless smile, a hot, searing kiss...

Logan held her own cool smile, even as she drew a slow breath to hide the frantic beating of her heart. "It shall be fascinating to see your home," she said, unbuckling her seat belt and rising, shifting Jax to her hip. "I consider it an adventure. I have always enjoyed a good adventure. And then it will be time for me to return home. As fun as it is to have a little getaway, I've a business in Los Angeles, and obligations there—"

"Your obligations are to your family first, and as the mother of my child, you and I will want to make the necessary adjustments to ensure that you and she are safe." His gaze never wavered. "Castle Ros is safe. If you do not wish to live here year-round we can discuss other options, but there is no place in the United States where you'd be safe right now."

"I don't wish to argue in front of Jax—"

"Then let's not."

She ground her teeth together, determined to keep her composure as an emotional outburst would only alienate Rowan and frighten her daughter. "You don't want me," she said softly, urgently. "And I don't want you—"

"You wanted me very much three years ago. You'll want me again."

Her gaze swiftly dropped to her daughter. Her voice dropped even lower. "Everything I cherished was stripped away by my father. Love is all I have left, and you are not going to take that from me. I deserve the chance to be loved, and we both know that is not something you're offering. And love is the only reason I'd ever marry. The only one," she repeated.

And then, desperate for air and space, she walked past him and headed for the plane door, too agitated to return for her purse and Jax's diaper bag. Purses and diaper bags could be retrieved…replaced. Her sanity was another matter.

Rowan followed Logan off the jet and took a seat next to her in the armored car. He was sure she didn't know the luxury sedan had bulletproof glass and extra paneling in the sides. She didn't need to know that. She didn't need to know that the perimeter of his estate was walled and patrolled and every security measure had been taken to make Castle Ros one of the safest places in Europe— whether for a head of state needing protection or his own woman and daughter.

His gaze rested on Logan's profile.

His woman.

She was.

She'd been his from the moment he laid eyes on her at the auction. She hadn't even known that he'd seen her long before she'd noticed him. He'd picked her from the others, chosen her from every woman there as the one he'd wanted, and he'd willed it, made it happen, focusing on her so that she couldn't help but know who he was...couldn't help but feel his interest and desire.

She, who was working that night at the auction, had scrambled to bid, and he'd kept his attention locked on her throughout the bidding, and she'd done what he'd demanded...

She'd won him.

And he'd rewarded her. All night long.

And as the night turned to morning, he'd lain in bed next to her, watching her sleep and listening to her breathe, and wondering how to keep her and incorporate her into a life where he was rarely in one place long.

He was a bachelor. He needed to be a bachelor. And yet with her he felt settled, committed. He felt as if he'd come home, which was impossible as he'd never had a true home. He'd never belonged anywhere—he'd shifted between continents and countries, languages and cultures. Rowan had been raised as a nomad and outsider, caught between his fierce, moody, ambitious Greek father and his kind but unstable Irish mother. After the initial love-lust wore off, his parents couldn't get along. He still remembered the arguing when he was very young. They fought because there was never enough money, and never enough success. His father was full of schemes and plans, always looking for that one big break that would make him rich, while his mother just wanted peace. She didn't need a big windfall, she just wanted his father home. And then his father hit the jackpot, or so he thought, until he was arrested and sent to prison for white-collar crime.

The time away broke the family.

It broke what was left of the marriage and his mother.

Or maybe what broke the marriage, and his mother, was losing Devlin, Rowan's little brother. Devlin drowned while Father was in prison.

Rowan tensed, remembering. Devlin's death at two and three quarters had been the beginning of the end.

Rowan's father blamed Rowan's mother. Rowan's mother blamed Rowan's father. And then Rowan's father was out of jail, and the fighting just started over again. Rowan was glad to be sent to boarding school in England, and he told himself he was glad when his parents finally separated, because maybe, finally, the fighting would end. But the divorce dragged on for years, and school holidays became increasingly chaotic and painful. Sometimes he'd visit one parent in one country, while other times neither parent wanted him and if there was no classmate to invite him home, he'd remain at school, which was in many ways preferable to visits with strangers, including his parents who became little more than strangers as the years went by.

After finishing school, he went to university in America, and then returned to Britain to serve in the Royal Navy and never again returned home. Because there was no home. He'd never felt at home, which is why the attachment to Logan had been unsettling.

How could she feel like home when he didn't know what home was? How could he care for her when he didn't know her?

It had been almost a relief to discover she was a Copeland. She had been too good to be true. His rage had been swift and focused, and he'd let her feel the full impact of his disappointment. But it wasn't Logan he was truly angry with. He was angry with himself for dropping his guard and allowing himself to feel. Emotions were dangerous. Emotions were destructive. He couldn't let himself make that mistake again.

And now she was back in his life, and she wasn't merely a beautiful but problematic woman, she was also the mother of his child.

And that changed everything. That changed him. It had to change him. There was no way he'd allow his child to be caught between two adults battling for control. Nor would he let Logan disappear with his daughter the way his mother, Maire, had disappeared with him after Devlin's death.

So there would be a wedding, yes, but beyond that?

Rowan didn't have all the answers yet. He wasn't sure how he'd keep Logan and Jax in Ireland. He wasn't sure how he'd ensure that they couldn't disappear from his life. He only knew that it couldn't happen. And it wouldn't happen. He'd keep Logan close, he'd make her want to stay, and if he couldn't do it through love, he'd do it through touch...sex. Love wasn't the only way to bond with a woman. Touch and pleasure would melt her, weaken her, creating bonds that would be difficult, if not impossible, to break.

Was it fair? No. But life wasn't fair. Life was about survival, and Rowan was an expert survivalist.

Fáilte abhaile mo bride, he repeated silently, glancing once more at Logan's elegant profile, appreciating anew her stunning gold-and-honey beauty. *Welcome home, my bride.*

CHAPTER FIVE

THE LUXURIOUS INTERIOR of Castle Ros hid its technology well. At first glance one didn't see the modern amenities, just the sumptuous appointments. The scattered rugs and plush carpets. The rich paneling and decoratively papered walls. The glow of lights in intricate fixtures. The oil portraits and massive landscapes in ornate gold frames. But then as Logan settled into her suite of rooms, a suite that adjoined Rowan's, she noticed the electrical outlets and USB ports tucked into every surface and corner.

There was a remote on the bedside table that controlled the temperature, and the blackout blinds at the windows, and an enormous painting over the fireplace that turned into a flat-screen TV. A refrigerator, sink and marble-topped counter had been tucked into one of the adjoining closets. On the white marble counter stood an espresso machine, and next to that was a lacquered box lined with pods of coffee. Milks and snacks filled the refrigerator. A small wine rack was stocked with bottles of red and white wine.

Apparently Rowan—or his estate manager—had thought of everything. There was no reason Logan couldn't be comfortable in the lavish suite.

Now Jax was another matter.

The castle wasn't child-friendly. There wasn't a small bed or even a chair suitable for a two-year-old anywhere, never mind the massive fireplaces—with fires—missing screens, and the steep stone staircases without a gate or barrier to slow a curious toddler's exploration.

But before Logan could voice her concerns, Rowan was already aware of the problem. "I recognize that the house poses a danger for Jax. While it's impossible to make the entire castle child-safe, I can certainly ensure that she has rooms—or an entire floor—that have been made secure, free of hazards, giving her plenty of space to play and move about."

And then he was gone, and Logan was alone with Jax in her huge suite with the high ceilings, crackling fire and tall, narrow windows.

Logan frowned at the fire. At least this one had a grate and screen, but the fire worried her.

But then, everything worried her. She'd lost control. Her carefully constructed world was in pieces, shattered by the appearance of Rowan Argyros.

He wasn't supposed to be in her life. She didn't want him in her life. She didn't want him near Jax. And yet here they all were, locked down in his high-tech, high-security castle.

She needed to get away. She needed to get Jax away from here as soon as possible. Logan didn't know how. She just knew it had to be done, and quickly. And while time was of the essence, strategy would be important as it wasn't going to be easy leaving Rowan's fortified home, nor would it be simple sneaking a two-year-old away.

After a bath and a light meal, Logan and Jax napped and then before Logan was ready to be awake, Jax was up and eager to play.

Logan's head throbbed. She needed sleep. Her body seemed to think it was the middle of the night—and back in California it was—but Jax was adjusting to the time change far better and Logan allowed the busy toddler to take all the shimmering silk pillows to the huge empty walk-in closet to play.

Logan made coffee and sat down with a notebook to figure out the next steps to take, and she was still sitting with the notebook—pages perfectly blank—when a knock sounded at the door.

Opening the bedroom door, she discovered a fresh-faced young woman in the hall.

"I'm Orla." The young woman introduced herself with a firm handshake and quick smile. "I've been a nanny for five years, but I'm not just a child minder, I'm a certified teacher, specializing in early education. So where is my lovely girl? I'm looking forward to meeting her."

Logan drew a short, rough breath, as Orla stepped past, entering the bedroom suite. "I'm sorry," she said awkwardly. "There must be a mistake. I haven't hired anyone."

"Your husband—"

"I don't have a husband."

Orla turned around and faced Logan. "Mr. Argyros—"

"Not my husband."

"Your fiancé—"

"He's not my fiancé."

The young woman didn't blink or flush or stammer. Her steady blue gaze met Logan's and held. "Your daughter's father."

Logan bit down on her tongue. She had no reply for that.

"He hired my services," Orla continued in the same calm, unflappable tone, her dark hair drawn back in a sleek, professional ponytail. Orla appeared to be a good five to ten years younger than Logan, and yet she was managing to making Logan feel as if she was a difficult child. "He said there'd been a recent death in the family," she added, "and you had matters to attend to. I'm here to help make everything easier for you."

Again, Logan couldn't think of an appropriate response. Somehow Rowan was getting the best of her, and he wasn't even here. "But I'm not working. I don't need any *help* with my daughter." She tensed as she heard her voice rise. She was sounding plaintive and that wouldn't do. "I enjoy my daughter's company very much, and right now I need her. She's such a comfort."

"But the wedding preparations will only tire her out. I can promise you she'll have great fun with me. I've brought toys and games and dolls. Does Jax like playing with dolls? I have a set of little fairies—they're a family and absolutely adorable—and most girls—"

"Fairies?" The connecting door to the massive walk-in closet flew open and Jax came running out, dragging one of the embroidered silk pillows behind her. She'd been happy in the closet, but apparently playing with fairies was far more appealing than tasseled silk pillows. "I love fairies!"

Orla was already on one knee, putting herself at eye level with Jax. "I have a whole family of fairies in my bag. Would you like to see?"

Jax nodded vigorously, and Logan held her breath, counted to five, and then ten, aware that her immediate presence was not needed here. "If you don't mind, I'll go have a word with Rowan."

Jax ignored her and Orla just flashed a cheerful smile. "Of course, Ms. Copeland. We'll be here, having a healthy snack and creating our fairy garden. We'll show you our garden when you're back."

Rowan wasn't surprised to see Logan at the door of his office. He rolled back from his desk where he'd been reading updates on situations he was monitoring and answering brief emails with even briefer replies.

He casually propped one foot on top of the other as she entered. "Everything all right?"

"No," she said curtly, crossing the floor. She'd changed since they'd arrived, and was dressed now in black trousers and a black knit sweater that clung to her high full breasts and hugged her narrow waist. Her thick, honey hair was parted in the middle, and the long, straight silk strands framed her face, drawing attention to the arched brows and haunting blue of her eyes.

He'd remembered she was pretty, but had forgotten how her beauty was such a physical thing. She crackled with energy, and just looking at her made his blood heat. "What's happened?" he asked, tamping down the desire. "Maybe I can help."

"You're the problem, and you know it." She stood before him, a hand on one hip, drawing attention to her lean figure, made even longer by her black leather boots. The heels on her leather boots were high. And incredibly sexy.

"Me?" he drawled.

Her arched eyebrow lifted higher, her expression incredulous, and Rowan didn't think she'd ever looked so fierce, or so desirable.

The fierceness was new, as was the crackling energy. She hadn't been fierce three years ago. She hadn't burned with this intensity, either. Becoming a mother had changed her.

He liked it. He liked her on fire. But then, he'd always loved a good fight, and she was itching for a fight now.

"Would you like to sit down?" He gestured to a chair not far from the desk. "We can talk—"

"You're not my partner or spouse," she said, cutting him short. "You will never be my partner or spouse, and you've no right to hire a nanny for my daughter without my permission." Temper flashed in her eyes. "Are you listening, Rowan? You need to understand what I'm saying."

His upper lip ached to curl. He wanted to smile but fought to hide his amusement, aware that she wouldn't appreciate it. "I'm listening, Logan."

"Good. Because you have an agenda—that's clear enough—but it's not my agenda, and I'm not going to be bulldozed into going along with your plan."

He'd found her impossibly lovely three years ago, the night he'd spotted her at the auction. She had an intent gaze, focused and watchful, and in her delicate silver and periwinkle gown, she'd shimmered, her beauty mysterious…that of a remote, untouchable princess. The untouchable quality drew him in. He saw it as a challenge. He couldn't resist a challenge.

Now there was an entirely different challenge before him. A different woman. And he understood why she'd changed. She'd had to be everything for Jax—mother and father, protector and nurturer—and she'd done it truly alone, cut off from family, mocked by society, and the pressure and pain had stripped Logan down and reshaped her, giving her an edge, giving her strength. This woman standing before him was no doormat. This new woman exuded power and resolve. This new woman was sexual, too, dressed head to toe in black, the light of battle blazing in her eyes, illuminating her stunning features.

"I don't want to bulldoze you. That wouldn't be fair to you or our daughter."

He saw her tense when he said *our daughter.* "She is *our* daughter."

"She's not a bargaining chip."

"I would never make her one."

She rolled her eyes. "I don't believe that for a second

and neither should you. You are the most ruthless man I have ever met, Rowan, and that is saying a great deal considering my father is Daniel Copeland."

"I spent ten years in the military as an officer. I have nothing in common with your father."

"Don't kid yourself. Nothing stopped him from taking what he wanted. And nothing will stop you, either. You take what you want, when you want, and discard—"

"I didn't discard you."

Her eyes burned overbright. She swallowed once, and then again, struggling to hold back words.

He sighed inwardly. "I treated you badly, yes. But it won't be like that with Jax."

"You're right, it won't be, because she is not part of this…she is not part of us. She is herself, and lovely and everything that is best in the world, and I will protect her from those who'd hurt her, and that includes you, Rowan Argyros."

"You don't need to protect her from me."

"I wish I could believe that."

"I'm not a monster."

Logan looked away, lips compressing, a sheen of tears in her eyes.

His chest tightened and it felt as if somewhere along the way he'd swallowed rocks. They made his stomach hurt. He'd hurt her badly because he'd intended to hurt her, and the unfairness of it made him sick. But it wouldn't change the outcome of this conversation. He wasn't going to lose Jax.

And he wasn't going to lose Logan.

They'd be a family because it was the right thing. Because it was the best thing. Because it would keep both of them safe, and that was the world he knew best.

Safety. Security.

No one would get to them, no one could hurt them. He knew it, and in her heart, she had to know it, too.

Rowan rose and moved past her to drag the tapestry-covered armchair forward. "Sit, *mo chroí*. You'll be more comfortable, I promise you."

She shot him a derisive look. "You want me to sit because it will make me more passive. But I'm not interested in being passive or docile. I'm not interested in being managed or accommodating you in any way."

She wouldn't like it if she knew he found her so appealing right now.

She wouldn't like it if she knew how much he wanted to touch her. How much he wanted to cover her mouth and drink her in, tasting her, taking her, making her melt.

He could make her melt.

He could.

He could do it now, too. Even when she crackled and burned. It'd be easier now, when she was on fire, her temper stirred, because anger and passion were so very close, anger flamed passion, anger made passion explode...

Logan straightened and stepped away from the club chair, closing the gap between them. It only took that one step and he saw the flicker in her eyes and the bite of teeth into her soft lower lip.

She was not so indifferent, this fierce woman of his.

She was not unaware of the crackle and fire in the room and the tension pulsing between them.

He gazed down into her upturned face, her eyes wide and blue, her breathing ragged. He could even see the erratic pulse beating at the base of her throat. They were so very close. If he drew a deep enough breath his chest would touch hers.

If he shifted, his knee would find her thighs. He'd be

there between her thighs. He very much wanted to be between her thighs, too.

One touch and he'd have her.

One touch and she'd be his.

"I want you to sit," he said quietly, gently, his blood humming in his veins, his body taut, hard. "Because I'm very, very close to stretching you across my desk and having my way with you." He stared into her eyes, the faintest of smiles creasing the corners of his eyes, even as he let her see the challenge in his eyes, and allowed her to feel his leashed tension. She needed to know that things were getting serious. This wasn't a game. "But somehow I think you're not yet ready for us to pick up where we left off—"

"That's not even a possibility."

And then he did what he knew he shouldn't do, not because she'd resist him, but because it wouldn't help his position—that he was good for her and Jax, and that he was the right one to take care of them.

But there was something about Logan that made him throw caution to the wind and he was done with restraint. Clasping her face in his hands, he captured her mouth and kissed her deeply, kissing her with that heat and hunger he knew she responded to, and she did.

Her lips trembled beneath his and her mouth opened to him. His tongue stroked the inside of her lip and then in, finding her tongue and teasing her until he felt her hands on his arms, her grip tight. She leaned in, leaning against him, and she was so warm and soft and…his.

His, but not his. Because he still didn't understand why he felt so possessive about this woman. He didn't understand the attraction and wasn't even sure he wanted to be attracted. The fact that she could even test his control, provoked him.

"I could make you come right now," he murmured against her mouth, as aware of his erection straining against the fabric of his trousers as he was of the hot, honey taste of her on his tongue, "and you'd love it."

She stiffened but didn't pull away, her chest rising and falling against his own.

He'd offended her, and it'd been deliberate. Just like before, he lashed out at her when truthfully he was frustrated with himself.

So really, he was no different from three plus years ago.

God almighty.

Rowan let her go and stepped away. He hated himself just then.

What was he doing?

This wasn't like him. His career had been built on defending and rescuing others. He was a protector.

Except when it came to Logan.

Rowan went to his desk, rifling through papers, pushing aside a stack of folders, needing time to calm down and clear his head.

He needed to be able to think. He needed her to think. They both needed to make the right decisions. Decisions about marriage and the future. Decisions about where they'd raise Jax together, protecting Jax.

This wasn't about love, but responsibility.

And yet he'd fulfill his duty as a husband. He'd make sure Logan's needs were met. He'd be sure she was satisfied.

"You can't have me," she whispered, drawing a rough breath and taking an unsteady step back. "And you can't have Jax, either." She retreated another couple of steps, arms folded tightly over her chest. "Just because you swept us out of the country and deposited us here in your Irish estate, doesn't mean we're yours. We're not."

"*She* is."

"You didn't want her. You didn't want anything to do with us—"

"You never told me I was a father."

"I phoned. You mocked me. Scorned me."

"You keep talking about you. You never told me about her. What about *her*?"

A shadow crossed her face and Logan's expression shuttered. He'd scored a direct hit. She knew he was right.

He shrugged impatiently. "In your heart you know you gave up too easily. If you truly love her as much as you say you do, you should have fought for her rights. Fought to do what was best for her."

"You think you're best?" Her chin notched up and yet her full lips quivered, the soft full lower lip swollen from the hard, hot kiss. "You think you're father material?"

His jaw tightened. "It doesn't matter what you think. What matters is the law. As her biological father, I have rights, and I intend to exert those rights, and you can be part of our family, or—"

"There is no *or*, Rowan. I am her family."

"Just as I am her family, too."

"You said you wouldn't use her as a bargaining tool."

"Correct. I will not bargain for her. I will not bargain with her. I am claiming my rights, and my right to parent my daughter, and we can either do this together, making these decisions together, or we can take it to the courts and let them decide."

"You wouldn't win custody."

He gave her a long look. "Your late father is a crook… one of the greatest of this century. You've hidden my daughter from me—"

"You're twisting everything."

"But can't you see how this will play out in court? Can't

you see that you've been duplicitous? Every bit as deceitful as your father?"

"No."

"But yes, love, you have. Legally you have." He fell silent, and the silence stretched, heavy, weighted, pointed. She needed to face the truth, and in this case, she was wrong. The court would take issue with her choices. The court would penalize her for those choices.

Silence stretched and Logan's heart beat fast as she watched Rowan reach for another sheaf of papers, carelessly flipping through them.

She continued to hold her breath as he leaned over and scrawled a few words—his signature maybe?—at the bottom of one page, and then flipped to another page and scrawled something again.

She hated this so much.

She hated bickering and fighting, especially when it was about a child. Her child.

And yes, Rowan was her biological father but it was impossible to wrap her head around the fact that he wanted to be in Jax's life. That he wanted to be a true father.

Or maybe she was misunderstanding. Maybe he didn't want to be hands-on. Maybe this was about power...control.

"My father rarely spent time with his children," Logan said flatly, trying to hide the thudding of her heart and the anxiety rippling through her. "He spent his life at the office. And then after the divorce, he saw Morgan, but not the rest of us. But that was because Morgan went to live with him, feeling sorry for him."

Rowan lifted his head, his gaze locking with hers. "But you didn't."

"It was his choice not to see us. Mother never kept us from him. He didn't care enough about us to maintain a relationship."

"But you view him as your father."

She struggled with the next words. "He paid our bills."

"So you really couldn't care less about him."

"I didn't say that."

"You want to attend his funeral."

"He was my father."

"Ah." Rowan dropped into his chair, and studied her from across the office. "And you don't think our daughter will care about her father? You assume she doesn't need one?"

"I never said that."

"But you've blocked me from her life. Kept her from knowing she has a father."

Logan closed her eyes and drew a slow breath. "There's a difference between paying for a child's expenses, and being engaged...and loving."

"And you assume I can only pay bills?"

Tension knotted her shoulders. Balls of ice filled her stomach. Logan flexed her fingers trying to ease the anxiety ricocheting inside her. After an endless moment she touched her tongue to her upper lip, dampening it. "You have assumed only the worst of me. You have judged me based on my name. You have treated me incredibly harshly, and it's difficult, if not impossible, to believe that you would want to be a father, much less a loving one."

"You were introduced to me as Logan Lane."

"Lane is my mother's name, and my preferred name. It is my name."

"Are you telling me you dropped the Copeland from your name?"

"I was in the process of legally changing my name. Yes. *Copeland* is a distraction."

He continued to study her, his expression impossible to read. He had such hard, chiseled features and his light eyes were shuttered. And then his mouth eased and his fierce expression softened. "No need to look so stricken. The good news is that we have the chance to fix things. You and I can sort this out without a judge…without the courts. It will be far less messy and painful if we manage our affairs privately. Surely you don't want your *distracting* name bandied about in the press? I would imagine that by now you've had enough media attention to last a lifetime."

Her stomach heaved. The very idea of being in the papers made her want to throw up. She couldn't bear to be chased again. It had been awful when the reporters and photographers shadowed her every move several years ago. She'd felt hunted. Haunted. And that was before Jax. No, Jax's picture could not be splashed about the tabloids. The reporters and photographers were merciless. They'd harass them, and terrify Jax by shouting at them, by pulling up in their cars, honking horns, creating chaos just to get a photo.

Logan exhaled slowly, clinging to her composure. "I have lived very quietly these past few years to stay out of the media."

"A custody battle will just put you right back in the headlines."

She stared at him, furious, frustrated, defiant.

His broad shoulders shifted. His gaze dropped to the papers in his hand. "The funeral has been set for a week from today. It will be held in Greenwich, Connecticut. Your sister Morgan is making the arrangements. Your mother and sisters will be there. It is hoped that you will be there, too." He looked at her once more. For a long moment he was silent before adding, "I hope we will be, but that is up to you."

"This is absurd."

"The grand service for your father...or that we'd attend together?"

"We're not a couple."

"Yet. But we will be."

"Many parents raise children in different homes—"

"Like mine," he interrupted. "And it was hell. I won't have my daughter—"

"Your daughter?" she interrupted bitterly.

"My daughter," he continued as if she hadn't spoken, "being dragged back and forth. It's unsettling for a young child. It's upsetting for an older child. We need to do better than that for her."

She hated that he was saying the very things that she believed to be true.

She hated that he was being the one who sounded responsible and mature.

Having grown up in a divorced family it wasn't what she wanted for Jax, but at the same time, she couldn't imagine a peaceful home, not if she and Rowan were living together in it. "It is better for a child to have two homes than one that is fraught with tension," she said tightly.

"That's why we need to put aside our differences and focus on Jax."

Logan looked away, a lump filling her throat. He made it sound so easy. He made it sound like a trip to an amusement park...but living with Rowan would be anything but fun. He'd hurt her so badly...he'd nearly broken her with his harsh rejection...

"I don't trust you," she whispered.

"Then I must win your trust back."

"That will take forever."

"We don't have that much time. The funeral is in a week."

She shot him a baffled glance. "I'm not sure I follow."

He dropped the papers and sat down in his chair. "We need to marry before the funeral because, if we're to go, we go united. You and me. A family."

"What?"

"We go united," he repeated firmly.

"There is no way…how could we possibly marry this week?"

"Not just this week, but tomorrow. That way we can slip away for a brief honeymoon before flying to Connecticut with Jax for the service."

"And if I refuse?"

"We stay here."

CHAPTER SIX

THEY'D STAY HERE?

Logan's legs went weak. Boneless, she sank into the chair behind her. Her voice was nearly inaudible. "You'd keep me from his service?"

His gaze was cool, almost mocking. "I could say so many things right now…I could say you never told me you were pregnant. I could say you kept me from my daughter—"

"Yes. This is true. But two wrongs don't make a right."

"So, Logan *Lane*, make this right."

Her eyes stung. She blinked hard and bit hard into her lip to keep from saying something she'd regret.

The only thing that had kept her going these past three years when it had been so hard was the belief that one day her life would be different. That one day she and Jax would have everything they needed, that their future would be filled with hope and love and peace…

But there would be no peace with Rowan.

It wasn't the future she'd prayed for. It wasn't the future they wanted or needed.

It wasn't a future at all.

Rowan leaned forward, picked up a thick stack of glossy colored pages and held them out to her. "Pick one or two that appeal and they will be here later tonight."

She took the pages before she realized they were all

photographs of couture wedding gowns. Fitted white satin gowns that looked like mermaids and slinky white satin gowns with narrow spaghetti straps, and princess ball-gowns with full skirts and gorgeous beading of pearls and precious stones...

The virginal wedding gowns were a punch in the gut and she nearly dropped the stack of designs before letting them tumble onto a nearby end table.

"We'll marry tomorrow night," he added, not sounding in the least bit perturbed by her reaction. "And steal away for a brief honeymoon, and then join your family in Greenwich."

"I'm not getting married like this. I'm not being forced into a marriage against my will."

"I don't want an unwilling wife, either. I want you to want this, too—"

"That's not going to happen."

"Not even for Jax?"

She took a step toward him and her gaze fell on the stack of bridal designs, the top one so outrageously fancy and fussy that it made her stomach cramp. "You don't know me. You know nothing about the real me. You and I would not be compatible. We weren't even compatible for one night—"

"That isn't true. We had an amazing night."

"It was sex."

"Yes, it was. Very, very good sex."

"But four hours or six hours of good sex isn't enough to justify a life together."

"Correct. But Jax is."

His reasonable tone coupled with his reasonable words put a lump in her throat. He was the bad guy. He was the one who'd broken her heart. How dare he act like the hero now?

She blinked away the tears and shook her head and headed for the door.

"We don't have a lot of time," he called after her. "If you won't pick a dress, then I'll have to select it for you."

She stood in the doorway, her back to him. "Your desire to protect Jax means crushing me," she said quietly. "And I know I don't matter to you, that I mean nothing to you, but you should be aware that I wanted more in life, and once I was a little girl, just like Jax, and on the inside, I am still that little girl, and that little girl within me deserves better."

Leaving his paneled study, she walked quickly down the long high-ceilinged hall and, spying an open door before her, went through that, stepping outside into the late afternoon light.

It was no longer raining but the sky was still gray, and the overcast sky turned the vast lawn and banked shrubbery into a landscape of shimmering emerald.

Logan descended the stone steps into the garden, feet crunching damp gravel. She began to walk faster down the path before her, and then she went faster, and then she broke into a run, not because she could escape, but because there was nothing else she could do with the terrible, frantic emotions clawing at her.

She dashed toward a stone fountain and then past that, focusing on the tall neatly pruned green hedges beyond. It wasn't until she was running through the hedges, making turn after turn, confusion mounting, that she realized it was a maze, and then abruptly her confusion gave way to relief.

It felt good to be lost.

There was freedom in being lost…hidden.

She slowed, but still moved, feet virtually soundless on the thick packed soil, so happy to be free of the dark castle with the thick walls and small windows…so happy to be far from Rowan's intense, penetrating gaze.

He didn't know her and yet he seemed to know too much about her, including the worst things about her… such as her weakness for him.

It was true that she couldn't seem to resist his touch, and it shamed her that she'd want someone who despised her. It shamed her that she despised him in return and yet she still somehow craved him.

This wasn't how it was supposed to be.

The physical attraction…the baffling chemistry…was wrong at so many levels.

She rounded a corner and nearly ran straight into Rowan. Logan scrambled backward. "How—" she started before breaking off, lips pinching closed because of course he knew his way about the maze. It was his maze.

His castle.

His world.

Her eyes burned. Her throat ached. She'd struggled for so many years, struggled to provide and be a strong mother, and now it was all being taken from her. Her independence. Her control. Her future.

She didn't want to share a future with him.

She didn't want to share Jax with him.

She didn't want anything to do with him and yet here he was, blocking her path, filling the space between the hedges, tall and broad, so very strong…

"What are you doing?" he asked, his brow furrowing, his expression bemused. "It's damp out. You don't have a coat."

"You've trapped me," she whispered, eyes bright with tears she wouldn't let spill because, God help her, she had to have an ounce of pride. "You've trapped me and you know it, so don't taunt me…don't. It's not fair."

And with a rough oath, he reached for her, pulling her against him, his body impossibly hard and impossibly warm as he shaped her to him. She shivered in protest. Or at least that's what she told herself when dizzying heat raced through her and the blood hummed in her veins, making her skin prickle and tingle and setting her nerves on fire, every one of them dancing in anticipation.

Her head tipped back and she stared up into his eyes, searching the green-gold for a hint of weakness, a hint of softness. There was none.

"I do not know what *fair* means," he said, his voice pitched low as his head dropped and his mouth brushed her temple and then the curve of her ear. "It's not a word that makes sense to me, but you, *mo gra*, you make sense to me when you shouldn't. You make me think that there is something bigger at work here."

"It's sex."

"Good. I like sex."

"It's lust."

"Even better." His lips brushed her cheek and then kissed the corner of her mouth. "I know what to do with that."

"But I want love, not lust." She put her hands on his chest, feeling the hard carved plane of the pectoral muscle and the lean muscular torso below. "I want selfless, not selfish. I want something other than what I've known."

"People are flawed. We are human and mortal and there is no perfection here. Just life." His mouth was on hers and he kissed her lightly and then again, this time the kiss lingered, growing deeper and fiercer, making her pulse jump and her body melt and her thighs press together because he was turning her on...again.

Again.

Just a touch and she ached. A kiss and she went hot and wet and everything in her shivered for him.

And when he bit at the softness of her lower lip, she knew that *he* knew. She knew that he understood her hunger and desire, and the worst part of all was that their history, that one torrid night, meant that she knew he could assuage it, too. But it burned within her, this physical weakness. It burned because she despised any weakness that would give Rowan the upper hand.

"I hate you," she whispered hoarsely.

"You don't." His hands twisted in her hair, tilting her head back, exposing her throat. His lips were on her neck and the frantic pulse beating beneath her ear. He kissed that pulse and then down, setting fire to her neck and the tender collarbone. "You don't hate me. You want me."

She gasped as his hand slid between them, fingers between her thighs, the heel of his palm against her mound.

And he was right. She did want him. But that only intensified her anger and shame.

She should be better than this. Stronger. Smarter.

Or at the very least, more disciplined.

Instead she let her eyes close and her body hum, blood dancing in her veins, making her skin warm and everything within her heat and soften.

She couldn't remember now why she'd found making love to him so incredible and so deeply satisfying, but her memory had clung to the pleasure, and his mouth on her skin was lighting fire after fire, making her legs tremble, dispatching what was left of her resistance.

"We can make this work without love," he said, his hand slowly sliding from her waist up her rib cage to just graze her breast.

She heard his words but they didn't compute, not when she was arching into his hand, longing to feel more, wanting the pressure of his fingers against her sensitive skin, wanting more friction everywhere to answer the wild heat inside of her.

"We don't have to be best friends to find pleasure with each other, either," he added. "We just have to agree that Jax comes first. And I think we can do that."

Then he kissed her so deeply that her brain shut up and her heart raced, silencing reason. She shouldn't want this, but she did. She shouldn't crave the intensity, and yet it ached and burned, demanding satisfaction. With their history, she should know that nothing good would come of this…sex would just be sex…and afterward she'd feel used and hollow, but that was the future and this was the present.

"So is that a yes?" he murmured against her mouth.

"No," she whispered, wanting the pleasure but not the pain.

"You want to be mine."

"No."

"You're mine already. You just need to admit it."

Her lips parted to protest but just then his hand brushed the swell of her breast and the words died unspoken. She shuddered, and the ripple of pleasure made her acutely aware of him. He was tall and muscular and hard. She could feel his erection straining against her. He wanted her. This…chemistry…wasn't one sided.

He brushed the underside of her breast again and she sighed, even as her nipple tightened, thrusting tautly against the delicate satin of her bra.

"*Rowan,*" she choked, trying to cling to whatever was left of her sanity, and yet the word came out husky and so filled with yearning that she cringed inwardly.

"Yes, *a ghra*?"

"This is madness. We can't do this—"

"But we already have. Now we just have to do right by our daughter." He released her, and drew back, his hard handsome features inexplicably grim. "So the only real question is, do you intend to select your bridal gown or am I to do it?"

With the distance came a breath of clarity. "I refuse to be rushed into marriage."

"We're short on time, Logan."

"We're not short on time. We have our entire lives ahead of us. Jax is so young she doesn't know the difference—"

"But *I* do. I want her to have what I didn't have, which is a family."

"No, you had a family. They were just dysfunctional… as most families are." Logan's voice sounded thin and faint to her own ears. She was struggling to stay calm, but deep down had begun to feel as if she was embroiled in a losing battle. Rowan was strong. He thrived on conflict. Just look at his career.

High risk, high stakes all the way.

"You are so focused on the end goal—getting Jax, being with Jax—that you don't realize you're crushing me!"

"I'm not crushing you. I'm doing my best to protect you. But you have to trust me—"

"I don't." Her voice sounded strangled. "At all."

"Then maybe that's what you need to work on."

"Me?"

He shrugged, as if compromising. "Okay, *we*. We need to work on it. Better?"

Back in her suite of rooms, Logan paced back and forth, unable to sit still. It was late, and Jax was asleep in the modified bed that had been assembled earlier against one wall of the huge walk-in closet, which had been turned into a bedroom for the toddler with the addition of a small painted chest, large enough to hold toddler-sized clothes, and provided a place for a lamp. It was a small, brass lamp topped with a dark pink shade that cast a rosy glow on the cream ceiling chasing away shadows and gloom. A framed picture of woodland fairies hung on the wall over the chest, giving Jax something to look at while in her snug bed. Rowan had even made sure Jax would be safe from falling out by adding a padded railing that ran the length of the bed.

But with Jax in bed for the night, Logan had far too much time to think and worry.

And she was worried.

She was also scared.

She was caught up in a sea of change and she couldn't get her bearings. She'd lost control and felt caught, trapped, pushed, dragged about as if she were nothing more than a rag doll.

But she wasn't a doll and she needed control. And if she had to share power, she'd share with someone she liked and admired and, yes, trusted.

Someone with values she respected.

Someone with integrity.

Rowan had no integrity. Rowan was little more than a soldier. A warrior. Great for battle but not at all her idea of a life partner…

Logan swallowed hard, trying to imagine herself wedded to Rowan. Trying to imagine dinners and breakfasts and holidays, never mind attending future school functions with him…

She couldn't see it.

Couldn't imagine him driving Jax to school or returning to pick her up or sitting in the little chairs for parent-teacher conferences. She couldn't see him being that father who was there. Present.

And then a lump filled her throat because maybe, just maybe, she didn't trust Rowan to love Jax because her father hadn't loved her. Maybe this wasn't about Jax at all—history was full of men who were good parents.

Logan had grown up surrounded by men who knew how to put their families first. Men who were committed and involved. She'd envied her classmates for having devoted fathers…fathers who routinely made it to their daughters' soccer games and dance recitals. Men who zipped up puffy jackets before they took their little girls outside into the cold. Men who'd put out an arm protectively when crossing a busy street. Men who didn't just show up in body but were there emotionally. Men who taught their daughters to ride bikes and drive cars and navigate life.

Logan's eyes stung. She held her breath, holding the pain in.

She'd wanted one of those fathers. She'd wanted someone to teach her about life and love and boys and men.

She'd wanted someone to tell her she was important and valuable. She'd wanted someone to say she deserved to be treated like a princess…like a queen…

Logan blinked, clearing her eyes.

But just because she didn't have a loving, attentive father, it didn't mean that Jax couldn't. Maybe Rowan could be a proper father. Maybe Rowan could teach Jax about life and love and boys…

And men.

Exhaling slowly, Logan glanced from the door of the closet—open several inches so she could keep an ear open in case Jax needed her—to the bedroom door that opened onto the castle hall.

She needed to speak to Rowan.

She didn't know what she'd say, only that she needed to speak to him about the whole marriage thing and family thing and understand what it meant to him. Was he going to be a father in name only or did he really intend to be part of Jax's life?

Because being a father had to be more than carrying on one's family name. Being a father meant *being* there. Being present. Being interested. Being patient. Being loving.

Logan peeked in on Jax and in the rosy pink glow she could see her daughter was fast asleep, her small plump hand relaxed, curving close to her cheek.

Jax's steady breathing reassured her. She was sleeping deeply. She shouldn't wake for hours—not that Logan would be gone hours. Logan planned to find Rowan and speak to him and then return.

She'd be gone fifteen minutes, if that. It'd be a short, calm conversation, and she'd try to see if they couldn't both discuss their vision for this proposed...marriage... and find some common ground, create some rules, so that when she returned to the bedroom she'd feel settled, and perhaps even optimistic, about the future.

At the foot of the staircase Logan encountered an unsmiling man in a dark suit, wearing a white shirt and dark tie.

"May I help you?" he asked crisply, revealing an accent she couldn't quite place.

"I was just going to see Rowan," she answered faintly, brow knitting, surprised to see someone so formally dressed at the foot of the stairs, and then understanding seconds later that he wasn't just anyone in a suit and tie, but a bodyguard...probably one of Rowan's own men. Which also meant he was probably armed and dangerous. Not that he'd pose a threat to her.

"Is he in his study?" she asked, nodding toward the corridor on the opposite side of the stairwell.

"He's retired for the night."

She didn't know how to respond to that, unable to imagine Rowan *retiring* from anything.

"His room is upstairs, just down from yours," the man added.

She knew where Rowan's room was. It was just on the other side of Jax's closet. The suite of rooms all had interior connecting doors, with the closet being shared by both bedrooms, but the door to Rowan's room had been locked and the chest of drawers had been placed in front of it, making the closet more secure.

It had been Rowan's suggestion.

He'd thought Logan would sleep better if she knew that no one could enter the room without her permission.

He was right. She did feel better knowing that the only way in and out of her suite was through the door to the hall, a door she could lock, a door she could control.

She'd been grateful for Rowan's understanding.

"Did he turn in a long time ago?" she asked.

"Quarter past the hour maybe. I can ring him for you, if you'd like."

"Not necessary," she answered lightly. "I can just stop in on my way back to my room."

She hesitated, glancing to the heavy front door across the entry hall.

She wondered just how far she'd get, if she ran for the door. Would she be allowed out? Somehow she suspected not. She sensed that this bodyguard wasn't just there to keep the bad guys out of Castle Ros, but to keep her and Jax *in*.

Rowan wasn't taking any chances.

And just like that she thought of Joe, and how Joe once upon a time must have been a bodyguard very much like this, a tall, silent man in a dark suit. That is, back before Rowan sent Joe to her, and Joe dropped the suit and intense demeanor to become her Joe, the recent college grad grateful to have a job…

Even though he was already employed, and apparently drawing two salaries. Her mouth quirked. She ought to speak to Joe about that.

"I'll head back upstairs," she said. "Good night."

His head inclined. "Good night."

And then she retraced her steps, footsteps muffled on the thick carpeting on the stone steps. The same carpet ran the length of the second-floor gallery with the corridor stretching east and west, marking the two wings of the castle.

Rowan opened his bedroom door just moments after she knocked, dressed in gray joggers and a white T-shirt that stretched tight across his chest and then hung loose over his flat, toned torso.

She couldn't help wondering if he'd been expecting her.

"Can we talk?" she asked.

He nodded and opened the door wider, inviting her in.

As she crossed the threshold, she flushed hot and then cold, her skin prickling with unease. She wasn't sure this was a good decision. She wasn't sure how she'd remain cool and calm if their conversation took place here.

As he closed the door, her eyes went to his oversize four-poster bed and then to the heavy velvet curtains drawn against the night. The room was close to the same size as hers and had the same high ceiling, but it felt far more intimate. Maybe it was the big antique bed. Or maybe it was the thick drapes blocking the moon. Or maybe it was the man standing just behind her, sucking all of the oxygen out of the room, making her head dizzy and her body too warm.

She drew an unsteady breath and turned to face him,

thinking she'd made a mistake. She shouldn't have ever come here, to him.

A tactical error, she thought. And worse, she'd voluntarily entered dangerous territory.

Swallowing her nervousness, she glanced to the chairs flanking the impressive stone hearth. "Can we sit?"

"Of course."

"It's not too late?"

"Not at all. I was just reading. I don't usually sleep for another hour or two."

Her gaze slid over the bed with its luxurious coverlet folded back, revealing white sheets.

She wanted to leave. She wanted to return to her room. It was all too quiet in here, too private. "Maybe it's better if we talk tomorrow. I'm sure you're as tired as I am—"

"Not tired yet. But I will be, later."

"I'm tired, though. Probably too tired to do this tonight. I just thought since Jax was asleep it might be convenient, but I'm worried now she'll wake and be scared…" Her voice drifted off and she swallowed, her mouth too dry.

He said nothing.

Her heart hammered harder. She felt increasingly anxious. He was so intense, so overwhelming. Everything about him made her nervous, but she couldn't tell him that. She couldn't let him know how powerless she felt when with him, and how that was bad, really bad, because she needed control. She needed to be able to protect herself. And Jax.

Logan grasped at Jax now, using her as an excuse to leave Rowan's room. "Let's schedule a chat for the morning. It would be best then. I wasn't thinking when I came here. I really don't want Jax to wake up and be frightened."

"I have security cameras. We'll know if she stirs. You'll be able to be at her side before she even wakes up."

Logan straightened, shocked. He had cameras? *Where?* "You're watching our rooms?"

"I monitor the entire castle. There are cameras everywhere."

"You've been spying on us in our room?"

He sighed and crossed to a wall with dark wood paneling. Shifting a small oil landscape, he pushed a button, and suddenly the wall split, opening, revealing a massive bank of stacked TV screens. There had to be five screens across, and five down, and some of the screens were blanks, while others showed interior castle rooms and corridors, and others revealed exterior shots: entrances, garden paths and distant iron gates.

She walked to the wall of monitors and searched for her room with the pretty canopied bed, but the only thing she could see was the closet door, slightly ajar, just as she'd left it. And then she found another monitor showing the hall outside her room.

No bed shots.

Nothing that indicated he was watching her. At least, not until she'd exited her room and approached his.

So he could have known she was coming to see him. He could have watched her leave her room and walk toward his.

She turned to face him. "You knew I was looking for you. You saw me downstairs talking to the bodyguard."

"I knew you'd left your room. But I don't have the sound on. I never do. It'd be too distracting."

"So you didn't know I was asking for you?"

"I thought maybe you wanted a snack."

She just stared at him, trying to decide if she believed him or not. She wanted to believe him, but there was no trust, and that was a huge problem. "So you closed the door on the cameras when I knocked on your door?"

"Yes."

"You didn't want me to see them."

"I don't want anyone to see them. Security is my business."

"But you showed me."

"I thought you should know they are there. I thought you'd be reassured that Jax isn't alone or in danger."

"But if the door is closed on the screens, how do you monitor movement in the castle?"

"The cameras also alert me to movement, and I get those alerts on my computer, my phone and my watch."

"Can you turn those off?"

"I can disable them or mute them. Usually I just glance at the screen, note the alert and then ignore. I never disable them. It defeats the purpose of being secure."

She turned to pace before the fire.

Rowan said nothing for several minutes, content to just watch her. Finally he broke the silence. "What's on your mind, Logan?"

He didn't sound impatient. There was nothing hard in his tone and yet she felt as if she was going to jump out of her skin any moment now. "I thought maybe we could discuss your proposal," she said, unable to stop moving. Walking didn't just distract her, it helped her process, and it minimized her fear and tension. She didn't want to be afraid. She didn't want to make decisions because she was panicked. Those were never good decisions. "I thought we could see if we couldn't come to some agreement on the terms." She paused by the hearth, glanced at him. "Clarity would be helpful."

"The terms?" he repeated mildly. "It's not a business contract. It's a marriage."

She stiffened at the word *marriage*. She couldn't help it. It was one thing to imagine Rowan as a father to Jax, but another to consider him as her husband. "Relationships have rules," she said cautiously.

"Rules?"

She ignored his ironic tone and the lifting of his brow. The fact that he sounded so relaxed put her on edge. "Most relationships evolve over time, and those roles, and rules, develop naturally, gradually. But apparently we don't have time to do that, and so I think we should discuss expectations, so we can both be clear on how things would… work."

He just looked at her, green gaze glinting, apparently amused by every word that came from her mouth. His inability to take her seriously, or this conversation seriously, did not bode well for the future. "This isn't a game," she said irritably, "and I'm trying to have an adult conversation, but if you'd rather make a joke of this—"

"I'm not making a joke of anything. But at the same time, I don't think we have to be antagonistic the night before our wedding."

She shot him a fierce look. "We're not marrying tomorrow. There is absolutely no way that is going to happen tomorrow, and should we one day marry, we will not need a honeymoon. That is the most ludicrous suggestion I've heard yet."

"I thought all brides wanted honeymoons."

"If they're in love!" Her arms folded tightly across her chest. "But we're not in love, and we don't need alone time together. We need time with Jax. She ought to be our focus."

"An excellent point. Now please sit. All the marching back and forth reminds me of cadets on parade."

"I'll sit, but only if you do," she said, gaze locking with his. She wasn't about to let him score any points on her. She hadn't survived this long to be beaten by him now. Her father's betrayal and abandonment had been one thing, but to be betrayed and abandoned by her first lover? That had opened her eyes and toughened her up considerably.

"Happy to sit," he replied. "I imagine we will have many future evenings in here, in our respective chairs, you knitting, me smoking my pipe—"

"You don't smoke and I don't knit."

He shrugged. "Then we'll find another way to enjoy each other's company."

She was fairly certain she knew what he meant by *another way to enjoy each other's company*. He'd always been about the sex. Maybe that's because that was the only way he could relate to women. "You're being deliberately provocative."

"I'm trying to get you excited about the future."

"Mmm." She arched a brow. "Are you also going to sell me beachfront property in Oklahoma?"

"No. That's the kind of thing your father did. I'm honest."

Her jaw tightened, hands balling into fists. "You don't have to like him, but I ask you to refrain from speaking of him like that in front of Jax. She doesn't need to be shamed."

"I'm not shaming her. And I'm not shaming you, either—"

"Bullshit."

"I'm just not going to be fake. If I'm upset, I'll tell you. If I'm content, you'll know. And since we're going to raise Jax together, it's better if we're both forthright so there is no confusion about where things stand." He gave her a faint, ironic smile. "Or sit, since that was the whole point."

She shot him a look of loathing before crossing to the hearth and sitting down in one of the large leather chairs, watching as he followed and then took his time sitting down in the chair across from hers.

He smoothed his T-shirt over his lean, flat stomach before extending his legs and crossing them at the ankle, and then he looked up into her eyes and smiled.

"Better?" he asked.

She ground her teeth together. Rowan Argyros was enjoying himself immensely.

"My father was the breadwinner," she said flatly. "My mother was a homemaker. It meant that when they divorced, she still had to depend on him to provide. I will never do that. If we marry, I'm not giving up my career."

"When we marry, we won't end up divorced."

"I'm not giving up my career."

"You barely scrape by. I make millions every year—"

"It's your money. I want my own."

"I'll open a personal bank account for you, deposit whatever you want, up front, and it'll be yours. I won't be able to touch it."

"It will still be your money. I don't want your money. I'm determined to be self-sufficient."

"Why?"

She gave him a long look. "Surely you don't really have to ask that."

"You're the mother of my child. You've struggled these past few years to provide for her. Let me help."

"You can help with Jax's expenses. We will split them. Fifty-fifty."

"What if I provide for Jax and the family, and then you can use your own…money…for your personal expenses?"

She leaned forward. "Why do you say *money* like that?"

"Because you have virtually nothing in your bank account." He rolled his eyes, apparently as exasperated with her as she was with him. "I'm not hurting financially. According to the *Times*, I'm one of the wealthiest men in the UK. I can afford to make sure you're comfortable."

"My work gives me an identity. It gives me purpose."

"Being a mother doesn't do that?"

"This isn't about being a mother. It's about being a woman, and I don't want to be a woman who depends on a man. My mother spent her life living in my father's shadow, and as we both know, he cast a pretty big shadow. I don't want to be defined by a man, and I like being able to contribute to the world."

He said nothing and she added more quietly, a hint of desperation in her voice. "Work makes me feel valuable. It tells me I matter." She looked away, throat working, emotion threatening to swamp her. "I need to matter. I must matter." Her eyes found his again. "Otherwise, what's the point?"

"But you do matter. You're the sun and moon for Jax. You're her everything."

"And what if something happens to Jax? What if—God forbid—there was a tragedy, and I lost her? I'd be lost, too. I'd be finished. There would be nothing left of me." Her voice cracked but she struggled to smile. She failed. "She's everything."

"Nothing is going to happen to her," he said gruffly. "Why would you think that?"

She couldn't answer. She bit down into her lip, her heart on fire, because bad things did happen. Her parents had divorced when she was young and her father had virtually forgotten her and then later it turned out that he was a criminal…he'd stolen hundreds of millions of dollars from his clients…

"Nothing is going to happen," Rowan repeated more forcefully.

She nodded, but tears were filling her eyes and she was pretty sure that she hadn't convinced either of them of anything.

For a long minute it was quiet. Logan knit her fingers together in her lap, knuckles white. Rowan didn't say anything, deep in thought. She glanced at him several times, thinking he'd lost the glint in his eyes, aware that his hard features had tightened, his mouth now flattened into a grim line.

She couldn't handle the silence any longer. "Maybe I shouldn't feel that way. Maybe it seems irrational—"

"It doesn't." His voice, pitched deep, cut her short.

She looked at him, surprised.

His broad shoulders shifted. "My little brother's death destroyed my mother, and it ended my parents marriage."

"You lost a brother?"

He nodded. "I was seven. Devlin was two, nearly three."

Jax's age.

He knew what she was thinking. She could see it in his eyes.

"But that won't happen to Jax," he added roughly, his voice as sharp as ground glass. "I will make sure nothing happens to her. And that's a promise."

She couldn't look at him anymore, couldn't stomach more of the same conversation. Jax was so valuable. Jax was perfect and innocent, not yet hurt by life or other people. She didn't yet know that people—even those who claimed to care about you—would fail you. Hurt you. Maybe even deliberately hurt you.

Logan hadn't remained a virgin so long because she didn't have options. Her virginity wasn't kept because there weren't men available but because she wanted to hold part of herself back. She wanted to save herself for the right person. She'd wanted to give that one thing—that bit of innocence—to a man who'd value her.

How she'd gotten that wrong!

Being disappointed was a fact of life. Learning to deal

with that disappointment, another critical life lesson. And it was fine to learn about life, and have to accept loss and change, but far better if those lessons came later. If the individual self was shaped and formed. Strong.

"You and I can make sure Jax is safe," Rowan said quietly, drawing her attention to him. "With vigilance we can give her the life I know you want for her."

Logan blinked tears away. "What life do I want for her?"

His gaze held hers for an extra long moment. "You don't want her crushed. You don't want her broken. You want her to remain a child as long as possible—safe, loved, cherished." He hesitated, and the silence hung there between them, weighted. "You want to give her the childhood you never had."

His words cut, pricking her when she didn't have the proper defenses. Startled, uncomfortable, she left her chair, crossing the floor a ways to stand before the bank of monitors. Jax's door remained ajar, just as she'd left it. She suddenly wished she could see Jax, though. She wanted to be sure the little girl was still soundly sleeping.

"Do you have sound, if you wanted it?" she asked thickly, keeping her back to him even as the threat of tears deepened her voice.

"Yes."

"Can you turn it on in her room? Or in my room? So we can check to see if it's quiet or if she's crying?"

"I could turn the camera in her room on. If you'd like?"

She glanced at him now. "So there is a camera in the closet?"

"I disabled it earlier, but I can turn it on."

"I didn't see one in the closet. Where is it?"

"It's positioned in the crown molding, hidden in the shadows of the woodwork."

"It's very small then?"

"No bigger than the head of a writing pen."

"Are cameras truly manufactured that small?"

"Mine are."

"You make cameras?"

He shrugged. "One of my companies manufactures cameras and security equipment. These small cameras are now used all over the world, in every big hotel, casino, government building." He crossed to her side, tapped several buttons on a panel and suddenly one of the dark screens came to life, and then he tapped another key on the panel and she could see Jax in her little bed, still sound asleep, although she now lay on her back, arms up by her head.

Logan shot him a troubled look. "I hate that you can spy on us."

"I don't spy on you. I haven't spied on you ever."

"Joe…?"

"Protection. And the cameras that remain are for protection.

"I deactivated all of the cameras in the closet, the bathroom, the bedroom, but the one positioned on the closet door. I thought it was important to know if Jax wandered out."

Logan shot him another assessing look. "Or if someone wandered in."

"Yes."

"Does that include me?"

"You're her mother."

"Which is why you're afraid I might try to run away with her."

He made a soft, tough mocking sound. "It's crossed my mind," he agreed. "More than once."

The smiling curve of his firm mouth just barely reached his eyes. His green gaze wasn't as warm as it was challenging. She didn't understand what she saw, didn't understand the tension or emotion…if it was emotion. But then he was an enigma, and he had been from the start.

That night at the auction he'd given her the same look— long, searching, challenging.

He'd looked at her with such focus that he didn't seem to be standing across the room, not part of the auction, but all by himself, and it was just the two of them in the room.

Everyone fell away that night in March.

The music, the sound, the master of ceremonies at the microphone.

There was just Rowan standing on the side of the stage looking at her, making her go hot and cold and feel things she didn't know a stranger could make her feel.

"And why would I run from you?" she asked, her chin lifting, her voice husky. She wasn't going to be the one to break eye contact. She wasn't going to back down. Not from him, not from anyone.

"Because you know when I take you to bed, it'll change everything. Again."

Her stomach flipped and her head suddenly seemed unbearably light, as if all the blood had drained away. "That's not happening." Thank God her voice was relatively firm because her legs were definitely unsteady.

"You sound so sure of yourself."

"Because I know myself. And I know you now, and I know how devastating it would be to go to bed with you— and not because you're good in bed, but because you're cruel out of bed, and I don't need more cruelty in my life."

"That was three years ago."

"Perhaps, but standing here with you, it seems like yesterday."

He shrugged. "I can't change the past."

"No, you certainly cannot."

And then he was reaching out to lift a heavy wave of hair off her face, his palm brushing her cheek as he pushed the hair back, slipping it behind her ear. "But I can assure you the future will be different."

His touch sent a shiver coursing through her. "I don't want—" she started to say before breaking off, because he was still touching her, his fingers sweeping her cheekbones, his fingertip skimming her mouth, making it tingle.

"Mmm?" he murmured, eyebrow lifting. "I'm listening, love."

She stared up into his eyes, her heart racing even faster, beating in a hard, jagged rhythm that made it difficult to catch her breath, much less speak. But how could she speak when her thoughts were scattered, coherent thought deserting her at the slightest touch?

"You know," he said thoughtfully, combing her hair back from her face to create a loose ponytail in one hand, "I never asked you about relationships you might have left behind…is there someone significant…?"

He was seducing her with his touch. She couldn't resist the warmth, couldn't resist the tenderness in his touch. She hated that she responded to his caress this way, hated that she felt starved for affection. He wasn't the right man for her. He'd never be the right man. "No."

"Why not? You're young and stunning—"

"And a mother with a young child dependent on me."

"You didn't want to meet someone…someone who could help you, make things easier for you?"

"No."

"Why not?"

"Surely it doesn't surprise you that I don't have a lot of confidence in men? That the men I've known—" she gave him a significant look "—cared only for themselves, too preoccupied by their own needs and their own agendas to take care of anyone else."

"You're not describing me."

"Oh, I most certainly am."

"Then you don't know me, and it's time to change that. Starting now. Tonight."

CHAPTER SEVEN

He captured her mouth with his, shaping her to him. The kiss had fire and an edge that revealed far more of his emotional state than he preferred her to know, but right now he was damned if he cared about anything but taking what he wanted. And he wanted her.

He would bed her tonight.

He would claim her as his.

He wondered if she even realized that she didn't stand a chance because, now that she was here at Castle Ros, he wasn't about to lose her.

He'd made the mistake once. He wouldn't make the same once twice. And, no, his feelings weren't tender or loving, but passion and possession didn't require love. Passion and possession needed heat, and there was plenty of that.

"Mine," he murmured against her mouth, making her heart race.

She heard him but couldn't decipher it, not when heat flooded her, making her weak.

His kiss did this to her. His kiss turned her inside out, confusing her, making her forget who she was and why they didn't work...

Because right now they did work. Right now he tasted like life and hunger and passion, and she wanted more, not less. And no, it wasn't safe, but she hadn't lost control in years…not since she was last with him…and suddenly she was desperate to be his…desperate to feel him and know him and remember why she'd given herself to him.

What had made him the one?

He shaped her to him, his powerful body hard against her and his mouth firm, nipping at her lip, parting her lips, tasting her. He wanted more from her, too. More response. More heat. The insistent hunger of his kiss made her head dizzy and legs tremble.

She clung to him, feeling one of his hands at the swell of her breasts. She shuddered and then shuddered again as he cupped her breast, sending sensation rushing through her. She made a hoarse sound of pleasure and he practically growled with satisfaction.

She felt his hands on the hem of her sweater, lifting the hem and tugging it up over her head, and then he was at the waistband of her trousers, tugging the zipper down before glancing at her feet and noticing the boots. He pushed her back onto the bed so that he could remove one boot and then the other, and then the trousers were gone, leaving her in just her bra and matching pantie.

She reached for his coverlet, wanting to hide, but he leaned over her, pinning her hands to the mattress.

"I want to look," he growled, his voice deepening, his Irish accent becoming pronounced.

She felt shy and she closed her eyes, but even with her eyes closed she could feel his burning gaze, which drank her in the way a parched man drinks a tall, cool glass of water.

His head dipped, and his lips brushed her jaw and then the column of her throat.

Air bottled in her lungs and her toes curled as he kissed down her throat to the hollow between her collarbones.

She shouldn't like this so much. She shouldn't want his mouth and his tongue and his skin...but she did.

She loved his firm grip on her wrists and the way he pinned her to the bed, his body angled over hers, his knees on the outside of her thighs.

His mouth trailed lower, his lips between her breasts and then light on the silky fabric of her bra, his breath warm through the delicate fabric, teasing the pebbled nipple with the lightest scraping of teeth, making her arch up, and her hips shift restlessly.

He worked his way to the other breast, teeth catching at the edge of the bra, and then sliding his tongue along the now-damp fabric, his tongue tracing the line of her bra against her skin.

She could feel the rasp of his beard and the heat of his mouth and as erotic as it was, it wasn't enough.

Her hips rocked up. She felt hot and wet and empty.

He could fill her. He should fill her. Hard. Fast. Slow and fast.

Anything, everything.

"You know what I want," she whispered, licking her upper lip because her mouth had gone so dry.

His head lifted, and he gazed down at her. "And you know what I want," he answered.

"I want sex and you want a wife." She'd meant it bitterly but her voice was so husky the words came out breathless. "Something seems wrong here."

"It's easy to have sex. It's harder to find the right wife."

"I'm not the right wife."

"You are now."

"Because of Jax."

"Because of Jax," he agreed, head lowering, his mouth capturing one taut nipple and sucking hard on the sensitive tip.

He worked the nipple until she was writhing and panting beneath him.

"Rowan, Rowan—"

"Yes, *mo chroí*?"

"You're torturing me."

"Just as I will torture you every night in my bed." He blew on the damp silk of the bra, warm air across the pebbled nipple. "I'm going to do this to your pussy, until you come."

"Rowan. I want you in me."

"I know you do, but I'm not ready to give you what you want. I think you need to be punished—"

"For what?"

"Where do I start?" He bit down on the nipple making her cry out. "You should have told me who you were… you should have told me you were a virgin…you should have told me you were pregnant…" He looked down at her, green-gold eyes blazing. "Should I go on?"

"But that's it. That's all. There's nothing else I've done wrong."

"So you admit you were wrong."

Her eyes closed as she felt his hand on her hip, caressing the hipbone. "I could have been better at communicating," she whispered, pulse racing, thinking she should tell him to stop even though she didn't want him to stop.

And then his hand was between her thighs, cupping her mound, the heel of his palm pressing against her, filling her with hot sharp darts of sensation, and his mouth was taking hers again, all heat and honey and mind-drugging pleasure.

She'd wanted him that first night they'd met, and oh, she wanted him again now. Maybe even more because she knew how good he felt, his body buried deep in hers, making her body come to life with each maddening thrust, the slow deep strokes making her hope and want and feel, and she'd cling to him just as she had then, and for those moments they were joined, there was nothing else she needed…

And then his head lifted and his heavy-lidded green-gold gaze searched hers. "You want me."

It was impossible to deny when her arms were now wrapped tightly around his neck. "Yes."

"You need me."

Her body was on fire. "Yes."

"But you don't like me, you don't trust me and you won't marry me."

"We don't know each other. We're just…good in bed."

The corner of his mouth lifted. "But it's a start."

"We can't base a marriage on sex!"

His broad shoulders shifted and yet his eyes bored into hers. "There are plenty of couples who don't even have that."

A lump filled her throat. She loved the feel of him against her, the weight of his muscular body and the heat of his chest where it rested on hers and she dug her fingers into the short, crisp strands of hair at his nape and tugged. "I'm tired of being grateful for small mercies."

"Sometimes all we get are small blessings."

Her heart did a painful thump. "I want more." It hurt to speak but she forced herself to add, "I refuse to settle for less."

And then after a long moment where she felt as if he was staring deep into her soul, his head dropped and he was kissing her again, his hand sliding around to unfasten the hook on her bra and peeling it away. His lips captured an exposed nipple, and her breath caught in her throat as he licked the tip, making it wet and then moving to the other nipple. The combination of warm wet mouth and then cool air made her belly clench and her thighs press tight. She tugged on his hair, holding him to her breast, as he began to suckle harder.

It was impossible to silence her husky groan of pleasure, impossible to not lift her hips to find his. She needed more from him. She needed all of him.

She'd gone years—three years—without his touch... without any touch from any man...and yet now, together like this, she felt as if she'd shatter if she didn't have him tonight.

He was peeling off her panties, dragging the scrap of satin down her bare legs and then tugging off his own T-shirt and joggers.

His erection sprang free and her gaze went to his torso with the sculpted muscle, the hard taut abdomen, the corded thighs and of course, the thick, long shaft at full attention.

The air caught in her throat as she took him in.

He was beautiful.

Her first. Maybe her last.

It didn't make sense and yet in some ways, it was exactly as it should be. She'd lost her head over him, giving him not just her virginity but her heart.

And she had given him her heart.

She'd fallen for him hard, so hard, and she'd imagined that he'd cared for her, thinking it was impossible to make love the way they had without feelings being involved...

She'd been sure there were feelings, the lovemaking so intense it'd felt somehow as if they were soul mates. Perfect and perfectly made for each other.

And now, here they were, three years older and wiser and yet she still craved the feel of his mouth and the taste of him and the feel of him...

"Look at you, such a bold thing," he drawled, shifting over her, his knees pushing between hers, making room for him between her thighs. "Getting an eyeful, are you?"

Her lips curved faintly. "There's a lot to look at."

"Disappointed?"

"You know you've got the...goods."

"Small blessings, *mo chroi*."

"I wouldn't say small in this case." She reached out and touched his rigid length. He was warm and silken and hard all at the same time. She heard his sharp inhale as she stroked the length of him so she did it again. He pulsed in her palm, straining against her. Just the feel of him made her ache on the inside. "Definitely not small."

His eyes gleamed as he lowered himself to kiss the valley between her breasts and then down her rib cage to her belly. He'd slipped a hand between her thighs, parting them wider and giving him access to her delicate skin and tender pink folds.

Logan sucked in a breath as he found her, gently exploring her sex, and she was ready for him, already so wet. Her eyes closed as she felt his hands moving, touching, stirring her up, making her shiver.

She was ready for him, so wet, and she could feel him slipping a teasing finger over her dampness and then tracing the softness, lightly dragging the moisture up over silken skin to her sensitive nub. He knew just how to touch her and the pressure of his finger against her clit made her heart pound. Sparks of light filled her head while honey poured through her veins...

He kissed her taut, tense belly as he stroked her, and then he kissed down her abdomen, until he was parting her inner lips to lick the tender clit. She gasped as his tongue flicked across her, making her go hot and cold. The pleasure of his mouth on her was so intense it was almost painful. Her toes curled and she buried her hand in his hair, her breath coming faster, shorter as he pressed fingers into her core, finding that invisible spot that heightened sensation. He thrust deeper into her, stroking that spot as he sucked on her nub and did it again and again so that she couldn't hang on to a single rational thought, her body no longer her body but his to play with and control.

Logan dragged in great gulps of air as he brought her closer and closer to orgasm. She dug one heel into the bed, trying to resist, doing her best to hold off from climaxing, in part because she wasn't ready for something so intense, but also because it felt so amazing she wasn't ready for it to end. But Rowan wasn't about to let her escape. He was far too clever with his fingers, and he knew how to control her with his mouth and teeth and tongue, and then the tip of his tongue flicked over her so slowly that she broke, the orgasm so intense that she almost screamed, but caught herself in time. Tears filled her eyes instead.

Hell.

He took her to heaven and then dropped her into hell.

It wasn't supposed to be this way. It wasn't supposed to feel this way. She shouldn't want him when he'd wounded her so deeply.

And then he was stretching next to her, his large powerful body pulling her close, and he kissed her, deeply, and even though he'd yet to bury his body inside her, she knew he was staking claim. His hands cupped her face, his mouth drank her in.

Mine, his fierce carnal kiss seemed to say. *You belong to me.*

But then he was drawing back, and he studied the tears slipping from her eyes. "What hurts?" he asked.

She looked up into his eyes. It was hard to breathe when

it felt as if a concrete block rested on her chest. It took her forever to answer. "My heart."

He held her gaze for another long moment and then his head dropped and his lips brushed hers. "Hearts heal." And then, kissing her, he shifted his weight, his hips wedged between her thighs.

She felt the thick smooth head of his shaft against her, pressing at her entrance and it felt good. He felt good.

She hated that.

She wished she could tell him to get lost, to go screw himself, to leave her alone but she didn't want that. She didn't want him anywhere but here, against her, with her.

"You make me want to hate you," she choked even as his thick rounded tip just pressed inside her body. She was wet and he was so warm and smooth and even though the tip was just barely inside her, intense pleasure rippled through her. It was the most exquisite sensation, him with her.

"You hate me because you like it so much," he answered, nipping at her neck, finding more nerves, creating more pleasure.

He was right. She shouldn't welcome his touch when she didn't like him, but separating sensation and reason was impossible when he was close to her. Something happened when he was near…something so intense it was like a chemical reaction.

He was a drug.

Potent. Dangerous.

Like now.

He was there at her entrance, the tip just barely inside her. He didn't thrust deeper. He didn't even move his body. And yet her body was going wild, squeezing him, holding him, desperate to keep him with her, in her.

"So hate me," he murmured, slipping in just another inch, if that. "I don't mind."

Her body pulsed. She struggled to get air into her lungs. Her skin felt so hot that she wanted to rip it off.

"You love this," she gritted, her nails raking his shoulders.

"I love that I can make you feel so good."

"If you really wanted me to feel good, you'd do something."

"I think you're feeling really good right now."

She didn't know about that. Her body felt wild. Her inner muscles were convulsing, squeezing the thick rounded tip of his shaft, again and again. She'd never felt anything like this and she couldn't figure out if she loved it or hated it, so hard to know what she wanted when everything within her was so turned on.

"It's not enough," she said breathlessly.

"What would you like then?"

"You know."

And he did know, because he did it just then, thrusting hard into her body, seating himself deeply.

She nearly groaned out loud. *This*…this was what she wanted. Her arms wrapped around his shoulders and she held him tightly to her, her eyes burning and her throat aching because she felt overwhelming emotion…

She'd missed him somehow.

She had.

Even though he'd broken her heart, she'd missed him and this…

And the tears seeped from beneath her lashes, as she struggled to contain the emotion and the pain.

"Don't cry, *mo chroi*," he said, shifting his weight to his forearms to pull out and then thrust in again, slowly, deeply. "It's not bad to feel good. Let me make you feel good."

Her head knew everything about this was dangerous.

Everything would just fall apart later but right now she couldn't think clearly. She had no defenses against this... against him. He made her come alive. He made her feel. Her spine tingled. Her skin prickled.

"Make me feel good then," she whispered, giving in.

He began to move, burying himself deeply just to draw back out, his length so warm inside of her. Each thrust brushed against that sensitive spot within her, and each thrust put pressure on her clit, so that he stroked nerve endings inside and outside and there was no way to resist the tension coiling within her. It was just a matter of time before she'd come again.

It was just a matter of time before he'd make her shatter again.

His tempo increased, and his body thrust harder, faster, and she clung tighter, answering each thrust with a lift of her hips, pressing up against him to create the most tension and friction.

He growled his pleasure, and from his quickening tempo, she knew he was close to coming but he held back for her, determined to give to her, and she wanted to hold back just to defy him...it seemed so important to defy him...but his hand moved between them and he was stroking her clit and there was no resisting him. She climaxed just seconds before he did and he bore down on her, driving into her, filling her with his seed.

It was only then that her little voice whispered, *This is how one gets pregnant...*

Of course.

A great way to trap her was to put another baby into her womb. Give them another life to protect.

She didn't want to cry now. She wanted to hit him. Fight him.

"You may have made me pregnant," she said hoarsely

as he shifted his weight, settling onto his side on the mattress next to her.

"Yes," he answered, pulled her onto her side so that he could hold her close to his chest, his long legs tangling with hers.

She stiffened. "That's not a good thing."

"Jax would like a brother or a sister."

"How can you say that?" She struggled to sit up but he didn't let her escape. "You don't even know her!"

He shrugged, his arms like iron bands. "All kids benefit from a sibling."

And then when he said no more, she glanced back at him and his eyes were closed, his long lashes resting on his high cheekbones. His even breathing told her he was already asleep.

She told herself she'd never be able to sleep like this. She told herself it would be impossible to relax. How could she doze off when her mind was racing? And yet somehow, minutes later, she was asleep, still captive in Rowan's muscular arms.

CHAPTER EIGHT

ROWAN LAY AWAKE, Logan sleeping at his side. He'd been awake for the past hour, listening to her breathe and thinking about the night.

It'd been years since he'd felt so much hunger and need, years since he'd wanted a woman the way he wanted Logan tonight.

Just remembering the lovemaking made him hard all over again. He'd found such erotic satisfaction in the shape of her, the softness of her skin, the scent of her body, the intensity of her orgasms.

He loved the taste of her and the urgency of her cries as she climaxed.

He hadn't felt this way about a woman since…

The March 31 when he'd first bedded Logan Lane.

The corner of his mouth pulled and he lightly stroked her hair where it spilled across his chest.

She wanted things he couldn't give her—romance, love—but he could give her other things, important things…stability, security, permanence.

He wasn't going anywhere. He wouldn't abandon her. He'd never betray their daughter, either.

And just because he couldn't give love, that didn't mean their relationship had to be empty or cold. This physical connection was hot. There was no reason they couldn't enjoy the heat and pleasure. They should take pleasure in each other. There would be no other.

Marriage was a commitment. He would be committed. Love wasn't necessary. In fact, love was a negative. It added pain and unnecessary complications. They didn't need the emotion. He didn't need it, and she'd be fine without it, too.

Logan woke and for a moment she didn't know where she was.

The bed was strange. Huge and imposing with its monster antique four-poster frame—and yet the white sheets were so soft and smooth they felt delicious against her skin.

Stretching, her body felt tender. Between her thighs it felt very tender.

And then she remembered it all. Rowan's mouth on her. His cock filling her. His expertise that made her come once, and then again.

And in the next moment she remembered Jax and she glanced at the wall of monitors to check the camera in Jax's room, but the screens were dark. The monitors were turned off.

Logan flung herself from bed, panicked. She grabbed the nearest piece of clothing—Rowan's T-shirt—pulled it over her head and raced back to her room. The curtains were open, sunlight poured through the tall, narrow windows, the sky beyond a hopeful blue.

Jax's bed in her closet bedroom was empty.

Logan tried to calm herself, knowing that in this place nothing bad would happen to Jax. The Irish nanny, Orla, probably had her. They were undoubtedly playing fairy-something somewhere, but until Logan saw Jax, and knew without a doubt that Jax was safe, Logan couldn't relax.

She stepped into shorts and dashed from her room, running down the stairs by two.

There were no bodyguards at the foot of the stairs today. The huge stone entry was empty. She went to Rowan's study. That was empty, too.

Where was he? Where was everyone? Had Rowan taken Jax and gone? Leaving her here?

She retraced her steps, returning to the impressive staircase but turning left instead of right and kept going until she reached the castle's kitchen. It was a cavernous vaulted space made of stone and dramatic arches. The huge commercial oven was tucked into what once must have been a medieval hearth, and a bank of tall, sleek stainless-steel refrigerators took up another wall. The kitchen was warm and smelled of yeast and warm bread. A woman had been bent over in front of the wood-topped island and now straightened. Startled by the appearance of Logan, she plunked her mixing bowl of rising dough on the island and wiped her hands clean on a nearby dish towel. "Hello. Can I help you with something?"

"My daughter," Logan said urgently. "I can't find her."

"Your little one is with Mr. Argyros." She turned to the stove, and pulled out a tray of golden scones and then another and placed them on top of the stove. "You'll find them outside in the garden." The cook nodded toward the garden beyond the kitchen door. "You can go that way. It's quickest."

"Thank you."

The air was cool and the gravel path hurt her feet. She should have worn shoes but Logan wasn't going back until she found Jax. She hurried down the path, trying not to shiver, telling herself there was no need to be afraid, but what if Jax was scared and Rowan wasn't patient? What if Jax was in one of her toddler moods—

She stopped short as she rounded the corner.

There between the hedges and the castle's kitchen herb garden was a little round table with matching painted chairs. A delicate lace cloth covered the pale blue wooden table and in one chair sat Jax, a tiny crown on top of her head, and in the other sat Rowan, looking beastly big in his pixie-sized chair. He was holding a miniature china cup and Jax was reaching for her cup and beaming up at him as if she was a real princess and Rowan her prince.

Logan couldn't breathe. She'd never seen Jax look at anyone like that. Not even Joe, whom she adored.

Logan's pulse still raced but her heart felt unhinged, flip-flopping around inside of her, hot emotions washing through her, one after another.

They were having a tea party in the garden. A father-daughter tea party.

And not just a casual affair, but this one had an arrangement of purple pansies in a little milk pitcher, and a silver tiered tray of sweets filled with little iced cakes and fragrant golden scones.

Someone had gone to a great deal of effort. Had Orla planned this? It seemed to be the sort of thing a professional nanny would think of, and yet there was something about the way the pansies spilled out of the pitcher that made Logan think this wasn't Orla, but someone else…

Her gaze settled on Rowan. He was smiling at Jax, his expression infinitely warm and protective. Doting, even.

Logan's eyes burned and she struggled to get air into her lungs but she couldn't see and she couldn't think, not when she was feeling so much.

Rowan looked like a giant in the small blue chair, his shoulders immense, drawing his shirt tight across his broad back, while the fine wool of his black trousers outlined his muscular thighs.

But Jax wasn't the least bit intimidated by the size of Rowan. If anything, she was delighted with her company, beaming up at Rowan as she sipped her tea, her chubby fingers clutching the little cup before she set it back down to ask if he needed more tea.

He nodded and Jax reached for the pot to top off his cup. As she started to pour the tea, she noticed her mother, set the pot down with a bang, and waved to Logan. "Mommy!"

"Hello, sweet girl," Logan said, blinking away tears before Jax could see them.

"We're having a party!" Jax cried, reaching up to adjust her tiara. "I'm a princess."

"Yes, you are." Logan walked toward their little table, but avoided Rowan's gaze. He was too much of everything.

Jax frowned at her mother's bare legs. "Where are your clothes, Mommy?"

"I need some, don't I?"

"Yes. You look naked." Jax sounded scandalized.

"I know, and it's a princess party. I'm terribly under-dressed. I'm sorry."

Logan leaned over and dropped a kiss on her daughter's forehead. "Is that real tea you're drinking?"

Jax nodded vigorously. "Yes."

"If apple cider is tea," Rowan replied, his voice pitched low, but even pitched low she heard the amusement in it.

She darted a glance in his direction, not sure what to expect, but thinking he'd be smug this morning, after last night.

Instead his expression was guarded. He seemed to be gauging her mood.

Logan wished she knew how she felt. Everything was changing and she felt off balance and unable to find her center. "Is this her breakfast?" she asked, noting the little cakes and miniature scones on the tiered plate taking center stage on the table.

"It's *tea*, Mommy," Jax said sounding a bit exasperated. "Breakfast was at breakfast." She then looked at Rowan, and her expression softened, her tone almost tender as she asked him, "More tea?"

"I haven't drunk my last cup," he answered Jax regretfully.

"Then drink it." Jax turned back to her mother, earnestly adding, "We only have two cups. Sorry, Mommy."

Logan couldn't help thinking that Jax didn't seem the least bit sorry that her mother couldn't join them. The little girl was soaking up the attention. "That's okay. I should probably go dress." But Logan found it hard to walk away. The party was so charming and Jax had never not wanted her company before. It was new, and rather painful, being excluded.

Rowan glanced at her, looking almost sympathetic. "You don't have to leave. We can find you a chair, if you'd like."

The fact that he seemed to understand her feelings made it even worse. He wasn't supposed to be the good guy. He was the bad guy. And yet here he was, dressed up in black trousers and a white dress shirt, balancing himself in a pint-size chair, and drinking apple cider in a cup about the size of a shot glass.

"How nice of Orla to arrange this," she said, injecting a brisk cheerful note into her voice. "I'll have to thank her when I see her."

"Orla won't be here for another half hour," Rowan answered.

Logan frowned, confused. "But she made arrangements for the tea, yes?"

"No," he said.

"My daddy did," Jax said, casting another loving look on Rowan.

Her daddy.

Daddy.

He'd told her.

Logan shot Rowan a disbelieving look, and he was prepared. He didn't shy away—instead he met her gaze squarely, apparently utterly unrepentant.

She felt completely blindsided and her lips parted to protest, but she swallowed each of the rebukes because this wasn't the time, not in front of Jax.

"We'll talk when Orla arrives," he said casually, as if he hadn't just pulled the ultimate power play, rocking her world again.

How dare he? How dare he?

She was so shocked. So upset. Anger washed over her in hot, unrelenting waves. "Is that what this party was for?"

"Orla will be here in thirty minutes." His voice was calm and quiet but she heard the warning underneath. *Don't do this now. Don't upset Jax.*

She bit back the hot sharp words that filled her head and mouth, battling the sense of betrayal.

He played dirty. He'd always played dirty. He would never change.

Her eyes stung and her throat sealed closed and it was all she could do to hold her emotions in. No wonder he'd been so successful in his career. He was extremely strategic. And he had no conscience. He didn't care who he hurt, not as long as he won.

"You've time for a hot bath and a light bite," he added conversationally. "I'm sure you'd feel better with some coffee and food in you. It's already past lunch. You must be hungry."

"It's past lunch?"

"Yes. It's already after two."

"Two?"

"You had a good sleep-in, and a well-deserved one." He briefly turned his attention to Jax as she'd just offered him a little iced cake from her own plate. The cake was now looking a tad sticky but he accepted it with a smile of pleasure.

He held his smile as he focused back on Logan. "I'm glad you slept. I think you were…spent."

She heard his deliberate hesitation and knew exactly what he was implying. She was spent because he'd worn her out with his amazing performance last night.

"It was a grueling day," she agreed shortly, turning away because there was nothing else she could do. She wasn't wanted at the garden party and she was cold in just the T-shirt.

Shivering, Logan returned to the kitchen to see about coffee and one of those scones she'd spotted coming out of the oven.

"Do you think I could get some coffee and one or two of those scones?" she asked the cook.

"I'll send up a tray immediately," the cook promised.

The tray with coffee and scones, and a bowl of fresh berries, was delivered just minutes later to Logan's bedroom, and Logan sat cross-legged on the large bed, enjoying several cups of coffee and the warm flakey scones slathered with sweet Irish butter and an equally thick layer of jam, before bathing and dressing.

By the time Jax returned to the room, Logan was very much ready to shift into mommy mode, but Jax had other ideas. After giving her mother a big hug and kiss she announced that she and Orla were going to watch a movie in the castle theater.

"But wait, how was tea?" Logan asked.

"Lovely."

Lovely. Now that wasn't a word American toddlers used often. "Did Orla teach you that word?"

"No, my daddy did."

Once again, *her daddy.*

She ground her teeth together, struggling with another wave of resentment. For the past two plus years she'd been the center of Jax's world, fiercely vigilant, determined to be both mother and father, and yet overnight her role had been changed. She'd been nudged over—no, make that shoved—and she was supposed to be good with it. She was supposed to just accept that Rowan was now in their lives, making changes, shifting power, redefining everything.

"What do you think of him?" she asked carefully.

"My daddy?"

"Yes."

"He's nice."

Logan smiled grimly. "He is, isn't he?"

"Orla says he's lovely."

So that's where she learned the word. Wonderful. "And where is Orla?" Logan asked, determined to hide her anger from Jax, even as she made a mental note of yet one more thing to discuss with Rowan. It was unprofessional for nannies—even cheerful Irish ones—to refer to their male bosses as lovely.

"Outside, in the hall."

Logan went to the door and opened it, and yes, there stood Orla with her ready smile. "Good afternoon," Orla greeted Logan with a lilt in her voice. "Did Jax tell you we're going to go see *Cinderella* in the theater?"

"No." Logan was finding it very difficult to keep up with all the twists and turns in the day. "There's a theater here?"

"Yes, ma'am. Downstairs in the basement."

"Castles have basements?"

"Well, it was the dungeon but we don't want to scare the little girl." And then she winked at Logan. "Or the big girls, either."

And then Orla and Jax were off, walking hand in hand as they headed for the stairs, both apparently very excited about the movie. The movie, undoubtedly, being Rowan's idea.

Which meant it was time to deal with Rowan.

Logan stepped into shoes, grabbed a sweater, and went to find him. It wasn't a simple thing in a castle the size of Ros. She checked the study and then outside, walking through one garden and then another, before returning to the house and climbing the stairs back to the second floor where she opened the door of his bedroom to see if by chance he was there.

He was. And he was in the middle of stripping off his clothes and he turned toward her, completely naked.

Her gaze swept over him, lingering on the thick planes of his chest, the narrow hips, the tight, honed abs and then below. He was gorgeous.

He knew it, too.

"Come back for more, have you?" he asked, his smile cocky.

Logan flushed but didn't run away. She closed the door behind her. "You had no business telling her you were her father—"

"Oh, I absolutely did." His smile was gone. "You were in no hurry to tell her."

"I had a plan."

"I'm sure you did. One that didn't include me." His dark hair was damp. His body still gleamed with perspiration. He made no attempt to cover himself. "But I'm not interested in being shut out or being relegated to the background as if I'm on your staff. I'm her father, not a baby-sitter or hired help."

She wished he'd put his clothes back on. How could she argue with Rowan when he was naked? "I've never said you were hired help," she snapped.

"You certainly haven't treated me as an equal, have you? But you're a Copeland. Why should I expect otherwise?"

"Not that again!"

He walked toward her, muscles taut, jaw tight. "Not that again? I'm not allowed to be troubled by your family? By your sordid history? I'm not supposed to care that your father destroyed my family?" He made a rough low sound, correctly reading her surprise. "Yes. Your father quite handily dismantled my family. It's embarrassing how quickly he ruined us. I blame my father, too. He was the one who chose to work for your father."

He paused to search her face. "Yes, my father once worked for your father. Did you know that?" He laughed shortly, mockingly. "And your father was underhanded even then, already an expert in white-collar crime."

Her heart raced and she held her breath, shoulders squared, bracing herself for the rest.

"Your father has been a sleazy con artist forever. But he was able to get away with it for years, hiding behind his big Greenwich house, with his big Greenwich lifestyle."

Logan swallowed, pulse thudding hard, and yet she refused to say a word, aware that he wasn't done, aware that anything she said would just infuriate him more. The fact that he couldn't accept that she and her father were two different people was his problem, not hers, and it had been his problem from the very beginning. She also understood now that it would never change.

He would never change.

"He was able to hide, your dad, by creating a veneer of

sophistication with money. Other people's money. Taking their incomes and their nest eggs and draining them dry so he could pose and preen, a consciencless peacock—" He broke off, and looked away, toward the window with the view of the rolling green lawn and the dark hedges beyond.

"There is power in money," he added flatly, harshly after a moment. "It provides an extra layer or two of protection, allowing your father to continue his charade for decades, whereas others, those who worked under him, or for him, were caught up in the schemes and exposed. And those men paid the price early. They went to jail. They served time."

His voice roughened, deepened, and Logan's skin prickled as she suddenly began to understand where Rowan was going with this.

His dad had worked for her father years ago.

Her father had been a con artist even then.

Her father had gotten away with the…schemes…while his father hadn't.

Finally she forced herself to speak. "Your father," she said huskily, "he served time?"

"Yes."

"How long?"

"Long enough." He faced her, expression hard. "It destroyed his reputation, while your father escaped unscathed."

"I don't remember any of this."

"It happened before you were born. I was just a boy, and my brother was a toddler."

She balled her hands into fists, her fingernails digging into her palms. "Why would my father be able to escape unscathed? Why did just your father take the fall?"

"Because my father was paid to take the fall." Rowan's voice was as sharp as glass. "And it wasn't a lot, not even by a poor man's standards, but your father didn't care. It wasn't his problem how the Argyros family survived. It wasn't his problem that a young Irish wife with two young children wouldn't be able to get by when Mr. Argyros went to prison, taking away income. Depriving the family of a father, a husband, a breadwinner."

For a moment there was just silence.

"If your father had been exposed then, if my father had refused to take the fall alone, your father wouldn't have been able to defraud thousands of people billions of dollars. Your father's career as a con artist would have ended. Instead, my father caved and took the blame and served the time, destroying all of us, but leaving you Copelands privileged, spoiled, glamorous and untouched."

And this is why he hated her father so much.

This is why he'd scorned her when he'd discovered who she was.

She was a privileged, spoiled, glamorous, untouched Copeland girl, while he was the son of a man who served time for her father's machinations. "I'm sorry," she whispered, and she really, truly was. She felt the shame of her father's actions so strongly. She'd been deeply ashamed for years, and the weight of the shame had almost suffocated her years ago. It's why she'd moved from the East Coast to the West. It's why she'd pushed her family away. It's why she'd dropped the *Copeland* from her name. Not to hide. She wasn't an ostrich. She'd never buried her head in the sand. She knew how selfish her father was. But it was impossible to survive mired in guilt. The move to California was a desperate, last-ditch effort to shift the pieces in her heart and head so that she could have something of a life. So that she could be someone other than Daniel's daughter.

But Rowan would never see her as anyone but Daniel's daughter.

For Rowan she would always be the enemy.

He shrugged carelessly, callously and turned around, heading for his en suite bathroom. As he walked away from her, she didn't know where to look or what to think or how to feel.

From the back he looked like a Greek god—the very broad shoulders, the long, lean waist, his small tight glutes.

But he also had the cruelty of the Greek gods.

He would punish her forever. He'd never forgive her. She'd spend the rest of her life punished and broken.

Hot tears stung the back of her eyes. "I'm not my father," she shouted after him. "I have never been him, and you are not your father!"

He disappeared into the bathroom. He didn't close the door, but he didn't answer her, either.

"And you have been punishing me from that very first morning in Los Angeles for being a Copeland, and you're still punishing me, and I'm tired of it. I'm tired of this. Your motives aren't pure—"

"No, they're not." He reappeared in the doorway, still stark naked, the hard, carved planes of his body reminding her of the large marble statue of Hercules she'd seen in Rome years ago. "But I take being a parent seriously, as I know how important parents are for young children, and you had no right to cut me out of my daughter's life. I just thank God that your father did die, and I was the one to come for you because otherwise I'd still be oblivious that she even exists."

Fine, he could be livid, but she was seething, too. "I should have been part of that conversation today, Rowan."

"Theoretically, yes, but you weren't there."

"So wait until I am there."

"I'm done waiting," he ground out.

"I should have been there when you told her," she shot

back, walking toward the bathroom. "I should have been part of that conversation."

"Theoretically, yes," he answered, leaning against the door frame, all taut, toned muscle and leashed power. "But there was a moment during our tea when she told me she didn't have a daddy and I was right there, and what was I to do? Pretend I hadn't heard her—"

"She did not say any such thing!"

"She did, *mo ghra*, and so I told her that I was her daddy." He shrugged, straightened. "I didn't make a big deal out of it. I didn't want to overwhelm her. I simply told her I was her father, and I was very sorry to have been away so long, but I wouldn't leave her in the future. I explained that we will all live together now, and we'll be a happy family, the three of us, and hopefully with time, she'd have a baby brother or sister, or both."

Her gaze had been sliding down his body but she jerked it back up, taking in his chiseled jaw, faintly smiling lips, and that impossibly smug expression. "You did not!"

"Oh, I did. And she was excited. She said she'd love a baby brother or sister. Or both. Maybe twins. Twin boys. Twin girls. The more the merrier." He gave her a searching look. "You do want a big family, too, don't you?"

"That's not funny."

"Jax and I are quite serious."

"Don't include Jax in this. She's just a baby herself, which is why you shouldn't lead her on. You'll just disappoint her—"

"But, love, think about it. We didn't use protection last night. You could very well be pregnant already."

She didn't know what to respond to first, his continued use of the word *love* or the suggestion that she could be pregnant. She focused on the second one since they'd both already established that he didn't love. "It takes longer than that for the sperm to travel to the egg," she retorted frostily.

"Maybe I have super sperm." And then flashing her a maddening smile, he turned around, displaying more of his assets, and disappeared into the bathroom.

Logan stood there, fuming, clenching and unclenching her hands. He was so satisfied with himself and so infuriating. And yet, to be fair, she couldn't blame him for feeling victorious. Rowan was proving to be an expert at getting things done, *his way*.

"By the way," Rowan suddenly called to her, even as she heard the shower turn on. "I heard from Drakon earlier today. There seems to be some drama in your family at the moment, and he hoped you could call Morgan after dinner, and I hope so, too, since you've no reason to fight with me—"

"You're trying to pick a fight with me right now."

"I'm trying to get you to focus on the big picture. Your family is in turmoil. You don't need to quarrel with me."

"So just marry you and be done with it. Not want anything for myself. Not need love or kindness."

"I'm very kind to you."

"Rowan!"

"I am. I made you feel so good last night."

"That's not kindness. That's sexual expertise. You're experienced. Technically sound. Big deal."

"It was last night." His voice was somewhat muffled but she still heard the hint of laughter.

"And this is today," she snapped, walking closer to the bathroom. "So what is happening with my family?"

"Your sisters are fighting."

She rolled her eyes. She wasn't surprised. She didn't even need to ask him which sisters. "I warned you that Morgan and Victoria don't get along."

"They seem to have done all right for a day, but then they began discussing the memorial for your father and things fell apart."

"I'm sure I know what happened there. Morgan wants a service and Jemma and Victoria don't, and Morgan's hoping she can convince me to take her side."

"Yes. How did you know?"

She grimaced and rubbed her knuckles over her chin. "It's the story of our family. Even when we try, we can't get along."

"But the news always depicts you four sisters as being very close."

"Lies, all lies," she sang and then her mocking smile slipped. "We've spent our lives being painted as those scandalous Copelands, but we're a family much like anyone else. We have problems. We struggle to agree on things. We have different goals and dreams. But that is far less interesting to the media. I'm afraid we'll always be tabloid fodder."

"Explain the family dynamics to me."

"That would take all day."

"Give me the short version."

"The judge allowed us as children to choose which parent we would live with. We all initially chose to live with Mom, but then Morgan—the most tenderhearted of us—felt sorry for Dad and decided to go live with him, even though he had zero interest in being a father or being there for her. But once she made her decision, she stuck with it, and to this day, she's tried to side with him, which actually just means taking care of him."

"Even though your father stole millions from Drakon?"

She grimaced. "It certainly complicated their marriage, didn't it?"

"So why are Morgan and Victoria so antagonistic? That doesn't make sense to me."

"Morgan wants everyone to forgive Dad, but Victoria isn't sure she can forgive Morgan for siding with Dad. It's endless and exhausting, and between us, I'm tired of it. That's why I moved to California, to get away from the family and the drama."

"Hmm." His deep voice was a rumble from inside the bathroom. "So if Morgan was Team Daniel, and Victoria was his archenemy, where are you on the spectrum?"

She tipped her head, rested it on the door frame. "Probably closer to Victoria, but not as extreme. It's hard because there was Dad and the bitter divorce, and then there was Dad, the investor turned swindler. He made a lot of really bad decisions in his life and now there are five of us trying to move forward, burdened with his…legacy."

Rowan was silent for a bit. "Do you have any good memories of him?"

"Not that I can remember."

"So the memorial service isn't important to you."

"I don't think we need one, but you can't tell Morgan that. She had such a different relationship with him than the rest of us did."

"She's your twin."

"Fraternal. We're nothing alike."

"But weren't you close growing up?"

"Yes. Until she left to go live with Dad." She fell silent a moment, thinking about the complex dynamics. "I do love her, though. She and I have a good relationship. I don't like her being upset."

"According to Drakon she's very upset, but then, so is Victoria."

"And they're still together, under one roof?"

"No, as a matter of fact. Victoria is now on her way

to Jemma's, and based on what I heard from Drakon, you're not going to get your sisters together anytime soon, whether for a memorial service or anything else."

Jemma was married to the powerful King of Saidia, Sheikh Mikael Karim, who'd married her against her will. He was seeking revenge on Daniel Copeland, but by the end of their honeymoon, Jemma and Mikael had fallen in love. He still was not a fan of her father but Mikael was fiercely protective of Jemma. "So they won't be attending our wedding?" Logan said.

The water turned off.

The bathroom was silent except for the drip, drip of water.

Logan grimaced and shook her head. Why did she just say that? What was she thinking? "I was making a joke," she called to him. "Trying to lighten the mood."

He said nothing.

She squirmed, giving herself a mental kick. "That was a joke," she repeated. "We're not getting married. I was trying to be funny."

"I'm sure Drakon and Morgan would come for the wedding," he answered, turning the water back on. "Mikael and Jemma would, too. And probably your mother—"

"Rowan, stop. It was a joke. A bad joke." She peered into the bathroom, unable to see all the way in, but she got a glimpse of the large mirror, clouded with steam. "But speaking of family members. How is Bronson? You haven't said much about him."

"I've been waiting for an update from his doctors." His voice was muffled. The shower sounded louder than before. "There was a setback early this morning."

"A setback?" She waited for him to add more, but he didn't. She took another step into the bathroom. "And? What happened? What's going on?"

"Come all the way in so I don't have to keep shouting."

"I don't want to come in. You're showering."

"I'm sure you've seen a man shower before."

She hesitated. "Actually, I haven't."

For a moment there was just silence and then she heard his low laugh. "Then you *definitely* must come in. Consider it remedial education."

"Not necessary. My education was excellent, thank you. I attended some of the best schools in the world."

He laughed softly again.

CHAPTER NINE

ROWAN'S WARM, HUSKY LAUGH sent a ripple of pleasure through her, unleashing butterflies in her middle and a rush of warmth in her chest. Why did she respond like that to him? Why did she have to find him so appealing?

He'd simply laughed. That was all. And yet his laugh made her feel good. His laugh didn't just turn her on, it warmed her from the inside out. Damn him.

Logan hovered inside the bathroom doorway and tried to force herself to focus. "How serious is Bronson's setback?" Rowan didn't reply immediately, and she took another tentative step into the warm, humid bathroom. "Is Bronson okay?"

"He's getting the best medical care possible but he's not responding as well as the team hoped." He paused, before asking, "When was the last time you saw him?"

She had to think. "It's been a while. A couple years, maybe. I was pregnant, and then I had Jax, so I wasn't traveling and Bronson is always working. He's spent the past three years working tirelessly to pay back as many of Dad's clients as possible. It's a thankless job, though. Most of the clients are so angry—and yes, they have a right to be, I know—but Bronson didn't steal from them. Bronson had nothing to do with Dad's company, and they don't realize, or maybe they just don't care, that he's sacrificing everything to pay them back."

Water just sluiced down. There was no reply. Not sure if he'd heard her or if he was done talking, she cleared her throat "Why did you ask? Is there something I should know, something you haven't told me?"

Again silence stretched before Rowan said, "He's almost destitute…just one step up from living on the streets."

"No."

"He's been ill, too. He's not in good shape."

"I had no idea. Poor Bronson. So who is with him? Mom?" She found it difficult to reconcile her tall, handsome, successful brother with the one in the hospital. "Are there any leads on who attacked him?"

"Your mother isn't there. She's been fighting something and isn't strong enough to travel."

"So he's alone?"

"Yes, but there is good news. The London police have taken someone in for questioning. It looks like the attack was an isolated incident. Victoria should be able to return home soon."

"That *is* good news."

"So Jax and I could return home soon, too."

"You're free to travel wherever you like."

"Seriously? So I could go to my room and pack right now?"

"Yes."

"You're not worried about losing me?"

"No, because you'd return frequently to see Jax—"

"I'm not leaving Jax here."

"I'm her dad. She needs to be with me."

"I'm her mother, Rowan. She belongs with me."

"Then I guess you might not want to travel for long periods, because this is her home now. And it's your home, too, Logan. That's why we're getting married. We both want Jax to have a family, and stability. There shouldn't be confusion on that." He was silent a moment before adding, "Do you want to come in and give me a hand?"

"A hand doing what?" she asked suspiciously.

"Well, you could wash my back...or something."

She went warm all over, picturing the *something*, and picturing the something growing larger, heavier.

She definitely was curious, and she squirmed a bit, listening to the water stream down, but she didn't like him and didn't trust him, and she hated how he used sex and temptation against her.

"You don't play fair," she called to him, trying not to wonder if he used a lot of soap or body wash, and if he'd lathered himself everywhere. Would he stroke himself as he lathered? Was he stroking himself now? But going down that road...exploring any of those questions would just lead to trouble. He was trouble. Hot, sexy, serious trouble. The trouble that made her drop her guard and lose her reason and she had adorable little Jax as proof. "So, no. Not interested in washing your back. Or anything *else*."

"Should we talk about the wedding then?"

"Rowan."

"Jax *is* expecting brothers and sisters."

"Then Jax is going to be disappointed," she answered firmly.

"And what if you are pregnant?"

She really didn't want to think about that. She wasn't pregnant. She couldn't be pregnant.

But he had gotten her pregnant the first time they were together. It could happen again.

"We have to use protection from now on," she said firmly. "We can't take these risks."

"I was thinking we'd get married tomorrow. Jax should be there, of course—"

"No!"

"It's her dream."

"It's also her dream to be a fairy and fly, but that isn't going to happen, either."

"You have no sense of adventure."

He was such a jerk.

Taking a breath for courage, she entered the steamy bathroom. It was a modern bathroom with stylish finishes—marble everywhere, even up to the high ceiling, a huge mirror running the length of a double vanity, and a shower the size of a walk-in closet, the spacious marble shower outfitted with multiple heads to give him an overhead soak as well as a full body spray.

Rowan was standing directly under one of the faucets, dark head tipped back, muscular arm lifted as he ran fingers through his hair, rinsing the shampoo out. His thick biceps was bunched and his flat, hard abdomen was a perfect six pack.

The man was too attractive.

He opened his eyes and looked at her. "You're sure you don't want to wash my...something?" His green eyes glimmered.

"No."

"Fine. But do you mind if I do?" he asked pouring body wash into his hand.

Her eyes widened.

Laughing softly he spread the liquid across his chest and then streaked it down his stomach, and then lower to his cock, which was coming to life.

"I did not come in here for a peep show," she said sternly.

"Just trying to get clean, love."

She grimaced, and looked away, not wanting him to
　　　　 ‌‌at it was fascinating watching his shaft spring to

life and even more fascinating to see how he held it, fisting the length, paying special attention to the thick knob at the end.

And she knew how he was gripping his erection by the reflection in the clear glass shower doors as those hadn't fogged up.

"What's going on with my sister?" she asked, trying to focus on what was important.

"Why didn't you see her for a couple years?" he asked.

From her position she could see his reflection continue to work the soap over his erection. He was slowly, firmly stroking down, working his hand up over the head. Her breath caught in her throat. She squirmed on the inside. "Um," she said, unable to think clearly. "Because I was pregnant…"

"Right." He was stroking down again, the muscles in his forearm cording.

God, he was sexy.

Awful. And sexy. Awfully sexy. Damn him. She dragged in a breath. "So…what's your point?"

"Think about what I'm saying."

"I can't. Not when you're doing…that."

"I knew you were watching." His deep voice was even huskier now than it had been a few moments ago. "Do you want to watch me finish?"

"No!" And then she turned around quickly to look at him. "Are you really going to come?"

His gaze met hers, and one dark eyebrow lifted. "Is that a problem?"

"It just seems…rude…since I'm standing right here."

"You're in my bathroom."

"You invited me in."

"Because you wanted to come in. You were curious. Admit it."

"I wasn't," she protested and then realized he'd stopped handling himself. He still had a huge erection, but he was rinsing off the suds and lather, and then turning off the water.

She glanced uneasily at his erection. "You're just going to leave that, that way?"

"Yes." He leaned out of the shower and grabbed a plush towel from the rack.

"But doesn't it hurt?"

"Not that much."

She couldn't stop looking at him, watching as Rowan dragged the towel over his face, mopping his dark hair and then down his body.

He stopped toweling as he reached his cock. "Sorry. Maybe I'm being dense. Did you want to finish me off?"

"No!" she cried, pretending to be horrified, but then ruined the effect by grinning. "But you should know that that *thing* is very distracting."

He held his arms open, as if giving himself to her.

Logan backed up a step. "I wouldn't even begin to know what to do with it."

"I think you did just fine last night."

"That's because you took the lead on everything."

"I just touched you, love."

That was true. And it had felt wonderful.

She eyed the long, smooth, thick length of him, capped by that equally thick head. She wondered what he'd feel like in her mouth. She wondered what that rounded cap of his would feel like against her lips. She wondered what he'd do if she put her mouth on him.

Pulse quickening, she took a step back toward him. "Can I touch you?"

He nodded, his lashes lowering, hiding his intense green gaze. She was glad. His eyes had a way of seeing too much.

She took another step toward him and, having closed the distance, she put her hands on his chest, his skin so warm beneath her hands, and slid her palms down from his pecs over his ribs to his pelvis with that impressive V-shape.

And then after stealing a peek up into his face—his expression was shuttered and impossible to read—she knelt down in front of him, and dragged her hands down over his hips, along the front of his thighs, his quadriceps rock hard.

His cock bobbed in front of her mouth. She looked at it a little bit warily even as her pulse jumped, adrenaline getting the best of her.

And Rowan, to his credit, just stood there, waiting.

Leaning toward him, she kissed the tip lightly, curious. He was firm, but the skin was soft, warm. She kissed him again, leaving her mouth against him, drinking in his heat and the silky softness as she opened her mouth to touch him with her tongue.

She thought he made a hoarse sound, and she looked up at him, but his expression was blank and so she opened her mouth wider and covered just the tip, and then sucked gently.

He grew even harder as she gently sucked, pulling on him, creating warm wet friction around the head, and then using her tongue to taste and tease the underside of the head.

He made another hoarse sound, and this time she smiled to herself. He didn't hate it. That was something.

Emboldened, she swallowed him even deeper and wrapped what she couldn't take into her mouth with a hand, holding him tightly, and stroking him with her mouth and hand the way she'd seen him touch himself in the shower.

She continued to work him, struggling to get a rhythm

going, but feeling awkward as she ran out of air more than once and needed to pull away so she could get another breath.

He groaned as she broke the rhythm a third time, and she froze, looking up at him apologetically. "I'm sorry. I'm not good at this and you're so big—"

"Don't apologize," he ground out, drawing her to her feet before lifting her up onto the bathroom counter.

He flipped her skirt up and spread her knees wide and then put his mouth on her, over the satin of her panties, and then, pushing the fabric aside, his tongue found her between the slippery folds. She gasped and arched as he flicked her sensitive nib.

"You're already so wet," he said, thrusting a finger into her.

She rocked against his hand, helplessly grinding against him as his sucked on her clit, already close to climaxing. "Sucking on you turned me on," she panted.

"It turned me on, too." His voice was rough, hoarse. "But don't come yet. You have to wait until I tell you."

"I don't think I can—"

He abruptly pulled away and she gasped as he left her. She struggled to pull down her skirt but instead he was taking her off the counter, peeling off her panties and turning her around, bending her over the slab of marble covering the vanity so that her bare butt was exposed.

"Watch me take you," he said. "Watch me fill you. Watch how good we are together."

And then he was parting her legs and running fingers over her, finding her where she was wet. She felt the moment his arousal replaced his fingertips, his thick insistent shaft pressing at her hot core. Her senses spun as he took the thick head and rubbed it up and down her, taking her creamy heat and spreading it over the tip, making them both slick.

"Watch," he commanded, putting a hand into her hair and tugging her head back to see her face in the mirror. "Watch as I fill you."

And then he was there, entering her, pressing the thick tip in, stretching her, slowly pushing deeper and deeper.

Her lips parted in a silent gasp of pleasure. He felt so big, and so hot inside her. It was hard to feel anything but him buried deep inside her, her body still trying to accommodate his size.

But then Rowan's hands were on her hips, stroking the outside of her hips and then over the round curve of her backside, kneading her ass until she wiggled, ready for more, wanting more.

His hands were under her now, cupping her breasts, rubbing the nipples, making her gasp.

"Look at you," he growled. "You're so beautiful."

"No."

"You are, and you're mine. We belong together, *mo ghra*. Can't you see that?"

She didn't know where to look. She was pressed close to the mirror, and she felt so much that it was hard to take in what she was seeing. Instead she got impressions—her pink cheeks, her bright eyes, her lips parted and swollen, while behind her Rowan was all hard, taut muscle. He looked powerful and primal and…happy.

It crossed her mind that he might just like her.

That he might truly want her.

She exhaled in a rush as he rubbed her sensitive nipples, kneading them, making her hotter, wetter, making her tighten convulsively around him.

"Keep watching." His deep voice was practically purring. "Watch us."

Her breath hitched as he slid a hand from her breasts, down over her belly, to settle between her thighs, and then hitched again as he parted her curls and the soft inner lips to stroke her swollen clit.

He played her clit without moving his hips and it wasn't fair—to feel so much fullness within her while he teased all those nerve endings—she wouldn't be able to resist him long.

"I'm going to come," she said breathlessly. "I can't stop it this time."

"Yes, you can."

"No, I can't."

And just like that his hand fell away, and he pulled out of her, and she nearly screamed with frustration at the deep intense ache within her that was part emptiness and part pain. Tears started to her eyes and turning around she beat him on his chest. "I hate you for doing that. Why do that?"

"Because when you delay an orgasm, it makes it even stronger when you do finally come—"

"I don't *want* it to be even stronger. I just want you." She beat one more time on his chest, this time for emphasis. "So stop messing around. Give me you." Her hands reached for his neck and she pulled his head down to her and she kissed him desperately. "I want you, you awful horrible addictive man." And then she was kissing him again, kissing him as if her life depended on it.

The kiss felt different.

Rowan had kissed Logan before. He'd kissed countless women before. But there had never been a kiss quite like this one.

It was hot and fierce and edged with a hunger that stirred his blood, but there was something else in it, too. Something…open. Something vulnerable.

Not that she was giving herself to him, but instead asking for something of him. And it wasn't a sexual commitment. It was bigger than that. Deeper.

She wanted *him*.

As his hands rose to clasp her face, his palms cradling her jaw so that he could kiss her more deeply, it struck him that she was looking for truth. She was looking for safety. She was looking for someone who would accept her, offering herself in return.

She'd been like this that first night together, the night of the auction…fierce, intense, warm, open.

He hadn't known her then. He hadn't realized she was a virgin. Hadn't understood that she hadn't merely been offering her body, but she'd been giving him her heart.

He understood it now. He understood her.

And this time, he wasn't throwing her gift away.

Rowan scooped her up in his arms and carried her through the bathroom to the bedroom where he placed her on the bed.

He stretched out over her, and she parted her knees for him, making room for him.

"I won't stop this time," he murmured. "And I'm not going away. I'm going to make you feel good, and I'm going to keep making you feel good until you and I are finally on the same page."

"That's going to take a lot of sex."

"Good thing we both like it."

He positioned himself between her thighs, finding her where she was so soft and wet and ready for him. He heard her sigh as he slid in, felt her hips tilt to welcome him. He nearly growled with pleasure as she accepted him, taking him deep. She was tight and hot and her body clenched him, holding him.

He loved being buried within her. Everything felt right

when he was with her like this, and everything would be perfect if he knew he hadn't hurt her.

But he had.

And he couldn't go back, and he couldn't change his re-action that morning in her kitchen, and he couldn't change the fact that he'd scorned her when she phoned weeks later, but he could give himself to her now. He could be real with her now.

He pressed up, resting his weight on his forearms, then he slowly drew out of her before burying himself deep again. He kissed her as his hips thrust, his tongue prob-ing her mouth, stroking to match the friction of his shaft.

It felt so good being with her. He felt so good with her. He didn't want the pleasure to end. This was sex, but not merely sex, it was more. He couldn't explain it, and didn't want to try. He just knew that he'd taken so many women to bed, and no one had ever felt like Logan. No one had ever made him feel the way Logan did. With her, he felt settled. Calm. Whole.

Logan was trembling. She was so close…so close to com-ing but she couldn't come. The two almost times in the bathroom had made it impossible to go over the edge. In-stead she was restless and aching, everything inside her wound so tight that she couldn't stop her legs and body from trembling.

Rowan's mouth covered hers and his large, powerful body rode hers, but she felt almost frantic as the orgasm remained out of reach.

Her hands slid down his back to cling to his hips. She flexed her fingers against his firm butt, his skin so warm, his body creating friction everywhere—his chest against her breasts, his cock inside of her. And yet the friction was just that, delicious sensation, but she couldn't reach the point that would give her relief.

She whimpered, muscles tight, need flooding her. She closed her eyes, trying to concentrate to see if she could find relief, but his hard heat inside of her wouldn't push her to that pinnacle.

"Rowan," she pleaded, gripping his hips. "Rowan… I can't…"

"You can." And then he slipped his hand between them, finding her sensitive nub and one, two and the sensation focused and narrowed, tension building, tightening, until there was no turning back.

She shattered, and kept shattering, the orgasm going on and on as if it would never end.

In a distant part of her brain she registered Rowan's deep groan, and his hard thrust, reaching release, before holding still, and just holding her.

She didn't know how long they lay there, warm and spent. She was truly spent, too. Her eyes closed. She exhaled and was soon fast asleep.

Logan didn't know how much time had passed when she finally opened her eyes because the room was swathed in shadows but it wasn't completely dark outside. She must have slept a good couple of hours though because she'd been dreaming until just a few moments ago, and the dream was good. She woke up feeling happy.

Stretching slightly she shifted, and became aware of Rowan's arm wrapped around her waist. She turned to look at him. He was awake and watching her. "Do you know what time it is?" she asked, her voice rough with sleep.

"Almost time to get up," he answered, kissing her forehead. "We're having dinner with Jax soon."

"We are?"

"Yes."

"You make it all sound so normal. As if we're a real family."

"We are a real family, and it is our new normal," he answered quietly, but there was no smile in his voice or eyes. His expression was somber. Even his green eyes looked dark.

We are a real family... And this is our new normal.

"We don't feel like a family," she said carefully, after a moment.

"Not yet maybe. But we will, with time."

She stared into his eyes, wishing she could see past the beautiful dark green color, wishing she could see him. "I know nothing about you, you know. We've only had sex."

"And a child."

"But it's really just been sex—"

"We did talk about your family earlier. It could almost be considered a real and meaningful conversation."

She felt like punching him in the chest again. "So tell me about your family. Open up about your world. Have a *meaningful* conversation with me."

"To be honest, I'd prefer to make you come again."

"Yes, I'm sure you would."

"Sex isn't a bad thing," he answered mildly, reaching out to stroke the swell of her breast and the firming nipple. "Sex creates life, and intimacy—"

"So does conversation, and sharing. And it's your turn to share. Tell me more about your family. Where are your parents now? What happened to your father after he served time? Do you see either of them often? And why did you go into the military? What was its appeal?"

He rolled onto his back and drew her with him so that she lay on top of his chest. "I'd rather not talk about boring things when we can talk about us. Did you like seeing us together in the mirror? How did it make you feel to watch me take you?"

"We're not discussing sex!" She shoved up, pushing away from his chest. "And you have to tell me something about you. I can't keep sleeping with a complete enigma!"

"You can if you like him."

"I don't particularly like him." She glared down at him, frustrated and yet aware that he was really handsome, and really appealing, and she could maybe see a future with him, but not as a married couple...rather, as lovers. Lovers that coparented. Or something of that nature. "And you have to share relevant things that I want to know. Otherwise, we can't keep doing this."

"Now you're just punishing yourself. We both know you like doing what we do."

She gave him a thump on his chest. "What were your parents' names?"

He sighed. "Darius and Maire. He was Greek American and she was Irish American, but neither lived long in the US. My mother was from this area, and my father from Rhodes, Greece, and they both had strong accents, hers Irish, his Greek. They drank hard, they loved hard, they fought hard, and they seemed determined to make it work, even when Dad went to prison, but when my little brother died, the love died, leaving just hard drinking and lots of fighting."

She closed her eyes and rested her head on his chest. "Do you remember Devlin?"

"Yes."

"What was he like?"

"Sweet. Happy." He paused, drew a breath. "Devlin was a truly happy little boy. He was always smiling. He had a huge laugh." His voice deepened, roughened. "I remember I used to love to carry him because he smelled good. He still had that baby smell."

Logan blinked back tears. "You must have taken his death so hard."

Rowan didn't answer but she felt the tension within him.

After a moment he said quietly, "Jax looks a lot like him. It's a bit disconcerting. If I could find a picture of Devlin I'd show you."

"I believe you."

He smoothed her hair. "What else?" he asked after a moment. "What are you aching to know?"

She smiled at his choice of words. "Do you like having dual citizenship?"

"I had three passports at one point—Greek, Irish and American, but I tried not to travel with three. It's confusing for border agents."

The corner of her mouth curled higher. "And your parents? Are either of them still alive?"

He hesitated. "Dad died of lung cancer a couple years ago, and she has dementia but I go see her every week or so when I'm here."

"She still lives near here?"

"Yes, she's in a care facility just down the road."

"You didn't want her here?"

"She was here until six months ago when she escaped her minder and tumbled down the stairs." He was no longer smiling. He looked tense and grim. "Her new home is top-notch and provides excellent care."

"I'm not judging."

He exhaled slowly. "No one wants to put their mother in a home. It doesn't feel natural."

Logan said nothing, sensing that he wasn't done, and she didn't want to stop him from saying more.

After a moment he shrugged. "I'd like to take Jax to

meet her. You can come, too. But Mother rarely recognizes me these days. She thinks I'm that nice man who plays the piano for dancing."

"Do you play the piano?"

"No. But she and my father met at a party and there was dancing, so maybe she thinks I'm my father." His brow furrowed. "Or the piano player."

Logan leaned up and kissed him. "They both sound like nice people," she whispered, kissing him again. "And I think it's a lovely idea to take Jax to see your mother."

They ended up making love again and it was different than it had been so far, sweeter and calmer but emotionally more intense.

Logan felt connected to Rowan in a way she hadn't felt before.

Maybe it's because she'd had a glimpse behind the mask. She was grateful he'd shared with her, even though it was clear he didn't like sharing. She was also touched that he'd tried to keep his mother with him, at Castle Ros, and that it had been a struggle putting her in a care facility.

Clearly he wasn't all bad.

Clearly he was rather good...maybe even very good...

She held her breath, scared to admit to everything she was feeling. It was confusing and overwhelming. So much was happening but she wasn't sure if any of this was right. She didn't want to go through life on her own, a single mother forever, but at the same time, sharing Jax would mean relinquishing control.

It would mean trusting Rowan to do the right thing.

It would mean trusting that she would do the right thing.

It would mean compromising and yielding and sacrificing independence, too.

Could she do that? Did she even want to do that?

Which brought her back around to the issue of control.

Control was such a huge thing for her because the loss of control always resulted in loss. As soon as she lost control, bad things happened. Without control she wouldn't be able to protect herself, never mind Jax.

Panic building, Logan rolled away from Rowan. "Time to get dressed," she said, rolling off the bed and heading for the bathroom.

She was quickly gathering her clothes when Rowan followed her in. "I feel like you're running away," he said, blocking the doorway. "Why?"

"Not running away. It's just getting late, and I need to shower and dress for dinner," she answered, unable to look at him.

"Everything was fine and now you're shutting down again—"

"I'm not shutting down!" she snapped, shooting him a fierce look. "And I'm certainly not running away, either. How can I run when you've brought me to your high-tech castle with bodyguards and security cameras and massive hedges everywhere?" Her voice cracked. "Look at me, Rowan! I'm naked in your bathroom with you blocking the doorway. I'm trapped."

"You're not trapped," he retorted impatiently, moving toward her.

She retreated, moving away until she bumped into the thick glass shower enclosure. "No? Then what do you call this…" she gestured wildly at the shrinking space between them because he was coming toward her again, rapidly closing the distance. "You're everywhere and you're overwhelming and overpowering, and I can't breathe or think or feel when you're with me—" She broke off as he pressed himself against her, his knee between her legs, his hands capturing hers, pinning them to the glass above her head. "See?" she choked as his fingers entwined hers and his head dipped, his mouth on her neck, setting her skin on fire. "You're doing it again…confusing me…overpowering me…making it impossible to think."

"What do you need to think about, *mo chroi*?" he murmured, kissing higher, just beneath her earlobe. "And why do you need to fight me? We work, you and I. We fit."

She shuddered against him, her breasts firming, nipples tightening as heat flooded her. She ached on the inside again, ached for him again. She loved the feel of him, loved it when he was in her, making her body feel so good, but he had the opposite effect on her head and heart.

He wasn't good for her. He wasn't right for her. He wasn't what she wanted—

No, not true.

She wanted him, but that didn't make it right. She needed a man who allowed her to be calm. She needed a man who made her feel safe—not safe in terms of keeping the bad guys of the world away, but safe emotionally. Safe as in loved.

He touched her and created energy and passion and excitement, but it was all so wild and dangerous.

And then he was kissing her, his lips on hers and there was so much heat and hunger that all the wild, chaotic emotion rushing through her slowed, thickened, turning to honey and wine in her veins.

He made her feel so much…

He made her want so much…

He made her want everything…and that included love. The more he touched her, the more pleasure he gave her, the more she wanted love.

His love.

Tears burned the back of her eyes, and her chest squeezed tight, her heart turning over. Making love made her want his love, and he was the first to admit he didn't love. No, he just offered sex. Lots and lots of hot sex, but sex without love was empty, and it would hollow her out, leaving her empty.

"Your idea of a happy relationship is sex," she answered, her voice faint. "But my idea of a happy relationship is love. Do you love me? Can you love me? Can you answer that?"

"When I touch you, do I make you feel good? When I hold you, do you feel desirable?"

"I want love and you want sex!"

"I want you, and I feel close to you through sex." He swore, and he rarely swore. "Hell, I am close to you during sex. I'm in you, love. We're as close as two people can be."

She didn't know how to respond to that.

"Sex can be a lot of things," he added. "Tender, rough, sweet, aggressive. It changes, just as we change, but sex creates a bond, creating something we only have together."

"But that's the problem. I don't want to bond through sex. I want love because love is the ultimate bond. It is the thing that keeps people committed when desire fades or someone is ill. If all we have is sex, what happens when sex isn't available? Does the relationship end? Are we done? What will keep us together?"

"Jax," he said promptly. "She'll keep us together."

She made a rough sound. "And what if something happens to her?" He said nothing and she searched his eyes, and she had the answer there.

Nothing would keep them together. Their relationship would end and the time they spent together would have meant nothing.

Logan shook her head. "This is why I keep repeating myself—I'm not settling. I'm not getting married for sex. If I marry, it will be because I've made a commitment for life to a man. That's the only reason to marry. Because I want to be with him. Forever."

His hands fell away. He stepped back.

She swallowed the lump in her throat. "Can I please dress now?"

He let her dress and go.

CHAPTER TEN

THEY HAD DINNER with Jax in the castle's "small" dining room, a room that still featured massive wooden beams and a huge iron chandelier and tapestries on two walls depicting a violent medieval battle, not to mention two suits of armor.

Jax was fascinated by the armor and the stone fireplace and the tapestry with the violent battles. She was the one to point out that even the intricate carvings worked into the mantel were of "fighting."

"Ireland is a very old country," Rowan explained to her. "It has a long history, and fortunately, or unfortunately, there have been many battles fought here."

Jax turned her wide blue eyes on him, studying him now with intense interest. "Fighting is bad."

"Fighting isn't good, no," he answered, "but sometimes you fight to protect things…your country, your family, your home."

She digested this in silence and then just moments later, slid out of her chair again to go study the fireplace once more.

In the end, there was very little real eating done, and mostly explanations and exploration, but Logan didn't mind. She'd found it difficult to eat tonight, her emotions still raw, her thoughts painfully convoluted.

And Jax was even doing her a favor, providing a diversion, keeping Rowan occupied with all her questions about war and Ireland and the coats of armor at both sides of the room, keeping Logan and Rowan from speaking to each other very much.

But finally, after dessert had been served, Orla appeared and offered to give Jax a bath and read her a story, promising Logan and Rowan that she'd let them know when Jax was ready to sleep, so they could come up and kiss her good-night.

Rowan glanced at Logan as if to let her decide.

Logan looked at her daughter who was already talking animatedly to Orla and seemed more than happy to leave the dining room and return upstairs.

Logan nodded consent, unable to argue with the plan, while at the same time aware that once Jax was gone, she and Rowan would be left alone together and they'd have to address the uncomfortable tension that had hummed in the dining room since the beginning of the meal.

"What do you want?" he asked her, breaking the silence. "What will make this better? What else can I tell you about my family, or my past, to show you who I am and help you believe that I'm committed to you—to us— and that I think we can be happy without all the hearts and fuss and romance."

"I'm not asking for hearts and fuss," she answered. "And you mock me when you imply that my needs are so trivial."

"I'm not trying to mock you, or trivialize what you feel. If anything I'm frustrated that you don't understand that what we do have is good. What we have physically is explosive and intense and deeply satisfying, and it's not often like this. To be honest, I've never known this with any other woman. I've only ever found this with you."

She froze, not certain what to do with that. She searched his face, scrutinizing his hard, masculine features, wishing she could believe him.

Would he lie to her?

Her brow creased, as she struggled to remember if he'd ever lied to her. He'd been harsh...cruel...but she didn't think he'd ever lied before, which was key. She hated liars. Hated to be played...

Her father had played them. Her father had turned them all into fools.

"But maybe I'm wrong," he added after a moment. "Maybe you've found this...connection...with someone else. Maybe there was someone who made you feel better."

"I've never been with anyone but you, so I wouldn't know," she answered flatly.

She saw the moment her words registered.

"You've only *ever* been with me?" he asked.

Her shoulders twisted. She kept her voice cool. "The night in California and then here."

He exhaled slowly, his forehead furrowed, expression troubled. "So you really don't know about... You have nothing to measure this—us—by."

She didn't know what he meant by that or how to answer something like that, and so she didn't.

Thank God he didn't ask why, because that would mean he truly didn't understand how difficult the past few years had been. That would mean he still believed she was that spoiled, pampered, selfish Copeland girl...

But he didn't ask why and she didn't have to defend herself. She didn't have to throw in his face that society continued to ostracize her and her siblings, making it almost impossible for them to make a living.

No, life had not been easy, and especially for her, once

pregnant, it became downright brutal. There had been no time for men. There had been no time for herself.

And even if there had been time to date...she wouldn't have. She didn't want another man. She'd wanted him. She'd fallen for *him*. Which, in many ways, was the greatest shame of all.

"We can make this work," Rowan said abruptly, leaving his chair, and walking toward her. "We can give Jax something better than what I knew and better than what I had. I want her to have stability and laughter and fun and adventure, and that can happen, but you and I, we have to get along."

"Isn't that what we're doing now? Trying to figure out how we can make this work?"

"I'm not sure anymore. I worry that you've already decided that it won't work, and you're just placating me until you can leave." He stopped in front of her, expression brooding. "But if you leave, it means Jax won't ever have one home. She'll end up like me, bouncing back and forth between homes and countries...different cultures, different customs, different schools. It's a lonely life for a child—"

"As well as a lonely life for me. Do you think I want my daughter living halfway around the world without me? Do you think I want to miss Christmas with her or a birthday celebration?" She was on her feet, too, her dinner chair between them, because God help her, he couldn't touch her again. She couldn't let him close because every time he reached for her, she melted, but giving in to him only made things worse. It made her hate him despite herself. "I don't want to live without my daughter. But I won't be forced into living with you, either!"

"I'm not forcing you. I want you to want to be here—"

"But I don't want to be here. I didn't choose to be here. And I didn't choose *you*."

"You did once."

She flushed, remembering the auction and how she'd put herself into a terrible financial situation just to be with him.

Even then, she was weak.

Even then, she was a fool.

"Yes, you're right," she whispered, heartsick all over again. "I did choose you and then you crushed me. Like a bug under the heel of your shoe." She gulped air, arms folding tightly across her chest to keep from throwing up. "And I'm just supposed to forget about what you did, right? I'm just supposed to act like it didn't happen. Well, it did happen! And it *hurt*. You almost broke me, Rowan. You made me question my own sanity and I'm not interested in ever feeling that way again."

She drew deep rough breaths as she backed away from him. "For one night I was yours, Rowan. All yours. And then I discovered what it means to be yours. And I have no desire, ever, to be yours again."

She started for the door, walking quickly to escape the room as fast as possible, but his voice stopped her midway.

"Forgive me, Logan," he said quietly. "Please."

For a long moment there was just silence. She couldn't bring herself to answer, and she wouldn't let herself look at him, either.

Finally when the silence had become suffocating and her body quivered with tension, she shook her head, and without a glance back, walked out.

But once at the stairs, Logan choked on a smothered cry, and dashed up the steep steps, taking them two at a time, trying to escape the hot, livid pain streaking through her heart.

Jax was asleep when Logan reached the room, and after saying good-night to Orla, Logan changed into her pajamas, but she couldn't get into bed—she was too wound up.

She paced until she couldn't take another step, and then she finally sank onto the plush rose-and-ruby carpet in front of the fireplace, and closed her eyes, trying to clear her head and get some much needed calm and perspective.

But every time she drew a deep breath, she felt a sharp ache in her chest and it hurt so much that she couldn't focus.

He'd asked her to forgive him, and she'd refused. *Refused.*

That was horrible. She felt horrible, but if she forgave him, truly forgave him, then she'd have no way to resist him, because she already cared too much for him. She was already far too invested.

Her anger was all she had left to try to protect herself. Without her anger she'd have no armor, and without armor, he could break her all over again.

But hanging on to the anger would destroy her, too. Anger was so toxic. It was poison for the soul.

She didn't want to be angry with him, but she also didn't want to stay here and give up the last of her dreams. She wanted a family for Jax, but she also wanted love for herself and it wasn't enough to be Rowan's sex kitten.

As much as she enjoyed being in his bed, she wanted his heart more than his body.

It was time to leave.

She'd pack tonight and leave tomorrow. Rowan would have to let her go. She rose and went to pull her suitcase out from beneath her large canopy bed but was stopped by a knock on her bedroom door.

It was Rowan, she was sure of it. She could feel his very

real, very physical energy on the other side of the door and her pulse quickened in response, her heart beating faster.

She retrieved the suitcase, placing it at the foot of the bed, and then went to open the door.

Rowan was not a masochist, and he was not looking forward to another conversation with Logan tonight. The last one had been more than sufficient for a single evening. But he'd promised to let her know if there was news regarding her brother, and there was news. And it wasn't good.

Logan opened the door. She was wearing red and pink plaid pajama pants and a pink knit top that hugged her breasts, making it clear she wasn't wearing a bra. But there was no smile as she looked at him, her jaw set, her eyes shadowed.

"Hope you weren't asleep," he said gruffly.

"No." Her lips compressed and her chin lifted. "I don't want to do this with you, Rowan. I don't want to keep fighting—"

"Bronson's not doing well," he interrupted quietly. He gave her a moment to let his words sink in. "His body seems to be shutting down."

She blinked, and looked at him, clearly confused.

He hated this next part and drew a swift breath. "They suggested it might soon be time to think about saying goodbye."

"What?"

"Are you comfortable leaving Jax with Orla? We could fly to London first thing tomorrow and be at the hospital by nine."

"No. *No.* He's only in his midthirties. How can his body be shutting down?"

"He wasn't strong before he was shot and he's not responding well to treatment."

Logan struggled to speak but the words wouldn't come. She looked away, eyes gritty, throat sealing closed. "Why isn't he responding to treatment?"

"He'd been ill for weeks before he was shot. His body just can't keep fighting."

"I want to go to him now."

"They have him sedated. You won't be able to see him until tomorrow."

"I want to be there when he wakes up."

"You will be. We'll go in the morning—"

"I'll go in the morning," she corrected. "Jax and I will go. This is a Copeland family matter, and you hate the Copelands."

"You can't take Jax to the hospital."

"We're going, Rowan." She stepped aside and gestured to the suitcase by the bed. "I'd already planned on leaving. You just need to put us on a plane and get us to London so I can see my brother. He needs me."

He heard the words she didn't say. Bronson needed her, whereas he, Rowan Argyros, didn't. "And what about Jax?" he said gruffly.

Her eyes suddenly shone with tears. "You'll miss her, but not me," she said with a rough, raw laugh before shaking her head. "Don't worry. I won't keep her from you. I promise to sort out custody and visitation rights, but surely we can do it later, when my brother isn't dying?"

Rowan's chest squeezed. He felt an odd ache in his chest. And looking at her in the doorway, in her pink-and-red pajamas, wearing no makeup, her long hair in a loose ponytail, she looked young and impossibly pretty, and it crossed his mind that one day Jax would look just like this: fresh, sweet, pretty. Little girls did grow up. Little girls became grown-up girls and grown-up girls should never be crushed. Not by anyone.

"We can make this work, Logan. You just have to give us a chance."

She made a soft, rough sound and blinked away tears. "I did. And the sex was great. It was fantastic. But I don't want your body, Rowan, not without your heart."

CHAPTER ELEVEN

THE FLIGHT TO LONDON was short, just an hour and fifteen minutes long. Rowan had let them go, putting them on his plane first thing in the morning. But he hadn't sent them off alone. He'd sent Orla with them as well as passports, including a brand-new Irish passport for Jax.

She had no idea how he'd managed that feat. But then, he had incredible connections, having worked for several governments.

Logan looked from Jax's new passport to Jax where the little girl sat quietly in Orla's arms across from her, and then to Orla herself and suddenly something about the Irish nanny made Logan stare harder.

Orla looked less like an Irish nanny this morning and more like…

Protection.

Logan frowned slightly, brows pulling.

Orla must have read Logan's expression because she suddenly asked Logan, "Are you okay, Miss Copeland?"

Logan nodded once, but she wasn't really okay. Her heart hurt. And she was worried about Bronson. And she couldn't see the future. And she wasn't even sure the nanny was a real nanny anymore…

"Orla, are you really a professional nanny?" Logan

asked, feeling foolish for voicing the question but unable to stop herself.

"I did go to nanny college, and I have worked for quite a few years now as a nanny. Why do you ask?"

"Because you remind me a little bit of Joe."

Orla's eyebrows arched.

"Joe was my assistant in Los Angeles," Logan added. "Or I thought he was my assistant. It turned out he was a former member of an elite military group and an employee of Dunamas. And I just wondered if maybe you were also Dunamas."

Orla just looked at her.

"Because I don't see Rowan letting us leave Ireland without security. I can't help thinking that maybe you're... security."

Orla's lips curved, her expression amused. "You know Mr. Argyros well."

Castle Ros felt empty without Logan and Jax. Rowan felt empty without Logan and Jax. He missed them already and they'd only been gone four hours.

He paced his study and then the library and then the length of the castle and finally the gardens, ignoring the drizzly rain.

He shouldn't have let them go. It was a mistake to let them go. And he'd been the one to put them on the jet this morning. He'd personally escorted them onto the plane, checking seat belts, trying to do whatever he could to keep his family safe.

He'd come so close to telling Logan that he'd changed his mind, that they couldn't go. Or at least, they couldn't go without him. But she'd refused to look at him, refused to speak, other than to murmur a quiet, taut thanks.

And then he'd walked off the plane and the crew shut

the door and the jet raced down the runway, before lifting off.

He felt as if his heart had gone with them, which was so odd as he didn't have a heart. He was, as Logan mocked, worse than the Tin Man...

But she was wrong. He had a heart and he did care. He just didn't know how to prove it to her since he didn't trust words. He'd never liked them. Actions always spoke louder.

Actions, not words.

Once on the ground, they transferred into a waiting car. It was raining and the city streets were crowded but the driver navigated the traffic with ease, getting them to the private hospital in less time than the driver had anticipated.

Logan, who had been calm until now, was nervous, her stomach doing uncomfortable flips. She leaned down to kiss the top of Jax's head, trying not to let her anxiety get the best of her. Bronson had to be okay. Bronson was the most ethical, moral man she knew. He'd spent the last three years trying to pay every investor back, working tirelessly to make amends.

She looked up and her gaze met Orla's. Orla's expression was sympathetic.

"I'm scared," Logan confessed.

"It'll be all right, now that you're here," Orla answered firmly.

"You think so?"

"Everyone needs family. He'll do better now that you're at his side."

Logan nodded and exhaled, forcing a smile. "So what are you and Jax going to do while I'm with Bronson? Go straight to the hotel or...?"

"I think we will go check in and maybe have a snack

and perhaps a nap. Don't worry about us. Focus on your brother."

She nodded again, hands clenched as she glanced out the window at the streets of London, but she couldn't focus on the city, not when she kept thinking about Bronson, and then Rowan.

Rowan who'd let them go.

Rowan who'd stopped fighting her and given in.

Funny how he finally gave her what she wanted, but she felt no relief. She felt just pain.

Just waves of sorrow, of deep aching grief.

The driver slowed before the hospital and then parked beneath the covered entrance and came round the side of the car to open the passenger door.

Logan kissed Jax goodbye and then stepped from the car, squaring her shoulders as she faced the hospital's front door.

There were several rounds of desks and locked doors to pass through, some of the locked doors security to protect Bronson from outsiders, while the last was the hospital's intensive care unit, where they were fighting to keep Bronson alive.

After checking in at the desk in ICU, she went to Bronson's room. She stopped in the doorway and struggled to process everything. The hospital equipment. The monitors. The patient in the bed.

Tears filled her eyes. She drew a quick fierce breath, and then entered, going straight to the side of the bed, where she leaned over Bronson and carefully, tenderly kissed his cheek.

For the next four hours Logan sat next to Bronson's bed. He slept the entire time she was there. The doctors and nurses came and went, checking the monitors, changing IV bags to keep him hydrated, shifting the bed a little to raise his head to ease his breathing.

She felt so guilty as she sat there next to him. He'd spent the past three years fighting to repay debts that were not even his. He'd battled alone, determined to clear the Copeland name.

It was an unbearable burden.

A thankless job.

And he'd never once complained.

Blinking away tears, she reached for his hand again. He needed to be okay. He needed to recover and have a life that mattered, because he mattered. But it wasn't easy keeping vigil. He wasn't the brother she remembered.

Bronson was handsome, heartbreakingly handsome, and yet he'd never paid the slightest bit of attention to his looks. He wasn't shallow or superficial. He had heart. And integrity. So much integrity. He was nothing like their father...

"Hey, Lo," a rough voice rasped.

She sat up quickly and moved closer to him. *"Bronson."*

His blue gaze met hers. He struggled to smile. "What brings you to London?"

"You." She leaned down, kissed his forehead and then murmured, "Oh, Bronson, what's happened to you?"

"Doesn't matter. I'm just glad to see you. I've missed you."

Tears filled her eyes and she couldn't stop them. "I've missed you, too, and I'm so sorry I wasn't here before."

"You're here now," he rasped, before closing his eyes again.

Bronson slept for another three hours and Logan just sat next to him, unable to imagine leaving him here alone.

She was grateful she didn't need to worry about Jax. Grateful that Orla was there. Grateful that Rowan had sent Orla. Grateful that Rowan wouldn't let anything happen to Jax...or her.

Bronson woke up again just before dinner. He seemed

pleased, even relieved, to see that Logan was still there. "Still here, Lo?"

She smiled at him. "Where else would I be?"

"Home, taking care of your baby."

"She's not much of a baby anymore. Jax is two, and she's here in London right now, not California."

"I'd love to meet her. I'm sorry I haven't been out your way—"

"We've all been busy. It's not been easy. I know." She reached for his hand and gave it a squeeze. "Bronson, I need you to get better. And I'm going to do whatever I have to do to make sure you have the right care…the best care—"

"I am getting it," he rasped, gesturing up toward the equipment. "I couldn't get better care than this, and it's because of you."

"Not me."

"Yes, you. Your friend Rowan did this. Arranged this. I'm alive because of him."

Her friend Rowan.

Her eyes burned and her throat sealed closed. She gripped his hand tighter. "He's not my friend." Her voice was hoarse and unsteady. "But he is the father of my daughter."

Bronson's gaze met hers. "Why isn't he your friend?"

"He's not. He's never been my friend."

"Then why would he do all this? Get me this help? Fly you here?"

"How did you know he flew me here?"

"Well, you're here, and he's here, so…" His voice faded as his gaze lifted, his attention focused on the door.

Logan turned around, glancing toward the door, and yes, there was Rowan, on the other side of the observation glass.

Her heart thudded extra hard. She had to blink to clear her eyes.

"Jax's father," Bronson said even more faintly, clearly tired.

"Yes." She turned back to her brother. His eyes were closed. "Sleep," she murmured, giving his hand a squeeze. "I'll be here when you wake."

Logan left Bronson's side and stepped out of his room into the hall. Rowan was no longer outside Bronson's room but heading for the elevator.

She raced after him, catching him before he could take the elevator down. "What are you doing? Where are you going?" she demanded breathlessly.

"I left some things for you. Some snacks, a toothbrush, a change of clothes. Knowing you, you're not going to want to leave him tonight."

Her chest squeezed, making her heart ache. She searched his face, trying to see what he was thinking or feeling but Rowan was so damn hard to read, never mind reach. "But why were you leaving without speaking to me?"

His powerful shoulders shifted. "I think everything has been said already."

Her eyes burned and frustration washed through her, hot and fierce. Not true, she thought. He hadn't yet said the things she needed to hear.

She saw him look past her, down toward her brother's room. "How is he?" Rowan asked.

"Weak, but mentally clear." She swallowed. "He said you arranged for his care. That he's here in this hospital because of you."

Rowan shrugged carelessly.

Logan struggled to find the right words. "He thinks

you're my friend. I had to correct him. Because we're not friends. We've never been friends."

He just looked at her, eyes bright but hard. Just like the rest of him.

She pressed on, emotion thickening her voice. "We were lovers and then enemies. And now parents."

"What do you want me to say?" he demanded tautly.

She was silent a moment, thinking. "I just want to understand."

"Understand what?"

"What would have happened that morning if we'd had coffee and breakfast in my kitchen, and you'd glanced at the magazine and my name had simply been Logan Lane… what would have happened with us if I hadn't been Logan Lane Copeland?"

He didn't take long to answer. "I would have married you," he said flatly.

She went hot then cold. It was the last thing she'd expected him to say.

His green gaze darkened. "You weren't just sex. You were never just sex. You were home."

She couldn't breathe. She couldn't think. She just stared at him, numb.

"I'd never felt that way with anyone before," he added curtly. "And I doubt I'll ever feel that way again." His strong jaw tightened. "I've only ever wanted you. And I still only want you."

I still only want you.

"Because the sex was so good?" she whispered.

"Because you were so good. You were…are…the other half of me."

Her eyes burned and she didn't know where to look or what to say. If that wasn't a declaration of love, she didn't know what was, and yet she'd told him so many times that she wanted love. She wanted to be loved. And it suddenly crossed her mind that maybe they were just using different words for the same thing. *"Rowan."*

But he took a step back, putting space between them, and pushed the elevator button again. "Go back to Bronson. Know that I'm with Jax and everything is fine."

But everything wasn't fine.

Nothing was fine.

They weren't ever going to figure this out, were they?

They were just going to keep getting it wrong.

"Why did you come?" she whispered. "Why bring me a snack and clothes and a toothbrush?"

"Because you needed them." He stepped into the elevator, the doors closed and he was gone.

Logan spent the night in a recliner in Bronson's room. She dozed off and on, wanting to be available should Bronson wake up, but he didn't wake again until morning, and she stepped out as the doctors and nurses made their rounds and did what they needed to do.

Her hair had come down and she felt tired and disheveled but grateful Bronson was getting such excellent care.

He would be all right. He would be.

She used the visitor restroom to wash her face and brush her teeth and try to wake up. She craved coffee but didn't want to go all the way to the hospital cafeteria. Eventually she'd need to leave to see Jax and shower but she'd return. Hopefully her sisters could come soon, too, so Bronson would know he was loved and supported. It was time for the family to come together and be a proper family again. She loved them. All of them. Her mother. Bronson. Her sisters. Jax.

Rowan.

A lump filled her throat.

Lovers to adversaries—but maybe they could be friends. Maybe they could find a way to get along for Jax's sake. There was no reason they couldn't figure this out.

She stepped out of the ladies' room to discover Rowan standing guard outside Bronson's door. The nurses were still with Bronson, changing bandages and linens.

Her pulse jumped when she spotted Rowan and kept pounding as she walked toward him.

"Thought you might like this," he said, handing her a tall paper cup. "With milk and just enough sugar."

She'd thought she'd wanted coffee, but now that he was here, she only wanted him. Gorgeous, horrible, awful, wonderful Rowan Argyros. "Thank you," she said, accepting the cup while wishing he'd hug her instead.

She felt so sad. All night she'd been so sad. Why couldn't they make it work?

"How is everything?" he asked.

She glanced through the observation window to her brother. "He slept all night," she said. "The doctors seemed pleased earlier."

"That's good news."

She nodded. She struggled to find the words that would move them forward. Or back. Or to whatever place they needed to be so she could be close to Rowan again. She loved being close to Rowan. She'd never felt safer than when in his arms.

But Bronson had seen them and was struggling to sit up.

Logan shot Rowan an intense, searching look before turning away to enter Bronson's room.

"Don't do that," Logan said, moving to the side of her brother's bed and gently pressing him back. "Save your energy for getting better, not for entertaining us."

"But I do feel better already," he answered, his voice still raspy but significantly steadier than yesterday.

"You sound better," Rowan agreed, standing next to Logan. "And I know the police want to ask you more questions, but they're waiting until you're stronger. I've told them they need to give you time. They have a suspect in custody and he's confessed to shooting you, even though you were in the process of writing him a check."

"He really confessed?" Logan asked.

Rowan nodded. "He blames Daniel and Bronson for the collapse of his marriage and other problems."

"He didn't understand that Bronson was trying to pay Dad's clients back?"

Rowan shrugged. "Over 63 percent of your father's clients have been reimbursed, not from Bronson, but from money the government was able to seize from offshore accounts your father established. Bronson has been working on paying the remaining clients back, but it's taking him a while and many of those clients need money now, not in the future."

"It's true," Bronson said unsteadily. "I get letters daily from clients who have nothing—they lost everything. They're hurting. They've lost their retirement money, and the seniors have nothing else. They're old and vulnerable, and because of Father they're losing their homes." His voice was rough. "I've been getting these letters for years and every time I get one, I wire money and try to cover the bills. But no matter how much I send, there are still hundreds of people who need help."

"Dad embezzled the money, Bronson, not you."

"But I'm a Copeland. I couldn't live with myself if I didn't try to make amends."

"But you've worn yourself out."

"I'm not a victim. I won't play the victim."

She took his hand and held it tightly. "Bronson, you weren't the one who hurt those people—"

"It doesn't matter. I accept responsibility—"

"And so do I," Rowan said, interrupting. "It's my turn to help. You've done enough. I've spoken with Drakon and Mikael, too. We are taking over, and we will make sure the rest of your father's clients receive restitution."

Logan's jaw dropped. "Are you serious?"

Again Bronson struggled to rise. "That's not necessary—"

"But it is." Rowan's deep voice was flat and unemotional. "We have the ability to do this for the family, and we want to."

Bronson sagged back against the pillows. Logan just stared at Rowan. "Why would you do this?" she whispered.

He shrugged. "Because I can, and I want to."

"That doesn't make sense." She was truly baffled. "You hate my father. You hate him so much—"

"But I love you so much more."

Logan's lips parted but no sound came out. She stared up at Rowan, not just bewildered but overwhelmed.

"I grew up without money," he added, "and I've discovered that money can make life easier. It buys things and gives one the ability to do things, but it doesn't buy happiness, and it doesn't buy love. I would rather give away what I have, and help the people I love, than sit on a fortune and let you and your family suffer."

She blinked back tears. "You love us."

"Yes."

She rose and moved into his arms. "You really love us?" she repeated, even more urgently than before.

"Yes, *mo chroi*, I've been trying to tell you that for days."

"But you never used those words!"

"I told you that you were home."

"But *home* doesn't mean love—" She broke off, hearing herself, and made a soft, hoarse sound. "But it should, shouldn't it?"

"Yes." And then he was kissing her, and they forgot about Bronson until he made a rough sound and they broke apart, embarrassed but also laughing.

"So, you are friends," Bronson said with a faint smile.

Rowan looked at Logan, a brow arched.

Blushing, smiling, she nodded. "Yes." And then she moved back into Rowan's arms and whispered. "I love you. You know that, don't you? I've loved you from the moment I first laid eyes on you."

He grinned. "And you thought it was just great sex," he said huskily, voice pitched so low that only she could hear him.

And then he was pulling her out into the hallway to kiss her again. And again. And again.

"Marry me, *mo chroi*," he murmured against her mouth. "Marry me, please. I need you with me. I want you with me. Tell me you'll come home with me, please."

"Yes." She smiled up into his eyes. "Yes, yes, yes!"

EPILOGUE

THEY WAITED THREE MONTHS to marry because Logan insisted that Bronson be the one to walk her down the aisle, and he needed time to recover.

The three months also gave them a chance to plan the wedding so that it wasn't a rushed affair, but the wedding of a lifetime.

After receiving her invitation, Victoria had at first sent her regrets, citing an unfortunate work commitment, but in the end every Copeland was there, flying to Ireland to attend the intimate ceremony at Castle Ros.

They were married at twilight in the castle's chapel with dozens of tall, ivory candles glowing at the front of the church, with more candles on each of the stone windowsills. The flickering candlelight illuminated the stained glass and the dramatic Gothic arches that formed the ceiling.

Logan wore an off-white silk gown that Jax picked out because Jax was the expert on princess gowns. The bridal gown's bodice was fitted through the waist and then turned into a huge bustled skirt.

The gown had needed last-minute alterations because the snug bodice became too snug. Logan was indeed pregnant, with twins.

She and Rowan had elected not to find out the sex, and

they were waiting until after the wedding to share the news with the rest of the family.

They'd tell Jax first, of course, because this had been her wish after all.

Logan's wish was that the babies would be healthy.

Rowan said he had no wishes because they'd all come true already. He had his wife—his *m' fhiorghra* or true love—his babies and his family, and he was referring to the Copelands as his family, too.

And so the beautiful candlelight wedding ceremony marked the end of the scandalous Copelands and the beginning of the happily-ever-after Copelands, as each of them moved forward with hope and love.

* * * * *

LET'S TALK
Romance

For exclusive extracts, competitions
and special offers, find us online:

 facebook.com/millsandboon

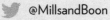 @MillsandBoon

@MillsandBoonUK

Get in touch on 01413 063232

For all the latest titles coming soon, visit
millsandboon.co.uk/nextmonth

MILLS & BOON
MODERN
Power and Passion

Prepare to be swept off your feet by sophisticated, sexy and seductive heroes, in some of the world's most glamourous and romantic locations, where power and passion collide.